THERE ARE NO STARS HERE

J.S. THOMPSON

REALITY
—LIFE—

Library of Congress Control Number: 2025919196

ISBN 979-8-9988304-0-2 (hardcover)
ISBN 979-8-9988304-4-0 (softcover)
ISBN 979-8-9988304-3-3 (Amazon/Kindle)
ISBN 979-8-9988304-2-6 (eBook)

Published by RealityLife, LLC
8401 Mayland Dr #8223
Richmond, VA 23294
United States of America

Cover Art by Julia at AuthorGenius.net
www.jsthompsonauthor.com

To Julian,
The creator of Ronnie and the founder of HERA.
My best.

To my parents,
Bernard & Sylvia

&

For all those who fight.
We were born to see the stars.

"Those who would give up essential Liberty, to purchase a little temporary Safety, deserve neither Liberty nor Safety."

- Benjamin Franklin, 1755

PROLOGUE

Manuel

When Manuel was ten, the federal government tore his family apart, and when he was twenty-three, the earth did it again.

He sat alone in his bedroom while Ronnie, the helpful artificial intelligence embedded in his thin tablet, sat propped on the edge of his desk. Ronnie was trying to teach him about photosynthesis—how plants turn the sunbeams into energy—but he couldn't focus. He wished his mother were there. She knew a lot about plants but hadn't been home in three months.

This was two months longer than usual.

It wasn't abnormal for Sylvia, his mother—a short, proud woman from Mexico City—to vanish to San Antonio to see her sister. When he had asked why she was always gone, his mother would simply give that shy smile and say, "We help people, Manuel, with the time we have." She would then dig her hands into the soil of the massive terrarium—her monstera, the one she called 'her beauty' and had tended for decades—near the window. She cared for that plant as if it were Manuel's brother, checking the soil, spraying the leaves, and adjusting the grow light as needed. "When we have time, we give."

Manuel's father would simply stand in the doorway, his arms

I

crossed and grimace tight. He never said it, but Manuel could tell he hated it when she left him, even if he loved her for it.

But today, as Manuel's father leaned against the doorway, his arms were not crossed. His eyes were wide, his hands gripping his tablet. "Manuel..." His father's voice was like sandpaper—harsh, rough. He cleared his throat. "Manuel. May I come in?"

Manuel nodded. His father never asked for permission to enter his room. "There are no locked doors in my house," his father would say as if he was the warden of apartment 293B. "You are a guest here until you've earned something."

The bed sagged to the right as his father sat. The scent of after-shave, tobacco, and peanuts tickled Manuel's nose.

His father should have been at work, helping fix the digital dark spots that cropped up in the barracks near the center of Denver, Colorado. Those homes, for the neediest around them, had been built by the government. Men like his father repaired the notoriously faulty infrastructure that blocked tech like Ronnie and SatTech from their dark, concrete interior. If his father was home early, who was fixing the homes?

"I... Son..." Manuel's father wrung his hands. "Manuel, something happened." He cleared his throat again and glanced back toward the door. "Your mother will not be back for a while." His father nodded, mostly to himself. "She's okay. She's safe. She's in San Antonio with her sister. She wants to come back, but she can't. She's stuck."

"Why?" Manuel asked.

His father let out a heavy sigh and affectionately squeezed the back of Manuel's neck, pulling him close. Manuel didn't look at his father; he just stared at the snow globe on his desk—a replica of la Plaza de la Constitución—as it reflected light around the room.

"It doesn't matter," his father said. "What matters is how we react." His father stood and gestured for Manuel to do the same. "You have one job, hijo. I will get your mother out, and we'll be fine. Do you understand?"

His father looked proud in the light—the sun making a halo around him, the heavens anointing him. But all Manuel felt was a twinge in the pit of his stomach, a hole growing deep inside. He started to breathe faster. His chest hurt. When would she be back? What if she was gone forever? Why did she—

"Manuel," his father said, holding out his hand. He held it at waist level and slowly lowered it, his palm facing the ground. "Tranquilo."

"When am I going to see her again?" Manuel asked, his breathing stabilizing.

His father glared at him. "What is your job?"

Manuel looked down at the floor—his father's boots, worn and brown.

"Manuel," his father demanded, placing a hand under his son's chin and holding it up. "We are men. We are strong. We work for solutions. We don't take shortcuts. Now is not the time for weakness. What is your job right now?"

He gritted his teeth. "Get good grades and finish school."

"And tomorrow?"

His voice cracked. "To apply and share that knowledge."

"And thereafter?"

His eye twitched—an involuntary reaction every time his father preached his *today, tomorrow, and thereafter* philosophy. His father was a proud man who demanded his son focus on three goals that evolved over time. If he followed the plan, the philosophy, he'd achieve his preordained purpose.

Manuel met his father's eye. "So I can change the world."

———

MANUEL WAITED for his father to go to bed before he collapsed onto his own and asked Ronnie what had happened. Ronnie chirped away and fed him results that said the nation was at war. A woman named York had declared much of the southern part of the United States free and stopped all travel between America and South Texas, Louisiana, Mississippi, and Alabama—all the places beyond what she called the York Line. Manuel's mother was on the other side of that line in the Free Republic of South Texas.

Manuel scoffed. *FROST.*

He tried to call his mother, jabbing his finger on the display over and over until Ronnie suggested he leave a message, and his mother could respond when the networks were restored.

Manuel was about to record a message when his father's voice nagged him from his mind. Would calling his mother be weak? He decided yes and instead glared at the red light of his old alarm clock on the wall. He could cry now, under the blanket of darkness, and be strong with the sun.

Manuel cried when his mother made contact with him a few weeks later. He didn't cry on purpose. It was as involuntary as his eye twitch. Her face was thinner than it had been the last time he'd seen her, but her hair was still the same comforting dark black curls framing her face. When she brushed it back, he ached. Her nails were not done. She'd always had her nails done.

"Mom," he said, clutching Ronnie as if he could pull his mother through the screen. "Where are you?"

His mother smiled. "It's good to see you, mijo."

Warm water spilled somewhere inside of him.

"We were in San Antonio with Tia Rodriguez," she continued. "But they've moved south where it's safer." She looked around and said something to someone off camera. She reconnected with him. "Some-place by Three Rivers. But we need to get to Laredo. There should be a safe place near there."

While she spoke, Ronnie served up a map and images of San Antonio—buildings on fire, people huddled together as they fled the city. He had expected to see the shells of buildings. But FROST looked like every other American city, save for the black, red, and blue flag flying over the State House.

His mother's voice pulled him forward. "Manuel, I'm fine, okay?" Her image skipped and jerked. "Manuel, look at me."

He made eye contact with her through Ronnie.

"I am okay. Your father is working to get us back home. Stay strong and look after him while he does. Okay?"

He nodded. "What happened?"

"Oh, Manuel. Governments fight, people suffer." She smiled. "But you are okay and safe. That's all that matters. I am okay. Listen to Sebán."

4

Manuel rarely heard his father's name spoken out loud like that. It was always *sir*, but his mother—when the name Sebán escaped her lips —made it sound warm. Like the tea they'd drink for breakfast. When they'd been together.

The fire behind his eyes crackled as he cried. He wanted her home. Why couldn't she just walk past the York Line and join them in Denver? Why was she going farther south? Why wasn't his father working faster? It had been an eternity.

"You're going to be okay," Silvia cooed into the tablet. "I will see you soon. Don't cry." Her face dropped with sadness. "Sebán won't like that."

Manuel sniffed heavily and nodded. "I'm sorry."

"Don't apologize to me." She smiled, her dark eyes getting that mischievous look. "You have nothing to be sorry for. Now, tell me. What is your job?"

His eye twitched.

The connection cut out.

PART I

NOW

1

AIRLOCK

Solanis

When the great window cracked, Solanis Tailor felt, for the first time, that she had made a mistake that would cost her and her brother their lives.

The pressure in their Boston compound had slowly dropped over the span of a few hours. Ronnie, the AI, had noticed first. It was tapped into the sensors in and outside of their home—the massive fortress in the supposedly protected gated community of Seaport. Once drowned by the floods, Seaport rose—a hybrid of fortified homes, compounds, soaring towers, and green corridors; a stark departure from the chaotic urban density of the past. Ronnie was supposed to let them know when the air pressure didn't match, which would indicate a leak. The compound's pressure systems were designed to keep her home slightly over pressure.

Pressure would keep Haze outdoors. Even a hairline crack could destabilize the balance, allowing the abrasive, razor-like particles to infiltrate their safety.

Both she and Greg had rushed to the living room and examined every corner of the cathedral-high ceilings, wooden walls, and glass fixtures.

Where was the leak?

He had found the crack—a small, curved fissure that tilted upward like a twisted smile. Solanis could hardly see it. But just because you couldn't see something didn't mean it wouldn't kill you.

Earthquakes were invisible, but one had killed her parents. All she had seen were the side effects and the consequences. Falling rocks. Bodies. Denver, fucking Colorado.

She shivered.

"I've got the sealant!" she yelled, running toward the basement steps while her brother headed for the airlock.

"Ronnie!" Greg yelled. "You didn't close the shutters?"

The intelligence responded no. It was having a hard time connecting to StarLight; the satellites couldn't penetrate Haze very well. Access to information was limited.

How did it always sound so nonchalant?

There had been a malfunction in the closing mechanism. The shutters that would protect the great window were stuck open.

Solanis stumbled her way downstairs, her hands vibrating as she searched for the sealant on the shelf with the emergency Haze supplies. Everyone had this kit in their home, issued by the Haze Emergency Response Agency—HERA. But she hadn't expected to need it. Haze wasn't usually deadly for people like her. People with means.

Haze wasn't new. The dark, human-manufactured hurricane was just Mother Nature's way of kicking everyone in the balls—a consequence for using plastic straws that killed turtles, forests, and birds. It was made up of ultra-fine particulates laced with the remnants of toxic industrial compounds that could cause respiratory distress. It was the perfect disaster—just small enough to fly through the air but heavy enough to cut you. When people in Seaport described it, they called it the lightest of the worst. Others compared it to the winter wind in Chicago—cold enough to cut your skin if you didn't bundle up. Denver called it business as usual. Worthington called it an excuse to build more Domes.

Solanis found the glue gun, checked the battery, found it full, and sprinted back upstairs. Greg was near the airlock—the massive secondary room they'd hastily added to the side of their compound earlier in the year—zipping up his light gray jumpsuit while clutching a mask under his arm.

"Seal from the inside," he said. "I'll fix the gears." He put the helmet over his head, turned on the air canister, and then slid a finger over the display next to the airlock room. It indicated his suit was sealed correctly. He gave her a cheesy thumbs-up—the same one her mother used to give her before she toured the stars—and vanished behind the massive door.

Solanis grabbed the ladder, climbed to the creepy smile of a crack, and began her work. "Ronnie, show me Greg," she demanded, powering up the gun.

The wall lit up, and the cameras outside their compound searched for her brother in the dark.

She inspected the window. How could one little line, about five centimeters long and no thicker than a hair, cause so much trouble? It mocked her. The upward curve sneered at her.

She leaned forward to fill the fissure, keeping one eye on Greg. Her hands wouldn't stop vibrating. She had to run her arm across her forehead a few times to steady the stream of sweat that would sting her eyes.

The display showed her brother's silhouette trudging toward the shutter's closing mechanism, hidden in a box next to the great window. His gray jumpsuit was stained dark as he moved, sullied by the grittiness of Haze. He stepped deliberately, fighting against the hurricane the gods sent up into the world, until he reached the box and pulled a tool from his Velcro pocket.

Solanis looked back at the window, determined the seal was applied correctly, and asked Ronnie to check the air pressure inside. The tablet indicated the pressure was normal. Good. Her job was done.

Greg cranked the shutters by hand. They were almost closed when one of the arms snapped, sending the now free shutter hurling toward him.

He reflexively tried to block the shutter with his hands, but it smashed into his helmet, throwing him backward across the front yard. Ronnie gave an alert to emergency services, but Solanis already knew that was useless. The wait, even with his insurance, would be significant.

She ran to the airlock, grabbed the extra jumpsuit, and desperately stepped into it. Greg struggled on the monitor, his hand covering his face.

She did not have much time.

His mask had shattered. He reached into his other pocket, pulled out some duct tape, and hopelessly began to try and tape over his helmet—a pathetic attempt to plug the hole. But instead of heading back inside, he began to make his way back across the yard and toward the now flapping shutter.

Another alarm went off. The window struggled. Solanis's ears popped. Pressure was rising in the room to compensate with the outdoors.

"Come back inside," she urged Greg through the monitor as she pulled her arms through the jumpsuit's sleeves and grabbed a mask repair kit from the shelf. She then began the time-consuming process of checking the seals on her jumpsuit; she'd never had to do this before.

Greg went outside. She didn't.

She didn't want to go out.

Please don't make me go outside.

She didn't want to face Mother Nature.

She willed Greg to finish his work and come back as quickly as possible. But her brother struggled. One hand still covered the makeshift patch while his other arm weakly pushed the shutter closed. He stumbled forward and fell again.

He was going to die.

And then she'd be alone.

She would not be safe if she was alone.

Solanis tied her dark wavy hair into a bun, slipped on her helmet, powered the air canister, and pressed the door to release the airlock.

A red warning alert came on. She ignored it and yelled, "Override!" The system unlocked, and she slid the door open and stepped down into the airlock.

The door had a hard time closing behind her, so she put her shoulder into it, forcing it closed. She knew if this door wasn't shut, the outer door would never open. The indicator above the door turned green.

The massive white room was normally only used during the twice yearly Haze storm. She'd always wondered why the designers made the airlock look like a padded cell. It was all flat walls and air canisters in case of emergency. There were large analog buttons on the walls, and if you looked closely, you could see backup emergency doors embedded in the ground and ceiling of the unit near both entryways. If you were forced to, you could probably live in an airlock this size. At least until you ran out of food.

Greg had once called the room dummy proof.

"Ronnie, let's go," she demanded, crossing the room to the exterior door. "Let's go."

The room filled with more oxygen, increasing the pressure inside just enough to provide an air barrier against the swirl outdoors. She'd feel the push and step outside into the black snow.

The floor vibrated slightly, and the door indicated she could exit when she was ready. There was a flashing red indicator next to the door, its needle pulsing to the right. She told Ronnie to override the warning light, pushed down on the handle, and exited the airlock into the Boston Haze.

The door screeched closed behind her.

Haze was like ash, gray snow swirling in the sky.

It pressed down on her from all sides, like a plate on her back at the gym.

Instead of the bright, calm Camelot air of the reconstructed Seaport, her home was all gray and dark shadows. Small red, green, and blue embers exploded around her like tiny, silent supernovas. The experts had said this was the flammable compounds inside Haze that lit and fizzled. It was a blizzard of ash with the grittiness of death, cloaking the world in an amateur gray and black.

Ronnie beeped happily, and a small pulse filled Solanis's ears as the AI tried to lead her by sound. It would know where Greg was, so she just needed to follow.

She could maybe see a foot in front of her. The airlock was

supposed to light up, but even the beacons were faint in the darkness. She wrinkled her nose; her suit smelled like burnt plastic.

Ronnie chirped, coaxing her to follow its audio guidance. She walked to the left, lifting each foot carefully. Her mother had done this once during astronaut training. She'd walk in the giant pool, the weight of the water forcing her to move slow. In those moments, Solanis would be glued to the edge of the tank, watching through the bright blue and leaving fingerprints on the glass as Greg just sat bored, reading.

She missed her mother. The way she smelled like wood, grapes, and barbecue. If she was still alive, she'd give Solanis a thumbs-up and remind her that there are harder things in the universe.

"Nuclear pasta," Solanis's mom would say, peering cleverly at Solanis as she giggled at the idea. "Hardest substance in the known universe."

This felt harder.

The beeping faded. Solanis pivoted to the left. The beeping grew more confident.

There he is.

Greg hobbled toward her. She couldn't see his face properly, but she knew he noticed her because he began gesturing with his free hand for her to go back. She ignored him and continued walking forward. He needed the patch.

When she reached him, she forced her brother to stop moving. She pulled out the patch kit, placed it over his helmet, and watched as it expanded and covered the hole in his mask. The sheeting bowed outward—a sign of positive air pressure. At least, that was what Ronnie said. She was a communications executive, not a fucking scientist.

She gave her brother half of a thumbs-up, and the two made their way back to the airlock together.

Greg leaned on her, hard. He drifted sideways into her, his body shaking, as he dragged his right leg in the dirt.

The lighthouse that was the beacon for the airlock came into view. She didn't have to tell Ronnie they were coming back in. It would know where they were.

Greg collided with the door, his shoulders heaving up and down. He tried to pull the handle but instead pitched forward.

She frowned. So, maybe Ronnie didn't know where they were.

"No!" she yelled, grabbing Greg around the middle and pushing him onto his back. She pulled the door, and the power operation assisted, sparking a grinding noise from the track. She stepped inside and grasped him under his shoulders and pulled hard to get him inside the airlock. All that lifting in the gym had finally come in handy.

Once his feet crossed the threshold, the outer door tried to slide shut but jammed on the track. They should have maintained this better.

Solanis stepped over Greg. "Come on!" she yelled to no one. "Come on!" She pulled the door, forcing it to close. The light on the door oscillated between green and red until she shoved her shoulder into the door, and it stayed green.

But she wasn't done yet. They'd need to depressurize the chamber to make it equal to their home. Then decontaminate, strip, and decontaminate again. And she needed to see how badly Greg was hurt.

The hissing was back as the air pressure rose. But there was a metallic groan behind her. She spun around and stared at the door.

The indicator was red again. The interior door shuddered violently, bowing outward. The klaxons sounded.

"Pressure irregular," Ronnie said.

No. "Ronnie?" Solanis asked.

"Integrity compromised. The pressure—"

Why the fuck was it always so cheerful?

"Fix it!" Solanis pleaded.

That was dumb. Ronnie would listen to her.

She threw herself on top of her brother as the airlock exploded. The walls buckled around her, and the inner door bent to the side, cracking. Her mask shattered on impact. Glass cut her cheek.

The seal hadn't held.

There was too much pressure in the chamber. Her home couldn't keep up.

The lights flashed crimson and white.

There was an emergency protocol. What was it? Ronnie spoke to her, but all she could hear was her heart thundering in her ears.

She knew this. She'd read the manual. What had it said?

The second explosion rocked the chamber, this time from the exterior door. The door bowed in, and the force threw Solanis and Greg against the wall. Something inside her broke.

The darkness bullied its way into the chamber, blanketing the walls, the sky, and anything that wasn't already grayscale. She groped for her mask, trying to cover any gap. But it was futile. The lights in the room strobed.

The weight of the darkness pulled at her. Her skin itched as thousands of pieces of glass, shards of the past, tore at her.

Another explosion as the spare oxygen tanks mounted on the wall combusted, filling the already crowded air with shrapnel. She knew what had happened—oxygen-rich air and Haze creates fire.

All it took was one spark.

She inhaled.

But it wasn't air that went in. It was the metallic taste and the grittiness of sand and iron. Stars crowded her vision as Greg shook beside her, in shock.

There was an override. She needed the emergency doors to fall. She needed to purge the chamber.

Solanis tasted iron. Blood.

She gasped. "Ronnie, push it out. Push it out."

A loud grinding noise filled the room as she clutched her brother's weak hand, and the room vented the air from the airlock. She realized her mistake. She'd forgotten to take a breath. There was no air left in the room. She clawed at her broken helmet, ripping it off her head. Her ears popped. The emergency doors slammed shut on either side of the room, and a cool mist filled the space as the compound began pumping fresh oxygen into the room.

She was going to die here. The air would not arrive in time. Her esophagus contracted as her throat became sticky and bitter.

Then came the breeze.

It wafted over her nose, and as if by instinct, she took a deep breath. She inhaled glass but also cool, crisp fresh air.

She coughed. Dark burgundy spilled from her mouth.

She was alive.

But she wasn't finished.

Greg was still on the floor, jerking and seizing.

"Greg!" she yelled, her throat screaming at her. "No, no, no." She got on her knees and pulled at his mask. "Ronnie," she gasped. "Decontaminate."

The suits were still dangerous.

Liquid fire fell from the sky.

She recoiled. The gash across Greg's face was deep. Dark lines protruded from his cracked face. He gritted his teeth and shuddered in pain as orange liquid poured in from the ceiling.

She unzipped her suit, pushing it down past her torso and began working on her brother. She knew what to do. She'd always found it difficult to ignore pain, even during her time in the National Service— the consequence of York's war with America.

She was overwhelmed.

Solanis blinked through the orange decontamination fluid, coughing but working quickly. Anything less than fire wouldn't neutralize Haze.

What was it HERA had said?

Decontaminate first. That was the fire rain.

Then treat.

This would hurt.

She pulled the jumpsuit over his torso and waist as he grunted in pain. "I'm sorry," she said. "We have to."

He grabbed her shoulders as she pulled the stained jumpsuit down past his legs and exposed his full body to the fluid. The black snow, the red blood, and the orange-tinted water pooled beneath them. It would drain eventually.

"Ronnie!" she yelled as she held Greg up under the flow of chemicals. "Medical consult."

They needed more time under the blast of the scalding heat of decontamination to ensure nothing got inside.

Those thirty seconds were an eternity as Greg howled in pain.

The water stopped.

Ronnie announced decontamination was finished. The light on the emergency door leading back to the compound turned green, and the door slid out of the way. She confronted the bowed and damaged internal door and threw her back into grinding it open. She returned to Greg, got her arms around his torso, and gasped as she pulled.

"Come on. Help me."

Greg convulsed as she crouched and forced him up to walk. She nearly slipped, her feet still wet from the shower, as she jerked him toward the living room and through the debris in the room. Not much Haze had gotten inside thanks to the pressure difference, but the chairs, tables, and lights had been shoved around. There was glass on the floor.

Ronnie had already set up instructions from HERA on how to treat Greg. Solanis leaned over, dumped him onto the floor, and looked to the screen, which flashed the words *offline mode*.

Fuck.

Ronnie still couldn't see the sky. It would need to use its internal memory for treatment. But in her state, she couldn't read all the instructions.

"Read the steps to me, Ronnie," she said, running half naked back to the airlock and dripping orange. She grabbed the white box with the cross on the front.

"You need to clean the wound," Ronnie said.

She placed the kit on the floor next to Greg who twitched and jerked. Something was wrong.

"Elevated heart rate suggests patient is in distress. HERA recommends administering a sedative. Oxygen level is low."

She watched as the display lit up—bruising, toxicity, and other damage due to rapid decompression and Haze poisoning.

Solanis slid the kit in front of her and pulled out a sealed packet that matched the one on the screen. Inside was a box about the size of a keycard. She placed it on his arm and told Ronnie to go. Her brother winced as the needles in the packet stabbed him. He jerked hard once, gasped, and then fell silent.

She didn't think as she worked. Her arms were tools for Ronnie, working to get Greg's injuries under control. She sprayed the antibiotics and skin growth stimulants onto the gash on her brother's face. She worked with Ronnie to find the shrapnel that was embedded inside him. Ronnie showed her the location of the bits she could yank from his body. She wouldn't get them all. Many of the particulates were too small to access. They'd have to come out over time.

After about an hour, Solanis fell back in relief, her hands sore. The little animation on the screen told her she was finished for now and read her instructions for post-traumatic care.

Ronnie said to look out for side effects from the face injury and that Greg's workplace—Half Dome Enterprises—would be sending some pills to help with the side effects. At least he had good insurance.

She draped a blanket over her brother, whose chest was now rising and falling with an acceptable cadence. She stroked his red hair softly and told him it would be okay.

She stared at the wall with the great window, now shuttered from the outside. Doubt crawled under her skin. Like the sinister smirk in the window, her uncertainty was spreading.

Maybe Greg was right. Maybe they should have left. Should have gone to Philadelphia.

Solanis pulled on the medical cuff from the kit that would diagnose her before she fell back onto the couch, exhausted.

The universe ate her, and she surrendered to a dreamless, dark sleep.

2

FLIGHT FROM BOSTON

Solanis

The first thing Greg said when he opened his eyes was, "What the fuck, Star? Your eyes."

Solanis nodded.

It had been two days since the botched airlock incident, and the side effects were still manifesting themselves. She had noticed her eyes about a day ago—how the scleras had become gray. Where white had been, there was just a milky darkness. Her vision had become more crowded, the darkness threatening to steal her eyesight. She was seeing red ghosts and fireflies around her home that she tried to wave away with a swat of her hand.

The fireflies ignored her.

She had covered all the mirrors when the entire eyeball had turned jet black. "Yours are like that too," she said, reaching for a cup of water. "Drink this. HERA says it's normal."

He sat up, using his arms to push himself straight. He accepted the cup and took a sip. He moved slower than usual, gingerly. "I don't give a fuck what Montgomery-Chavez has to say." He had only been awake for a few moments, and he was already imitating the news feeds where they cursed the HERA administrator's name.

She reached onto the side table and handed her brother two bright blue pills, stamped *ACER*. "Worthington sent these. Said it would help with your condition. Take two every four hours."

He inspected the pills. "How did they know?"

"Ronnie messaged Half Dome, I guess."

"You get pills?"

"Said they were for you."

He scowled and then crossed his arms.

"Gregory," she snapped. "Take them."

"Don't call me that."

"Take the pills."

"I hate it when people call me that."

"I hate it when you don't listen to doctors."

Her brother pouted. Then dry swallowed the pills. He ran his hand over the rough edge of the scar that was fading on his face and waved his hand in front of his eyes. He inspected his palm. "Mine black too?"

"Yes," she said. "But they said—"

"Normal. I know." He scowled and closed his eyes. "We need to leave."

She shook her head. She didn't want to say.

"Star..." He gave a slow blink and breathed deep. "Did you ask yourself the question?"

She rolled her eyes. "Not this again."

"Star, come on."

"*What do you know?*" She rolled her eyes again in bitter imitation of her brother. "It doesn't always come down to that."

Greg would always say that awful line when trying to solve a problem. "What did we know about Haze and the last couple of days?" He grabbed his tablet from the side table and began flicking through it. "People are dead."

"Put it down. You need to rest."

"Star, what do we know?"

Solanis tugged her black hair and let it fall over her face.

"You look like Mom when you do that." His smile was gentle. "Now. Come on. What do we know?"

"Haze has been in Boston for a few weeks now."

"Right, and it's only gotten worse."

"But they said—"

"*They?*"

"HERA said not to leave." Solanis felt a twinge of annoyance. "Stay in your home."

"But?"

"We are running out of food."

"And we are sick." He pointed at their eyes. He coughed again, hard. Black bile stained his lips. "We can't stay here for much longer."

She didn't want to talk about this. She didn't want to leave. This was her home. "Maybe we should have moved into one of those Domes. You know, the ones your boss makes."

His laugh dissolved into a hacking cough. "No, Star, no." He put down his tablet. "Absolutely not."

"But they can protect me from Haze."

"And you end up locked in that thing forever." His eyes shimmered for a second, and she thought he had rolled them. But it was hard to tell with eyes so dark. "Not worth becoming an Evergreen over this. Abandon your life. Live inside a Dome."

"They're not dying like we are."

"They're not living either."

The silence was a rickety chair.

Solanis pushed a little more. "They protect us from Haze, right? Your boss is probably in one."

"The boss can do whatever he wants."

"Have you been inside a Dome?"

Greg winced. "You won't catch me in there."

"You won't use your own product?"

"I enjoy living life on the edge." He opened his arms, grinning. "Boston. Where Haze is just a breeze away."

Solanis frowned. "Maybe leave the PR to the professionals."

He hacked another laugh.

"Take the pills, rest, and drink water. I have work to do."

"Of course you're working." He gave her a mocking look.

She shrugged. "What else am I going to do?"

"Solanis Tailor. Ever predictable."

"Go shower," Solanis shot back. "You smell like sweat. And your workshop."

Greg gave her a light nudge on the shoulder, ignoring her jab. "Come on... Predictability isn't always a bad thing." He sniffed his armpit and shrugged.

Solanis didn't smile. Her ex-boyfriend had called her predictable once.

But Greg was right.

He was never wrong.

————

SOLANIS HAD BEEN UNEMPLOYED for a year once, and every day was a nightmare. She spent the hours applying for jobs, working out, and wandering around Boston to try to get her mind to stop reminding her how much of a failure she was. But just being in downtown Boston had been enough to make her feel better.

Boston was home. The Boston pulse was familiar.

If she closed her eyes, no matter where she was in the city, she'd feel grounded. The pulse moved with her soul: the way the buildings groaned under the weight of history; the feel of the people streaming around her; and the way the city smelled, smiled, throbbed. The pulse was consistent with its breakfast rushes, rush hours, and weekend gatherings. Even though everyone scrambled around, addicted to Ronnie or staring at the massive displays on the side of buildings that showed public news feeds, Boston had an element of personal intimacy to Solanis. The pulse was constant like her heartbeat—unnoticed until it skipped or stopped entirely. Everything had a place.

But with Haze now in the streets, Solanis was trapped in her home office, video conferencing her team of engineers to keep them on track. As the communications director for RealityLife, a tech start-up famous for holding the patent for the first fully functional mechanical prosthetic that looked real, Solanis's job was to communicate Reality's priorities to the world. That meant getting Omer, her director of technology, to yank his head out of the clouds and focus on what she needed—the bigger picture. Or, as her CEO Val Reality called it, *changing the menu*.

Omer's distraction was understandable. His work wife Theresa had been missing for months. Sentinel, the private security in Boston, had been searching. But no luck.

Omer fumbled over his words as he tried to follow the formula Solanis had insisted everyone on the technical team use when presenting to her. The format—problem, cause, solution, use case—was the only way she'd listen to presentations. It made her life easier, kept things organized. This was the safe way of doing her job.

"BlackBox really is, technically speaking, an incredible piece of technology," Omer said, his eyes moving side to side behind his glasses—a sign he was reading his notes while he spoke. "BlackBox is built off a frequency of patterns that are constantly rotating. This one device can block and regulate all signals going in and out of a city. It can also keep everything safe."

"Everything?" Solanis asked, leaning forward in her chair. The fire-flies were dancing. She had to brighten her display so she could see him better. "It'll protect you from another blackout?"

He nodded. "We've tested it, and it works. It's blackout-proof. You won't lose your data."

She raised an eyebrow. "You're serious?"

"Absolutely. After the blackouts fifteen years ago, this is what people have been demanding. Solanis, this is it. This is the product. This is changing the menu."

They had lost everything in the cyberattacks fifteen years ago. Everyone had slept through their alarms because the very foundations of their lives had been shaken.

She had been in the National Service at the time, serving her oblig-atory two years by pounding out press releases and communications materials for the army near the York Line. The United States had been at war then, and for a moment, she thought they'd revert to throwing sticks over the border. She hadn't gotten paid that day because, without Ronnie, everything had ground to a halt. While the hackers never revealed themselves, for nineteen hours, people panicked when they realized all their devices were empty. No more names, numbers, contacts, photographs, or porn.

After, people had rushed to build new hardened infrastructure. A lot of it was cheap and not made to last.

Val Reality knew that if she could bring a product to the market that could be hardened against attacks in the future, RealityLife could become one of the most profitable companies in the world. If Solanis's team could devise something that worked and actually protected data, even from invisible hackers, she could become chief communications officer—a remarkable achievement for someone only in their first career.

Solanis would need to study the fact sheets and learn more about the product and how to position the device. She'd need to speak to the analysts about pricing. There was so much to do.

"When will it be ready?" she asked.

Omer looked off screen for a second. "Nine months. We could go faster."

"Don't move too fast. This is going to pay us our bonuses." She grinned at him. "I'll buy the first round of drinks when the money hits the bank."

He smiled back. "You should know, we are working on a way to crack it—"

She shook her head. "No, I don't really care about that. The shareholders won't take lightly to our uncrackable box being crackable."

He took off his glasses; he didn't need to read his script anymore. "I didn't say it was uncrackable. Nothing is uncrackable. If you had a few centuries and enough processing power, you'd be able to crack anything."

She raised an eyebrow.

"My point, Solanis, is that you need a way to turn it off. BlackBox, it is built on a frequency of patterns. Solve the pattern, and you can turn off the box. Only it's just a lot of invisible patterns you can't see. You'd need a key and a way to see those patterns."

"Invisible?" She rubbed her eyes; they were sore again.

"More or less." He nodded. "You and I can't see them, but maybe if butterflies still existed, real ones anyway, they might be able to see the patterns in the sun."

She nodded and forced a smile; he was making this too complicated. "Whatever. Just keep that to yourself, the butterfly stuff. Same time next week?"

Omer raised a finger. "There is one more thing. Our missing colleague. Theresa. They found her. She's in one of those Domes."

She frowned. "And she didn't tell anyone?"

"Looks like it. But when you get a chance, watch the interview with her mom and that news feed reporter guy. Something's off about the whole thing."

Solanis sighed. She knew he was sensitive. He'd liked the new girl a lot, and her vanishing had wrecked him. "Omer, you've got to move on."

He grimaced. "Her mother Aiesha is demanding an investigation. You donate to her channel?"

"I'm rolling my eyes, Omer."

"I can't tell," he said quickly. "They're too dark. They just shimmer."

"Good." She rolled them. "I can't donate to her channel. You realize Theresa's an adult. It's a lost cause."

"Be nice," he insisted. "There's something off about all of this."

"Don't let me catch you wearing red and holding her portrait. Louder Than the Earth have been causing problems around that second Dome. What's it called?"

"Shalina," he said a little too quickly. "LTE means well. They've just been through it."

Solanis raised an eyebrow. "They brand their victims."

"Every movement has radical factions." Omer was dismissive. "Theresa used to say it all the time. That's"—he looked at the ceiling and then back at the camera—"the crucible, right? You go through it and the squeeze. And the person who comes out is either a phoenix or a monster."

"And you're saying Louder Than the Earth is filled with…"

"Monsters maybe. Both creatures—they're not real of course, but the way Theresa used to tell it—both creatures are made of fire, but the phoenix can do good. The monster can destroy the planet in its anger."

"LTE are going to destroy the planet?"

"They're trying to save the planet."

"You might be onto something. Did you see the one who set herself on fire? I'm pretty sure they blew up one of Worthington's Waystations. You've seen them, standing outside our offices with the massive photos of Theresa. They don't speak. Monsters."

His nod was stiff. "I just don't get it. Why would Theresa just leave and not say goodbye? We need to do something. Aiesha will. Rumor has it she's running for Congress."

"When she does, maybe she can get us better jobs. Tell her we know her daughter. Theresa the Evergreen."

He didn't say goodbye when he ended the call.

———

WHEN GREG COUGHED, the blood clot spattered onto the small black disk he'd been working on. Both he and Solanis stared at the disk before he quickly wiped away the dark red blood and ran his hand over his mouth. She could tell he was scared.

"I've been taking the pills," he insisted as he wiped down the rest of the workstation and stashed the disk into a safe behind him. "You take them too?"

"I didn't get any. Employees only." Despite the warmth, she shivered.

She checked the news feeds. There were others like her brother. Coughing blood, black and thick. Some had dark eyes. "Maybe we should..." She shook her head and pointed at her tablet. "There are bodies in the street. This is our home."

He didn't respond.

But she saw it—what was happening. Even if she didn't want to.

During dinner, he ran his fingers through his hair. Clumps of it were falling out.

He stopped going to his workshop.

He started missing door handles, light switches.

She was certain they needed to stay inside. The time to evacuate had passed.

Only, Boston had other plans.

The city caught on fire.

Greg awoke her in her room, groping for her in the dark and mumbling that they needed to leave.

The city, the world, was on fire. She could hear the screams, the thundering on the walls.

He grabbed the tablet from her hands and hobbled back toward the door. He missed the center, smashing his face and tablet into the wall, and growled. His head pitched back as he grabbed his nose. Black blood leaked from his face.

She stared at him as the lights rose and fell, caught between their nighttime and emergency alert settings. "Greg?" she asked, her breath ragged.

Was he okay? He needed to be okay.

He groaned and grabbed her wrist, dragging her from the bed and into the hallway. She didn't want to leave, but even she could see the tints of acid green, the red fires, and the electric blue flames shooting through the darkness as the house rumbled around them.

She kicked, trying to wrangle herself out of his wet but firm grip. She couldn't go outside. That was the danger. That was the threat.

That was the cave.

Greg fell down the stairs, dragging her down with him. Her face hurt, her wrist hurt, and her fingers hurt. Everything hurt. He stood, howling in pain and grabbing at his shoulder blade.

A bone protruded from his back, cutting through his shirt.

She stared, her eyes huge, as she watched the deformity grow.

Howling with pain, he whirled around, hoisted her up over his good shoulder, and stumbled his way to the carport. She bounced, watching the back door that led to her home get smaller and smaller. He placed her in the car, slammed the door, and hobbled over to the other side. Haze pounded on the garage door, demanding entry. All she could feel was Haze around her, the rocks from the earth collapsing in on her and the taste of iron in her mouth.

Please don't turn on the lights.

Solanis screamed and clawed at the door handle. She needed to go back inside, where it was safe. There was nothing in the black snow for her. She didn't want to wander in the dark.

But Greg knew her. He'd locked the door from the outside.

There was no air in here.

Why couldn't she inhale?

She was going to collapse with dizziness.

She would die.

Her body shook.

There were tears on her face, yet her eyes were dry.

Solanis snapped her head to the right as the light in the car came on. Greg was in the driver's seat. He was looking at her, his dark eyes barely visible through the thick darkness.

"I got you," he said. "I am here. What do we know?"

His voice was clear. Not raspy. Not coughing.

Crystal.

She shook her head, gripping the armrest. "No," she moaned. She clawed at her throat. The air was too thin. "No."

"Star." He grabbed her arm. His hand was devastatingly cold. "It's like I said in Virginia. You are safe when we are together."

She clamped her mouth shut and closed her eyes. *Don't remind me of Virginia.*

"Say it, Star."

Take me back inside.

Why couldn't she speak?

And then it was easy. She summed it up in her soul, and the words came out. "I am safe when we are together."

There we go.

He instructed the car to take them south.

———

Boston was dying.

The lime, electric, and scarlet flames erupted into the air, forcing the car to tint the windows as it jerked and accelerated down the streets.

Screams followed the flames.

29

The thick Boston Haze pressed against the car windows like pounding protestors as Solanis held herself in the passenger seat. The car complained that it had lost its spotty connection to StarLight, forcing Greg to grab the yoke and navigate manually. Her brother, with the bone in his back and his sticky hands, squinted through the darkness, relying on the car's night vision to navigate.

The car swerved and jerked forward under his guidance. Bodies littered the streets as people choked, gasped, and pleaded for help. Soldiers, in masks and protective gear, gestured for them to head toward I-93 to get out of the city. As they crawled onto the expressway, the car chirped, insisting it had found a connection to StarLight again. But Solanis didn't trust the link.

Greg made it fifty-nine kilometers before she had to drive.

By then, her brother was squinting, blinking hard, and shaking. Blood came from his eyes. A blood vessel in his arm had burst, giving his skin a purplish red tint.

There was an almost milky gray glint coming from his left cheek.

Red embers and fireflies swirled around Solanis. The screens in the car spewed out red waves. Everything sent light her way. The corners of her vision were collapsing.

———

AFTER HOURS in the car with a shivering, coughing, dying Greg, he and Solanis reached a checkpoint with a group of soldiers. The car greeted the National Guard, throwing up a safety signal on the dashboard and happily requested permission to send their identification information to the soldiers.

A soldier pulled down his mask and tapped at his tablet. The device glowed red as fireflies swirled around the device. "Tailor?"

"My brother. Please. He's not doing well. We were in Seaport. Boston." Solanis coughed and clutched her brother's shaking, sticky, cold hand.

Greg was in bad shape. There was now a jagged, growing dagger of bone protruding from his arm, the sharp edges cutting through the skin as the surrounding tissue pulsed hot and red. The bone glowed against his body. Each time he breathed, the wound expanded.

She whimpered.

"He's your brother?" the soldier asked, his eyes shifting between Solanis's tan skin and Greg's pale, beaten complexion.

Solanis yelled, "Help him!"

The soldier gave a curt nod and motioned for two of his colleagues to join them. The other two soldiers, guns in hand, jogged in their direction.

Greg muttered something and pressed his hand against the car's dash. In an instant, the windows slid back up and turned black.

"What are you doing?" she cried, raising her hand to unlock the doors.

But he grabbed her.

His grip hurt.

His hand was cold.

There was banging outside the car.

He yelled as the bone in his arm split the skin further. He coughed. A blood clot splattered on the window. She jumped in her seat, recoiling and fighting the urge to comfort her brother.

He shook.

The banging grew louder.

The car happily asked if he could comply with law enforcement.

He reached around his neck and yanked the chain he'd been wearing. He gave her a hard look. His eyes were pitch black, nearly vanishing, as he squinted and spoke through heavy, wet, gasping breaths. "You have to keep this." He thrust the flat disc into her hands. It was the disk he'd been working on in his workshop—small, round, and smooth. He spoke through gritted teeth. One of his canines cracked and broke. He clutched her with freezing hands.

Solanis accepted the disk.

He gagged and then coughed again. "Keep it."

Her face was sticky with blood.

"Hide it," he said.

From the passenger's side, the banging grew louder still.

"Keep it until I get back."

The passenger door exploded open, and one of the soldiers, now wearing a mask, sliced through Greg's seatbelt while another dragged him from the car.

She covered her ears at the noise of the explosion and blinked several times, trying to get her bearings.

"Come back," Solanis said weakly as she scrambled over the seat. Her knee clipped the middle console, sending pain up her leg. But as she tumbled out of the car and into the light, she tried again. "Where are you taking him?" Her voice was no more than a whisper. She could see Greg, still being dragged away from her.

He convulsed, his legs cutting into the grass.

"Where are you?" She stumbled forward. Her legs weren't working properly. She tried to call again, coughing as she spat grass. "Greg..."

A firm hand wrapped around her arm and pulled her back.

She wanted to throw up. Her stomach flipped.

She squeezed the disk.

I am safe when we are together.

Solanis rapidly breathed through her nose, the stink of cut grass flooding her senses. Greg moaned as the soldiers kicked his legs out from under him. He fell backward with a thud, blood flowing from his mouth and nose.

With the practiced efficiency only the trained army could muster, one of the soldiers pulled a large black bag forward and placed it under Greg's legs. The unzipping noise tore through her soul.

For a second, Greg locked eyes with her.

The universe moved in slow motion, every single frame in front of her articulated so boldly and precisely that she could have reached up and adjusted the lines that made up her brother's face.

Was he smiling? That clever hint of a smile he always gave her.

The smile that told her he'd be back as soon as he was patched up. As soon as he had some oxygen in his body. As soon as they fixed his eyes. The smile that told her exactly what she knew—that they were safe when they were together.

She blinked, and the smile was gone. It was a lie.

Reality came crashing down on her as the soldiers zipped the bag shut around Greg and dragged him away.

She screamed, clutching the grass beneath her.

The earth was moving too fast.

3

THE GREAT EARTHQUAKE

Manuel

The elevator always felt slower after a double shift. A day investigating a new outbreak of the flu that threatened to cross FROST's border into the United States meant more tests, more protocols. Manuel didn't enjoy working as part of the military machine, but rent was due by the fifth of the month. And getting paid meant long days laboring over the steel tables in the lab, and only getting high on the weekends.

He wanted to go home.

He wanted his mother home.

At least tonight, he would be able to speak to her again.

Over the past thirteen years, he'd spoken to his mother off and on. Mere moments at a time. But his own government had demanded SatTech block all connections between the United States and the Free Republic to stop "the enemy" from communicating. That meant his mother couldn't call home. How his mother was "the enemy," he didn't know. But once again, he was the victim of powerful people who didn't think things through. The anxiety that built up inside him caused him to develop crease lines on his forehead—lines that his father insisted were proof that he was a man, maturing.

"Men worry about the world around them," his father had said from his seat at the table as he managed the weekly household budget. "You need to protect people around you. That's masculinity. Not this other shit you see in the news feeds." He wagged his finger at Manuel. "You can cry. Alone. In your room. With your sweetheart or confidant if needed. No shortcuts in life or emotions. But never in front of them." He had gestured toward the window. "In front of them, you turn pain into something productive. Like your job for the thereafter."

His father would then ramble on about how there were three kinds of men. "The ones who fold under pressure like a baby giraffe, wobbling on its legs and tripping over itself. The second is the monster, the one who, under pressure, destroys the world. But the most brilliant is the phoenix."

Manuel would fight the urge to roll his eyes.

"The fowl that would rise from the ashes, lead everyone to the thereafter." Sebán would get that glint in his eyes when he spoke of the phoenix.

Manuel had done his job. He completed his two years of the National Service. He graduated from college, securing a decent job at the lab. But his father always demanded more. He'd brought home his certificate on the dean's list, and Sebán took one look at him and asked if he could keep it up for all four years. Manuel was a valedictorian, and his dad was asking him if he'd applied for graduate school. During the ceremony for honors at the lab, his father had shoved his hands into his pockets and simply nodded. He didn't even get a knowing look of understanding or approval.

Just a curt nod.

Manuel's mother had become a freeport for his achievements. He'd jot down lists and lists of things so he wouldn't forget during their nearly monthly calls. When he spoke of his accomplishments, she'd smile through the camera and announce to her room that her son was doing excellent work back home. They'd tell him stories, tales of long ago. Mostly fiction, but the tales of warriors and heroes eased the pain. The women of the Free Republic would fawn over him.

In those moments, he would glow.

The women always looked frail, too thin with hollow cheeks.

"Spaceman," a woman with dark curly hair playfully said to Manuel, jerking him back from his thoughts. Her arm held the elevator door open.

"Thank you," he said as he stepped inside.

Another man followed them into the elevator, took one look at Manuel, and stepped closer to the woman, casually leaning his head forward. "You doing anything tonight? A few of us are headed to the bar across from The Pig & The Sprout."

Manuel rolled his eyes. Everyone was jockeying for position to speak to the new woman from Washington, DC.

She stole a look at Manuel, chuckled, and opened her mouth to respond—only for the earth to choose that moment to fall from under them.

In an instant, the three were airborne. Pain radiated through Manuel's skull as he smashed into the lights above his head, shattering the covers. He flung his arms up to try and shield his eyes from the thin glass rain, but he was too late. The woman screamed. His face burned from the hot shards.

His knees buckled as he slammed into the ground, collapsing under the weight of gravity. The elevator came up to greet him and then bucked to the left and the right.

As quickly as it started, the world became still.

He blinked a few times, trying to regain his bearings. He pushed himself up from the floor, glass embedding into his palms. Pain shot up his arm.

The floor was sticky with blood.

He tested his voice. "Is everyone okay?" It sounded strangely muffled in the settling box.

The woman whimpered from the corner of the elevator as the man groaned, face down in the glass. Blood dripped from his head.

The ground sped away from them again.

Manuel yelled, and his elevator partners were flung to the ceiling. This time, he threw his hands over his head, and his arms took the brunt of the impact. Glass, flecks of metal, and blood swirled around him as the elevator sped toward the bottom of the shaft. The ceiling pushed them further down until weight was restored, and they smashed into the ground with a wet thud. Something crunched.

"Stay down," Manuel groaned through the flashing lights as the woman tried to stand. He pushed himself up and grabbed the handles embedded in the elevator walls. "Come here." He motioned toward her. "Grab this." He pulled off his tie and looped it around the handles on the side of the elevator, creating a better grip. "Just in case."

She crawled to his side of the elevator. Her forearms were streaked with blood. Glass glittered her dark curly hair, and her skin was stained with paint where the elevator had come apart. He had seen the look on her face before.

Fear.

The air tasted of iron.

"What's your name?" he asked the woman, trying to calm his breathing. He reached his arm out and slowly lowered it to the ground. *Calm.*

"Cassie," she said, giving him a quizzical look. "Cassie. From Washington."

He tried to smile. "Manuel. I'm from here."

She gave a slow, stiff nod. Her breathing was stabilizing. "I'm here on a work trip. I'm not a scientist. It's all government affairs. I shouldn't even be here right now. I was subbing in for Eric, but his kids were in school, and—" She forced a smile, but it just looked like a grimace. "I think he's dead." She pointed at the man who lay still, the oscillating red and white flashing lights hiding and revealing the growing pool of blood around his head.

The elevator told them to stay put. Emergency assistance was on the way.

Both of them held on to the elevator handles.

He groped the floor for Ronnie, but his hands shook too much. *What is happening?*

The elevator shook again. He grabbed Cassie's arm and pulled her close. He wanted to believe he had grabbed her to shield her from the danger, but he knew the truth.

He didn't want to be alone when he died.

When they were freed from the elevator, they left their dead colleague behind.

———

AFTER SUCCESSFULLY DODGING STAR SERVICES, the private security who had put up caution LEDs out front, Manuel and Cassie climbed the twenty-nine floors to Manuel's childhood apartment.

There didn't seem to be too much damage.

"Dad?" he said into the darkness. He paused, listening for a response.

His father would be sitting at the table in the back room, composing his daily letter to the president and telling Ronnie to reach out to FROST's president too. But all he heard was a monitor somewhere deep inside the home.

He took a few steps forward. "Dad?" he yelled again, dragging his sleeve over his face. He wanted to sound authoritative when he encountered his father, not the dribbling mess from the elevator earlier.

But the apartment was silent.

Sebán's body was wedged between the floor and the heavy bookcase that had taken up the far wall in their seating area—the bookcase where his diploma from the University of Colorado had sat.

The bookcase where the last photo he had taken with his mother and father had always been.

The Colorado heat had dried the bloody crown around his father's head. Ronnie lay shattered next to him, the display still flickering the last letter he'd been composing, the one demanding his wife's freedom.

Cassie screamed.

Manuel stared at the contorted body and frowned. "Dad?"

His father didn't answer him.

He wouldn't.

Manuel got down on his knees, suddenly aware that his heart was beating in his ears. His blood was pumping through his body, and the cadence was regulated through his heart muscles.

Manuel sucked in air so quickly he felt dizzy. He brushed back his father's hair. "*Dad!*" he yelled. "Get up. We have work to do."

Something warm gripped his shoulder. He jumped. It was Cassie.

"Manuel," she said quietly. She had taken off her blazer and held it in her right hand. "He's gone."

He shook his head. "No. He would have said goodbye first. He wouldn't leave like this. We have work to do. We haven't gotten her from there yet." He gestured toward the display that had fallen off the wall. He couldn't read it; the world was all blurry. "She's still there. He hasn't gotten her out." His ears rang. The lights hurt. Something metal buzzed behind his eyes. His head swam. He looked back down at his father. "Dad, come on. ¡Despierta!"

But his father didn't move.

Cassie stepped in front of him and put her blazer over his father's face, covering him. He felt himself collapse into her arms as he leaned backward. She held him.

Now that his father couldn't see him, he cried. The heat inside of him released, and he shook.

Hard.

She kept holding him, her chin resting on his shoulder. He felt the wetness of her tears, but he didn't mind.

He looked up at Cassie. "He's gone."

But she wasn't looking at Sebán or Manuel. She stared at the display that was tilted on its side, where Washington, DC had flooded. The dome of the US Capitol had collapsed. The city had cracked as it slid into the swelling Potomac River. The news feed showed a map of the United States, where the East Coast was reforming. Great chunks of Virginia, Delaware, and North and South Carolina were simply gone.

It wasn't just Denver. The Earth had shaken. The planet had tried to kill them.

Manuel reached above himself and squeezed Cassie's shoulder. "I..." He didn't know what to say.

Behind the table, a glint of light caught his eye. His mother's monstera sat undisturbed in its terrarium, its leaves full and green. He stared at the plant and, for a moment, could smell his mother. The scent she'd always wear. The way no dirt would stain her long, beautiful nails. The way her hair cupped her face.

He needed to find her.
Before the earth shook again.

4

WALTER

Solanis

When Solanis first glimpsed the camp HERA had set up nearly five hundred kilometers from the checkpoint where her brother was zipped into a body bag, she was struck by the attempt at organization. The camp was rows of tiny rectangular shacks shoved together with the massive HERA seal—an eagle glaring at a hurricane spiral—stamped on top. On the hills around the camp were the massive green tents— trademarks from the Evergreens.

Worthington's devotees were here.

Solanis had heard of the camps before—the government's well-intentioned, organized way to deal with the side effects of the two Haze clouds that roamed North America. But Big Brother was over-whelmed. Everything started in clean, Denver-like grids but soon gave way to barrack-like, haphazard placements. There were dirt roads that simply ended as if HERA had forgotten to give them a destination, or they'd been eaten by the pure volume of people.

Solanis was given three tokens in her account that she could use for meals, a place in a shack filled with four bunk beds, a folding chair, and a cabinet that looked like it would give you an infection if you rested your hand on it for too long.

Her roommates, who seemed to be having an equally bad month, took one look at her and scoffed when she asked them if there was a bar where she could get a drink, clearly deciding it was better to ignore her than to engage. The old woman on the top bunk shoved her purse under her pillow.

It was fine.

Solanis could hear her fellow refugees sobbing into the night. The pillows weren't as thick as they thought.

———

"YOUR EYES ARE NOT SHOWING any signs of clearing up. We need a more aggressive path of treatment." The doctor who visited Solanis and her roommates on a weekly basis gazed at his tablet while instructing her to blink and look up and down.

"Can you clear the darkness?" Solanis fidgeted, giving serious side-eye to the fireflies clustered around the doctor's tablet.

"Doubt it," the doctor said, tapping the screen a few times. "You're not the only one. You're using the eye drops, right?"

She nodded.

She'd been using them for the past month since she'd been at camp. She never really got used to calling this refugee center a camp. They weren't singing songs and chanting around a fire. Just crying and nursing their wounds.

Nothing was getting better.

She just wanted to go back to Boston.

She wanted to see her brother.

"No matter. We won't give up." The doctor tapped at his tablet a few times, swept back the canvas flaps, and forced the door open with his shoulder. He reached up and snatched a package out of the air, delivered by a small drone. The box, stamped *ACER*, was white and contained several bright blue plastic vials. "Try these twice a day for a month to make sure you don't lose your vision." He held up the vials. "They're experimental. But we gotta throw everything at this."

She accepted the package. "Can I at least see him?"

The doctor breathed heavily and peered at her from over his

42

glasses. "I have nothing to do with your brother, Miss…" He looked at his tablet but came up empty.

She scowled. "Tailor."

"Yes." He tapped the display. "Solanis Tailor. I'm supposed to ask about your mood, but the answer seems obvious."

"I'm done yelling," she said.

He raised an eyebrow.

"I am."

"Good."

She had yelled enough the first few days at camp.

The first day she'd arrived, she'd hiked up the hill to the hospital and demanded to see Greg.

"My brother," she begged to the nearest nurse who screamed when she saw her. "He was just taken by them. Is he here? I need to see him."

The nurse dropped her tablet. "Your eyes."

"Get over yourself." Solanis glared at her.

Another nurse—a heavyset man wearing a HERA badge—held up his hands. "Ma'am, if you're looking for someone, you'll need to speak to the concierge. A doctor should be able to look at your eyes—"

"He's tall, red hair, and his eyes are black. Like mine. There were these…" She squeezed the bridge of her nose as the image of the bones protruding from her brother's arm and shoulder slipped into her mind. "Tell me where he is. I need to see him."

The man shook his head and pointed back at the front desk. "You're not a princess. Everyone speaks to the concierge."

The concierge gave her a sympathetic look and said the hospital hadn't processed anyone fitting Greg's description. "The military doesn't usually bring their personnel here," the woman said, looking at the screen in front of her. The fireflies clustered there too.

Solanis gripped the top of the plastic reception desk and begged the woman to check again. "I was with him yesterday," she said. "There were these soldiers. People. They pulled him into a bag."

But the concierge had already begun looking at the line that had formed behind her. She'd have to sign up for the registry, and someone would alert her when and if he arrived.

43

Solanis ignored the woman and stormed to the back of the hospital, tripping several alarms and forcing the security team to scramble after her.

When the security team finally calmed her down to a point where she had stopped crying and was sitting quietly in a booth with a sympathetic-looking counselor, she realized how she must have looked to the world.

Like a woman who bit glass on purpose.

None of these orderlies, technicians, or doctors had seen her in her prime—as the fit, confident, fantastic woman she was before Haze ate away at her. They had probably assumed she was this erratic figure— the typical angry Black woman who was willing to cause a scene to get what she wanted.

So, she spent her days in limbo. Refusing to move on until she heard more about Greg. She did the recommended breathing exercises, used her eye drops, and did her best to get into a routine so she wouldn't go completely insane. She would drag herself awake from nightmares of her brother, bones jutting out of his arm, shoulder, and face. She'd do her exercises, stare into the mirror at her ruined eyes, and listen to people cry. The old woman in the bunk above grinded her teeth in her sleep.

What unsettled Solanis the most was the children from Boston—all of them with their little black eyes, playing around her feet, holding out their tablets, and asking for money.

The innocent ones.

Like her.

Solanis still visited the medical center each day, asking the concierge if they'd seen Greg. Each time, the concierge would type a few keys into the console and kindly say, "No."

Sometimes, Solanis would take the back entrance into the center and wander. She'd pay off a janitor or a nurse and check every single bed, fearful she'd discover— No. She didn't want to consider it.

Yet the routine continued.

She slept, she worked out, she ate, she roamed the hospital, and she slept some more.

Haze still ravaged Boston.

The kids with black eyes sang for her.

Solanis distracted herself. She got back to work again in the spring —calling into conference calls and producing releases for BlackBox, which was now on the market. It changed the menu. But she didn't care. At least the fireflies had faded.

She wrote letters to her alderman.

She wandered.

She slept, she worked, she worked out, she ate, and she roamed the hospital.

Over and over.

Day after day.

Week after week.

Month after month.

Springtime turned into the heat of summer.

Boston smoldered.

She slept.

Worked.

Worked out.

Ate.

Slept.

When her doctor told her Greg was dead, she thought she'd misunderstood him. He just walked in and said it.

She squinted. "I'm sorry. Did you just—"

"Your brother, Gregory Tailor, is dead." The doctor looked down at Ronnie and thumbed at it a few times. "Patient 89762. The National Guard sent a photo if you want to see."

She shook her head and flapped her arms to push back the world that was suddenly too heavy, forcing itself on her. She was suffocating in the sweltering heat.

This was it. Her mother had warned her. The universe had come to kill her, smashing her inside her own personal black hole. The world was spinning too fast, and it was all she could do to hang on for dear life and stop from falling from its gravity. She needed to go outside and ground herself, cling to the grass so she didn't get ripped from the planet.

Greg was in front of her. His smile planted on his face. He was helping her up when she fell. There he was, falling down the stairs and insisting it never happened. He was looking at her again, silently communicating through their unspoken bond. Saying she had been chosen, not abandoned when she was adopted.

He flickered out.

Just the wall, the door, and the doctor.

And then he was back. Greg's bone, stained with deep black blood.

Somewhere in the back of her mind, she knew she wasn't suffocating, even if it felt like death had come to claim her. This was just her mind rebelling. She pulled in more air, her eyes hot. Her chest itched, and her heart expanded and then exploded, the fire cascading through her arms, stomach, and legs.

But beneath the pain, the squeeze of the black hole, and the fire of her panic attack, her mind and soul let out a warm, low wail.

Relief.

Solanis found herself crying. Under sadness's gravity, she found a pocket of relief. Greg wasn't suffering anymore. There were no more protrusions from his back. No more jutting bones.

No more black blood.

The doctor didn't know Greg, yet he found it perfectly sensible to call him Patient 89762. As if her brother was just a lab animal—some failed experiment.

"You're an asshole," she told the doctor.

"Am I?" He raised an eyebrow.

"*Patient 89762?*"

"You're quick to judge. Yet you don't even ask my name."

"Don't you have someplace else to be?" she shot back. Her mind was on autopilot, the gears whirring in her head. Her fingers clenched tightly against her palms. The water he had handed her spilled.

The doctor shrugged.

And then it dawned on her.

This wasn't his first death conversation today.

This was his job.

So, Solanis grieved.

Her mind hurt.

Moving hurt.

Being alive hurt.

She moaned, the sound echoing like a weak car horn as it crept down the street.

Her body was lead.

Zippers scratched her skull.

She flinched.

Why hadn't anyone told her it would be the last time she'd see her brother alive? She would have said something profound. She would have told him that she loved him. At least that much.

This tasted bitter. What was it—bile, regret? Stale bread?

Was she safe now?

They were not together.

Could she be safe again?

———

SOLANIS REFUSED to go to the monthly memorial service, where the camp honored those who died. It would be a bunch of politicians and mopey people saying nice things about the dead.

They didn't know Greg. They'd probably call him Gregory.

Instead, she opted to head to the cafeteria and use one of the meal tokens that had been piling up in her account.

The old woman above her, the one who ground her teeth in her sleep, had asked her if she had any extra meal tokens. Solanis, suspicious of the slippery slope of welfare, insisted she was all out.

"Liar." The old woman jabbed one bony finger into Solanis's face. "You haven't left in days." But after a glare from Solanis, the teeth grinder had climbed back into her bunk and focused on huffing whatever was in a paper bag that she kept tucked in her purse.

The cafeteria, located in a long tent near the center of camp, was thankfully empty. Solanis had taken to wearing a hat and pulled it low to mitigate the effect her dark eyes had on people. The hat was a transparent shield from the glances—comfortable but hardly effective. She had expected more people to be suffering with Boston Eyes, but the doctor had reminded her that haze scleral hyperpigmentation, or HSH, had never been a thing

---

before. He kept asking her to donate her medical records for study.

She had impolitely declined.

Solanis approached the long table where trays of food sat behind the glass barrier. At the serving line, a bored-looking young adult sat, reading. His long-sleeved HERA shirt was rolled up to where it showed off his forearms. There was a tattoo on his arm, a snow capped mountain. His lean frame, probably sculpted by a life of lean proteins and leafy greens, would have intimidated her if she were weaker.

Astonishingly, he held a real paper book. The cover looked leather, the embossed words nearly lost to the constant groping of eager hands. There was something odd about seeing a young man staring so intently at an antique. Usually, it was professors and grandparents who kept paper books on dusty shelves, clinging to the good old days when they were tools and not trophies.

The man was ignoring her.

Solanis cleared her throat, startling him. "Are you going to give me food or keep reading that book?"

He wobbled backward in his chair but successfully regained his balance. "Ma'am," he said, meeting her gaze. "Resting." And then, "Apologies."

Ma'am, huh? "Where'd you get the book?" She nodded toward the novel in his hand.

He looked down at the book and snapped it shut. "My grandmother."

"What's it called?"

The man tilted his head, lowering his jaw as if trying to see her better. "You do much reading?"

She shook her head. "I don't usually have time."

"Everyone has time," the man said. He was still trying to see her face better.

She shook her head. "Clearly you do. What's it about?"

He scratched his chin and flipped the cover over. "It's called *The Tiger and the Dragon*." He leaned against the serving table. "Evidently, there's like five of these stories. Martial arts and that stuff. Love story too."

She nodded slowly. It was *there are*, but she wasn't going to correct him. "Is it good?"

He frowned, examining the cover of the book. "Can't tell. This Chinese lady loves this man, but I don't think he realizes it. He's disciplined. But stupid." He set the book down and pointed at Solanis. "There a reason your hat is like that? You rob someone?"

Solanis bristled. He really wanted to see her face. "It's better this way."

He reached behind him, pulled a bent HERA cap from his back pocket, and jammed it on his head so it covered his eyes. "You sure? Can't see shit like this."

Her own laugh caught her off guard. "It's my eyes."

"What about them?" He picked up a scooper and a biodegradable bento box with the HERA seal stamped haphazardly on the side and attempted to scoop some chicken. He missed the side of the container. "Can't see what you're doing if you are hiding from security."

"I'm not hiding from security."

"Let me see." He pulled off his cap and ran his hand through his hair. He put down the box and strolled around the table. He was so smooth with his movements that the next thing she knew, he was directly in front of her. "Come on. Let me see."

It couldn't hurt.

Maybe then he'd stop flirting with her.

But maybe—and this was a big maybe—she didn't want him to stop.

Solanis pulled her hat off and looked down at her feet. How was it possible that he'd never seen anyone with Boston Eyes before? Or was he about to say something stupid to her? Remind her that she was tainted now that her beautiful eyes had been replaced with deep pits of darkness?

He leaned toward her. "Let me see," he urged, kindness carrying his voice. "Come on." His words were soft clouds.

She made eye contact.

His eyes were a rich coffee with a little too much cream inside. The lines on his face were evidence of constant unrestrained smiles. His dark hair, especially the curl that strayed from order, begged for a trim. He wasn't boyish. When paired with his biceps, he was...

What was it?

Helpfully masculine.

"Ah." The man smiled. "I see the problem. Do you mind?" He reached one hand up toward her face.

Solanis took a step back.

"No, no." He smiled. "Your hair. There's an insect nestled in here." She let him pull out the bug, and he set the insect down on the ground and stood back up, gazing at her. "No wonder you hide your face. I'd never forget if you robbed me in the street."

The tingle crept up her spine. She pushed back her hair behind her right ear.

He grinned. "You like chicken?"

She nodded as he returned to the other side of the serving table and resumed fixing her a box.

Why hadn't he said anything about her eyes?

She stared at the man as he added some chicken, greens, potatoes, and a hunk of bread to the box.

"I added some extra potatoes in there," he said, the grin still on his face. "I like potatoes, and you look hungry."

"I'm not a child."

"No, you're not." He handed over the box. "No. You're not." He elongated his words.

"Token?" She accepted the box and held up Ronnie.

The man snorted. He'd picked up the book again. "I'm not the government." Then he grinned once more. "I mean, I am, but not today. Today, I'm just Walter."

Walter. "So, you're going to just give me a free meal?"

He looked back at his book. "No one gets a free meal. You pay taxes."

She laughed, thanked him, and began to walk over to the rows of tables that mimicked church pews, a cruel manifestation of the old traditions of her grandparents. The sanctuary of solitude in lieu of communal eating was inviting, but today, when she knew Greg's headshot would be grinning at her from the front in the other room, she did not want to sit alone. No. That wasn't right. She *could not* sit alone.

She turned back to Walter and opened her mouth. When he looked back at her, there was a tingling inside her that forced her to take a small step back.

She opened her mouth again.

He spoke first. "Want company?"

"How did you know?"

He walked toward her, his book tucked under his arm. "No one wants to eat alone." He stood next to her, took the box from her, and tapped the book lightly on her back. "I'll tell you about this book." He gave a heavy sigh, like an animal that had just settled down for hibernation. "Or we can sit, and I can gaze into those pools of brilliant darkness you have for eyes."

Solanis blinked.

He was laying it on thick.

But the way he spoke to her and her eyes was the same way she spoke about Boston. The soft upturn in his voice, the eagerness. That grin. There was a word for that feeling—the blanket that waited for her after a long day of work. Or her favorite treadmill.

Familiar.

Yes. There it was.

Familiar.

———

OVER THE NEXT THREE MONTHS, Walter became constant. Daily, he ate with Solanis and told her stories about his growing up in the barracks and his career as a junior HERA officer. He hadn't scored high enough to make it into Augustus, West Portia or any of those other schools that claimed to train the young leaders of tomorrow. Instead, he'd taken the skills exam where he was placed as an operations associate at the refugee camp. Now, several years later, he was in charge of day-to-day operations.

"The recruiter said I had leadership potential," he said over dinner one night. They were eating chicken, potatoes, and broccoli. Again.

"I'm pretty sure they tell that to everyone. I like my job. It's good enough."

He tended to say that a lot. Things were always *good enough.*

"Don't need houses the size of a compound." He took a sip of water from the cup he constantly carried on his waist. He said it was better to reuse than to toss.

Solanis didn't have the heart to tell him that she had lived in one of those compounds with the massive walls for security and the security systems that armed themselves every night. A lot of good the compound had done her. Even now, in the shacks that were Little Boston, as they called her part of the shantytown, she could remember her father asking her to check the front door to make sure it was locked.

Back then, Ronnie hadn't been around to do it for her, so she'd walk over to the front door and twist the bolt to the left and then to the right to hear the satisfying click as the door confirmed it was locked. The tiny green light on the knob would blink sleepily at her, and she would look back at her dad and nod.

"All safe," she would declare with glee, basking in the glow of her father's approving nod.

Her parents were giants then.

Her mother would double-check the other doors before retiring to her study, where she'd spend the night reading star charts and deciphering the puzzles of the universe.

Wood, grapes, and barbecue.

Walter recycled everything, meticulously pulling apart, rinsing, and separating containers into the proper bins when it was time to discard their bento boxes.

"You recycle enough to join the Evergreens," Solanis observed as he used his spare water to clean his reusable fork and stowed it into his pocket.

"The environment is important, Solar," he said simply, walking out ahead of her and holding his hand out behind his back so she'd grab it.

Solar.

She liked it when he said his name for her. It was also so deliberate, as if he was testing it out.

Walter's name for her had come when he had asked her how she'd gotten her name.

Solanis had been playing with his hair, running her hands through the back where it was slightly curly. "My mother gave it to me."

"It's different. Does it mean anything?"

"Every name has meaning."

"I know. I'm named after my first father."

She frowned. "First?"

"You have multiple parents in the barracks. He's the first one in order of importance," he said. "I have about eight parents, you know. Five mothers, three fathers. Tax breaks if you're part of a village."

That didn't make sense.

"But Solanis," he continued. "Does it have meaning?"

She nodded. "My mom was an astronomer."

"Did she go up?"

She instinctively looked toward the sky. A flat ceiling greeted her instead. Walter had stuck those little glow in the dark star stickers on the ceiling. She didn't have the heart to tell him he'd gotten all the constellations wrong. "She went up about once a month. You know, hopping on the moon to take photos. It was really cool. She met my dad that way."

He nodded. He closed his eyes, seemingly lost in the continued stroking she did to his hair. His hand clutched her arm, his thumb tracing a line on her skin.

She liked it when he touched her.

She smiled. "She named me after the stars."

He raised an eyebrow. "One star?"

"All of them."

"You're the solar system then."

"The stars."

He had opened his eyes. "Solar. I like that."

Warmth.

Whenever they walked, he stood close to her. He showed up at her shack in the mornings and walked her to breakfast before heading off to some command room to no doubt manage the influx of refugees who were still streaming in from parts of the East Coast. Haze was still

53

tearing apart the northeast. A new Haze storm was sprouting just off the coast of Louisiana.

RealityLife announced their relocation to Denver, a move Solanis refused to even consider.

"Fuck Denver," she said to no one, dizzy at the thought.

The bunk above her was empty. The woman had left a few days ago.

A father and daughter occupied the bunk beds on the other side of the room. The little girl played with Ronnie nonstop during the day while her father covered one ear and tried to get the insurance company to pay out a larger settlement so they could move. On his second day, Solanis's new roommate had asked her how long she'd been at camp and shook his head at the answer.

"It's foolish," he had said before dragging his daughter to lunch. "This isn't a holiday."

—————

WALTER TOOK Solanis to the forest on Friday morning. As they made their way through the thick trees, the smell of the morning sap and whatever cologne he had sprayed on for this occasion casually took over her senses. The underbrush crunched under her feet as she hurried after him.

"My parents used to love spending time in the forest," he said, pointing up at the trees around them. "They were thicker back then. Lucky to have one near our apartment. They'd always go on walks and stuff after their shift."

"Is that why we're here? To imitate Mama and Papa Walter?"

He laughed. It was a nice, husky sound. "No. I got a spot for you all set up." He gestured forward and continued walking. "Your parents ever spend time on land? You know, when they weren't in space?"

"My dad was a scientist. He spent all his time on the ground. Research. Worked with animals. They have some great stories from their adventures." She had told him that they had died, and he'd usually step over the subject, like he stepped over the branches that littered the forest floor. But today, he didn't.

"Can I ask—"

"How they died?" She cut Walter off. She hadn't meant to. She'd just hadn't wanted to talk about it. She never wanted to talk about the caves in Virginia if she could help it.

"You don't have to if you don't want to."

"I know." She again spoke too fast. She caught his gaze, the hurt look on his face. "I'm sorry," she said softly, grabbing his arm. "They died in one of the aftershocks. I don't know." She shook her head. "It's hard to…" She waved a hand. *"You know."*

He nodded, his arm slipping around her shoulders. "It's okay," he said. "I got you. If the earth shakes, I'll cover you."

She nodded, suddenly feeling chilly. She blinked quickly to push the image of the wet cave walls waving and bucking from her mind. The sound of organic shrapnel as it attacked her face as she sprinted for the cave's exit.

She shivered and focused. She listened for the sound of Walter to drag herself back to the present.

"You know, my grandmother, my real one, used to tell me the story of this island off the East Coast." He stopped walking, catching the incredulous look on her face. "Just hear me out."

She raised an eyebrow.

"Stay with me. The way the story goes is one of those islands, the ones off the East Coast, the edge, if you go during the right time, when the Earth is tilted just right, you can spend the night with one person you lost."

"Walter." She tapped him on the shoulder.

He plowed ahead. "But you can only do it once."

"Come on." She shook her head.

"She said it's real." He reached into his chest pocket. "Besides, there's proof. I have this."

He pulled out a remarkable item—a real photograph. One on real photo paper.

She took the delicate paper and studied the photo closely. There was a middle-aged woman standing in the jungle next to a young man, both smiling at the camera. The man made a heart with his fingers.

"These your parents?" she asked.

"Grandparents." He pointed at the photo. "My grandma took this photo when they met up on the island."

She examined the photo closely. There was joy on the woman's face. She was gripping the man so tightly there were marks on his midsection. He held a familiar book.

Walter shrugged. "She tried to find the island again after, but she never could. But it was worth it. Closure. Didn't need to go back anyway. But she was pretty clear. The island, the one where she saw *him* again... The moment you step on it, you'll know."

She gazed at the book held by Walter's grandpa. "Walter, is this..."

He nodded. "He brought it back for her."

"Your book."

"My book."

So, her boyfriend had an imagination.

Boyfriend. She hadn't said it out loud yet.

Walter stopped. They'd come to a rocky hill. It led upward to a flat plateau that would have excellent views of the camp. "We'll go to the top. Ready to climb?"

She looked up at the rocks. She had never been much of a climber. But he insisted that he'd be right behind her. She nodded, grabbed hold of a gap in the rock, and began the ascent.

The rocks weren't difficult to grip. Walter stayed behind her, giving her the silent boosts she needed to get to the next set. At one point, he held her foot as she tried to pull with her arms.

"Use your legs," Walter said. "They're strong."

She adjusted and pushed with her legs, suddenly aware that he was getting a face full of ass as she moved.

He didn't complain.

She reached the top and turned back around to see his hand reach over the edge of the boulders. He poked his head up, grinned, and hit a wet patch, causing him to lose his grip.

Solanis lunged forward, tried to grab him, and missed.

She leaned over the rock to see how far he'd fallen, ready to run back to camp and get help. She knew how to run.

But instead, she saw Walter with his left arm clutching a gap in the rock, hanging on. He pulled himself up and grinned again. "I've never fallen before."

She grabbed his hand and helped pull him over the top. Heavy, he tumbled forward on top of her.

She stared at him, seeing every feature on his face, clear and defined. The coffee, the joy lines, the dirt on his chin from their walk. He had remarkably long eyelashes for a man.

He was…familiar.

His breathing was fast as he recovered from his brush with death. The noise coming from him was husky. He grinned at her once more.

"Your eyes are brilliant dark pools," he said quietly as he ran a hand through her hair. "The universe is inside of them, you know?"

Solanis smiled.

She wanted to hide from his gaze. Intense. Piercing. He could see her. What was it he saw when he looked at her? Could he really see all of her?

Walter's hand had stopped at the nape of her neck, his thumb caressing her jawline. He was so close.

"I am going to kiss you now," he said.

Their lips met.

He pulled her toward him as they kissed, refusing to let gravity hold her to the ground. He pulled her with his other arm until she felt as if all of her was supported by all of him. His strength was only matched by the intensity of his mouth as she felt the subtle give-and-take of him. Her tongue danced with his. Her blood felt like gentle solar flares radiating through her body as she too pulled him toward her.

And then, he was back in his own universe, grinning at her.

She exhaled.

"Again."

She wasn't asking.

———

THE LITTLE GIRL in the bunk with her father wailed, ruining some of the only decent sleep Solanis had gotten during the year she'd been in the camp.

Solanis sat up, blinked a few times, and peered over the edge of her bed. She'd stolen the top bunk a few weeks after the woman had left. The wind kept picking up, and with the door that wouldn't shut, she was done with waking dusty and coughing.

The little girl pulled her father toward the door of the tent. "Go get her!" she screamed. "Go get Mommy! Go get her."

But her father looked back at her as she kicked up dust around his feet and shook his head. "My sweet Tabitha," he said, reaching over to pull her into an embrace. "Tabitha, she's gone."

But the little girl squirmed harder and wiggled out of his embrace. She yanked his arm—hard for her, but for a man his size, the movement did nothing. Solanis couldn't remember his name. She'd only spoken to him to be polite, especially after his stupid question.

"Go get her!" the little girl wailed again, her sweater stretched and ruined in the scuffle.

He tried again. "Please, my darling, sit down. Let me tell you what happened."

But the little girl refused to listen and instead made eye contact with Solanis. Both of them stared at each other for a moment, the girl smiling wide. "You can get her. You look just like her. Go get her!"

Tabitha's father shook his head. "Tabitha, she's dead. She's not coming back." His tone was sharp.

The little girl shook her head and ran to Solanis's side of the room. Before anyone could react, she crawled into Solanis's bunk and planted herself at the foot of the bed.

"My mommy would not leave," the little girl said. "Can you find her?"

What was she supposed to say? You couldn't reassure a child who had lost their mother.

Adults could barely handle death as a concept.

"Tabitha, come on," her father said. "We have to go. We'll be late for the bus."

Solanis looked over. "The bus?"

"Before we move in, we're going to stay with my brother for a few months." He grabbed the back of his neck, pinching the skin between his fingers. He looked at his tablet. "There's a bus every day, and it leaves in half an hour."

"Move in?" she asked.

"Inside," the man said, shaking his head. "We're going to Shamut."

She frowned. She'd heard that name before.

The little girl shook her head. "Not without Mommy, we aren't. No. We aren't going without her." She slid back down the ladder and grabbed her father around the legs. "No. No. No."

Solanis frowned. "Where are you—"

"Have you been?" he said. "To Worthington's Dome centers? A Waystation?"

Oh. That was where she'd heard it. They'd pushed information to her during her first week here. A year ago.

Shamut. One of Worthington's Domes. She'd seen the massive green tents at the edge of camp but didn't have a reason to go inside. If she went anywhere, it would be Boston.

The door opened.

Walter.

His grin slipped when the little girl threw a temper tantrum on the floor.

Solanis nodded toward the pair. "They're leaving."

"Headed out, Barto?" Walter asked the man.

"Worthington made us an offer." Barto shook Walter's hand, but Tabitha grabbed their hands and pulled down hard. "We're going in one of those Domes."

Tabitha continued to say no.

"Oh?" Walter said.

She cried harder.

He kneeled. "What's the matter?"

"Her mother," Solanis said.

Tabitha put her arm on Walter's shoulder. He was now face height with the little girl.

"Please find her," she said. "I don't want to leave without her. Please?"

He looked down at the ground and then back at the girl. "Tabitha, isn't it?"

"I know you can find her. I've seen you with the foods. The adults. You work here. Find her please." She tugged his polo, stretching the neck. "Please?"

He scratched his chin and smiled at her. "It's not up to me. You need to talk to your father."

She backed up from him, the betrayal clear on her face, and then looked at Solanis. "Can you help me? Please? She looks just like you. She would listen to you."

Solanis looked from Tabitha to Barto and then back again.

But Tabitha could see it. She'd lost. She burst into tears, burying her face in her hands. Walter kneeled next to her and patted her shoulder. He pulled her into his chest. She hugged him, crying harder.

Barto stood uncomfortably behind them. He had resumed packing, exhaustion's gravity pulling at his shoulders.

Tabitha sniffed hard and backed up, snot on her face.

Walter pulled a tissue from his pocket and wiped it away. He looked up at Barto. "If it's okay with your father, we can go down to the center." He was referring to the main building near the center of camp where the kids would hang out, pretending they had more freedom than they had. "Your friends will be there. Maybe we can go there. I think we have some ice cream still."

She, seemingly distracted with the idea that ice cream was nearby, nodded.

Barto did the same. "I'll catch up. We can get tomorrow's bus." He looked at Solanis. "Just give me a second."

Tabitha's father began shoving a few things into the tetanus cabinet and then reached for his shoes. Walter and Tabitha left the shack, and Solanis climbed down onto the floor.

"It's hard," she said, lacing up her shoes. "For me, it was."

"Hard?" Barto closed his suitcase.

"When my mother died. My parents, really. It took me time. But eventually—"

"Excuse me, Tailor. I'm going to stop you." The man kicked his suitcase into the corner and deadpanned. "No, it didn't."

"Excuse me?"

"No. It. Didn't. Take time, I mean. You're still not over it. And you won't be."

"That's not what I—"

"I see how you stare. The way you clutch that tablet of yours, drooling over Boston." The man gave a bitter laugh. "You're not over it. Boston's dead. It's not coming back."

Solanis tilted her head to the left and then right. What the fuck? "I am over it," she said.

"No." Barto shook his head. "Lie to yourself all you want. But I see it. I can see it. Boston is dead."

"They can fix Boston."

"There it is. Proof." He shook his head. But it wasn't in anger. It was slow, sad. "I'm not trying to be an asshole. But think. She'll have to accept her mother is gone one day. Tabitha will. And you'll have to accept that you're not going back to Boston. Don't believe me? Ask your boyfriend." He gestured toward the door. "He's the government. He knows."

She pinched the bridge of her nose. Her head was heavy, and his anger was coming harder than she'd like.

He took a step forward and grabbed her hand. His grip was warm, soft, and authoritative. "Do what it takes to forget Boston. You can't stay here forever. You've been here too long. We are going inside. Because we need to move on. I'm tired of this. And you need to do the same. I don't want to go. But I have to protect Tabitha. You figure out what your job is. My advice? Ask him what he wants with you. Why he chose you. Is it because you're broken? Men like that love broken girls. They're fixable. My wife was made of china. I have the glue to prove it. Or is it because he wants a future with you? And if he wants the future, then you need to get out of here with him." He squeezed tighter; her hands ached. "This camp is purgatory."

Solanis opened her mouth, but he shook his head.

"You read the story," he continued, "about the journey from hell? Orpheus and Eurydice?" He didn't wait for an answer. "Never mind. The point is, the ending was inevitable. The journey may be difficult. But the ending is inevitable. This is the best advice you will ever get. I don't care about you, so I have nothing to lose here." His left eye twitched. "I've watched you since we arrived and am not surprised you haven't punched your ticket out. You have two choices. You can keep looking at the past..." He gestured to the tablet. "Or you can move forward. Go someplace like Denver or Shamut or wherever the fuck you need to hide or thrive. But crying into your pillow at home is better than at the train station."

She clenched her jaw. Was this grief? A warning?

Barto pulled out his tablet and fetched hers from her bed. He held the two next to each other and transferred a file. "Here," he said, his voice softening. "Talk to them. Tell them what you want. They'll give it to you. All you have to do is be ready to give up everything. They're going to save the Earth. You should be willing to go through fire to come back stronger." He handed the tablet back to her. "You've seen the Haze cloud coming this way."

The door swung open.

Walter had returned. "She's at the center." He sent Barto the info. "Give them the code. They'll give her to you."

Barto nodded, gave Walter a knowing nod, and walked to the door. Pulling back the flaps, he pointed to Walter. "Ask him. And then go speak to them. Then decide."

The door jammed when he left.

"Ask me what?" Walter asked.

Solanis looked down at her tablet, staring at Barto's invitation to speak to the Evergreens—the ones in the green tents around camp. She shook her head. "It's nothing. Just nonsense."

Oh. So, she'd lied to him.

First time for everything.

5

EVERGREENS

Solanis

The Evergreens were…eccentric.

Besides their green uniforms and their unfettered devotion to Worthington—a man they sometimes referred to as the Man from Denver—they were determined to save the planet.

Solanis spent her night scrolling through Ronnie while Walter slept next to her. One of his arms was thrown over her waist. Combined with the deep rumble of his snores, she was warm.

Worthington's digital pamphlet explained he'd invested billions into the development of the Domes—the solution to stop the decay of a planet that would die if they didn't act fast enough.

Four of them were complete: Porciúncula outside of Los Angeles, Shalina in the Midwest, Jericho near Henderson, Nevada, and Zenos in Arizona. Shamut would be modeled off Boston.

Solanis scrolled down the page and paused at an image of Worthington. He stared directly into the camera, the emeralds he had for eyes gazing deep into her. Maybe it was the screen, but there was something empty about those green gems. He wore a stern yet kind expression, his skin proof he'd done some work outside in his life. She pushed her earbud in her ear and watched as Worthington gave an interview in a popular news feed.

He insisted the Domes were humanity's last great hope in the fight against the climate crisis. "The planet doesn't trust us anymore," he had said to the interviewer, the strict staccato of his voice clear over her earbuds.

Her mother sounded like that.

Rapidly precise.

"We switched to electric cars, we gave up meat, and we even used the oceans to power our cities. And yet, the dark clouds roll in and murder us. Haze roams the earth. Mother Nature is sending us a message. She doesn't trust us. The earth doesn't believe us. It's time we regain that trust again. We need to drastically cut everything about our footprint and give the earth time to heal. The Domes are the first step in doing this."

"Wait." The interviewer raised an eyebrow. "You're telling us you're making more?"

Worthington smartly tapped his temple. "We must think big. By the time we are finished, this entire planet will be covered in them, and then the real healing will begin."

The interviewer nodded. "We've seen reports you have shadow investors—"

He had cut him off with a wave of his hand. "We are focusing on saving the planet. Everyone should be involved. Everyone's money was once green."

Solanis scrolled through some more testimonials from smiling people, families, and singles among images of children playing in wide open green spaces. They all wore small leaf pins on their chests and lived in shared housing. She scrolled some more and discovered the Domes would assign you a job upon entry.

"When you open yourself up for the better, you realize you don't need the distractions of the past," one man said. "This is what we need. Set yourself free." He stood with his wife at a place called Waystation, Los Angeles. His job title was *motivator, Happiness Directorate.*

She laughed. *Happiness Directorate.*

Wasn't her old colleague Theresa in one of these? Poor Omer. Wait.

He had asked her to watch a specific interview.

Solanis thumbed through the tablet a few times until she found the link Omer had sent her a while back. She tapped the screen, and a woman appeared who had clearly been crying—her eyes red, a tissue balled up in her hands. She recognized the host, Matthew Matthewson, from a popular news feed.

The lower third identified the crying woman as Aiesha, Theresa's mother.

Aiesha stared into the camera in front of her. "I'm afraid one day Theresa will die in one of those fucking Domes. And I will get her out before that happens. If it's the last thing I do. I will get her out. Worthington needs to let her go." Her voice was warm with an edge of tension.

"Die?" Matthew raised an eyebrow—too thin for his face.

She nodded. "I'm her mother. I know she's in danger. I can feel it."

"You're saying the Domes are not safe?"

"I don't know yet. But I can feel it. It's like a sickness. A hangover. An addiction. I need to do more research. But I'm her mother. Every ounce of me knows she's in danger. I need to get her out."

"How?"

Aiesha looked up. "There's an election soon. Maybe I'll run. I'm not the only one who feels this loss. The loss of our people. Of our families."

"So, you'd work with LTE?"

She slowly tilted her head to the left and then to the right. She swallowed and gave a grimace. "I don't condone violence. But whatever it takes. People say Worthington brings people together. But he's sure helping to pull them apart."

"And what if you can't get her out? Will you go in?" Matthew stared straight into her eyes.

"In?"

"To be with her? Join the Evergreens."

The camera focused on Aiesha again, only she was fuzzy around the edges. The camera corrected, zooming out slightly, and then refined the focus. She looked down at her hands and then back at the lens. There was a tear making its way down her cheek when she regained her composure. "Theresa will not die in vain." She shook her head. "Theresa will not die in vain."

The screen went black.

———

WALTER STIRRED in the darkness but still held onto Solanis as if she'd fly away at any moment. But she wouldn't fly away. Gravity kept her pinned to the camp, to this moment. What was it Barto had called it? Purgatory. Or was Walter trapped in her gravity?

What did he want from her?

It wasn't a bad thing to be in Walter's orbit. This relationship had always felt like a fast, uncontrolled fall to someplace familiar. But what did she want in the long term? Or even the short term? Did he choose her because she was broken? Was he really the man Barto insisted?

She usually wouldn't put too much stock in a stranger's assessment of her relationships, but Barto seemed to know Walter. They'd been friendly enough together, but Walter was friendly toward everyone.

The idea that Walter loved her because of her sickness was the sleep paralysis demon in the corner of the room.

Walter was awfully fixated on her eyes, he was ten years younger, and his job as a junior officer was "good enough." She'd never dated *good enough*. His barracks banter was eons away from the strict staccato of her people.

Maybe she needed to accept the fact that despite the butterflies, Walter Mustafa might be a fling. A temporary refuge in a period of confusion.

She had tried to learn what her boyfriend wanted—even if putting a label on their relationship caused her to bite her nails and tug at her hair. He'd responded with a sappy "for you to be happy." But she'd done a poor job of communicating. Asking your boyfriend anything after sex was like asking a starving man if he'd like a steak.

So, this time, she just told Walter what *she* wanted.

She wanted to go back to Boston.

He had other plans.

But she insisted.

———

SOLANIS AND WALTER had been stargazing in the grass when she'd the mistake of suggesting the return to Boston. She'd been watching the news feeds—the ones that suggested the city would be ready for cleanup any day now. She'd been trying to tell Walter there was hope of returning home.

And he would come with her.

"Look at this." She handed him the tablet.

He took one look at the display and handed it back to her. "No, Solanis. No." He sounded cold.

"Walter, just look." She pushed the tablet into his hands. The host was pointing to charts and graphs that showed Haze was dissipating.

"Solanis." He held up his hand, refusing the tablet.

"Just look. We might be able to go back. Right? I have a home there. We can fix it. You'd love it. Come with me."

He rolled over, his back to her, and she shivered. "No, Solanis. You don't understand. We aren't going back. Ever. It's not happening."

She reached over and tugged, rolling him back over. "Don't say that."

"Have you been paying attention?" He reached for her tablet. He squinted at the cracked screen as he tried to get it to keep up with his movements. "You really should get a new one."

She rolled her eyes. "I'm fine."

But he plowed on. "You realize in Boston you still can't breathe without protective equipment, right?" He flipped the tablet over for her to see a massive Haze weather pattern—the dark hurricane off the coast of Massachusetts. "This is what it looks like. It's just waiting to sweep back into the city. You know this danger."

Solanis stared at the screen—a dark storm around a crystal clear eye. She pulled the tablet from him and swiped a few times, searching for the news feed she'd seen before. "It can move," she said desperately. "It can move away."

"No," he said. "It's not moving away. And even if it does, recovery will take years."

She shook her head. "It always goes away."

"This one isn't. Years, Solar."

Something lurked behind the anger in his eyes. But she couldn't tell what it was. It wasn't fear. It wasn't quite pity. Was it anger?

"Fine. Then what do we do?"

He tugged his tablet from his pocket. "People are going to the capital, Denver. It's growing."

She froze. Then shivered. The salty scent of pickles wafted by. "No. Not that."

His eyebrows went up. "Solanis?"

"Not Denver."

He sat up. "Did something—"

"I'm not talking about it. But we aren't going to Denver."

He nodded. "Or Boston."

Was that bitterness?

They sat in silence. How did he know? There was no way he could declare it, here and now, that she wouldn't be going home.

"Because I work for the government," he said at last. "And we are there every fucking day."

Shit. She'd spoken out loud.

"Solar, I'm telling you Boston won't be back." He placed the tablet on the grass. "Are you listening to me?"

She squinted her left eye toward him. "So, now you're the government."

"I always have been."

Gravity was heavy here.

"Look, Solar." Walter sat next to her and put his arm around her shoulder. "I'm on your side. I want you to be able to go home. I want that for you." He paused, holding her tightly. "I want that for us. You know that." He rested his chin on her shoulder. "But it's not going to happen for maybe five, six years."

"No," she said. "You don't. You want me to stay here. Broken."

"Stop. I don't know what that means." He shook his head. "What can I show you?" He pulled out his own tablet. "Look at this."

She gasped.

On his screen was her compound in Boston. At least what was left of it.

The exterior was stained black, and the windows had been boarded up. Two HERA employees paced inside her home were pointing to the damage. She couldn't tell what they were saying as their masks obscured their faces. The walls were scarred where Haze had scraped off the wallpaper, scratched the mirrors, and shattered her things. Her mother's office and Greg's workshop were destroyed.

Solanis looked away.

Walter had been in her home. And he hadn't taken her with him.

"When were you there?" she demanded.

"It doesn't matter."

"Tell me."

"Solanis..."

"You lied to me."

He shook his head. "No."

"You lied. Turn it off."

"Look at it," he said.

But she was done. She stood. "Turn it off, Walter. Now."

The screen went dark.

"I knew you'd need to see it to believe it," he said, standing in front of her.

"You went to my home and filmed this? For what? To win an argument?"

"It's not like that."

"Then what is it?"

"You needed to see to believe. I know you."

Barto's words nagged at her. *Men like that love broken girls. They're fixable.*

Walter wanted her broken. He knew seeing her home in its dilapidated state would break her.

She refused to look at him but spoke anyway, the shaking in her voice surprising even herself. "What am I supposed to do now? I have no home."

He leaned over and tried to raise her chin. But she refused. She'd start crying. She knew the look that was in the back of his eyes now.

It was pain.

He knew he'd hurt her.

She ached.

"What am I supposed to do now?" Solanis repeated, her mind knocking down solutions. She grabbed his hands, tracing his knuckles with her fingers.

"We can figure it out." He squeezed her hand. "There's always —"

She shook her head, cutting him off. "If you say Denver..."

He recoiled.

Ah. There it was. The pain.

Something light fluttered inside of her.

Walter took a step back—an awkward movement considering how hard she was gripping his hand. He looked like a kicked puppy. "Why won't you tell me what happened in Denver?"

"Because, Walter..." She closed her eyes and breathed deep. "It hurts too much."

She let go of her boyfriend's hand.

She was running out of options.

―――――

THE JOURNEY TO get to the Evergreens was filled with red.

Solanis walked up the hill to the green tent and through the people who stood silently in red around the path. They were like trees, the way they stood still. Their red uniforms blew in the breeze. Each of the members of Louder Than the Earth held a large burgundy and black photo of someone who had gone on to live in one of Worthington's Domes. Phrases like 'If you died today, who would thrive?' graced the massive boards of faces that gazed back at her.

Solanis tried to ignore them, looking down at her tablet and pretending to read an important email. But their silence was heavy.

AMBASSADOR ZEBULON WICK seemed to be allergic to blinking.

Wick, as he insisted Solanis call him, sat in his chair across from her in a room the size of a large trailer. There were digital panels on the walls that made the space look infinite. He had this habit of placing his elbows on his knees like some thick green spider folding itself up. He placed his hands in a steeple position underneath his chin.

The director of all Shamut's communications watched Solanis carefully, unblinking, as she did her best to look unbothered. But she was bothered. Scheduling this meeting after her first real fight with Walter was like shopping while hungry.

Wick's buttons strained against his vest as he sat. It wasn't because he was fat; he was like one of those guys she'd seen at the gym who were simply growing too fast to see their tailor every weekend.

Ambassador Wick let the silence stretch between them.

She gave up. "You wanna give me the pitch?"

"Before we start, I wanted to offer my condolences for Gregory," he said. "I know he worked for Worthington, and we are very sorry for your loss."

"Greg," she said quickly.

He nodded. "Of course. Greg was a valued member of our family."

She nodded.

He leaned back in his chair. His fingers were at his chin again. "I usually ask people what they want out of these sessions, but you already know what we have to offer. I doubt my speech about a dying earth is going to convince you to make the perfect sacrifice."

"Perfect?"

"Yes. One small choice that will set you free." He opened his arms. "Our self-sustaining, safe, trade-based economy is designed so you have everything you need. Shamut is healthy. No bad things like smoking or processed food. There's no money, no cars. Everyone plays a role in our safe circular society."

"Safe?"

The room fell silent for a moment.

"Yes," he said. "No Haze inside. Unlike here." He narrowed his eyes. "Why are you really here, Solanis? Why did you come?" He sounded like a man who had never had to ask a question twice.

Why was she here? The question was deceptive in its simplicity.

"I don't know," she said. "I don't think I know."

"Let me show you something."

She hadn't noticed, but the walls had shifted to show a silent video of a young Worthington kneeling in a river with a group of children around him, the scarves around their faces and necks blowing in the wind. She'd seen this image before in the textbooks—the kids ruined because of the war. The Man from Denver held the notorious water filter in his hand while standing knee-deep in the amber and black water.

"We've all seen the great miracle," Ambassador Wick said, the weight of the past causing his voice to adopt a rough husk. "I was there, you know. When he did this."

More and more children gathered around Worthington, who was filling some of the cups, pots, and pans they had brought with them. The kids pushed and shoved, eager to get water. He didn't seem bothered. He worked as if on autopilot.

Wick continued. "I had been in the Free Republic, like the other illegal relief efforts, doing what I could." He raised a hand. "I know you consider them traitors. All part of York's failed ambition. But the kids didn't ask for any of this. Every day, I'd see what reckless government wrought over the innocents, both theirs and ours. There was a child an hour earlier who had tried drinking from the water. You remember school? The water was so toxic, so vile, that it would catch on fire in the right conditions. As I watched, it leaked from a burned hole in his esophagus. The kid had been drinking creek water for as long as anyone knew."

More families gathered around Worthington in the river. There were nearly a hundred trying to get close to him.

"I ran to him," Wick said. "The child. And that was when I saw him. The Shepherd. On the hill, looking down at us. The valley was the perfect spot. You'd see the drones coming. In his hand, the filter. The one Worthington built. It could filter out that wretched chemical that no one had been able to get out of the water. The chemical that forced the Free Republic to come back to the union. The chemical that had littered everything south of the York Line with bodies."

He stood and walked over to the screen. He pointed to the speck that was Worthington. Solanis could barely see him now—the video had continued panning out until he was just a dot in a sea of children, families, and onlookers with a dilapidated ranch in the distance.

"This man walked straight to the river, dipped his filter inside, and drank straight from the river. He let the water flow directly into his mouth and looked right at the children and said, 'Come drink. Be thirsty no more.' And they came."

The screens changed again, showing Worthington back in Denver with the president as he received the Presidential Medal of Freedom. He did that thing he always did, where he held out his hand to the eager crowd.

"And the world saw what I saw. He would save us all." Wick didn't blink as he gazed down at Solanis. "All he asks of us is to do one thing. Make the perfect sacrifice, and he'll keep us safe. He'll set us free. You ever see a miracle? Because I did. You can too."

He sat back in his chair.

Was she supposed to get emotional? She wasn't sure what he expected her to do next. Should she throw herself on the floor, begging for salvation?

But he just sat in the silence.

"Can Haze get inside?" she asked.

"You mean the storm that's on the way here?"

She shivered. "Can it get inside? It's important."

He stared at her. "What is this really about?"

She could see Greg again. "I lost my brother. No..." She frowned. "He was stolen from me."

Ambassador Wick nodded.

"And..." She paused. "I think it was my fault."

He nodded. "Is that what you believe?"

"I insisted we stay."

He nodded. "Why?"

She hadn't spent too much time in self-reflection. But her brother's word came to mind. *Predictability.* "It was what we always did. When Haze came around. We'd lock the door, close the windows, and turn on the filters."

73

The images on the screen had changed again—people sobbing in a crowd as Worthington stood in front with his hand out, reaching. The image faded into a whirl of colors—abstract patterns of greens and whites—casting the room in an ethereal glow.

"But this time, it didn't work. Greg went outside. Got hurt. I got hurt. That's why these are black." She gestured to her eyes. "It's why people stare." She sighed, shaking her head. "You want to know why we stayed, sir? Er, Ambassador? It's because home was safe. I'd read the reports. I'd listened to the administrator when they said that going out would be dangerous. We'd always been safe. Denver wasn't safe. Out there wasn't safe. And I wanted to be safe." She stopped. "I wanted to make sure we were safe. That's all. And it didn't work. I failed that."

Wick nodded. "There's nothing wrong with safe. You'll find there is no one here who is going to say you're responsible for your brother's death either."

She squinted at him. Had she said she felt responsible? Should she?

"Shamut is a chance to start again," the ambassador said. "Isn't that what you want?"

She thought back to her home in Boston—the videos Walter had shown her. The way everything in the videos from HERA showed the microplastic stains, the bodies. The great window boarded up. That was hers once. That was stability.

"No," she said. "I want to go back. Back to before any of this happened. Back to when everything was...whatever it was. I thought maybe this place, Shamut, will never be home. I know it's not home. But it's..." Her tongue played with her teeth.

He raised an eyebrow.

She shook her head. Why did this feel like therapy? What else did she want from him?

And it clicked.

"It has to be safe," she said. "I want to make sure it's safe. Because I can't go through this again." She gestured to the door. "I don't want that to happen again."

He nodded. "Solanis, I will be living there. My wife and kids are coming with me. It's safe. And as a member of the leadership team, I'll be recruiting people who are accomplished in their fields to help lead us inside."

She nodded.

"And I think you should consider joining our team. You'd help ensure the people around you are safe too."

She considered his proposition. Was it possible? A way to steer toward the light. A way to sit with the captain and lead the journey. "I don't think I'm the right person—"

But Wick cut her off. "Solanis, you escaped Haze, and the fact that you've come here, to this room, in this moment, means that you've already taken the first step in building a new future. I am offering you a chance to keep doing what you do best. Join the Communications Directorate with me and my team. Become a leader. Who knows? One day, you might become an ambassador yourself. Helping save the planet as we focus on the thereafter."

She almost rolled her eyes at the idea of saving the planet. She wasn't one of those hippie Evergreens who walked around hugging trees. But a chance to lead, a chance to determine her own destiny... She'd at last be able to control her universe.

No one was left to steer.

She could be safe.

For the rest of her life.

This could be Boston.

Ambassador Wick was smiling at her when she nodded. For the first time, she noticed his eyes were green—but not naturally green. He still had those dark brown circles that surrounded the cornea where he'd had them surgically redone. Maybe they could redo her eyes too.

"Let me show you your new home," he said.

The walls morphed. She could see the city.

Shamut looked like Boston, only cleaner. There was more green than she was used to. She felt the soft breeze and could smell the grass of the country, even though she was in the center of the city. All around her, people walked and rode bikes. Kids played.

There was laughter again.

There was a pulse.

There was no Haze.

"What do I have to do?" she asked.

He smiled. "Orientation is a start. But first, you have to set yourself free."

———

WALTER DIDN'T YELL when Solanis told him—she knew he wouldn't. He just stared back at her, his right ear twitching, and said, "You sure?"

Something inside of her wanted him to fight. Why couldn't he demand they stay together? She had prepared an answer that would convince him to come with her.

She grabbed both of his hands and smiled at him. She'd need to do this right. "There's space for both of us. We get a place to live. We keep this going. You love me, don't you?"

"I..." He stuttered, looking confused. "Of course I do. You know I do. That's not—"

"Then we do this together." She pushed harder, her eyes wide and a smile playing over her face. "You're right, Walter. I agree. We can't go back to Boston, and you know Denver is not an option. And Haze, it's everywhere. If we go inside, we can build that future together. This is us." She needed to paint that picture—the one of the future she could almost see.

She'd come home every day, greet him in his workshop, lock the doors at night, and retire to her mother's study. There would be kids if they wanted.

But he refused to dream with her. He let go of her hand instead, scratching the corner of his eye. He didn't take back her hand when he finished.

Solanis reached back out to him. She was cold.

He didn't bite. "So, you decided?" His voice was thick.

"Come on," she said, widening her eyes some more and then trying to get them back to normal size. Why wasn't this working?

Oh. Her eyes. They were broken. Like her.

Like the kind of women Walter liked.

"Come on," she said, speaking quickly. "I can't do this without you. You've fixed me. But I'll fall apart without you."

He shook his head. "Shamut isn't real. It's not Boston, Solar."

She frowned. "It feels like Boston though. Come on. We just need to go together. We can do this together. I am safe — no. Walter. We are safe as long as we are together. The Dome should be finished soon, and we can move in. It's safe."

But he was silent.

It was because of her eyes, wasn't it? She'd lost her ability to bend the universe to her will. And now, she'd have to pay the consequences. The future crumbled in front of her like the caves in Virginia when they'd claimed the lives of her parents. The future instantly renovated into a new plan. One that hurt more. One without Greg. One without Walter.

Heavy price.

Was this the cost of safety?

Solanis rubbed her chest. It hurt.

He wouldn't stay behind. He loved her. Right?

She didn't want him to stay. "Please, Walter?"

"You sure you can't do Denver?" he asked.

"Walter..."

He grabbed her hands, gripping them tightly. "Solar, we can go to Denver. I will leave this. There are jobs over there with the agency. We can be happy, Solanis."

"Walter," she said, harder this time.

"Solar." He let go of her hands and grabbed her face. "Solar..." His eyes were wet. "Please. What is it about Denver? We can fix it. I can fix it. Whatever it is, we can fix it. We can go someplace else too. Please? It doesn't have to be Denver."

"Someplace without Haze?"

He dropped her face. "You know I can't do that." He pulled her into an embrace. "You're scared, Solar. I get that. I can protect you out here." He whispered urgently into her ear. "I can't protect you if you're inside a snow globe."

"Come with me, Walter. Please."

"Which means you'll never see me again," he said, the heaviness weighing down his words. "I'll never see you again."

Her heart collapsed as Walter released her.

"You can't leave once you're in." He scratched his eye and then pressed the bridge of his nose. "You know what, Solar? I'm not okay with that." His words were shaky. "I'm not okay with that."

This was a breakup.

It wasn't supposed to be.

"Can we just sit here?" he asked, looking away. "For a while. Just sit here?"

Solanis's pulse moved so fast she thought she was going to die. She walked toward the couch and fell next to him, her arms wrapped around him and pulling him close. "Are you sure?"

She felt his body shake as he covered his face, their arms contorted around each other. She closed her eyes as he spoke.

"You are."

———

THE NEXT FEW DAYS, Solanis worked with her insurance company to put the money into a hidden trust, where it would be safe far away from Worthington's people. She wasn't giving up everything. Besides, Walter could use the money to buy his own place. She packed her bags, wandered the camp, and signed the paperwork.

She cried herself to sleep for weeks.

Walter held her.

He didn't ask about Denver.

He didn't ask about the Domes.

In the early morning, the day before she was supposed to leave, he opened the tent flap and pulled her outside. He kissed her on the lips, deep and hard.

When he came up for air, he pointed to the scattering of stars above them. "That one..." he said, pointing toward Sirius, hovering just south of Orion's Belt. "That one right there. I don't know what it is or how it got there. But when you look up, I'll look up too."

She nodded, the organic planetarium of the stars scattered above her.

She stared at Walter hard. She needed to remember him, all of him.

"Tell me how your book ends," she said, wrapping her arms around him. "What happens in the end?"

He shook his head. "I never finished the book."

"But it looks like you did."

"It does. But there's a movie."

"Is it any good?"

"Almost as good as us."

"Tell me the ending, Walter. Please?"

He looked up at the stars again, their light reflecting in his eyes. She knew he didn't understand them or what they meant to her. But when he looked back down, she saw he'd been crying.

"Li Mu Bai dies from his wounds," he said. "Jen Yu jumps off Wudang Mountain. There's this old story of an old man who jumped from the mountain to make a wish come true. So, she jumps. She's at peace, accepting her destiny. Or fate. They might be the same." He looked down at her, his finger on her chin, and eased her up until she met his lips. "If I could, I'd jump now." When he came back for air, he nodded gently. "It's a love story, Solar. A really, really good love story."

He sighed like the hibernating bear.

"Maybe one day, we'll jump together," Solanis's voice was hardly a whisper.

Walter simply nodded.

Solanis took him to bed.

They tangled into the sheets together. He lifted her as he entered her. He bit her nipple and gripped her butt with his warm, calloused hands. He thrust hard as she squeezed her thighs around him, her body begging him not to leave.

She pulled him into her, closer than she'd ever known. Her moan shoved him over the edge with a primal aggression—an aggression she happily accepted. She saw the stars, all of them, when the orgasm flooded her body, and when the morning light trickled into the refugee housing, she knew leaving would be a mistake.

But she had to leave.

And so she did.

And Walter let her.

6

SPROUTING

Solanis

"The Sprouting is how each of you will start your journey inside the Dome. When you wake up, you'll be in Shamut, ready to start your new life," an eager Evergreen said to Solanis on Potting Day.

Solanis had laughed the first time someone had told her about Potting Day—the day she was supposed to go from here to there. Over the past several hours, the Evergreens had picked her up from the refugee camp and brought her south to what she was pretty sure used to be Lancaster.

The bus teemed with excitement. The group sang songs and clapped, eagerly looking through the windows to see if they could get a glimpse of the Dome. They wouldn't. Rumor had it seeing the Dome up close could make you sick.

Ronnie had been busy preparing Solanis for the journey. It had given her the packing list; she was allotted one bag to take with her. Everything else, like clothes, snacks, and her eye medication, would be provided once she was inside. But as Ronnie was busy ensuring all the arrangements of her previous life were squared away, her tablet told her she needed to bring something with her to sacrifice.

It was what Worthington wanted.

She simply stared out the window as the bus hummed its way through a forest and into a large clearing where a slew of bright white buildings were nestled together. This would be the space between her old life and her new life.

"Welcome to the Waystation," the bus announced happily as the light rose, and the UV filters faded from the windows. "Please remember to take your belongings with you."

She followed the group and was surprised to exit into a throng of Evergreens, all wearing green and clapping and waiting to receive them.

A woman with bouncy blond curls, who looked like she wanted nothing more than to greet Solanis, approached her and gave a half wave and a nod. "Solanis Tailor?"

"That's me."

"Welcome to the Waystation. We have so much to do before you enter Shamut. I'm Yolanda." Without asking, the woman grabbed Solanis's bag and guided her inside.

"Hold on." Solanis took one last look at the sky. The trees were long and thin like the fingers of some underground god, clawing for the heavens. She took a deep, cool breath of crisp air and stepped inside.

———

THE WAYSTATION WAS a hub of movement. Plants grew from the floors, their vines snaking their way up desks and other fixtures.

The Waystation smelled like soil.

There were rows of personal table consoles embedded in each space —enough for two or four people. Evergreen officials hovered around, wearing darker, nearly black suits. She'd never seen their type before. Their jackets were longer, trailing behind them.

Ronnie chirped in her ear, telling her those were healers—the doctors of Shamut.

"Come on," Yolanda said as they made their way to an interview table near the center of the room.

As Solanis sat, the noise of the room simply faded away as if someone had closed the door to a busy hallway.

But Yolanda pretended not to notice her shock and instead folded her hands in front of her and offered her a warm smile. "You ready?"

"You've been inside?" she asked. Butterflies of excitement fluttered at her fingertips.

Yolanda laughed. "No. You can't leave once you go in. We're all Worthington's virgins here. But they pair those of us who have served with new transplants like yourself."

Solanis nodded, although she didn't like the idea of becoming one of Worthington's virgins.

The console in front of them lit up and went through a series of questions for her to answer. Did she consent for the medical exam that day? Had she transferred her assets to Worthington? Had she told her family she was taking this step? Did she consent to her medical records being transferred to Half Dome?

The console also told her she wouldn't have to worry about taking pills for her eyes. They'd automatically put the medicine in her food.

She took her time going through the prompts, and after about an hour of back-and-forth, the screen signified she was done.

"I know that was a lot, but you must be sure." Yolanda gestured back to the console that had lit up again.

Are you sure the Dome is your destiny?

Solanis paused. Destiny was doing a lot of work in that sentence.

"It's going to ask you a few more times as we go through this," Yolanda said. "The Shepherd wants all of us to be sure when we make the perfect sacrifice."

She shivered. She pressed yes.

Yolanda reached out and placed her hand on Solanis's shoulder. "It's okay to be nervous. Nothing worth doing is easy." She pointed back down to the console again.

It was asking for another confirmation.

She smiled. "This is my favorite part."

The console's screen faded to its neutral tone and, along with it, the rest of the room's noise. Everyone was still speaking, interacting and gesturing. But Solanis couldn't hear them.

"We isolate the frequencies so it's just us." She gave a sheepish smile. "We can focus together." She gazed at Solanis as if she was her most favorite person in the world. "Do you have any reservations about entering Shamut? Just one more confirmation."

Solanis stared into her soft brown eyes and smiled. "I think I am good."

Yolanda smiled. "You need to say yes or no."

She lied and said no.

The room came rushing back. Suddenly, the butterflies were gone. But there wasn't time to feel the relief.

Yolanda motioned for Solanis to stand and pointed to a healer who had appeared from seemingly nowhere. "We are going with her."

Solanis nodded and let the healer lead them through the Waystation.

Yolanda was in front, grabbing Solanis's hand and pulling her through the room. Her blond curls bounced as she weaved through the other people.

Their destination was a room that felt so warm and cozy that Solanis felt she could live there forever. No direct light shone on them. Instead, just two flat tables lay in the center. Soft tones filled the air. The warmth of music.

The healer instructed them both to lay on a table and fussed over them.

The table was so soft as Solanis lay down. The healer began pressing sensor stickers to her temples as she fidgeted. Even the stickers were warm.

Had the music gotten louder?

And why did it feel like it came from inside her?

A healer placed a warm hand on her shoulder. "You are going to feel a slight pinch, and then you'll fall asleep. If you get nervous, just let me know. Everything is perfectly safe. You are safe."

Yolanda, who Solanis had almost forgotten was there, grabbed her hand and gave her a firm squeeze. "Are you ready?"

————

SOLANIS WAS VERY MUCH aware she wasn't wearing underwear.

She let out a sharp intake of breath and grabbed for the necklace around her neck. With relief, she felt the soft smooth sides and sharp edges of Greg's last pet project.

Her breathing calmed.

A soft chime rang around her.

Three tones in melodic succession.

A soft male voice spoke.

Solanis Tailor.

You are safe.

You are free.

Welcome home.

She sat up. The voice told her that she was going to feel tired, but there was a pill on the nightstand that would help. The voice—firm yet kind and oddly familiar—told her she was safe.

Solanis reached over, took the pill, and swallowed. She downed the cup, blinked a few times, and looked around the room.

She'd remembered seeing the mockups of these dormitories in the brochure. The room was a light-colored wood. The sunbeams, from the gaps in the walls, gave the space an ethereal feeling. It was as if she was in heaven's waiting room. Small windows were nestled in the corners, flooring, and walls, making ceiling lights unnecessary during the day. There were more clothes in her closet, the various shades of green giving her limited options. But the far right of the room was her focus.

Like home, the window was great. Even though she felt steady, she moved slow. But she could see her home. Outside was the uncanny version of Boston she had longed for. She could see the parks, the historically tinted cobblestones. Plants crawled up the side of the buildings, clinging to the trellises. Down below, people clad in green walked around as they too acclimated to their new, domed surroundings.

Solanis checked the bathroom, finding a shower, a toilet, two sinks, and a recycler. There was another window—thankfully fogged.

She stared at herself in the mirror above the sink and nodded at her jet-black eyes.

Walter stood next to her.

No.

That wasn't right.

She blinked again.

Walter wasn't there.

She let out a nervous giggle. She didn't know what she'd expected. Had she really thought her eyes would just return to normal when she woke up? Not even Worthington could do that. He was from Denver, after all.

Yolanda met her in the living room, looking as refreshed as ever. Her blond curls were even more bouncy than they were on the outside. She smiled at Solanis as she showed her the community kitchen with the fruits and veggies that were grown inside Shamut and pointed to the photo of Worthington hanging in the living room. He gazed at them with his chin up and his knowing eyes—watching.

"Can you feel it?" Yolanda's warmth was like a blanket.

Solanis did feel something. Lucky maybe? It wasn't giddiness. But she felt flighty, airy almost. She took another look out the window and craned her neck upward, to see if she could see Shamut's structure. But there was only a bright blue sky. No clouds. No jets. Just clear blue.

"The dome is too big to see from down here," Yolanda said. "You can try all you want, but the Shepherd designed Shamut to be seamless with the world around us."

Solanis nodded as Yolanda showed her the community spaces. The quadplex had several wings where she and her roommates would be living, built with a central hub and a communal kitchen and screens to watch news feeds in the center. Her room was just one of many with its own private living quarters and bedroom.

Yolanda handed her a tablet. "This is the Voice. Our version of Ronnie. It's already connected to the network. All important updates will come here. If you lose it, you can acquire another at the vending machine. And it looks like you have your first message."

She looked down at the device, where an indicator waited for her response.

Worthington requests your presence in person at the Sprouting Ceremony in Worthington Park.

Yolanda gasped. "Oh, wow. You're going to see him in person." She swayed where she stood, fighting for stability, and then recovered.

"That's such an honor. You're going to see him. Not many people get to attend the Sprouting with the man who did all of this."

"Why don't you take my place?"

She seemed to consider it for a moment but then shook her head. "This is your moment. Your honor. You've been chosen. Just make sure you bring something special from before, so you can have a tribute to offer."

Right. The sacrifice.

"What if I don't have anything?" Solanis instinctively caressed the smooth sides of the necklace beneath her shirt.

"You'll think of something. Listen!" Yolanda pointed upward as soft music swelled around them. "It's all he asks for us in return. It's almost time. You need to go. There's a special train reserved for people who Worthington has chosen to witness in person."

———

As SOLANIS RODE, people sang, hummed, and rocked side to side like daisies in a field. There was a fuzzy, viral excitement in the air. She found herself being extra polite to the men and women around her as if she was a child before Christmas, hoping Santa would notice. There were kids inside Shamut, also in green, who ran around their legs while laughing as the train rumbled down the park.

There were no vendors on Yawkey Way. At least not today. Instead, there were dancers, all in green—spinning, twirling, and clapping in unison. Their skirts and pants and shirts blew in the wind as they welcomed the newest Evergreens.

The red bricks of the buildings were familiar. Banners graced their sides—but instead of commemorating the World Series victories and the names of players like Yastrzemski, Nichelle, and Ortiz, Worthington's name glinted down with his accomplishments and screens of him speaking and consoling the masses. In one frame, he was giving a woman who looked awfully like Solanis a hug.

Her fingers tingled.

Solanis flowed with the crowd into the stadium. No one asked to see her ticket; she just followed the signs to her seat. She and her fellow

Evergreens branched out to all parts of the stadium, and soon, she was sitting behind home plate. The Green Monster bloomed with plants and flowers, but instead of the Red Sox logo of before, there was just a leaf—a symbol she'd seen on flags around her new home. The stadium wasn't set up for baseball. No mounds or plates. Just a stage and aggressively green grass.

Solanis rooted herself into the plush seats that replaced the narrow wooden seats of Fenway Park—no, Worthington Park—and tried to get comfortable. She still felt lucky, as if her head was floating. She hadn't been to many ball games, but the lack of hot dogs and the smell of fried tenders was getting to her. She'd also never seen this much green in her life. All around her were plants, greenery, and green uniforms.

The singing grew louder as more people took in the tune and internalized it. The song blossomed from their mouths. The man sitting next to Solanis sang softly, the deep baritone of his voice sounding lovely in her ears.

"I don't hear you singing," he said.

"You don't want that."

He laughed and extended his hand. His breath smelled like peppermint. "Leonardo."

"Solanis." She smiled. "You go to Fenway a lot?"

He frowned. "You mean Worthington Park?"

She nodded. "Sorry. I forgot." She looked around and gave a nervous giggle as the singing continued to swell.

On the giant hovering screen that pollinated the stadium with light and noise, a video played, showing Worthington speaking to school children, world leaders, and others who seemed in awe of the man. She met Leonardo's gaze and realized he hadn't laughed.

"You would do well to remember that," he said quietly. But his grin came back. "I am not much of a baseball fan. Think we'll have a team?"

She forced a smile, the look he'd given her throwing her off. "I never asked. But I assume so. Imagine if your job is baseball. Also"—she gestured to the Green Monster—"what would their name be?"

Leonardo laughed. "The Greens? You have a job?"

"Communications Directorate."

He laughed. "You're a unicorn then."

"What's a—"

But he had already plowed ahead. "I'm with SPINE. We'll be partnering with you."

"SPINE?"

He nodded, sitting straighter with his chest puffed out. "Security Protection & Intelligence Network. I'm law enforcement. I was chosen to keep people safe." He looked around the nearly full stadium. "Should be easy enough. We all chose to come here, right?"

She nodded. "I came here because it was safe."

He nodded again. "That's the theory, right?"

Three chimes rang out through the stadium. Several people strode onto the field from first base. All of them were in the green uniforms that were standard for the Evergreens, but one look at the Jumbotron showed her they were important. They had a silver leaf over their hearts. Yolanda's had been gold.

"Those are the ambassadors," Leonardo said, clapping with everyone else. It was like thousands of leaves rustling in the breeze.

Solanis nodded, recognizing Wick and his straining buttons.

A man and a woman who had the energy of an overpaid motivational speaker at an ill-timed work retreat addressed them.

"My friends," the man said in a smooth voice. "Welcome to the Sprouting."

Applause echoed through the stadium.

"My name is Lijah, and this is Aenni." He gestured to his partner.

Aenni spoke now. "For those of you who are new here"—there was some laughter—"the Sprouting is how we welcome all of you to Shamut. It's where we all start together, as one community, to build the future we promised each other. Today, we will all pledge ourselves to the success of Shamut. We will meet our community, and then we will root ourselves into the work that will save the world."

The stadium rustled with applause.

Lijah took over. "But first, it's time for us to all plant our seeds into the ground. And for that, we have an honored guest. He is the man who ended the war. Who created the filter. The Man from Denver who set us free."

The stadium fell silent and dimmed to almost darkness. And then, from the tunnels where the baseball players usually exited to make their millions, came a tall man with a straight narrow face and eyes like emeralds. The screens that hovered overhead showed the green suit with a jacket that trailed behind him.

Worthington walked with the swagger of a man who had just been told he was king of the world. Indeed, the great peacemaker took his time—paused, strutted, and nodded at Lijah and Aenni while basking in the applause.

He raised one of his hands up at waist height in a gesture that looked like an attempt to calm the crowds. But he was reaching out to them, like a vine inching toward support. Receiving their praise, their energy, and their light.

He reached for them.

Solanis's face was wet.

Leonardo dropped to his knees and raised both of his hands to the sky. The woman in front of Solanis reached back, screaming, while another sobbed into his wife's arms.

"Citizens," Worthington said, still turning in a slow circle like a helicopter seed falling from the heavens. His arm was still outstretched, yearning for them. "Welcome home." He lowered his hand and stared out at them all, the hovering screens giving her the illusion that he could see into their hearts. "I have dreamed for this day longer than you can imagine." He spoke slowly, deliberately. "I know each of you have struggled in the darkness, toiled in fear, and have been broken by the failed promises of those who claim to lead."

Solanis rested her hand on Leonardo's shoulder. He shook.

Worthington continued. "Some of you have lost the ones you care about. Not to death but to something much more difficult. Ideas. You are here because you chose to believe in something bigger than you. Bigger than us. Because you decided to make the perfect sacrifice so our children's children can have a chance. They will write about this day when our descendants swing open the doors to a new, clean Earth. Your names will be etched into the marble of those who gave everything. A place of honor among humanity."

Someone a few rows back wailed into the void of the stadium. This hum of grief hung in the air.

"But be not afraid. Do not distress. Because you've put your hope in me, and I have invested in you. And starting today, each of you have set yourself free."

Leonardo hid his face, his shoulders still shaking.

"Each of you was lost, and now you are alive. You were lost and now... My sons, my daughters, my people, you have come home. Welcome home."

Solanis hurt for Walter, ached for him. The black hole pulled her inward.

She cried.

Why hadn't he come? Why had he stayed outside? She hadn't made a mistake coming here. He'd made the mistake of letting her leave.

"I am asking each of you to make the perfect sacrifice so our future can live. You will be tested, and you will grow and learn. Ask yourself every day—every moment—you spend building Shamut if you are willing to make the perfect sacrifice. Abandon the relics of the dying world and embrace the new of the world in front of you. Embrace the world that is sustainable. The world where we breathe together. The world where we can truly be free. A world where we work for us."

Worthington stepped back as a group of Evergreens escorted a family toward the stage. As they walked, the center of the stadium pulled open, and a glaring glow of light flooded the venue, forcing Solanis to squint.

Solanis knew that was a recycler.

The child clutched a teddy bear, his mother carrying him forward. As Solanis watched, the father greeted Lijah, nodded toward his wife, ripped the teddy bear from his son's hands, and tossed it into the recycler. The screens showed the bear being torn apart by the nanobots deep within the chamber until there was nothing left.

"You ever see a person go into one of those?" Leonardo asked, his voice thick.

She frowned at him and saw his eyes were red.

He grimaced and shook his head. "Nasty stuff."

The kid cried as his mother held onto him. The father shook Worthington's hand and fell to his knees, bowing at the man's feet. Worthington placed a hand on the man's shoulder, encouraging him to stand, and then sent them to the other side of the stadium.

Somewhere, a voice told them that Worthington was going to greet her section, and the Evergreens began escorting them toward the tunnels of the stadium so they could access the field.

Some had trouble walking—immobilized by the idea of meeting a living god. Others had to be controlled from running out onto the field. One by one, families and individuals walked to the stage and sacrificed an item to the recycler. A woman hugged Worthington, holding him tight. A man and woman knelt at his feet, the screens showing them thanking him profoundly. He pressed his lips to the head of a baby who couldn't have been more than a few days old.

As the line grew shorter, and Solanis realized she too would be asked to sacrifice something into the recycler, she began to panic. She'd been so wrapped up in the moment, she'd forgotten. The moment she'd awakened, she felt as if her mind was moving slower. It made sense. This was a lot to take in.

But what would she give away? She had nothing.

Her hand wandered to the black disc Greg had given her right before he'd been stolen. She closed her eyes and breathed deep, doing her best to keep her composure. Greg had never told her the purpose of this trinket, this last totem of him, even when he had demanded she keep it at all costs. No. She would not give away her brother's memory.

Gravity shifted under her as she opened her eyes, swaying slightly. She lost her balance. A set of strong arms caught her before she hit the ground.

"Walter," she said and looked back, only to see Leonardo grinning at her.

"I know," he said. "It's a lot. I might pass out too."

He must've thought this was all because of Worthington.

The singing was louder as she stepped onto the field. Around her, the Evergreens beckoned her forward, gently nudging her shoulders, pulling her, and passing her off to one another. They lightly rubbed her back, smiling at her.

Others cried with joy, spun, and danced. They twirled, told her how lucky she was, and purred. Some lay on the ground in ecstasy, moaning into the lights of the park.

Her steps were sure, but her knees were weak.

It wasn't just the musical tones and the sobbing that echoed around her. There was a voice that was omnipresent around them—a warm, friendly voice that was neither male nor female. A narrator for kings.

As she continued forward, through the encouraging waving from the Evergreens traveling with her, she tried to focus through their clapping and singing and dancing, all perfectly timed with her movements. She could almost make out the words.

Before she knew it, she was at the steps, gravity yanking at her as she met Lijah. He beckoned her forward, his hand helping her up. He looked at her, gave her a hug, and smiled.

He urgently whispered, "What will you be giving away?"

"I don't have anything."

"Don't worry." He handed her a small stone. "Just throw this in. He hates it when people aren't seen giving something up."

Solanis took the stone and stepped toward the recycler. Worthington watched her, his green eyes staring deep into hers. She took another step forward, the electricity of the recycler causing the hairs on the back of her neck to rise, and dropped the stone into the pit.

Worthington smiled at her. It felt like shoving her hand into a cosmic ray of energy. There was a coldness about him that felt like it was stealing her life force.

Solanis reacted violently. She shook as the Evergreens twirled, danced, sung, and cried around her. They mimicked her, some falling to the ground and others screaming in pain. Or was it ecstasy? Worthington's eyes, the pure emeralds, came into clear focus as he connected directly with her bottomless pools of darkness.

"Solanis," he said with a quiet intelligence she swore only she could hear. "Your brother told me all about you. And now you are here. You are free."

What?

Her world dissolved as suddenly Walter, Greg, Boston, her parents, and the stars—all unfurled around her, and she forgot how to breathe. It was as if Worthington had found the exact spot in her soul where he knew she needed to hear his voice and plucked the vine with his powers, and now, she was at his feet, raw. Sobbing and clutching him for dear life.

She didn't feel free in this moment. She was overwhelmed. Everything that had happened came pouring out of her. Foster care. Virginia. Denver. Haze. Greg. The black bag. She couldn't breathe. There was a zipping noise and a black hole threatening to crush her under its defiant weight.

She shook violently.

Her hands vibrated.

A shiver crawled up her spine.

A gentle hand touched her back, and a woman helped her limp to the other side of the stage, where the Evergreens waited to receive her. They cuddled her, they wiped her eyes, and they told her she was free.

"The world is right now," they said as they spun, danced, wept, laughed, and cooed.

The music continued. The waves of their uniforms swirled, and the lights sang. And through all of it, the words for kings that echoed across Worthington Park came into angelic focus.

As the world despaired, resigned to earth's last sigh,
He rose to heal with resolve of steel, insisting the world should not die.
He ended the war, revived the greens, and healed the sea.
This is the man who saved us.
This is the man who set us free.

PART II

TOMORROW

7

BIRTH

Eight Months After Solanis Entered Shamut

Solanis

Gabby faced danger for the first time seconds after she was born.

Solanis Tailor squatted over the birthing bed, her arms gripping the bar above as the healers surrounded her, murmuring words of encouragement. But she wasn't listening to them.

She would only listen to Katia.

Katia Delgado, her closest friend inside Shamut, stood in front of her. Silver hair poked through her hairnet as she trained both of her eyes on Solanis and gave a determined nod.

"It's time. Push one more time," Katia said, her eyes flickering over to the healers behind Solanis who fed her instructions.

Labor had been hours of work and anxiety with no firm deadline. Katia had held her hand throughout the process, squeezing her shoulder and feeding her frozen electrolytes, all while using an uncharacteristically soft and kind voice.

"Your baby will come when she's ready," Katia said. "Solanis." She looked her dead in the eyes. "You need to push. This is it. One deep, purposeful push."

Solanis nodded, her quads feeling tight, heavy, and wet as she used her forearm to wipe her brow. Her hair was a matted mess stuck to her forehead.

She was too hot.

Gripping the bar, she adjusted her feet and took a deep breath in and slowly let it out. The aggressive burning deep within boiled over as an intensity overwhelmed her. The room was red, and Katia's face was blurry.

Resistance.

A rush.

Relief.

The room returned to sharp focus as the pressure dissipated, relief pinpricking its way up her spine and through her arms and her cheeks. She wanted to sit. But not yet.

Katia nodded her approval and grabbed her under her armpits, propping her up. She helped turn her, careful not to snag the umbilical cord that snaked between the new mother's legs.

Solanis needed to sleep.

But the room was too quiet.

Wasn't her baby supposed to cry?

Solanis traced the wet, vascular cord up toward the doctors who swarmed around her daughter. She was so close, but she couldn't reach her.

"You're cutting the cord, right?" A healer broke himself away from the others. "The father's not coming?"

"Yes," Katia said, glancing down at Solanis. She made the cut, untethering the baby.

Her daughter was taken farther away to the other side of the room as the healers worked on her.

"Where is she?" Solanis shivered. She was cold.

"Give them a second," Katia said, craning her neck. "I've done this twice."

"She hasn't made any noise." She tried to shake the red fog from her eyes.

Gravity wasn't enough to pull her daughter back.

The distance ached.

"What's happening?" she asked, willing herself, as if by some miracle, to see through the healers. She caught a glimpse of Gabby's unmoving foot. It was so tan and small. But her baby was quickly blocked by another healer with a green blanket.

"Hold on," Katia said. Her usual aggressiveness was back. A darkness lingered under her voice.

Solanis had tried to speak again but was exhausted. It wouldn't matter; Katia spoke enough for the both of them when she was around. But this deep feeling of dread, the deep pit of the black hole, ate away at her.

Why hadn't her daughter cried?

"Doctor?" Katia's voice hurt her ears.

The room was a deep, obtuse burgundy.

The earth moved too slow.

A whimper cut through the air, followed by a wet cough, and then the loud, anxious cries of her little girl.

The lights were bright again.

Time returned to the right speed.

"There we go," one of the healers said, turning, smiling, and cradling the baby in her arms.

Katia squeezed Solanis's shoulder. "She's good. See?"

Solanis wiped away the tears and sweat that slicked her face. Her daughter was alive. She had cried.

Her daughter was safe.

Solanis reached out her arms. *Give her to me. I need her.*

The healer took a few gentle steps forward and placed Solanis's daughter gently on her chest as the baby squirmed and wiggled in her arms. The child fidgeted, her hands gripping and slipping on Solanis's skin until she squeaked and synced her breathing with Solanis's. Heart and lungs together.

As Solanis looked down at her perfect daughter, the universe shifted and centered around her. The baby's light brown eyes looked up at her and then closed again before she slept for the first time on this side of the universe, exhausted from being born.

It took everything in Solanis's power to tear her eyes away from her daughter and look at Katia, who gazed down to her with an approving, thin-lipped smile as she too marveled at the tiny creation between the two of them.

"She's all yours, Solanis," Katia said. "She's all yours."

Solanis gazed down at her daughter, feeling the remarkable pull of her gravity. "Your name is Gabby." She felt the tears and the smile deep and hard as Gabby squirmed and wiggled on her chest.

She was awake again, seemingly having recognized her mother's voice.

"I am Solanis, your mother. And I promise you we will be safe as long as we are together."

———

GABBY PROBABLY DIDN'T UNDERSTAND her mother's words spoken to her the moments after her birth, but as Solanis watched her grow older and go from a cute drooling infant to a determined, sassy toddler, she realized that while the center of her universe had changed, the real world didn't get any smaller. At least the real world as built by Worthington.

Each time Gabby cried, the universe tilted sideways until Solanis could remedy the problem.

When Solanis returned to work at the Communications Directorate —referred to as ComCen by her Shamut colleagues—she spent the day staring at the live feed of her daughter in day care, ignoring the engineers' briefing about a network outage caused by updates to BlackBox, the hub of their communications. Solanis didn't pay close attention, the ambassador was supposed to maintain the box. That had been made clear their first week on the job.

During a debriefing with the ComCen and SPINE ambassadors, where Wick and Kruger gave them another update on LTE's latest efforts to infiltrate Shamut, Leonardo had to carry the briefing on his shoulders. When she and Leonardo returned to the hallway, Leonardo asked her what was wrong. Solanis burst into tears and pointed to the Voice.

The Voice showed Gabby sleeping alone in her bedding station at day care.

"They haven't spoken to her in the last half hour." Solanis waved her hand over the tablet. "She's going to think the other kids don't like her."

Leonardo had looked from her to the tablet and pulled her into a hug. "She's fine," he said, pointing to the Voice. "Look, she's sleeping. That's a good thing. She needs to sleep."

"But what if she wakes up, and she's alone? She doesn't know they'll check in on her. She'll think I abandoned her." She shivered and pulled away.

The nights in Denver had been cold and lonely. Gabby wasn't going to grow up like that.

Leonardo gave her a pat on the shoulder and took away the Voice. She grabbed for it, but he held it just out of reach. Instead, he pulled her close to him and gave her a hug.

He was warm.

"She'll be fine, Solanis," he said. "You want to go visit her? We can go visit."

Her cheeks flushed. In her moment of panic, she realized she was at work and was blubbering like a woman who ate glass on purpose. Her colleagues were probably staring at her with pity.

Get it together.

But the overwhelming tidal wave of dread kept smashing her in the face. Each time she looked at the Voice, she felt drawn to her daughter. Gabby was a strategically placed magnet—too far to pull her anywhere quickly but close enough to cause some attraction.

But she ached for Gabby. The distance ate her alive.

Leonardo and Katia were helpful while she failed to adjust.

Leonardo made sure to join Solanis for the group morning work-outs ComCen and SPINE did together. He'd match his pace with hers, huffing and puffing as he spoke to her about the latest cases he was working on, how his brother had been an inspiring figure in his life, and why he thought Kruger was likely to retire soon. "Her sister joined LTE. She might want to leave and go find her. Bastards."

When Solanis casually mentioned that she thought the tattoo that said *Bullets For Breakfast* on his wrist was crooked, he gave her a dark look and picked up the pace.

He rallied several members of the SPINE team to stop in and say hello to Gabby while they were on their rounds. Each of the agents waved at the camera while holding an excited, giggling Gabby on their shoulders.

Solanis couldn't explain why seeing Gabby giggle, laugh, and demand more from them made her stomach fill with battery acid. But she grabbed an antacid from the cafeteria, determined to tamp that down.

Katia, who was with Shamut's Infrastructure Directorate, moved her daughter Tatiana from the day care center closest to her quadplex to the one Solanis was using. Tatiana, a year older than Gabby with the same thick platinum hair as her mother, took to sitting with Gabby and engaging with her as the days went on. Solanis had a sneaking suspicion Katia had only moved Tatiana because when her migraines came, Solanis would be the one to pick Tatiana up from day care. But before long, they, like their parents, had become best friends.

It wasn't unusual for Leonardo to pick up Gabby from day care if Solanis had to work late or for Katia to have both girls in tow, their backpacks dragging behind them as they ran onto the fields for after school sports.

The older Gabby got, the more she expressed her independence—an independence that manifested itself through concerning developments like talking back, insisting on dying her hair, and babbling to strangers.

Strangers like Childre Underwood.

———

GABBY AND SOLANIS had been cooling their feet in the park's fountain. Her daughter, seven at the time, got a kick out of swirling her feet in the warm water, watching the fish nibble on her toes. Her daughter had swirled her feet once, looked up, spotted a man on the other side of the water, and began calling for him.

Solanis looked to where Gabby was waving and shouting and watched as the man looked back at them with such a strong expression of familiarity that she had the urge to scoop up her daughter and run.

But she didn't want to be rude. She'd need to speak to Gabby about gesturing for strange men to engage with her during their time together.

Solanis simply smiled and gave the man a polite nod and then refocused her energy to make sure Gabby didn't fall into the fountain.

But the man didn't take the hint. He stood, walked through the fountain's water until he was soaking wet, and stopped right in front of her.

He was like an investment banker who had just come back from an all-night coke bender. Straight back, perfectly lined jaw with a sliver of scraggly hair peeking out from a five o'clock shadow that had been given permission to roam. His eyes were like ice but the type you'd see on a news feed that showed environmental videos with polar bears looking for land, doomed to drown in the ocean. His teeth were straight, but his Oxfords were soaking wet. He hadn't bothered to take them off.

This juxtaposition of quality and coke-addicted frat bro puzzled Solanis.

"Are you well?" she asked tentatively as the man gave her a look of realization.

"I think I know you," he said.

"I doubt that very much."

"I do though," he said. He held out his hand.

Solanis instinctively shook it.

Gabby jumped up and down. "That's Childre. He's really nice."

"Stop jumping. You'll slip."

"I am Childre," he said as if he hadn't heard Gabby. His hand lingered in the shake for just a moment too long.

"Solanis." She grabbed her daughter's hands. It was time to go.

She'd heard about this before—Dome sickness, where people seemed lost to themselves as they transitioned into Shamut. Some people had a harder time adjusting during their first few days.

Weak people.

Like the ones who wept during the Sprouting.

Gabby protested as her mother pulled her out of the fountain and headed toward their bike.

"I didn't know you had a daughter." Childre followed the two of them, grinning.

Gabby turned her head, smiling back. "This is my mom. She's always been my mom."

Solanis pushed aside her regret of teaching her daughter good manners, held Gabby's hand tighter and sped up. "We don't talk to strangers, Gabby," she hissed.

But he continued walking after them. "I know you though. You're Solanis, right?"

She nodded politely. She'd reached the bike and tapped the Voice on the handlebars. A chime signaled the bike had unlocked.

Childre walked around the bike and stood in front of them. "The stars, the stars," he said, completely deadpan. Then he laughed. And repeated it again. "All of them." He smiled as if expecting applause.

She nodded curtly and began strapping Gabby into the passenger seat behind her. "It's nice meeting you, Mr. Childre, but we have to get going." She checked Gabby's helmet and then her own and biked away.

Solanis continued to see the man around town for several weeks. She did her due diligence, of course, reporting her interaction to the proper channels to let them know someone might be Domesick and needed care. But she often saw Childre in his uniform, performing his duties around Shamut. He'd smile at her each time she walked by, say something profound about the stars, and then saunter back to whatever he was doing.

Childre became familiar, and Gabby waved and said hello when they saw "that strange man on the corner."

This was the pattern until the day Solanis got the phone call.

———

KATIA CALLED Solanis and asked her if she had dropped Gabby off at school.

"Of course," Solanis said. "I dropped both girls off."

"She's not here," Katia said with her usual bluntness. "I think they lost her."

She shook her head. "No, there's no way."

She felt the earth vibrate under her feet. She knew it, she knew it. Gabby never should have gone on that field trip without her. She should have trusted her instincts. And now her daughter was lost, wandering inside—

"Solanis?" Katia said.

"I'm on my way."

She excused herself from work and sprinted to the nearest cart, demanding it take her to the academy. She told the Voice to call Leonardo. He would know how to help her.

He met her at the academy with three of his colleagues and instantly began interrogating a distraught chaperone.

The academy was a sprawling campus with a massive rotunda in the center. The neoclassical marble and limestone columns held up the flat ceiling where tall arches gave onlookers a hint at the beauty inside. On the pathway leading toward the east entrance, emerald banners hung from massive poles every few feet, displaying happy, smiling students.

Of course, in the lobby was a four-meter-tall statue of Worthington. All government buildings had some of him inside. Here, he was made of white marble and was on one knee, speaking to two children holding various objects. One of the kids held a model of Shamut in their hand.

The chaperone cried under SPINE's interrogation. Leonardo would probably kill the woman if she didn't produce any useful information. The tutor insisted repeatedly that everyone had been safe and accounted for and that she had no way of knowing that Gabby was gone until the Voice told her. The woman was clearly rattled as he barked orders into his tablet to search for the little girl.

Katia patted her silver bun, rolled her eyes, and suggested that someone needed to be Recycled.

"Be nice," Solanis hissed at her but not disagreeing. Death was a good punishment for losing her daughter.

Leonardo spoke to his agents in the field through his earpiece, mumbling to himself about their incompetence. "They're all fucking academy rejects from back home," he groaned as he flipped through the screens on the Voice.

In his green uniform, crisp pants and dark blazer that stretched over his wide shoulders, he was authority. The man of confidence was a stark contrast to the weeping boy who worshipped the Shepherd all those years ago.

Leonardo looked up. "We found her."

———————

WHEN THE CART purred up to the fountain, Leonardo, Katia and Solanis found Gabby sitting with her feet in the water next to Childre, who was doing the same. He wasn't wearing shoes or socks. Instead, he had rolled up his uniform pants. Both of them were giggling like two kids who had decided to take the day off from school.

Solanis ran to Gabby, yelling her name, and scooped her out of the water. Gabby, startled, began to cry.

"I told you you can't talk to strangers." Solanis turned her back to Childre and carried her daughter back to the medical cart that had followed them to the fountain.

Leonardo rounded on Childre, peppering him with questions.

Gabby cried harder.

Childre yelled for help when a SPINE agent pulled him backward and onto the ground.

"You idiot, stop!" Leonardo yelled pulling the agent back.

"He found me." Gabby buried her head into Solanis's shoulder. "He found me!"

Katia tapped Leonardo on the shoulder, gesturing toward Gabby. "Give it a moment."

The other agent stood stupidly, pulling Childre with her and twisting his arm behind his back.

Solanis, still holding Gabby, yelled over to Childre. "Why did you take her? What's your deal anyway?"

"Mom, he didn't," Gabby insisted.

"Quiet, Gabby."

Katia tried to pull Childre out of the agents grasp, but the agent wouldn't move. Katia gave Leonardo a stern look, "Seriously?"

Childre was weeping.

Leonardo held up his hand. "Too much," he told the agent. "Just calm, okay?"

The agent nodded and loosened her grip.

"She was scared," Childre said, breathing hard, squirming under the man's grip.

"You can't just take someone because they're scared!" Solanis yelled.

"Hold on, Solanis," Katia said as another SPINE agent pulled out the zip ties and started toward Childre. "Leonardo!" Katia glared at him.

Leonardo squinted and gestured for the agent to hold off a moment.

Childre pulled hard, throwing the agent off balance.

Katia too her opening, pulling Childre behind her.

Solanis moved back quickly to avoid the scuffle.

But Leonardo raised a hand in the air, his eyes still on the Voice. "Calm. One second, guys."

SPINE stopped moving.

"I think he's telling the truth." He handed the Voice to Solanis.

She watched the display. Gabby had wandered off while her school group was headed toward the doors of the Higher Committee. She had found her mother's picture next to the other ComCen leaders. The girl had stared with awe, but when she looked back down the hall, her group was gone.

The camera feeds tracked her daughter until she wandered outside and began to cry when she realized she was lost.

It was Childre who had found her and held her and told her it was going to be okay. "Let's find the solar system," he said.

And they walked right back to where they had met the first time. Back to the fountain.

To cheer the little girl up, Childre had dipped her toes in the water, and they had watched the fish nibble at their feet together.

Solanis looked at Childre, and her anger evaporated. "Thank you," she said curtly to the man whose silver hair was now matted. There was a burn on his face from his cheek being scraped on the ground.

Katia scowled at Leonardo. "Maybe Childre should join SPINE? Might be an improvement. Why couldn't you find her anyway?" she asked.

"We don't put trackers in kids." Leonardo scowled. "Against the rules."

"Missing girls should be found quickly," she said. "My people clearly know what they are doing."

He scowled. "Give her an inhaler next time. We always track drugs." He walked back to the cart, his middle finger in the air.

Gabby copied him.

8

PROPAGATION

Nine Years, Three Hundred Days After Solanis Entered Shamut

Leonardo

Deputy Ambassador Leonardo Walkenshaw could never tell if the tattoo from the barracks on his inner forearm was crooked or not. The tattoo artist down the street had sworn to him he could etch the phrase *Bullets For Breakfast* over his superficial veins, but it always looked a little crooked.

The words were easy to read when he was slugging through desk work. He'd just flip his forearm over and see his brother's favorite phrase. But the letters were harder to read when pulling a gun on a suspect. His tattoo was an organic reminder that the only good thing about eating bullets for breakfast was that you didn't have to pay for lunch.

Heck, you didn't have to pay for much of anything after that.

Leonardo hadn't pulled his gun much in the nine and a half years after entering Shamut, Mr. Worthington's massive Dome project nestled somewhere in the heavily modified plains of rural Pennsylvania. His job as deputy ambassador with SPINE was to make sure people were safe. Worthington had told him so.

But most of the crimes he'd stopped so far were menial. Like people speaking about the outside or hoarding food. Most days, he felt like a beat cop who walked the streets, aiming for little more than a high step count. But Mr. Worthington had said, in the orientation video, that everything they did mattered. He had said that one little thing could bring the entire Dome down, so Leonardo was the tip of the spear in the battle against nostalgia. Nostalgia, Worthington had warned, was for the past. And it was the past that had gotten the earth to its current decaying state.

Nostalgia was a sweet, hollow poison.

But today was different. There was action in the air in the form of Childre Underwood, who stood on top of tables at the market, hurling pots and plants at innocent citizens who were just trying to shop and trade. There was no money in Shamut; reformed socialism, disguised as community, was the trade of the day. But throwing terracotta pots at poor old ladies who just wanted to trade blankets? Not on his watch.

If luck was with them, today's action would get him one step closer to the ultimate position inside Shamut.

Ambassador.

The Voice was a comfort each time it spoke directly to him. Even when the tablet was just giving him instructions as it was now—telling him more about Childre Underwood, and his alleged mental illness.

Leonardo felt grateful he could hear the Shepherd's voice every day, even if it was through the Voice that he carried with him every-where. He doubted he'd hear Worthington again in real life. The man was far too busy saving the world and ending wars.

Leonardo had met the Shepherd twice. First, when he was in prison. The second time was nearly a decade ago in Worthington Park, where he had forgiven him of all his sins and entrusted him to protect his beauty, his Dome. The mighty Shamut.

Leonardo rubbed his chest. The memory of that moment was an echo—faded but not lost.

He'd love to speak to the Shepherd again.

One day. When he became ambassador.

Leonardo checked his gun, finding it in working order, as the cart rolled forward. He'd never shoot Childre. That was how you did it in the old days. In the barracks, you'd gun someone down if they were too much hassle. If they were kids, you'd tranquilize them, wrap them up, and deliver them back to their parents after an overnight underground. A few days of darkness and nothing more than lukewarm water and biscuits were usually enough to get behavior modification to stick.

But this was Shamut, where the preferred tools were purple smoke and bureaucracy. Bureaucracy could bring anyone down. Besides, he was a reformed man. The was no nostalgia for the past here.

———

THE OPEN-AIR MARKET was complete chaos.

Usually, the market—a wide open street where people set up shop in the permanent booths on each side with goods to trade—was filled with people this early in the morning. But today, instead of the usual trading atmosphere, the citizens of Shamut cowered behind trashed booths, trying to escape the man on the table who flung pots and plants all around the market. Childre, their aggressor, had silver hair that was cut close on the sides and straight teeth. His eyes were a striking bright blue, clearly from expensive genetic selection, which meant his parents had money at some point to create this nearly two-meter-tall intelligent man. The silver hair was an anomaly though. Leonardo didn't know many people with silver hair that wasn't dyed, and as far as he could tell, there weren't any roots.

His hair was natural.

Childre wore a green jumpsuit that the Voice in his ear identified as the customary uniform of the infrastructure team. He yelled at the top of his lungs; picked up another of the reddish-brown pots; threw it toward a SPINE agent; and then wagged his finger at the officers.

Right in the center of it all was his partner.

Deputy Ambassador Solanis Tailor.

Solanis was the type of woman you'd see in a commercial for makeup. Not the kind that made women feel better about their insecurities. She would be the type who lied to them, telling them they didn't need men to be happy.

At about a meter and a half tall with dark curly hair and a complexion that made Leonardo feel guilty at the thought of sleeping with her, Solanis was a woman who walked like someone who should have an entourage. She was fit—a quality he liked—and about fifteen years away from her second career, which he found strangely enticing.

She had a tongue that could convince even the harshest critics to agree with her, and had managed to manipulate her green ComCen uniform in such a way that it flattered her. The other unicorns in her office looked awkward when they donned the ComCen blazer, close fitting top, and slacks.

Only her eyes ruined it all. They were jet black.

Not just the pupils or iris or whatever you called them. The entire eyeball looked like someone had spilled black ink and couldn't clean it up. Leonardo had heard about HSH, or Boston Eyes as people called it in Shamut. But he'd never actually seen anyone with the affliction in real life until he had met her.

He'd done a good job pretending not to notice. Over the years, the eyes seemed to be more of a cosmetic blemish, giving her no special powers. They just made her creepy to look at.

But it was something he could get used to if she wanted him to.

Solanis had somehow positioned herself between the suspect and the officers and was doing her best to reason with Childre. She spoke in a low, soft voice that could just be heard above the commotion.

"This isn't real!" Childre yelled toward her, his eyes focused firmly on hers.

"Childre, it's me. You know me." She brushed her hair back so the confused man could fully see her face.

"Solanis?" His shoulders slumped as his diabolical expression changed to something more cheerful. "The stars have arrived," he said, breaking into a smile and instantly dropping the pots in his hand.

Leonardo's agents shifted their positions as she urged the man to come down. "Why don't you join me down here, and we can talk?"

Leonardo narrowed his eyes. Childre might look like he was complying, but he had seen this before with people going through manic episodes. They could weave their personalities to fit any situation. Childre would wait for her to let down her guard and then attack her. That was what they did in the barracks.

Childre glared at Leonardo.

Leonardo gave a sarcastic salute. A dick move, but he didn't want Childre to think they were friends.

One of them was breaking the Shepherd's laws—the contract they'd made to this place. The other was protecting their home.

He'd seen Childre before—the vacant expression on his face. People who walked like that sometimes killed people for no reason. Got called harmless because they looked like investment bankers.

Leonardo grimaced. Investment bankers weren't harmless. Maybe Childre was a panda—cute and useless.

"You good, Solanis?" Leonardo asked.

She made eye contact. At least he thought she did. It was difficult to tell with people like her; they tended to always look like they were looking through you. The corners of her mouth turned down slightly.

Was that disappointment?

"Agent Walkenshaw," she said. "I think we've got it from here."

A few of the other unicorns stood around, looking like they were about to head into a press conference.

"You think so?" Leonardo asked, flashing a smile in her direction. "He's still on the table, and all these poor people are afraid." He placed his right hand on his hip, pushing back his jacket. He wanted Childre to see his gun; it would scare him.

Childre didn't react. He still gawked at Solanis.

"Yep," she said, smirking. "Besides, you're late. Just woke up?"

Leonardo laughed. "I've been up. We're busy. But I rushed over when I knew you'd be here."

"You missed me?"

"*Missed* is doing a lot of work in that sentence."

"What word would you use?"

"What do you call waking up in the middle of the night and noticing your blanket fell on the floor?"

She thought for a moment. "Heartbreaking, soul-crushing, devastating." She turned back to Childre. "Come on, Childre. Come down. We can speak here."

"You sure you have this?" Leonardo asked.

Childre had a hungry look on his face. There was an intelligence behind the manic way he was behaving, which meant he wasn't a panda. Leopards were like that. What if Childre leaped from the table and hurt her? Or himself? That meant paperwork and failure. He wasn't explaining to Kruger how he let this go sideways. That was how he'd miss a promotion.

Solanis simply nodded. "I'm in control." She turned back to Leonardo's SPINE agents, who had created a half moon circle around the table, and held up a hand. "Take a few steps back, guys. Give us some space, okay?"

Leonardo hated when she did this. She was right to command the scene, but she was putting herself at risk. The farther back his agents got, the less likely they were able to protect her. Lions still ate people in the African plains.

He unholstered his gun, his hand next to the trigger. "Solanis," he said gently, "I don't think—"

His earpiece lit up. "Sir." One of the agents buzzed him from back at headquarters. They were probably watching through the drones that hovered over the streets. "Should we step back?"

Solanis looked at Leonardo, her hands still up in that calming gesture toward Childre. "Leonardo..." She raised her right eyebrow.

Childre looked from Leonardo to the gun in his hand and back to Solanis.

Leonardo raised his gun, training it on Childre, and said quietly into the headset, "She owns the scene. Back up but be ready. I have a line of sight."

His agents took a small step back, confirming they had heard him over their earpieces.

"More," Solanis insisted.

Leonardo rolled his eyes. She was reckless. Completely reckless. Did she know she was putting herself in danger?

His agents complied.

"What the fuck is she doing?" one of the agents mumbled in his ear. "Leonardo, just get this over with."

"Quiet," he hissed. "Give her a second."

Solanis looked back at Childre and extended her hand. "Come on. Let's get off the table."

Childre looked back at Leonardo, frowned, and jerked his head toward her. Leonardo gripped his gun tighter, ready to aim. *Squeeze the trigger. Don't pull the gun.*

But Childre must have sensed it was safe. He climbed down from the cart and gave her a grin. But that didn't last long.

He clutched the side of his head, frowning. "I was supposed to tell you something," he said, screwing up his face in confusion. "The notes. Something about the notes." He looked up and then narrowed his eyes at her. He grabbed her shoulders.

There it was.

Leonardo didn't wait. He relaxed his grip on the gun, stepped forward, and said, "Take him out."

In an instant, the SPINE agents tackled Childre and held him down. One of his agents stood in front of Solanis and stepped backward, forcing her away from Childre.

Solanis stumbled, and Leonardo gently tugged her toward him. When possible, you never roughy handled your partners. But even though Solanis was a veteran, she hadn't seen *real* combat. She was a paper pusher. A flack. A unicorn. Sure, they'd trained together when they had first arrived in Shamut, but people like her never actually fought during the National Service. Even if everyone did their thirteen weeks of firearm and basic training. Paper pushers never understood that one stray bullet, and they'd be in the next recycler with everyone chanting their name.

Childre yelped and struggled, his face in the dirt. Blood came from his mouth as his hands were wrapped behind his back. One of the agents zip-tied his hands and jerked him upright. At some point, he must have been kicked in the face because a bruise began to appear on his cheek as he tried to yell and kick. But the agents got him moving, dragging him toward the waiting cart.

"Help me!" Childre begged to the market around him as SPINE marched him out. "They're hurting me."

Solanis stepped around Leonardo and tried to pull the SPINE agents off Childre, but they shook her off. She would never match their strength, and besides, their uniforms were designed not to be gripped by hands. She whirled around and stalked back to Leonardo, her eyes looking darker than earlier.

"Seriously?" she demanded. "You break protocol now? I had him."

"He grabbed you. At that point, you're in danger." Leonardo didn't yell. One thing he'd learned from the ComCen executives was how to keep his cool. "Besides, the bosses wanted this over with. And they're the ones judging us."

She gestured back toward Childre's cart. "You think we are going to get points for this?"

He nodded. "We get points for doing our jobs, not for being nice."

"The protocol is that when I am at the scene, I am in control." She was angry.

"Until you are in danger." He shook his head. "I know, I know. We can't let anything happen to you. You guys."

"I had this." She shook her head.

"You're never actually in control," he said. "You unicorns never see what could go wrong."

Solanis scoffed. "Don't let the others hear you say that."

"Pretty and dangerous. But mostly pretty." He looked down at the Voice and tucked it away. "We should check to see if he was a red coat before he came inside."

"LTE?" She had her arms crossed as she looked past Leonardo to where the cart was vanishing in the distance. People with black eyes always seemed to look extra angry. Though she was kinda cute when she was upset. "You actually think so?"

Leonardo nodded. "They'll do anything to bring this place down."

She didn't respond.

"Read the latest briefings. More threats. We have to stay vigilant. Besides, Chris—"

"Childre," she corrected.

"Childre." He clenched his jaw; she was always correcting him. "He's in my custody now, so you know what that means? I get to assign the caseworker. And that's going to be you, Solanis. We will interview him. You'll Propagate and collect the points."

She sighed, but a small smile crossed her face. "Okay, Leonardo."

"Come on," he said, resting both hands on her shoulders and feeling them relax. "I've got your back here."

Solanis smiled and thanked him. She had a pretty smile. "Just let me do my thing next time." She fished the Voice from her side pocket. "You sure Propagation is next?"

He looked down at his own tablet and clicked Childre's profile. "Yes."

She shook her head. "I really don't want to Propagate him."

"You want to be promoted?" he asked.

"Yeah, but we know him."

"Doesn't matter." He nodded and gently squeezed her shoulder. "We need to win. Remember what we promised each other?"

She nodded. "Ambassador or nothing. I know. We are a team. You're the tip of the spear, and I'm the handle. Blah, blah, blah."

Leonardo grinned. "See? I'm surprised someone as old as you can remember that tip of the spear bullshit from orientation."

Her eyes did something funny. They shimmered slightly—a movement you could only see in the light. But it didn't matter. She was smiling at Leonardo, and that made him feel warm in the cheeks.

"Careful," she said, tapping him on the forehead. "I might forget to back you up during review one day. Then you'll be out there, waking up with the red coats."

She walked away and gestured for her fellow unicorns to get into the cart with her.

The cart rolled away.

———

SPINE's HEADQUARTERS was located across the boulevard from the ComCen building. The Darkness—as the low four-story building was called—went deep into the earth, where the real work of SPINE was done.

You didn't have to scan your eyes, badge, or handprint when you walked into the Darkness. The building knew who you were automatically. The moment Leonardo entered the atrium with Solanis, their faces, weight, and other recent biometrics were scanned, and they gained the access they needed to step behind one of the many doors that would carry them into the bowels of Shamut.

While underground, bright lights that mimicked the sun came from every corner of the space, giving each floor of the building an earthy glow, an irony for a building nicknamed the Darkness. The soft gold and green covered the open floor plans and adorned the rows and rows of desks and monitors. Around him, Leonardo's agents reviewed cases and tracked leads for potential crimes within Shamut. While amateurs, they still managed to clear a significant amount of cases. Old ladies who steal blankets are not clever.

The room where they held Childre reminded him of the Waystation where he and his escort had lain on the table and were told that when they opened their eyes, they'd be inside of Shamut.

Leonardo had woken up without any underwear.

Childre was being tended to by a healer who rubbed a thick paste on his face. The tablet monitored the tube that was in the man's arm as some sort of solution was fed to him. Childre squirmed at the healer's touch making these pathetic squeaking sounds as the salve was applied. Leonardo's tablet told him they'd discovered no connection to the whimpering man in the chair and LTE. The Voice, burdened with Worthington's rapid, precise cadence, made it difficult to cast doubt on the truthfulness of the statement. Besides, the mewling mentally ill man didn't look like someone who was willing to brand his enemies in a desperate effort to purge the planet of sinners. LTE were killers. Radical killers.

Childre's eyes lit up when he saw Solanis, and he pointedly ignored Leonardo.

It didn't matter. Propagation was her responsibility. Leonardo was just here as backup, in case Childre wrapped his arms around her neck and began squeezing. Leopards didn't choke people. Monkeys did. Maybe Chris—no, Childre—was a monkey.

"I am glad you're back." Childre's swollen cheek made it hard for him to speak. "I didn't do anything. But they need to know. It's all not real. None of it is. There's a place outside of here. Don't you remember?"

He wasn't making sense.

Solanis spoke to Childre as if she were speaking to Gabby. "Childre, do you know where you came from?"

The man frowned and looked at the floor. The healer tilted his head back up so he could finish his work.

"Childre," she said again gently. "Do you know where you're from?"

He closed his eyes as if thinking. But he came up empty. "I was just here one day."

"This happens sometimes," the healer said in a low voice while smiling at Childre.

His patient began to cry. Leonardo glanced at Solanis, who looked concerned. Leonardo copied her, furrowing his brow.

The healer examined his work, stepped back, and then spoke to the room. "Give it an hour, and it'll be like new." The healer looked back at Childre, smiling, still addressing the weeping man as if he were a child. "Sometimes, when people transition from there to here, they forget. That's normal. You'll be okay."

Childre sniffed and nodded.

"We're going to Propagate you today. You'll wake up as if it's your first day, but you'll be like new. You should get your memories back. Deputy Ambassador Tailor will help in this process. Keep you calm."

The healer motioned for the rest of the room to get ready as Childre looked to Solanis. The man was afraid. You couldn't Propagate someone who was afraid. The drugs wouldn't work.

Solanis sat next to Childre. "Childre," she said as she helped ease the man's torso backward, so he was lying back on his bed. "I want you to think about the last time you were happy."

The man rested his head on the pillow and nodded.

"Can you tell me when that was?"

"The pool with the fish," he said, nodding happily toward Solanis.

You've got to be kidding me.

"Fountain," she corrected him. "Just focus on that. The way the fish nibble at your toes in the water. How fun is that?"

Childre nodded again. "They tickle."

Leonardo wanted to vomit. This was why no one took ComCen seriously.

"Yes, they do." Solanis looked at the healer who was getting the injector ready. "Just think about the fish."

Leonardo had a great respect for her, but this mopey dopey way of doing things made him want to rip his hair out. Why couldn't they just jab something calming into the man's neck, then inject the propagation serum into him, and plop him into a new housing unit? Was the hangover really that bad? They could just make the drug stronger if it was less effective on agitated patients. These rituals and protocols were a waste of time.

Childre stopped smiling. "I just keep thinking I have to tell you something."

Solanis's arm jerked.

The man motioned for her to lean forward.

The healer opened a port in the IV.

Childre leaned directly into her ear and whispered something.

The healer plunged the needle into the IV, and Childre went limp.

Solanis snapped her head up and looked at Leonardo.

"What did he say?" Leonardo asked.

She frowned and blinked. "I…didn't catch it."

The healer ignored them both and checked Childre's pulse. Abandoning the warm bedside manner he'd adopted earlier, the healer was now all business as he snapped off his gloves. "This happens sometimes. Get him upstairs so we can place him in a new housing unit and prepare him for a new Sprouting. We only get one more shot at this." He looked at Solanis and gave a slight smile. "DA Tailor, you're good at your job. Man was completely calm when he went under. Makes for a more effective serum. Good work. I'll tell Wick."

Solanis nodded in thanks.

The healer sighed and gazed at Childre who was breathing peacefully, knocked out on the table. "Poor guy. I'll have to check his files and see if there's anything in his medical history that might point to this happening. Regardless, that's tomorrow's problem. Another two hundred will be here for the Sprouting." He smiled. "Our community is growing."

The healer left, ignoring Leonardo, the gurney with Childre trailing after him.

Leonardo found himself left alone with a frustrated Solanis.

"Ugh, I hate that so much." She leaned against the table. "It's awful."

"You did great." He placed his arm around her. "Seriously, it was flawless. We'll get points for sure. This entire operation will get us points."

"You know Childre knows Gabby?"

He frowned. "This is the job. No room for feelings."

"It still doesn't feel good."

"He's a crazy guy who's Domesick. He could have hurt you."

She held up a hand. "I'm done talking about this."

Leonardo scoffed. "Don't be a jerk."

She was like this sometimes—the personification of the makeup commercial.

Solanis tugged her hair and crossed her arms. "I'm not. I'm just saying. You think Winston's done a Propagation yet?"

"He'll find a way to cheat," he said.

"Snowmen always cheat."

He shook his head. "They weren't all bad."

She didn't respond.

Leonardo tried again. "You think Chris—"

"Childre."

He barreled on. "You think he has a family?" The Voice beeped. He was needed back upstairs; Kruger had summoned him. "Never mind. I gotta go. You're still down for dinner later?"

"I should be," she said, looking down at her own tablet. "Can I bring Katia?"

In the world that was Solanis Tailor, Katia was a necessary, painful ambiance. He'd wanted it to be the two of them.

"Um... Sure," he said, resigned to an evening with annoying chatter that would go over his head. He could swear that Katia talked over him on purpose.

"Great. Don't forget to do your paperwork. I'll have my team sign off on my section by tonight." Without looking up, she left the room.

Leonardo shook his head. Every time he thought he was getting somewhere with her, she'd revert back to...whatever that was.

9

OATH

Solanis

The day after she Propagated Childre Underwood, Solanis had two problems. She had a pounding headache, and it was Tuesday. Tuesday was sprint day, where she and her fellow Evergreens would head to the athletic fields and run until they were about to throw up. The coach —a man who looked like he was in the middle of his second career with large round glasses and a head that wouldn't look out of place in an egg carton—explained to them that sprint day would happen until they died. Or turned one hundred years old, in which they'd die anyway. Everyone was Recycled at 100.

"Besides," the coach said, fondling his whistle. "The weather is literally perfect. You have nothing to complain about."

"It's always fucking perfect," Katia said, clutching a stitch in her side. Her tank top stuck to her as she tried to catch her breath. "I'm going to die if we keep this up."

Solanis bounced on her toes, her hands resting on her lower hips. She did her best not to copy Katia. Air struggled to stay inside of her, but she wasn't about to let Katia know she was suffering too.

"Then you should be able to run faster," the coach said, eyeing

Katia with disgust. "Maybe if you attended the weekly training sessions consistently, you wouldn't be in this position."

Solanis wrapped her arm around Katia's shoulders. Katia opened her mouth to shoot back, but she steered her away. "No use," she said. "He's gonna just get mad."

"I'm nearly forty!" Katia said, ignoring Solanis.

"And you're slower than you need to be," the coach retorted, his hands on his hips. "Move faster or the whole lot of you will do more straightaways. Your elderly friend is faster than you."

Elderly?

"Keep up the good work, Miss. Tailor." He nodded. "We'll make an ambassador out of you yet."

Solanis nodded, confused. Who used *elderly* as a compliment? But she lined up for the next sprint anyway, dragging a winded Katia next to her.

Solanis didn't mind Katia's attitude, as long as she could beat her each time they ran up and down the track. The unspoken competition between the two of them only worked because she was consistently faster and stronger than her silver-haired friend. She only bragged about it when she felt Katia needed to be put in her place, like when she pretended to know more than she did.

But it was Katia's own fault. She had a habit of vanishing for weeks at a time and wasn't consistent with her weekly workouts. A few years ago, she'd vanished for nearly a month, and Tatiana had to stay with her. She had claimed she had migraines, but there were pills for that kind of thing nowadays. Besides, Katia wasn't exactly *that* type of Evergreen; the kind that hugged trees, practiced free bleeding, and lusted after the idea of gasoline drying up once and for all..

It didn't matter though. Solanis suspected Katia could talk about the world out there, and no one would do anything about it. Katia had worked for Worthington. So, while the coach relished in being an asshole, he was also powerless to do anything about her spotty attendance records. "Besides," Katia would say. "Even if I vanished into the darkness, I'd be back. I always come back." It was not tradition. It was expectation.

———

AFTER THE EVENING WORKOUT, Katia and Solanis headed to the cafeteria for some food.

Katia hitched her workout bag up onto her shoulder. "I hope Leonardo won't be joining us."

"He's supposed to pick up the girls."

They walked into one of the many mess halls in Shamut. The room was filled with rows of long wooden tables and displays showcasing the latest news from inside of Shamut. It smelled delicious. But just because you could bask in the aroma of apple pie, chicken, or lab grown steak, didn't mean you were getting Thanksgiving dinner. Diets were managed by the dietitians and adjusted accordingly.

"He's always hovering." Katia tossed her bag onto one of the long tables, causing two young women near them to glare in disgust. They still moved over though. "Leonardo's like a golden retriever."

"I wouldn't let him hear you say that," Solanis said, indulging the game that she had to play constantly with Katia and Leonardo.

Friendship with Katia meant accepting that she and Leonardo were not going to be the best of friends. Tolerance was the work. Solanis had a suspicion the only reason Katia and Leonardo tolerated each other was because he was Solanis's partner at work, and Katia found Solanis to be a helpful escape from ball busting her husband. Solanis didn't mind. Katia was worth the trouble. She was entertaining. She'd been there when Gabby was born.

"He's only trying to help."

"I know he means well," Katia said, craning her neck to see the food options better. The walls of the cafeteria were lined with transparent boxes where you could grab a snack. "But he's so full of it. It's as if Worthington himself came down and appointed him to be our personal bodyguard."

"To hear him tell it, that's what happened." Solanis picked up an apple from the shelf and scanned the Voice. It would add the apple to her daily macro allotment. If she overate, she'd be on dry oatmeal for the next few days. "I think he's a true believer."

"What do you mean?" Katia inspected a protein bar, frowned, and settled on a cup of carrots with hummus.

"You've heard his story? How Worthington came to the barracks and—"

"Yeah, yeah," she said. "Told him that he was needed to protect his beauty. Gave him a second chance. Whatever the fuck that means. We've all heard the story. You'd think the Man from Denver gave him a blow job." She led the way back to their seats. "He loves that man. Probably why he's single."

Solanis raised an eyebrow. "Still?"

"Marrying him means you're asking for a threesome with Worthington. What does it matter to you anyway?" She dipped a carrot in the biodegradable container. "Almost ten years, and you haven't touched him once."

"Worthington is intense." Solanis took a bite out of her apple.

She ignored her pivot. "You have to be careful with people like that. You know, the ones with mindless devotion? The ones who just *do*." She sniffed hard and took another bite of carrot. "Those are the ones who really believe in all of this. These carrots are so small."

Solanis set her apple down. "Don't you believe at least some of it?"

She rolled her eyes. "The earth is dying. No shit. Do I believe Worthington will save us?" She snorted. "He can hardly build a subway tunnel that works. You know what I'm doing right now? We've been working on modifying some of the plans for the new subway beneath the outer edge of the Dome. You know the one that connects Wonderland to Central? Those old people want to go to the farmers' market. Anyway, I'm designing the train cars, and I point out that there are already tunnels under the Dome. Massive tunnels. But they're too small to fit a casual subway." She gestured wildly with her hands as she explained this offense to design. "Some of these tunnels are so small that you or I might hardly be able to fit through them. Who is the idiot who started digging and didn't just dig the right holes? Small tunnels mean small trains. Small trains means you have no place to put Ronnie. Anyway, I told my team they needed to just come back to me when they fix the holes. But what idiot designed this?"

Solanis gave Katia a look. She'd done it again, confusing Ronnie for the Voice. Nearly a decade in, you'd think she'd get her story straight. "You really think Worthington was poring over subway tunnels?"

"No, but his choice in general contractor leaves much to be desired." She ran her hand through her hair.

She reminded Solanis of the girls she knew in high school when she was in foster care—the ones from downtown. They had this way of speaking in this wandering fashion, where the words kinda smashed together sometimes. They were contrarian, lingering on the edge of what was an was not acceptable.

Katia threw her hands up in the air in dramatic disgust, causing a few people to frown in her direction. But she ignored them as usual. "I can't work like this, Solanis." She sighed. "But tell anyone here that the Shepherd is less than perfect, and you'd think I'd burned down a forest."

Solanis frowned, looking around the room. "Don't be too loud. I don't want to lose points."

She rolled her eyes. "You're being dramatic."

"They'll drag you into the Darkness. Never be seen again."

"I *always* come back." Katia scoffed. "The rules are idiotic."

But Solanis held firm. "Worthington's rules aren't completely *idiotic*. I mean, he has reasons right? He did build all of this. No Haze, plenty of food. We aren't getting a bad deal."

Katia scowled. "No, not at all all idiotic. Rules from the man who *raised the greens and fucked the seas.*"

Solanis laughed nervously. She wasn't getting anywhere with this. But she leaned in close anyway. "Hey, you're good at technology. You know I'm no good at it." She reached into her pocket and pulled out a small tile. "Any idea what this is?"

She handed Katia the tile, one of the tiny squares she'd been receiving for the past year. This was the square that Childre had to be referring to. But why had he called them notes? They were small, ordinary-looking tiles about the size of her palm. But there was a curious squiggle on the tile that bounced off the corners as if searching for something.

Was Childre sending these to her? Were they supposed to be gifts?

Even though Childre was clearly a few steps away from being locked in a home named after a saint, these gifts were pretty bad. You couldn't write on them, they wouldn't tear, and they had the consistency of hard silicone.

Omer would know.

Greg would have loved a good puzzle to solve.

Katia looked down at the tile and then back at Solanis. "They look like electric paper maybe?"

"Electric paper? No one uses that stuff anymore."

Electric paper should have been the replacement for real paper, but it was too expensive and impractical. Solanis had never seen it in real life before. So, she had twelve bits of electric paper sitting in the bottom of her underwear drawer and didn't know how to use it.

"Can you check for me? You know how bad I am with tech."

Katia nodded and then looked up. "You'd better put that away. Mr. Perfect is coming." She stood, blocking Solanis from view, and waved toward Leonardo.

Solanis tucked the tile back into her pocket.

Leonardo strode toward them with Gabby over his shoulders and Tatiana toddling behind them, laughing hysterically as he jumped up and down. Tatiana had her mother's trademark silver hair and hazel eyes. She always looked like someone had just put a little too much hair on her head. Gabby, on the other hand, had inherited her mother's dark skin, original light brown eyes, and freckles. Her nose and jaw were her father's. Her hair, a mixture of both, which Solanis hadn't quite managed to tame in her daughter's awkward phase.

Leonardo had a backpack on his front and back as he lugged their school supplies over to the table. He placed two square boxes—arts and crafts projects—on the table and sighed with relief.

"They're heavy sometimes," he said, referring to the backpacks.

Tatiana, in her excitable state, ran and gave her mother a hug while he helped Gabby off his shoulders.

"Luna." Katia stroked her daughter's hair.

Tatiana squirmed at her mother's nickname for her, but accepted the kiss on the cheek that came with it.

Behind her, Gabby bent down, picked up her backpack, and then tossed it onto the table. She picked up a cube and played with it.

"Hello, Gabby," Solanis said, brightly reaching out toward her daughter.

But Gabby ignored her, instead turning to Leonardo with the cube and showing it to him. The cube, which seemed to be made of some sort of thick paper, glowed from the inside. There was a lid on the box and what looked like interior flashing screens.

"Gabby?" she asked gently. "Give Mom a hug."

Gabby did this sometimes.

She looked up, dropped the cube on the table, and smiled at Solanis. Then walked over and gave her a quick hug before returning to showing him the cube. Solanis stole a look at Leonardo, but he simply shrugged.

"Gabby, did you want to tell your mother what you were telling me earlier?" he said.

Gabby pulled out a small Voice tablet from her bag and thrust it into her mother's hands. She didn't make eye contact. "We have a trip. We're going to visit the Fields." She pointed to the tablet where the permission slip waited for Solanis's approval. The Fields were a massive forest built at the edge of Shamut that served as a rest and recovery spa for those who had done remarkable acts of service.

Solanis's chest tightened. This was an overnight camping trip, where the class would learn about nature and what it would take to survive the outdoors. It looked like the academy was giving her nine-year-old a survival skills lesson.

"Tatiana is going," she said quickly. "All the other kids are going. Can you sign, Mom? Please?"

Solanis smiled at her. "We will talk about this when we get home. Okay?"

Gabby shook her head. "Permission is due by tomorrow."

"When's the trip?" Katia asked brightly.

"Monday," Tatiana said. "I want Gabby to be in my group. Please can she come? Please, please?"

Solanis gave Katia a look. This was an ambush. She was doing this on purpose, egging her on. "Gabby and I will talk about this when we get home, okay?"

Gabby rolled her eyes and crossed her arms. "I'm not going to get lost again."

Solanis kept the smile on her face, even though her heart sped up.

She pushed harder. "You're going to say no. You always say no."

Solanis stopped smiling. "Gabby…"

She had been doing this a lot lately. Challenging her.

Katia had insisted Tatiana had been through a similar phase, but the bite felt harder than the sting of Haze when it was her miniature duplicate. It was like she was looking into a mirror and playing a game of tug-of-war with herself. Could she win that battle?

Gabby's shoulders slumped, and she flung herself down on the bench next to Tatiana. Solanis ignored the temper tantrum. It was annoying, but Solanis wasn't her daughter's friend. She was her mother. And she needed to make smart decisions, not emotional ones.

"Hey." Leonardo turned to Solanis and nodded his head toward a nearby table. "You got a second?"

"As long as you're not going to ask me about the field trip."

He shook his head, put his hand on her elbow, and led her to the side of the room, away from Gabby. "You good?" he asked. He was giving her that sheepish smile he got whenever they stood close together.

She nodded. "What's up?"

"Gabby's teacher. He wants to speak to you. He cornered me at drop-off. You know. The one with the big glasses?"

"Everything okay?"

"He was angry," he said.

She frowned. As dramatic as Gabby could be, she was generally a model student. Her daughter tended to go with the flow and had a ridiculously loud laugh at times, but she was nine. She couldn't expect her to be a perfect little angel.

"It's the permission slip, isn't it?" she asked.

Leonardo shook his head. "He didn't specify. But he did say it was urgent. You should go by today before you head home?" He did this sometimes—end sentences with a question. As if he needed to get her to agree to what he was saying.

She folded her arms and looked back at the table where Gabby sat, giggling at something Katia had said. She was probably telling her daughter how uptight her mother was.

Katia spared no one.

But what could have happened that was so bad it demanded an immediate parent-teacher conference?

"Does it have to be today?" Solanis said.

He gave her a look. "Just see what he wants. Besides, the ambassador committee? They'll look for any excuse to dock points."

"And god knows if Winston finds out..." she groaned. "He wants my promotion. He's such a Snowman."

He nodded, resting his hand on her arm. "One more thing. When did you meet Katia?"

"Meet her?"

"Yeah, like before you came in here. Or after, like, me?"

Solanis laughed. "After, Leonardo." She smiled and ruffled his hair. "In fact, you're technically my oldest friend here if you don't count Yolanda. Best friends, right?"

He didn't respond.

But the joy faded quickly as she felt that familiar nudge in the back of her mind. This Gabby situation could hurt her. She couldn't afford to lose points if she was going to become an ambassador. Ambassador Wick had been clear. Everything they did—and that included the company they kept—mattered at a time like this. Worthington only selected the best.

"Gabby." Solanis motioned for her daughter to gather her things.

But Gabby was engrossed with the cube again. Somehow, she'd managed to make it fall apart, the screens on the inside glowing.

"Gabby," she said again, more sternly. "Let's go."

Gabby nodded, and the cube snapped back together.

Katia walked over to Solanis. "You let her go on the trip, and you and I can have a night out. Been trying to get you to Dirt anyway."

For a ridiculous amount of time, Katia had been trying to get Solanis to head to a venue on the outskirts of downtown Shamut whose slogan—*Worthington Doesn't Need To Know*—gave her all the ammunition she needed to say no. She didn't need an excuse to leave Gabby home overnight without her.

She repeated what she'd said every week for years. "I'm not sure if it's for me."

"Come on. Think about it. Tatiana is going. She's going to be fine. It's the Fields. It's one of the safest places inside Shamut."

Solanis shook her head and looked at the floor. "We don't know that."

"Gabby won't get lost again," Katia said quietly.

Leonardo helped Gabby put on her backpack, and before she joined Solanis, she turned and gave him and Katia a hug.

The pain was back again.

Because she could have sworn her daughter hadn't wanted to let go of Katia.

GABBY HUGGED Dr. Eritten as he shook Solanis's hand. He patted Gabby on the head and then motioned to the two chairs in front of the desk. He adjusted the nameplate, which read *Dr. Richard Eritten.*

"Thank you for your time, Solanis," Dr. Eritten said, settling into his own seat and enunciating every syllable.

"No problem, Richard." Solanis smiled gently. She didn't want him to see she was nervous.

He frowned and tapped his nameplate. "It's Dr. Eritten."

Okay.

His frown hardened.

"Is everything okay, Doctor?" she asked, giving serious side-eye to Gabby, who was absorbed in her book.

Gabby had stopped fidgeting while in the educator's office, almost as if she knew why she was there.

Did he make the students call him doctor too?

Was Gabby being teased? Were the other kids mean to her? Or did she ask too many questions of her professors? Solanis had done that when she was a kid. Mr. Nikielski had made her life miserable as a result. Or maybe it was the dreaded question. Had Gabby been asking about her father? She wasn't old enough for that conversation yet.

"Gabby is an aggressive student," he said.

"Hold on a second." Solanis held up her hand.

"And that's a good thing, Solanis. She clearly loves to learn, and she's hitting her marks academically. We can tell you're spending the right amount of time with her after school and working with her on assignments."

Dr. Eritten's smile was forced.

Solanis knew this look; she'd given it to many people when she was about to deliver bad news. His mouth might have been curled upward, but the smile didn't quite reach his eyes.

"But we do have an issue." The educator leaned back in his chair and pawed at his tablet. "Your daughter has recently expressed some reluctance to say the oath every morning."

She blinked. "Excuse me?"

"You're excused. But it's not your daughter's fault. We've noticed a few kids who suddenly seem reluctant to give their proper due to the Founder." The professor gestured toward the Voice. "Take a look for yourself."

She checked the console and watched as most of the students stood and faced the portrait of Worthington. They all began the Oath of Commitment.

Except her daughter and three others. They just sat there.

Of course, Tatiana was one of them. She was Katia's daughter, after all.

"We've done our investigation," he said, "and Tatiana is the instigator. Do you know her mother Katia?"

The screen zeroed in on the silver-haired girl who sat quietly with her arms folded, her face a perfect mimic of her mother's. Solanis suppressed a smile; Katia would probably be proud to see her copy her like this.

But Solanis wasn't antisocial like Katia. She looked over at Gabby, who had grown bored with the conversation and was once again reading.

Dr. Eritten continued. "We would like you to speak to your

daughter about the importance of paying due respect to the Founder every morning. He's the one who saved us and allowed us to live under the safe terrarium of Shamut."

He gazed up at the portrait of Worthington that hung on the wall. This version showed Worthington teaching students in an outdoor classroom. Solanis didn't remember Worthington being a teacher. Wasn't he a businessman?

"Everyone pays their respects, so we do not forget who he is, who we are, and the sacrifices we've made. We must remember."

She nodded. "Gabby?"

The girl looked up, seemingly sensing the change in her mother's tone. "Yes?" She was quieter than normal.

When Solanis was a girl, her father had once taken her to the lab where he tested new medicine on animals to check for side effects that might be dangerous to people. A mouse had been pressed against the corner of a cage when a robotic arm had sprung to life and began its soft, mechanical journey toward the animal. She could feel with every fiber in her being that the mouse knew the needle was coming, and it let out whimpers so frail and hopeless that she begged her father not to let the machine inject it.

She had asked as if her father hadn't been the one controlling the joystick that moved the mechanical hand toward the vibrating animal. But her father just smiled his knowing smile—the one that told children her age that he possessed some godly wisdom that she would eventually inherit. He pressed the button, and the two watched as the mouse squeaked over and over again in fear.

"The mouse doesn't understand we need to inject her with medicine to make her better," her father said quietly while Solanis watched in horror as the needle plunged into the creature's skin. "It can't see past the slight moment of pain that it needs in order to grow. Besides, it's not in any pain yet. It's simply afraid of the anticipation."

After an hour, her father encouraged her to look at the mouse, who was running around with the other mice behind the glass as if nothing had happened.

"See?" he had said, hugging an upset Solanis. "She's fine now. She needed to make it through that moment."

Here, when her daughter squeaked at her, Solanis felt exactly the way she had in the lab all those years ago.

It was the sound of pain.

"You know it's important you pay your respects to Mr. Worthington." Solanis gestured to the portrait.

Her daughter stayed quiet.

"Can you tell us why you haven't been paying your respects?"

Gabby's eyes darted back and forth between the two of them, her mouth glued shut.

"You're not in trouble," Solanis said gently.

The educator cleared his throat. "Actually…"

She shot doctor-professor-whatever-his-name-was a dirty look. "Give me a moment."

The man fell quiet.

Her eyes slid back to her daughter's face, which was now contorted in fear. She stood and kneeled in front of Gabby. "Baby…" She placed a hand on her daughter's leg.

Gabby was trembling like the mouse trapped in the corner.

She realized she was the needle.

The epiphany shot solar flares through her veins.

This wasn't going to be productive.

"We'll figure this out," Solanis said, hugging her shaking daughter as her tears wet her shirt. "Let's pick this up later."

"Solanis," Dr. Eritten said sternly, "there's something else."

"It's deputy ambassador," Solanis said, shocking herself at her harshness.

Her daughter, seemingly sensing the tense environment, cried harder.

She patted her on the back, encouraging her to quiet down and modulating her voice to be more even toned. She didn't want the mouse to shake anymore. "And I said we'll discuss this later."

"You're not hearing me." Dr. Eritten stood. "I have to report this to the Higher Committee. Because you're vying to become ambassador, this matters. The company you keep, the ones you hang out with, reflect your judgment."

"You're going to report me because my nine-year-old didn't say the oath?" She kept her tone deadpan and controlled.

"It's my duty to report. It's all of our duties. It's what they expect of us."

"Seriously?" She shook her head.

"If you can't control your daughter, how can you control a part of Shamut? We deserve leaders who will—"

"And I take it you think Winston would do better? The Snowman. The traitor."

"His daughter isn't refusing the oath."

"He doesn't have children."

"And that's why he should be ambassador," Dr. Eritten said stiffly. "Maybe you can focus on—"

"Nope." She shook her head. "Don't finish that."

Dr. Eritten folded his arms.

"I'll see you tomorrow."

———

SOLANIS'S STEPS were loud as she stalked past the sneering photos of the professors, all of whom had determined her daughter was an anti-social. Once in the rotunda, she glanced at the statue of Worthington, nodded, and stepped into fresh air. She found their bikes and made sure Gabby was safely on hers, and they headed toward the fountain.

By the time they arrived, Gabby had stopped crying. Gabby, now the mouse who had forgotten she'd ever been shot, laughed and purred as the fish nibbled her toes. As the fish took their pleasure in the dead skin they'd been craving, Solanis held one hand around Gabby and the other around the Voice. The tablet had cued up messages for her.

The first was from Katia, asking about the meeting with Eritten. Solanis looked up toward the sky, squinted at the fact that she couldn't even see the top of Shamut, and told the Voice to just answer for her.

The professor was mad about the oath.

Would Katia get a reprimand too?

Likely not.

Solanis knew what was going on here. Despite being far away, Shamut was pretty much Boston.

The second message was an automatic notice from ComCen. She was under status review.

That was fast.

Gabby was busy looking into the fountain as the fish worked themselves into a frenzy. "You should put your feet in too," she said, tugging on Solanis's blazer.

Solanis nodded, kicked off her shoes, and delicately placed her feet in the water.

She looked back at the tablet and read the full text of the notice. It explained to her that everything she did counted toward her promotion. She'd get points for finishing casework and performing Propagations and finally a Recycling. And she'd lose points for exhibiting less than admirable behavior, like hanging out with antisocials. Or having a daughter who acted like a nine-year old. At the end of the review period, she would be evaluated against her peers, and the one with the most points would win.

Solanis flipped back to another screen where the ranking stood. Winston and she were currently tied for first place.

What would happen if there was a tie? Would they flip a coin?

She could always tell everyone his dad fought for the Free Republic. That shit was bound to trigger someone inside and make him lose points. Most of Shamut's officials were from above the York Line. She'd seen the demographics.

Solanis tapped her nose and shook her head. She wasn't that kind of girl.

But her status as deputy ambassador was under review. Honestly, if she had it her way, she'd tell Doctor Professor Potentate Eritten to just bite glass and call it a day. But she couldn't do that. Maybe Leonardo could. He was one of the good old boys with a gun. He could do whatever he wanted. She'd need to be careful though. She'd seen what happened to those who were antisocial inside of Shamut. They got Propagated. And if you were Propagated too many times...

Propagation meant disqualification.

She needed to become an ambassador. It was the one goal she had inside Shamut. Control the world around her so Gabby could grow up healthy and safe. She would not allow the earth to shake and hurt her daughter as it had to her all those years ago. Haze would not invade her life again.

The third message said her team needed to discuss the Propagation with Ambassador Wick. This was normal. She told the Voice to get her team started on the report.

Katia pinged her again. *You're under review?*

Solanis stroked her daughter's hair while holding the Voice in her hand and swiping her fingers over the keyboard. She had a knack for typing without looking.

Gabby looked at her mother and frowned. "That's shivery, Mom."

The Voice chirped happily and sent the message.

"It's easier," Solanis said. "That way I can stare at you all day."

Gabby made a gagging noise and turned back to the fish.

"Sweetheart," Solanis said quietly, "why didn't you say the oath?"

"Tati said that he wasn't a god. He was like you and me."

"He is a person like you and me. But he's earned our respect."

"But why?" Gabby moved her feet in little circles as the fish tried to keep up. "I don't pledge to you."

Solanis smiled. "Because he built this. Gave us a safe home."

Katia's invitation had now been raised to the top of her queue.

Her daughter looked up at her. "But you made me, right? You gave me a home."

Solanis looked back, amused. "I did."

"Then why don't I pledge to you?"

She laughed and poked her daughter on the nose. "Maybe you should."

The universe inside her purred at her daughter's laugh. She wished there were more of these moments. More kind, innocent, mother-daughter moments.

The Voice chirped again. Katia had responded. *Come to Dirt. We can get that fixed. You can't have that. You need to win.*

Solanis frowned. How was Katia planning on fixing this? She left Katia on read. "Promise me you'll say the oath, Gabby. Please. For me?"

Her daughter nodded. "Does Luna have to say it?"

"Luna?"

"Tati's nickname?"

"Oh yeah." Solanis frowned. "Why does she call her that?"

"Why don't I have a nickname?"

"You don't need one."

"Do you have one."

"A few."

The rickety chair was back.

Gabby placed her head in Solanis's lap, nuzzling into her thighs as she got comfortable. Solanis stroked her hair as the Voice nagged her about Katia's remarks. The invitation had popped up again. Katia always marked her notes as urgent.

"You should never miss a message from me," Katia would say, smoothing her tight, silver bun.

Gabby said something else, but Solanis didn't catch it.

She was distracted.

Solanis thought she had seen movement from the other side of the fountain, only to be met with empty space. Daily, she used to see Childre there. The man would have waved at them, grinned, and splashed over. He would have scared away the fish by walking too fast, acted upset, and kept his feet in the water until they came back. Gabby would have laughed and said that maybe his feet were shivery.

Solanis shook her head.

Too much slang.

But this wasn't going to happen today.

Childre wasn't going to be near the fountain for another week. His usual spot was empty because he was resting so he could restart his life again. So he could try again at freedom.

Gabby had fallen asleep. Solanis stroked her hair, worrying what her father would have said about her little act of rebellion. No doubt the man would have been proud.

Solanis squinted. Or maybe he would have been worried the young girl was jeopardizing their safety. He had said he was the government. She couldn't quite remember how he would have thought anymore. The angry black hole tugged at her again.

Childre. Katia's daughter. The notes.

The forest was becoming dense.

Solanis pinched the bridge of her nose and tried to grip the ground with no success. She hadn't been able to ground herself for the past decade.

The Voice politely chirped again, waiting for an answer.

Solanis responded. *If we can fix this, I'll come.*

The Voice chimed happily and accepted the invitation.

————

SOLANIS SKIPPED dinner that night and spent the evening reading to Gabby. She couldn't help but marvel at her daughter—the way she was growing dreadfully fast and inheriting a rebellious personality from someone. In a year, she'd start her apprenticeship, hopefully in ComCen. Or maybe not if Winston was in charge. They could clean toilets together.

What would Walter say if he knew his daughter was cleaning toilets?

What would Walter say if he knew he had a daughter?

Baby steps.

Under the watchful eye of Worthington's portrait, she read to Gabby, telling her approved stories the Department of Happiness created.

Soon, Gabby's eyes were drooping as she clung to her mother. Solanis tucked her into bed, kissing her on the forehead. She turned on the night-light and closed the door behind her.

The darkness in the hallway obscured her bedroom door. It looked like the mouth of the cave in Virginia. The ones that had been a thousand years away. If only she could have run faster.

Solanis swallowed, the taste of iron in her mouth.

She didn't want to go inside, where she would fool around with the tiles that had the lines that squiggled around aimlessly. No matter how she pushed them together, they never said anything. Just the bouncing, wandering, inky snakes.

No sense in being so confused this late in the day. Instead, she walked to the hallway, past the kitchen and living room, and took the elevator down to the lobby. She exited the quadplex and looked up at the sky.

The star—the one Walter had told her to look out for—should have been right up there, hovering just south of Orion's Belt.

But she hadn't seen any sign of Sirius. Just the same three stars staring back at her with their steady light.

Solanis sat on the park bench and took a deep breath. She knew what was going to happen next. It happened every single night she was here. She relaxed, letting her spine elongate as much as it could on the hard bench outside their homes. She begged the universe to let her skip this moment, so she could pass it off as insignificant. She didn't know who might be listening. But maybe someone, somewhere out there, would hear her before she opened her eyes again. Or maybe not. Because she was inside a Dome.

Solanis opened her eyes.

Greg stared at her, the shards protruding from his arms and the bone striated with blood. His red hair was even darker—matted burgundy and brown.

She stared back.

Greg's black eyes never blinked.

She pinched the bridge of her nose.

They had always said that nothing could get in or out of Shamut.

Evidently, that included the star she'd been promised.

And that was almost true.

Nothing could get in or out.

Nothing except him.

10

THE ONE EYED MAN

Manuel

The first thing Manuel realized when he became a member of Congress was how little control he had over his life. The day after he'd been sworn in, he'd refused the offer to go to the temporary offices the federal government had set up north of Denver where Jackson Lake State Park had been. Instead, he headed downtown to his district office, where he'd play his role in the pageant Cassie had set up for him.

It was the usual nonsense. People would walk in, say they'd voted for him, take a few photos, settle on the couches in his office, and tell him that they'd love to partner with him on one issue or another. A round man with a bow tie and his business partner told him they were hoping for new funding for development in downtown Denver, while a thin woman with two children in tow explained that the expansion of barracks housing was getting out of control.

"Think of my children," she said, gesturing to two drooling fat babies nestled in a stroller between them.

Cassie stole a glance at Manuel at this moment. The woman had two children, so she could afford the taxes that came with that. Wealthy people liked to complain.

Cassie politely thanked the woman for coming, ushered her outside the office, and told the front desk assistant to give her a few small bottles of kombucha on her way out.

Manuel stood and stretched. The light from outside was at its evening auburn glow phase that happened as it trekked across the sky, turning the rebuilt Denver city streets into gold plates. He had the urge to go outside and soak the last seconds of sunlight into his bones.

"Surely that's all for today?" he asked Cassie, turning his back. He needed to focus.

"We have one more," Cassie said, and in a move uncharacteristic of her, she left the office without telling him the details of his next appointment.

The man who strolled in had a burn on the side of the face and was missing an eye. His dark hair fell over the burn, fluttering as he stepped up to Manuel and reached out a massive manicured hand.

"Congressman," the man said.

He wore black slacks that came down just above his black boots. His tan shirt, reminiscent of the ones worn by the kids who were drafted into the war, was neatly tucked into his pants. The collar on the top of the shirt wasn't creased; it lay perfectly flat. The man's hair and arms were well tanned, but Manuel could have sworn he saw a tattoo nestled on the left bicep.

Manuel automatically shook his hand and gave a pleasant greeting. He tried to add bass to his voice, to project the authority that came with the congressional pin on his dark green blazer.

"This is a nice office," the man said, letting go of Manuel's hand and gesturing to the two chairs, the unused couches, and the wide windows. "You planning on staying long?"

"Tonight?" he asked. "You're my last meeting, but Cassie might have other plans."

The man laughed. He sounded like he smoked. "I meant in this office, Congressman."

Manuel glanced at the empty door, wondering where Cassie was. He wasn't afraid, but he didn't know who this man was or why he seemed to be threatening him without threatening him.

"I will serve as long as the people of District 1 let me," Manuel said, opening his hands wide and showcasing innocence. If he moved quickly, he could lunge his shoulder to the right and knock this man off his feet.

But the man just rolled the only eye he had left and asked if he could sit.

"I'm sorry, sir, but I didn't get your name," he said.

The man settled onto the couch, lounging as Manuel took a few steps between him and the door.

"Did you have an appointment? I'm sure Cassie could get you time later—"

"You shouldn't stay in here long. It's beneath you." The man's good eye was still looking around the room. "You know why I put you here, right? Because of what you said about the Free Republic."

Manuel's blood went cold. Where was Cassie? "Sir, I think you're misunderstanding—"

"No." He pointed his finger at him. "I'm not. Your mother's over there, right?"

He didn't answer.

"You said, when you announced you were running for this seat, that you thought it was time we got the innocent people out." The man sighed and pushed back the unruly hair falling over his good eye. "I agree with you. Which is why I put you here."

He tilted his head forward and to the right. "Sir, I'm grateful for every voter who—"

"Please." The man held up a hand. "Shut up."

"Wait a second." He clinched his fists. "It's time to go."

"No. I paid for you to be here because of what you said."

"And I'm telling you it's time to go." He took a step toward the door and called for Cassie.

"And I agree it's time to bring your mother home."

Manuel froze.

"Now I have your attention."

He kept his face blank. "You have sixty seconds."

Cassie walked in behind him.

"Cassie. He has sixty seconds before security escorts him out of here."

She nodded and left the room. He'd have to deal with how she let this happen later.

"Your mother isn't the only one trapped behind the York Line," the man said. "And it's not York's fault you can't speak to her. It's SatTech. They own the stars. The president, *our* president, wants to starve them, shut them out, told SatTech to turn out the lights. Which is why you only get less than ten with your mom. You can only redirect satellites so much before they crash into each other."

Manuel crossed his arms. "Thirty seconds."

"SatTech needs to go. I can get rid of them. They are shitty tech. They don't work. I can buy them out. But they're partially owned by the feds. Any takeover will have to be approved by the federal government. By you and your colleagues. My people will update the satellites. They'll work again. Better. Faster. I'll rename the company to StarLight. It's a better name anyway. I'll take it private. The consultant says it sounds inspiring. And you'll be able to talk to your mom. It's the first step to bringing her home."

"You just want me to vote for approval on a sale?"

"No. I want you to give the people of the Free Republic a chance to speak to their loved ones again." The man smiled. His teeth were perfectly straight, perfectly white. Were they real?

"No. This is just for you to make money."

"Can't two things be true at once, Congressman?" The man gestured around the room. "You did all of this to help District 1, but you also did it so you can repeal the laws that make it illegal for your mother to cross the border. How are we so different?"

The man was mocking him. But he was right. Motivations be damned. But he wouldn't take a bribe. He wasn't that kind of person. He was a man. He had integrity.

The man stood. "You can say no. And nothing will happen. I'll find a way to buy the stars." He looked out the window where the amber glow was gone, replaced by the dark blue of night. "But it's in both of our best interests to put this country back together again, and I think you're the one to do it." He pointed to his eye socket. "Even I can see this office is too small for you."

Manuel paused for a second and then shook his head. "I'll have to review the terms of the deal before I can vote on it. Make sure it's—"

"What's best for the people of District 1?" The man laughed. "I know, Congressman. My team has unlimited resources. Come back when you need something. Unlike this office, my door is open to you. But you'll pay a price. The scales will shift. This is your chance."

The man nodded to the two security officers who entered the room. He brushed past them.

Once back on the sofa, Manuel glared at Cassie. "We're just letting anyone in here now?"

"Tiberian isn't just anyone," she said quickly. "He can help. He knows the other side."

He frowned at the absurdity of the name. "I've never heard of him. And what were you thinking? I don't want *that* in here. I want this room clean."

"He's heard of you," she said. "And you want to get those people home. The two aren't compatible."

"Yes."

She held up her hand. "No, Manuel. They are not." She sat next to him. "This is my world. I know this better than anything else. You need to keep trusting me."

"I don't want this to go wrong. My father would—"

"He's not here right now, Manuel." She gave his leg a small squeeze. "And I know that's terrible, but the one you can save is your mother. She's still out there on the other side of the border. She's our focus."

Cassie was right. It was just him. Only he could decide what was best for them.

"You told me your dad's mandate for you once. What was it?"

His eye twitched.

"To change the world."

"And to change the world, you need to speak the language. Money is the language of Washington and is now the language of Denver. Money will get you resources. It'll open doors. Cash opened this door." She gestured to the office around him.

"Was Washington always like this? Creepy men in your office?"

She sighed. "Not just in the office. But it's not always dark, Manuel. And Washington was more than the Hill and the political heartbeat of the nation. More than constitutions and monuments. We had the last Pandas on this side of the world. It's not always a political drama."

He nodded. "Just don't bring him back here. At least not right now."

She nodded. "Won't matter. When you need him, he'll extract a price. You should have used him when you could. Now, you'll pay. Men like Tiberian don't beg."

11

INVESTIGATING

Leonardo

In the barracks, it wasn't unusual to wonder which apartment to go to after school. Food could be found anywhere if you looked hard enough. Each apartment in the massive, curved complex that made up the rows of barely inhabitable housing was unique.

Some had foil covering the windows so the government couldn't see what they were doing; others had a large, illegal dog lurking in the corner, waiting for scraps. Leonardo liked animals. He'd always save a portion of his meal for the scraggly puppies that wandered around the winding narrow halls of the compounds. But the one thing all residents of the barracks had in common was their inherent suspicion for those who told what Leonardo's first mother, Mother Alice, called hard lies.

"Everyone lies," Mother Alice had insisted while reminding the young teen that he should wash his hands before dinner. There were sometimes toxic chemicals in the concrete they mixed outside when they expanded John Barracks's fulfilled promise of universal housing for all. "You need to know why they are lying to determine whether it's a soft lie or not."

At the time, Leonardo had nodded and shoved his hands under the sink. The soap foamed as he applied it to his gritty hands. He'd been messing around in the junkyard on the outskirts of his housing row. "What's a soft lie?"

"It's what you told me earlier," she said, nodding toward the table. "Don't worry, my little lion. Everyone lies soft. And I'll still enjoy my surprise party. Father Eric is just really bad at keeping surprises."

He turned off the water. "And the hard lies?"

She handed him a dishrag. "Those are the ones that have reason behind them and not good reason." She watched him wipe his hands on the rag and then took it back. "Like the lies politicians tell. They only do it to get power. More power."

He nodded.

"Both lies, you need to know the reason." She left the kitchen and sat at the table. She rubbed her fingers against a groove in the imitation wood. "It's not red and blue. Strictly speaking." She shook her head and gestured for him to come to her. She did this sometimes, getting glassy eyed. It meant she was going to speak about her sister. "My sister—god rest her soul—was swayed by one of them. Politicians, I mean. Chief of staff to a political giant. See where it got her? Dead. And that's because President Rosenbaum told a hard lie."

Leonardo nodded quickly. His mother did this sometimes—lived in the past. "A hard lie is designed to deceive with bad purpose?"

"Purpose or intent." Mother Alice closed her eyes and snatched the tear that had threatened to fall from her cheek. "Rosenbaum promised peace talks and instead shot York dead like a dog. My sister too." She shook her head. "Liars can be miracle workers, Leo. Promising change that they will actually try and get done. York was one of those liars. I believed her when she said she wanted to make the world better for people under her protection. But liars can carry snake oil. They don't have solutions, and they have no intent to have a solution. Spend your time with the soft ones, Leonardo. Not the hard ones. Or you'll wind up dead in the People's House, mumbling up at the ceiling as the angels carry your soul to heaven." She shook her head. "Never thought the United States would kill a sitting governor.

"They called her a traitor you know? We were fucked. Everything about us." She sniffed. "But we'll find the truth. We'll dig for it. And when we find it, you'll need to keep living. Redeem us Leonardo. And stay in line. Don't fuck it up. Be useful to someone."

Leonardo had nodded.

Mother Alice's words were why he became an investigator. And then a detective. And they were his weakness, his inability to let someone else— including that boy— hurt someone else. The incident, the one he tried to forget, was why he needed Worthington's redemption. Or maybe forgiveness.

Katia could not fuck things up for him. Not for Solanis. Not for what he, and he alone was entrusted to protect. If he broke that trust, he'd be no better than the dogs wandering the barracks, searching for food. Cute, but without purpose.

———

As EXPECTED, Katia didn't take too well to Leonardo asking her where she had been when she had vanished for a week or more at a time.

"It's antisocial behavior, Katia," Leonardo said.

"Did the coach turn me in finally?" Katia asked with a thick sass in her voice. "It's not antisocial. Nowhere in the rules does it say I have to attend workouts. Especially not sprint day." She shuddered. "As long as I hit my goals, I can do what I want. As far as the Man from Denver is concerned, I'm a good little girl."

Leonardo gave her a once-over. She wasn't unattractive, but her brashness was. He let his eyes linger at her hips—a move he knew would prompt an aggressive reaction from her. "I came alone, Katia."

She folded her arms and gave him the reaction he was hoping for. She was busting his balls. "You're for real. This is an official visit?"

He pulled out the Voice and glared at her. "Lightly official. Coach was concerned. I can bring someone else next time and make it official."

"Fire away then, officer. What do you want? I have work to do. There's a Dome to run, remember?"

"It's agent. You're not in trouble yet, you know," he said dryly. "Where do you go when you're gone for weeks at a time?"

"Yet?"

149

He glared at her. She tapped her foot, maintaining consistent eye contact. But he refused to speak. The longer he lingered on the pauses, the more likely he was to get her to crack.

He'd been around her long enough to know when she was lying. She tended to lean on her left foot, and she'd avoid touching her hair. She always played with her hair, so when she made an effort not to, it was because she was focusing, concentrating. He had seen her work and tug her hair when she was frustrated. Which meant that when she focused, she'd tug, and when she was nervous, her hand fell straight. People wanted to be in control when they were nervous.

"I get headaches," she finally said. "Migraines."

He nodded. It was a lie. "And where do you go during your migraines?"

Her hand twitched.

He shook his head. "We sent an agent here last month, and it was only Diego."

She laughed. "You've been stalking me?"

"Doing my job."

She fell silent.

"So"—Leonardo raised an eyebrow—"eighteen months of migraines?"

"I sometimes go to the caves. At the edge of Shamut. We built secret hot springs in there."

He nodded. "I didn't know that."

"Solanis hates the caves, and besides, there's a lot you don't know, my little lion."

What?

Suddenly, his insides were boiling.

"What did you say?" He needed water.

"I said there's a lot you do not know, Leonardo." Katia leaned forward from her position on the other side of the kitchen.

He shook his head. The room didn't feel safe anymore. He could have sworn she'd said...

He shook his head. Impossible.

He placed the Voice on the table. "What are you delivering to Solanis Tailor here?"

She leaned over the tablet. On the screen, she approached Solanis Tailor's quadplex and slipped an envelope into her mailbox. The same type of envelope she'd delivered for the past year and a half.

"Oh, that?" She grinned. "Girls pass notes, Leonardo."

He shook his head. "Paper is too rare to waste on notes. I've never seen her give one back to you." He scrolled to the next screen. "We've been watching you, Katia. What's going on?"

"Girl talk," she said, her eyes wide and innocent. She crossed her arms.

"Then you don't mind if I ask Solanis about them?" He did his best to sound super casual.

This would be the moment.

Katia's hand tried to jerk upward. But it couldn't because it was trapped against her armpit and her body. Instead, the entire right side of her body flinched. It was a slight motion—a twist in the shoulder, an unconscious jerking.

But it was there.

He was close.

"Come on, Katia," he said. "What is it? If it's porn, I won't care. I'll drop it. You bringing smut with you from the caves?"

"You're going to drop it anyway." She glared at him.

"Am I?"

"Yes," she said, "my little lion."

So, he'd heard it the first time.

"Let me make something clear to you, Leonardo." She took a step forward, the storm in her silver eyes brewing. "I'd hate to tell Solanis about James Seek."

The cuts in his stomach were open again.

But he couldn't show her that she was getting to him.

"Who?" he asked.

"Stupidity looks bad on you." Katia uncrossed her arms and leaned on the counter. "Everyone pays the tax eventually." She took a step forward, so she was right next to his ear and spoke quietly. "Solanis will run from you if she finds out what you did to the boy. Worthington's forgiveness means nothing."

The chill that went up his spine forced his leg to twitch. "You're going to get her in trouble, Katia. You know how much becoming an ambassador means to her. You giving her contraband—"

"Who said it's contraband?"

"Stop with the hard lies, Katia," Leonardo said, turning his head so he was looking directly at her. "You know what I'm talking about." He was bluffing, but she didn't need to know that. "We've seen what you've been doing, and we don't know why yet. But you'll go down. Alone."

Her face broke into a smile. "No. Choose your adventure. You drag me down for sending Solanis harmless notes, she doesn't become ambassador, and I have no problem telling her exactly why. You'll never sleep with her. Try and bring me down, and even if you manage to leave her out of it, you'll collapse too. You'll be the man who didn't do his job, threatening the *sanctity* of Shamut. You know, for *not* turning me in when you first discovered whatever you think this is. I know you've been watching." She pulled his face forward and kissed him deeply on the mouth.

Leonardo, violated, pushed her away and wiped his mouth, spitting. "What the fuck?"

She grinned. "Got you."

He shook his head, still rubbing the lipstick from his mouth. Compromised was too soft a word. Blackmail sounded better.

How did Katia know about Seek, the boy from the before?

"The before doesn't matter," he thundered, jabbing a finger in her face.

She raised an eyebrow.

"We get a clean slate when we come in here." He took a step forward. "You don't want to make an enemy of us."

"SPINE? Those amateurs? You're not the only one in here with bodies clinging to your jacket. But they don't matter. She matters."

"Solanis?"

"Keep up, soldier. You need to do everything you can to make sure she becomes ambassador. And then I don't let it slip that you killed a boy."

"His mother could have been killed."

"She won't care."

"Things don't always go perfectly."

They were bellowing at each other now.

"Seek was a child," Katia said. "Here's how this works. Solanis cares about Gabby more than anyone in the world."

"As do I," he said.

"I know." Her voice was soft. "And if you play ball, you'll have a chance. Just slow your investigation on the fucking tiles. They're nothing after all. Work to make her ambassador—"

"I am already working with her to become an ambassador."

"Then keep doing what you're doing. Get her to not sabotage herself." Katia reached over and pulled some lint off his uniform. "Besides, I'm sure she won't mind seeing you at Dirt tomorrow night."

He fought the dopey grin that threatened to make an appearance. He tried to counter it with a frown, but his face wasn't working.

"She cares about you, Leonardo. Just be on her side. Be there for her and Gabby, like you've been doing, and I'm sure she'll fall into your arms. That's how it works, right?"

He didn't nod.

Katia closed her eyes and then opened them again quickly. "I'll whisper in her ear for you."

"I don't want to hear about..." He paused. He couldn't bring himself to say Seek's name. All he could see was the boy's mother sobbing as she pulled her son into the light to find hope that didn't exist. "Don't bring him up again." His voice softened. "Please."

"Then stay in line. We don't have to be friends, Leonardo. She's my investment. Solanis Tailor."

Leonardo nodded. "Promise me there's nothing on those notes that will compromise her."

She shook her head. "Girl talk, Leonardo. It's nice that you care so much. I'm not even sure she knows how to read them yet. She sucks at puzzles."

He suddenly felt defensive. "I mean, she's older."

"Careful, Leonardo." She wagged a finger. "Ladies of a certain age don't like being called old."

He forced a laugh. Solanis looked younger than Katia, but he wasn't about to say that.

Katia pushed back her hair. "Get out of my house. We're done here. Diego will wonder why there's a strange man in my kitchen."

"Those notes better not be compromising."

She tapped her two fingers against her neck and rolled her eyes. "Bye, Leonardo."

———

ONCE OUTSIDE, Leonardo began his walk toward a bike station, where he could ride back to the Darkness. Where did Katia get the nerve to treat him like this? He should call Kruger and tell her to bring the hammer down on Katia. But that little breeze on the back of his neck— the melody that told him he could have Solanis if Katia wasn't far away—stayed with him.

Instead, he swiped the Voice a few times and ordered an officer to keep a close watch on Katia. Off the books, of course. Just see what she was up to. No reports would be filed. Watch the electric paper. If it was just innocent girl talk, then fine. He wasted his time.

And then maybe he could have her.

But experience had taught him that no one built threats on innocent foundations.

What animal would Katia be?

12

HEARING

Solanis

"Man spends all this time setting us free but can't save us from paperwork," Leonardo groaned while Solanis obsessed over her tablet.

He had swung by to show off a robotic dog SPINE had acquired to help them fight crime. The dog—which evoked a startling sense of déjà vu in Solanis—had a flat back, six legs, and a mouth that spun in circles where who knows what lay beneath. She wasn't quite sure what crime he would fight with a robotic dog that looked like it was designed to rip people apart. Were the old ladies in the market stealing blankets again?

"Watch this," he said.

She looked up from her desk in the open floor plan of ComCen. The dog marched around the bright, wide open space of the command center, its legs silent as it navigated corners and hopped on tables. A few of the other ComCen officers stopped their work to admire the create as it wandered and clicked around the room.

"It's how it sees," Leonardo said. "It's gathering data about the world around it. It could be pitch black, and it will still find you."

"I don't think that thing should be walking around in here."

Winston's voice came from behind Solanis. He had a knack for appearing suddenly in rooms where he wasn't the center of attention. The kid seemed to thrive off dramatic effect. He stepped forward, picked up the dog, and handed it to Leonardo. "These are pretty buggy, aren't they?" he asked, folding his arms.

"They're still being tested," Leonardo said. "The kill function is off. Can't tell between friend and enemy. So, you kinda have to worry about them eating your friends."

Click.

"I hear it eats, snowmen," he said to Winston.

Solanis snorted.

Winston frowned. "Don't be an asshole."

Click.

Leonardo tucked the dog under his arm, its legs flailing in the air. "I'll see you at Propagation review," he said to Solanis and then headed for the exit.

Winston shook his head, readjusted his ponytail, and wiped his brow. "Fucking asshole."

She smiled at him. "He can't hear you. He didn't mean it."

"He's garbage. Makes sense, being from the barracks and all. They're trash, the barrack beetles."

She was used to ignoring blatant classism and just leaned over her console and tried to review the report she was supposed to be presenting in a few moments.

But he crept up behind her and leaned over her shoulder. "You're not ready yet?" He motioned toward the display.

"I'm ready." She tried to brush him aside.

But he stayed in place, staring at her screen.

Leonardo had said he did this to intimidate her. It was the stuff guys did.

She rolled her eyes. "No Recycling on the calendar yet?"

"I have a lead on one," he said. "That should be enough to kick me into first place before the end of the week. Which means…"

Solanis shut off her console and adopted a poker face. She spun around and took an aggressive step toward Winston. "Means what, Winston? What does it mean?"

He took a step back from her. "I win. I become ambassador. Maybe I'll keep you on when I'm in charge. We might need someone to clean the toilets. You know, a job that's not directly in front of the public. Creepy eyes and all."

"You know what would be a shame?" She leaned forward, invading his space, her eyes boring into his. "For anyone to find out what your father was doing during the war. Remind me again. He was Governor Mercedes's chief of staff? Does the Free Republic ring a bell?"

He scowled. "You and I both know—"

"Know what? That your family are a bunch of snowmen?" She was loud on purpose. She wanted everyone to hear. She wanted them to know the rumors were true. She could fight back. "That while some of us were doing our national service, you were polishing old York medals?"

He opened his mouth to respond, but Ambassador Wick entered the room, and everyone snapped to attention.

Winston leaned forward so he was directly in her ear. "When I win, you can find a new job."

She snorted. "Bite glass."

———

PROPAGATION REVIEW WAS A WELL-REHEARSED DANCE. Solanis and her fellow ComCen officers would stand in the center of the room, present their cases to the ambassador, and then brace themselves for the seeds Ambassador Wick would throw their way. The short, quick innocent questions that could lead to larger, full breakdowns. Winston had never broken down before, but as Leonardo said, there was always time.

Propagation review was just the start of a longer, formal process. The findings of the review would keep Shamut safe from antisocials. From there, the Higher Committee would review the data and propose new solutions that would become law. Solanis and her team never learned what the Higher Committee decided. Ambassador Wick never volunteered to tell them.

One of the techs put Childre's grinning, innocent face on the screen and called Solanis and Leonardo—who had returned—to the center of the room. They both took their usual stances facing Ambassador Wick, who raised his hand, a choir director demanding silence.

"You know what?" he said. "Winston will do this one. I think it will be good practice for the future."

Solanis's heart sank. "Sir?"

"You're both vying for ambassador. Might as well get some practice in. I noticed you're both tied on the leaderboard. I've been getting lots of notes about both of you." Wick beamed at the two of them. "Well done. You can lead the next one, Ms. Tailor."

She gave a polite nod and exchanged glances with Leonardo. This wasn't going to go well. Fucking Free Republic Winston would do anything to cut her promotion. The room was tilting, the earth accelerating its rotation. What was it her mother had said? If the earth spun too fast, they'd get crushed. Or they'd fall off. She couldn't remember.

"Deputy Ambassador?" Winston's voice was a needle. "I asked you if you were ready to summarize the case."

So, Winston was going to be like this.

The information grazed the tip of her mind, just out of reach.

"Yes," Solanis said quickly. She clenched her fists and took a deep breath.

This nervousness. Where did it come from? It had to be Winston. He was burrowing under her skin with that stupid serious look on his face as he peered down at her from his seat.

She clenched her jaw.

Winston wasn't just threatening her; he was threatening Gabby.

Focus.

She summarized the case and let Leonardo walk through SPINE's role in everything. He emphasized their grand partnership, talking up her and her "invaluable work to keep Shamut safe." He really was a good partner, and his praise seemed to be working.

Ambassador Wick nodded along, smiling like a dutiful wife toward Winston. Maybe he had already decided that Winston was the guy. This whole hearing was a sham. He had said he'd done some time in the Free Republic. What was it he'd said when he had met her in the refugee camp? He was with the relief agency or something.

Leonardo tapped her on the shoulder. "DA Tailor can answer that."

Solanis nodded. "Childre has been in Shamut for a few years."

Winston fired more seeds. "What was his job?"

"Ration support, infrastructure."

"Did he show any signs of being antisocial before we encountered him in the market?"

She paused. The answer was there, right out of reach, hovering near the dark corner of the room. Her ego wouldn't let her look down at the Voice. That was a weakness. It would make it look like she didn't practice.

Wick raised an eyebrow.

Winston's serious face morphed into a grin. He had her, didn't he?

Was she the mouse?

"Did Citizen Childre show any signs of being antisocial before we encountered him in the market?" Winston sounded impatient. His teeth were fangs.

Solanis looked at Leonardo for help. Why was she shaking?

"Mr. Deputy Ambassador," Leonardo said, "Childre *did* show some signs of being antisocial. The deputy ambassador reported an incident near Worthington Fountain, where he seemed in distress." He pointed to the big screen in front of them, and the Voice pulled up the report.

"Thank you," Solanis said.

He gave her a professional smile and clasped both of his hands behind his back.

The ambassador scanned his tablet and then told the Voice to make a few formatting changes here and there. "It looks like the healers determined he was just Domesick. Health and Safety confirmed he was taking his meds, but they weren't working. Happens sometimes." He smiled smartly toward Solanis.

"It seems that the man is a problem," Winston said.

"He wasn't always like that, sir," Solanis said. She didn't want Childre Recycled. "He found my daughter, remember? I think he means well, but he's sick."

He shook his head.

But Wick nodded. "I remember." He smiled. "How is Gabby by the way? Is she doing okay?"

"She's well. Thank you for asking." Solanis smiled back. "She made the dean's list again. Really enjoying school."

"Ahh..." He grinned back at her. "That's excellent to hear. The future of Shamut really lies in the souls of young women like Gabby."

"Does it?" Winston asked.

Solanis glared at him, and the room shifted uncomfortably. "Of course it does."

"If you're going to be part of the future, shouldn't you say the oath every morning?"

"She's a child. I have it handled."

Ambassador Wick frowned and looked toward Winston. "What do you mean?"

Winston scrunched his brow, putting on his serious look-at-me-I-can-read face. "I spoke to her professor and he informed me that Solanis Tailor had not been encouraging her daughter to say the oath every morning."

"Don't lie," Solanis shot back. "And it's deputy ambassador."

But Ambassador Wick held up a finger, shushing her. "I'm not sure what that has to do with this."

"She's under status review," Winston said.

He thumbed his tablet a few times. "Hmm..." He scratched his chin. "That's true. But Gabby means well, I'm sure. Just have her say the oath, and you're fine. Children are wild cards, are they not? Mine really do test me."

The room joined him in laughing.

Solanis nodded. "Gabby is special. She means well. She really does."

Winston frowned. "I have another question."

"Seriously?" Leonardo spoke up from behind her.

He plowed forward. "What did Childre say to you at the market?"

She tried to keep her expression neutral, but this line of questioning was exhausting. She brought up the video and pushed it to the screen.

It showed Childre, a pot in his hand, as he spoke to her. "He was saying that the Dome is not real. He needed to get out. Something like that."

Winston raised an eyebrow and grinned. She was pretty sure the rats had looked like that before they chomped on cheese after finishing the mazes her dad made. Wide-eyed and focused. Drug addicts. "Something like that?"

"Yes. Something like that," she said. "The Voice has the exact language. It's in the report."

"I asked for it now."

The Voice repeated the phrases.

"Thank you, Deputy Ambassador," Winston said. "But I was referring to what he had whispered to you in the Propagation room."

"You asked about the market," she said.

The flicker of annoyance that crossed his face was worth the risk. This small break in character was her signal that she wasn't going down without a fight. "You know what I meant."

She widened her eyes. "Did I?"

He pushed a video toward the screen. It showed Childre whispering in her ear right before Propagation. "Here. What did he say here?"

Solanis paused for a moment.

She'd been in this situation before—people asking her questions they already knew answers to. This was a test. It was so obvious. But the hard part was deciding what kind of test this was. What point was Winston trying to make?

If she told the wrong story, Winston would have a rebuttal. He would win.

What did he know?

Winston had the video of the Propagation. Everyone had access to it.

He had spoken to Eritten.

She knew he would stop at nothing to become the ambassador, and this ambush was designed to raise his station in front of Wick. Which meant... What?

"He said that he sent me a note," she said.

It was a simple gamble. Assume Winston knows about the notes and reveal Childre had mentioned them. She could pass it off as some crazy man spouting nonsense. They already thought Childre was insane. You didn't Propagate mentally competent people. And if he didn't know about the information, all she had to do was say that she had omitted it from the report because it was so insane she didn't think it mattered.

"What was with the notes?" Wick asked.

"I don't know, sir," she said. "Childre was speaking nonsense."

"He was having a breakdown." Leonardo gestured toward the display. "He referred to Solanis as the solar system and suggested she was receiving unauthorized communications."

Winston raised an eyebrow, urging her to respond.

But she just stared straight ahead. Many had hurt themselves by answering questions that didn't exist.

Winston tried again. "Have you been receiving unauthorized communications from anyone?"

She lied. "Childre speaks nonsense."

"Are you sure?" he asked from behind her.

"Did I stutter?" Anger felt good.

He fell quiet.

The ambassador clapped his hands together, breaking the tension. The buttons on his vest clung on for dear life. "I think we have what we need. Great work, DA Tailor and DA Walkenshaw. And can we please give a round of thanks for DA Lancaster? Great work. Maybe next time, a little less forceful. One team, one Shamut. You get it." He clapped Winston on the shoulder and began gathering his papers.

"Of course, sir. Just making sure everything that's in the report is germane."

"Yes, yes, yes. Solanis is a great partner." The ambassador nodded toward her. "Deal with your status review. You're so close."

She nodded. "Yes, Ambassador. I spoke to Gabby, and she agreed she made a mistake."

Wick winked at her and nodded. He was always winking like a politician. "Can't have our best citizen suspended from duty in times like these. We have another Sprouting coming up. It will be Shamut's tenth anniversary, and I think..." The man smiled at the portrait of Worthington that graced the wall of the command center. "I think the Shepherd himself will be here to mark the occasion."

Solanis wanted out of the room.

He waved a hand. "I think that's the last one. You're all dismissed."

Winston scowled and headed toward the elevator. Without thinking, she followed. Leonardo yelled her name, but she didn't care.

Winston stepped into the elevator, and she and Leonardo slid in after him. She stood there for a second, counted to three, and jammed her finger on the stop button. Winston nearly fell over as the elevator jerked to a halt, emitting a harsh alarm.

"What the actual fuck, Winston?" She glared at him. "You're not fucking with my daughter."

"Solanis..." Leonardo said, holding up a hand.

"Back the fuck up, Leonardo."

He took a step back.

"Don't you ever bring her up to me or anyone again. Do you hear me? Put her name in your mouth again, and you'll forget how to speak."

Winston crossed his arms. "She's mad."

She rolled her head to the side, pinching the bridge of her nose. "You need to fight fair."

"No," he shot back, looking her up and down. "There's nothing unfair about this fight. We have the same job, and you let the mediocrity in." He laughed. "You've got to do better than that if you think you can lead. Ever consider going back home and playing Mommy? That's a noble profession."

"Why the fuck..."

But he wasn't done. He put his finger under his chin in a mock thoughtful posture. "Though that would require you to be good at being a mother too. I'm sure they teach classes in the Department of Happiness."

Solanis shook her head. "Careful."

He leaned forward. "Or what?"

"Look me in the eyes and listen closely."

"I would, but I can't see them now, can I?"

"Solanis, no!" Leonardo yelled. He pulled her back into the elevator door.

She had lunged at Winston, who smirked and pressed the button to restart the elevator. She clawed at Leonardo, but he pushed her backward against the wall.

Leonardo then spun around and punched Winston in the face just in time for the elevator doors to open.

Winston wiped his forehead, shook his head, and went to stand.

But Leonardo pulled him up and got in his face, shoving the leaf on his lapel into his cheek. "You see this? It means I have friends who carry guns. You keep your mouth shut, or you'll have new friends too. You'll be drinking your meals."

He pushed Winston backward and let him walk out the elevator.

Winston laughed. "Your agents are amateurs. Rejects. The good ones won't come inside. There's no crime to fight. Doesn't matter anyway," he said, throwing his hands up and rubbing the spot where the leaf had imprinted onto his face. "I have a Recycling coming soon. You two are fucked. Find a new girlfriend who isn't going to be stuck at deputy. Unless you like the shattered ones."

Solanis snarled, but Leonardo pushed her backward.

She didn't like the way that felt. "Don't fucking touch me."

He frowned and backed up. His eyes were hurt again. "Sorry. I was just—"

She left the elevator. How did she attract these types of men? Men who searched for projects with glue in hand.

"Wait..." He ran after her and leaned in close. "You weren't hiding anything, were you? About the notes? Like that's just bogus, right?"

The fire in her stomach flared. "Bite glass." She spun around and headed toward the doors.

She didn't need him to swoop in and be a hero. Worthington had put him here to protect them. But he was always hovering over her, suffocating her. This entire place felt like that. Did she look broken? Was it because she was a single mother? She'd chosen this, hadn't she?

No.

She didn't know. Had she known, Gabby's father...

Solanis tapped her nose and shook her head. *Stop. Focus on what's next.*

She needed to find Katia.

She needed the status review removed from her account.

That was what Gabby needed.

Not for her mother to pity herself.

13

DIRT

Solanis

There was no green in the club Katia dragged Solanis to. Just pulsing lights, shaking hips, and a floor made of dirt. Solanis followed her as she wove through the jumping, dancing, occupied crowd that had to be two thousand strong in the perfectly square room. The lack of green felt deliciously dangerous.

"Rumor has it they import it from outside," Katia had said, motioning to the dirt when they'd first entered the overstimulating box.

Solanis had nodded, the warm earth feeling familiar between her toes.

Leonardo was taking photos with a man who appeared to be a drink away from a bad decision, their arms slung over each other's shoulders. The woman next to him flashed a peace sign and grinned for the tablet. He then took a selfie with the man, passed him back to his friend, returned to a couch, and then fell into deep conversation with a woman whose hair was braided to one side with beads woven throughout. This new woman immediately began squeezing his upper leg.

He grinned at Katia and Solanis and beaconed them forward, a king holding court.

Solanis gave him a polite hug while Katia helped herself to a bottle from the table. The woman with braids gave Katia a sharp look.

"Solanis, Solanis, Solanis." He grasped her shoulders and took a hard look at her red dress, lingering at the slit that ended at her upper thigh.

Katia squeezed herself between the other woman and him.

"Congrats on a successful review. Feels good, right?" Leonardo said.

"I heard you punched Winston in the face." Katia leaned close to him, grinning.

Solanis hadn't seen her be this friendly to him before. "Katia!" she scowled.

"What?" She shrugged. "Winston's a prick. He deserves it." She turned to the woman who had been sitting next to Leonardo. "I'm Katia, and that's Solanis. Who are you?"

"Savannah," she said, turning her nose up.

"Nice to meet you, Nanna."

The woman tried again. "Savannah."

Katia nodded. "Nanna. I once had a dog named Nanna. A black lab. Very obedient."

Savannah frowned but didn't push the issue.

"I told the desk chick who hands out the assignments to make sure we get paired up for our next case," Leonardo said. "But she didn't seem too keen on that idea." He took a sip of his drink, bobbing his head to the music and still staring intently at Solanis. "You and me, Solanis. We're gonna get this. I'm close. I can feel it."

She didn't respond.

Savannah tried to reclaim her spot between him and Katia.

Katia didn't move.

"I had to watch one the other day," she said, looking at him. "It's tough."

"Watch what?" Katia asked.

"A Propagation."

"It's necessary." Leonardo grinned at Solanis. "You should have seen her with Chris. You know, you only have a Recycling left. And then we see where the seeds fall." His eyes glistened with eagerness. "I hear the Fields are incredible."

Solanis nodded slowly. "You been? And it's Childre."

He rolled his eyes. "You gonna let Gabby go for the overnight?"

She shrugged. "I don't know. Though maybe I should. I can't believe she gets to go before I do."

"Who is Gabby?" Savannah asked.

"Why don't you get us another drink?" Katia said loudly, pointing to the far table with more bottles of tequila, vodka, and mixers. She turned to Leonardo. "What is it they say about the Fields? Oh yeah. *Happiness grows here.*"

Savannah tried to insert herself back in the conversation. "Have you been?"

"Aren't you getting drinks?" Katia asked her.

She rolled her eyes but stood and began fussing with the drink table.

Katia frowned. "There's no way the trees in the Fields are real. What did they do? Build an entire forest indoors?"

"Aren't you infrastructure?" Leonardo asked.

"My point exactly. You can't grow what's in the ads inside. The giant redwoods, the massive oasis. Not enough light in this snow globe. Besides their uniforms are ugly. Boxy long robes." Katia shuddered making eye contact with Solanis and tilting her head to the empty seat next to Leonardo. "You're probably just given some juice and a few memory modifications and sent back to work."

He shook his head. "Kruger says they're real. She's been."

"Yeah. She looks like the type to need a strict memory wipe, among other things." She unleashed a diabolical grin.

Solanis gave her a look. "They don't really erase minds, right?"

But she was too busy handing Savannah a bottle opener. The woman had returned with two glass bottles. "Be a sweetheart and open this for us. Thanks, Shannon."

Savannah grumbled and began working at the top of the vodka.

Katia cleared her throat again and pointed to the seat next to Leonardo.

Solanis took her hint and sat next to him.

The group bobbed their heads to the music for a little bit and sipped alcohol as the room vibrated and bounced. The mint on Leonardo's breath mingled with the tequila. Did he always lean this close to people when he spoke to them? Or was he just getting drunk?

His arm found its way around her shoulder. It didn't feel bad. But she'd need to eventually remove it.

Katia continued feeding him more drinks like a host determined to hit a price minimum. "Solanis might lose her job," she said in such a matter-of-fact tone that even Solanis was surprised.

Solanis glanced at Katia who stood. "What are you—"

But he squeezed Solanis's shoulder. "What?"

"This is what I was telling you yesterday," Katia said. "Solanis is under review."

"Wait," Solanis said to her. "You spoke to him yesterday?"

She ignored Solanis. "You need to help her. I'm cashing in."

Leonardo narrowed his eyes. "It's just a review. Not a big deal."

She tossed her hair back. "I am making it a big deal."

Solanis looked from Katia to Leonardo. She knew they didn't like each other, but the tension had gotten so high it would fail a drug test.

"Go away, Savannah," he said quickly, his arm still dangling over Solanis's shoulder.

Dangling, not stroking.

"I have a clearance," Savannah said.

"This isn't about that." He stood and gestured to a passing host. "Let's talk."

Savannah rolled her eyes but sat back.

The host nodded and gestured for Solanis to follow him. Solanis, Katia, and Leonardo cut through the crowd toward a door near the side of the dance floor marked *Club Operations*. The host pressed a code in the door and nodded to him, and they entered the room.

The office was tiny with a small chair and console that displayed the club's interior. Worthington had a portrait here too. Solanis almost wished he'd been raving instead of staring stoically into the distance.

Leonardo sat at the console and gave her a look. Was he mad at her? Katia stood in the corner, her arms folded.

"You need my help?" he asked.

"No." Solanis said glaring at Katia.

"He's going to help us." Katia ignored Solanis and turned to Leonardo. "What can you do for us?"

He frowned. His eyes were on the console where Solanis's headshot smiled back at them, a blinking indicator next to her name. "Are you kidding?" he said. "I can't erase that."

"You're a SPINE deputy," she said, jabbing her finger toward the console. "Fix it. You owe me."

He glared at her and pointed to the console. "I can't do anything. It's not giving me an option, see?"

"Leo…" She shook her head. "Don't be dense. Find the investigator. The one who will be looking into it. I don't have to tell you this."

His hand flew over the console, and he pushed windows aside and investigated the glass. "I could lose my job for this… You're under investigation for Childre by the way. Something about notes. Not just Gabby." He glared at Katia and then turned back to Solanis. "You sure there's nothing there?"

Solanis kept her face neutral as her stomach boiled. Katia stared pointedly at her and then back at Leonardo.

"Move on," Katia said. "Or…" She nodded toward Solanis.

Whatever had happened between the two of them, Solanis wanted no part of. But he typed aggressively, digging into the menus.

He paused and snuck a look at Katia. "Your daughter caused this, you know. No public investigator's name."

Katia rolled her eyes. "Of course Luna didn't say the oath. She doesn't need to."

"She should," Solanis muttered.

She glared at her. "I'm trying to help you."

"You can't help me if I'm Propagated."

"You won't be Propagated. Leonardo can find the investigator and clear the infraction."

"Or," Solanis said quietly, tired of the back-and-forth, "you could tell your daughter to stop telling mine to skip the oath. It's your fault I'm here in the first place."

Katia shrugged. "A Band-Aid. I can't help it if Gabby has opened her eyes."

"It doesn't work like that," Solanis said. "I can't keep her safe. I don't have the same immunity you do. I don't work for Worthington."

Leonardo leaned back in his chair, his eyes flicking between the two of them.

But Katia ignored her. "You fix it yet?" she asked him.

He stood. "Tomorrow. But I can only do this once. Or I'll look stupid. Even the investigator will try and cover his ass if this happens again."

"She'll say it," Solanis said firmly, praying she was right.

Katia rolled her eyes, still glaring at Leonardo. "Throw your weight around or something. Those muscles need to be good for something."

He snorted. "We're even now, right?"

Solanis shook her head as Katia pushed harder.

"Is that a promise?" Katia said, blocking the door. "You'll fix it?"

He held firm. "Are we even?"

She nodded. "Solve this, and you're free."

He turned to Solanis and locked eyes with her. "You need to be careful with her. The only thing scarier than getting Recycled is this bitch right here." He jabbed a thumb toward Katia.

"You're such a lion," Katia purred, jabbing her shoulder into him.

For a moment, Solanis thought he was going to retaliate, but he just glared at her.

"You're lucky Katia's on your side." He left the room.

Katia pulled a vape from her pocket. After taking a deep drag, she offered it to Solanis, who stared at the pen and raised an eyebrow.

"You made a pen?" Solanis asked.

"You can thank me now."

She shook her head. "What do you have on him?"

"Enough."

"What do you know?"

"Doesn't matter." Katia pointed to the room beyond the door. "Commerce is everywhere. I can be the taxman."

Solanis frowned. "You're not suggesting he's crooked?"

"No more than the rest of us." She pocketed her vape. "Don't forget: Even SPINE agents needed to be set free." She stretched. "Besides, he's about to become an ambassador. I saw the paperwork yesterday. Kruger loves him. Both of you will sit on the super committee or whatever they call it."

"The Higher Committee," Solanis said.

Had Leonardo lived a different life in the past? They'd all come from somewhere, but she hadn't considered him being some sort of criminal. Assuming he'd been a criminal. Maybe he was a teacher. Just bored and wanting a change.

Did she owe Katia a favor now?

But Katia read her mind. "Don't worry. You don't owe me. Friends don't tax each other." She fished her vape out of her pocket again, took another hit, and smiled at Solanis. "My sweet Solanis, don't look so concerned. I've got you."

Solanis shook her head. "That's just so much at once. Everything is always changing."

She laughed. "We're inside a Dome. A snow globe. Nothing is changing here." She leaned forward and hugged Solanis. "You shake the same damn snow over and over. I'll tell my daughter to start saying the oath, but you tell Gabby to think for herself."

Solanis bristled at the feedback.

She noticed. "Don't get mad, Solanis. I'm not saying she's a drone. Far from it. Tatiana is one of the most brilliant young women inside this snow globe. She takes after her mother." She beamed with pride. "But your daughter is smart and needs independent thinking. When my daughter asked Gabby why we say the oath, she had no idea."

Solanis nodded. "Didn't you say the Pledge of Allegiance as a kid?"

"We all did. Everyone did because of the war. Gotta know who's loyal to us and...who's part of the Winston-York Coalition." She laughed.

Solanis did too.

"Does she know why we say it?" Katia asked. "Because it's not because Worthington built all of this. It's not because he's *the Man from Denver* who saved us or set us free. He's a billionaire like the rest of them. Just as bad."

She shook her head. "No. We say it because they want us to

remember what we are here for. I mean, most of us anyway. I didn't come here to recycle. But now that I'm here, now that we are here, we're a part of this mission. One day, Gabby's kids will open the doors and go out into a world that we saved. One free of Haze. I need that for Gabby."

Katia gazed at her. "You don't seriously believe they are going to thank us for saving the world? The people out there think you are crazy. They'll call it an invasion. We might all die in the war that breaks out. Our grandkids anyway."

She looked at the console in the middle of the room. "We don't need another war."

Katia wrapped her arms around her shoulders. "Wants and needs vary." She voice was hardly a whisper. "The reason we say the oath is because every generation we have inside this fucking Dome will remember just a little less than their parents. It's like electric paper. You've seen it before, right? The magnet you use to cause it to snap back together loses its power each time until..." Katia gave a grim smile. "Until it hardly reassembles at all."

The metaphor was lost on her. "Is that a bad thing?"

Katia took a step back. "Leonardo doesn't think so." She paused. "What do you think?"

"About digital paper?"

"Bite glass," she said, pushing Solanis playfully. "Think about it." Her eyes grew wide and hopeful. "Digital paper. The memories are important." She patted Solanis on the shoulder and then turned and exited the room.

Solanis stood quietly for a second and went to clear the console where her name was blinking with the *Under Review* status indicator. She didn't deserve that scarlet letter.

She paused, staring at the small arrow indicator at the bottom of the screen. Leonardo hadn't cleared everything yet. His mind must have been somewhere else. She was about to clear the screen for him when curiosity got the best of her. What exactly did SPINE see when they hovered over their consoles in the Darkness?

Solanis swiped the screen, and several windows popped up, filled with mundane data. There were screens and screens of reports from every corner of Shamut. Crime was down, but conversations about the outside were up. Somewhere downtown, a woman had been caught writing novels that mimicked a series from the outside. SPINE had warned her to make sure she stuck to her approved writing list, and it was recommended she transfer to a job at ComCen.

Typical Evergreens. Harness someone's power for the greater good.

Leonardo was talented. He had a very high customer service rating with most saying they found their engagements with him to be professional and well intentioned.

He did better than every one of his peers.

She stopped scrolling when she saw Winston's face alongside her own. Under his photo, it said *Ambassador Approval Pending*. She should stop reading. Just go back. But she couldn't help herself.

She dove further into the data and her stomach fell. Winston hadn't been bluffing. He had a Recycling scheduled in two days. Citizens Alberto Landingham and Ursula Carter-Landingham were scheduled for their end-of-life Recycling. They were going to be returned to the earth from which they were born as soon as they turned one hundred. This wasn't unusual; they'd all go back to the earth at one hundred. There wasn't enough room for everyone to live to a hundred and twenty.

During the ceremony, their family and friends would go to the Elder's Center, where their portraits would be hung, and they'd sit on thrones wrapped in vines and greenery in front of the room, and they'd be showered with tales from their lives. There would be tears, and they'd hear their favorite songs. Children and grandchildren would embrace them.

The ambassador of happiness, Montoya, would speak. He would show what type of tree would represent them in the Fields and the lives they would be enabling through their Recycling.

And then they'd be led to the back, where an ambassador from ComCen and a healer would be waiting. The healer was there to perform the ceremony, but it would be Solanis and Winston's job to ease the passing. To ease their journey toward whatever comes next. The meds needed to work.

Some would smile the entire time, relaxed and ready to go. Others would cry when they heard the people in the other room slowly chant their name, louder and louder. The applause always caused tears of fear, hope, and excitement.

She and Winston would keep them calm. They'd remind them of their heroism. Remind them that they had chosen death so others might live.

A perfect sacrifice.

The honor.

The ceremony was so sacred that she had never been herself. But if Winston was going to perform one in two days, did that mean he'd win the ambassador competition?

Solanis tapped the bridge of her nose.

She could find a Recycling.

Would she be held back at deputy ambassador permanently? Or at least until Winston decided he wanted a turn on the Higher Committee? By then, she'd be at least eighty. By then, she'd be preparing for her own Recycling in fifteen to twenty years.

Only she knew the truth.

One shot.

No second chances.

Unacceptable.

The console thanked her for her time and asked if she wanted to log out. She nodded, and the Voice happily closed all the windows, thanked Leonardo for his time, and then dimmed to an acceptable ambiance.

Star, what do you know?

She closed her eyes, pinching the bridge of her nose, and shook her head.

Winston was going to win the competition.

No, she didn't know that. She only thought that right now.

What did she know?

Walter would ask if her life as DA was good enough.

She had not seen Sirius since she had arrived inside of Shamut.

Unsettling, but...

What do we know?

She was under review, and Leonardo was going to help clear that for her. Katia had dirt on him.

Ambassador Wick was friendly toward her, and he'd be an ally in this fight, even if he was also helping Winston. She could go to the ambassador and ask for a Recycling assignment. Be proactive. He was the one who had suggested that the ambassador job would be for her. He was the reason she had become a citizen of Shamut.

If she didn't do that, she'd never become an ambassador.

The checklist told her as much.

Solanis stood, straightened her dress, and rejoined the room. She didn't get very far. Leonardo held two drinks in his hands, bobbing his head to the bass. Spotting her, he handed her a drink and got close—a tipsy cheerfulness on full display.

"You're being silly." She shook her head but accepted the drink.

"You need to relax a bit more," he said, his shoulders moving to the bass.

She took a sip out of the paper cup. The drink was smooth but chased with a bite in the back of her throat. She moved her hips to the music and let the lights and screens fill her vision. They were jumping with the crowd, waving with the rest of Shamut and getting lost.

"This is good!" she yelled in his ear.

He flashed her a thumbs-up. It was hard to speak when the DJ was so aggressive.

"You are going to be okay, you know?" he said. His lips grazed her ear, and she tingled. "I'll fix this."

She turned and faced him. She put her hand on his shoulder and neck, pulling him close. He smelled like tequila and sandalwood. "Thank you. This means a lot." She pulled back, leaving one arm on his shoulder. "You're all right," she said to his other ear.

"You deserve the best," he said. "Can't let this stuff get you. One more thing left, and we've got this. And then we can do what we want. We'll be set."

She closed her eyes and let the beat of the room guide her movements. He was in sync with her, his other hand flirting with her hip where the slit of her dress met her waist.

This was familiar.

Only she shivered.

It had been a long time since someone had been this close to her. But he was the predictable, reliable sentinel on the hilltop.

She opened her eyes. He had sealed the gap between them.

He was fine.

He looked down and tapped his forehead to hers, closing the gap completely. His chest was now directly on her. He leaned forward again. His lips tickled her ear, and she could smell the peppermint on his breath.

"You know, we've never tried this," Leonardo said.

"I know," she said. "You have Katia to thank for this."

"Really?"

"Yeah." She closed her eyes. She was okay. She was safe. "She has been begging me to come to Dirt."

"Oh." His laugh was a bit too loud. "Not that. This." He took a step back. The distance was so sudden. "Us. We haven't tried us."

She was suddenly aware how she was moving her body to the music. "What?"

Leonardo closed the gap between them again, making her warm. His mouth was near her ear, and his breath warmed her neck. "Us. The two of us. I mean, I've been trying for a while. But us." He gestured between the two of them.

The laughter didn't get caught in her throat.

He backed up. "I'm serious." His grin faltered. "Why don't you and I go out for real? A real date."

"Leonardo..." She raised an eyebrow. She was cold again. But she had no interest in feeling warm. What was he doing? Was it the tequila? The music? Men always had the audacity, but where was this coming from? "You're not serious?"

"I'm not joking. Let me take you out. To the Fields. I can get us a pass." He tried to close the gap again, but she backed up.

He wasn't the consistent sentinel—more like unfamiliar eyes in the darkness.

No. This wasn't going to happen. She wasn't going to let someone else in her life right now. Not when she had her hands full with Gabby and her attitude, when she was about to fail in her quest to become an ambassador. What was he thinking? Was he really into her? The age difference aside, they were friends. The music wasn't loud enough to shield her from his disappointment.

His smile vanished.

So cold.

She took a step forward to him. Her stomach twisted, and her ears rang. The warmth that came from him felt like an oven.

"Leonardo..." She grabbed both of his hands, their weight like lead in hers. "You're a great guy, but..." Her brain stumbled as she struggled. "You're one of my best friends for a reason. And I love you like a brother. Okay? Let's keep that?"

He took a few heartbeats to nod. "I know that."

He turned and faced the DJ. He bobbed his head to the beat, refusing to make eye contact with her. "I'm going to get another drink."

He didn't return.

14

RECYCLING

Solanis

"I don't need help," Gabby said, sitting at the dining room table with Solanis and her nightly homework.

Solanis figured it was in her best interest to monitor her daughter over the next few days so she wouldn't fuck up her promotion.

Gabby had several squares in front of her and a few different magnets. Evidently, she was supposed to be exploring something to do with the magnets and how they could charge various elements.

She was confused and kept prodding the Voice to help them.

"It's easy, Mom. All you need is to get them to stick."

"Stick?"

Gabby rolled her eyes—a gesture she hadn't learned from her—and pointed to the square lying on the table. "They make different shapes." She arranged the shapes and selected the magnet, and the squares instantly joined together to form a star. "This thing makes those things remember what they were supposed to do. So, they stick."

Solanis looked at the Voice again, which showed the proper terminology they should be using. "You're supposed to be saying it the right way."

Gabby sighed as if she had just been asked to build Shamut by herself. "The things are charged, and they pull the tiles together."

The things, the things, the things. The Voice didn't like that answer.

"Gabby," Solanis said. "Come on."

Gabby fell silent. The Voice made an encouraging comment. "The rock charges the paper, which then uses the memory that is programmed inside of it to snap to a shape." She spoke so quickly that Solanis almost missed it.

"What is the purpose of the magnet?"

She rolled her eyes again. Where was she getting this bad habit from? Tatiana? "You mean the rocks?"

"Gabby." Solanis pointed to the magnets. "Those are not rocks. They are magnets."

"All rocks are rocks, and rocks are magnets?"

"Gabby, no."

Solanis's father once spoke of the patience of a man named Job. What would Job do right now?

Gabby sucked her teeth. "The magnet charges the paper, which then uses the memory that is programmed inside of it to snap to a shape."

"Very good."

She moved the cards around and created various shapes with the magnet. Solanis picked up one of the tiles and flexed it in her hand. This one had a rough black snake bouncing off its edges. The shapes looked familiar; like the tiles tucked away in her bedroom.

Solanis stared at her daughter. "Gabby, does this work everywhere?"

"What do you mean?" Gabby was poking the magnets, making them chase one another across the table.

She forced a smile. "Explain it to me please. Does this magnet work with any type of paper? Pretend I don't know anything."

Her daughter picked up the small magnet and handed it to her. She then handed her the cards. "If they are the right kind of cards, they work. See?" She placed the magnet into the middle of the box, and the cards stood to attention and made a star. She then pulled a box with its dim pulsing lights from her backpack and placed the magnet in the center. The box stiffened, each side aligning perfectly.

She removed the magnet, and the box fell apart.

"Does this magnet work with any of these tiles?" Solanis asked.

The Voice pointed out to the two of them that electric paper came in different shapes and sizes.

Gabby laughed. "Mom, of course it does. Everyone knows that."

Her breathing was too fast. But she hadn't known. "Can Mommy borrow this?" she asked quickly, standing.

Her daughter nodded slowly, looking confused.

"I'll be back. I just need a second."

Solanis made her way down the hall, her feet padding lightly on the wooden floors. When she reached her room, she shut the door behind her and locked it.

She rarely locked her door; she wanted Gabby to have access to her at any time. But if this rock was a magnet, and the notes that had been in her dresser this entire time was a message...

Solanis pulled the box out of her drawer and dumped the contents onto her bed. The paper just sat there, the snakes bouncing off the edges of their flat cages. No wonder it looked familiar. Electric paper. She was about to place the magnet on her bed when she recoiled as if stung.

She paced the room. Was this a test in her step to become an ambassador? Was this a loyalty test?

No. There were no loyalty tests.

She approached her bed, staring at the scraps of paper lying innocently on the bedspread. They were puzzle pieces, waiting to be assembled. The squiggles bumped against the edges of the tiles.

Solanis shook her head, squeezing the bridge of her nose.

Was this a choice?

Childre had said this was important.

Solanis shook her head. So, there was something in the electric paper. There would be a message—a note she needed to read. She could read the note, and if she didn't like what it said, she could toss it in the recycler. This was easy. She was hyping herself up over nothing.

And yet, her hands refused to move.

Solanis took a deep breath, sat back on the bed, and placed the magnet in the center of the tiles.

The tiles stirred for a moment. Then several snapped together so quickly she nearly fell off the bed. Three of the tiles remained still.

The moment the paper connected, the black dots on each of the scraps wiggled faster. Now that they had the charge of the magnet, they began to twirl and dance together, creating letters. Then words…

Authenticate with your voice.

"What?"

The squiggles danced again, accepting her lame question as authentication, and wiggled around the tiles, now one unified slate of electric paper.

They took a century to form new words…

Solar. Come outside.

The lightning bolt shattered her.

No.

There was no way.

This wasn't real.

We don't talk about outside.

Any second, SPINE would come busting through the door, demanding she get on her knees and preparing her for Propagation. Did they Propagate you with your children if you had to go? She racked her brain to remember what she'd learned her first few days at ComCen.

Solar. Come outside.

She was going to be sick.

Solanis stumbled to the restroom and fell in front of the toilet. Her hands slipped off the edge of the bowl, almost causing her to hit her head. But she recovered. She didn't need to vomit anymore. Instead, she stood, faced the bathroom mirror, gave herself a moment to notice the water on her face, and wobbled back to the bed. She grabbed the paper, tossed it into the recycler, and watched it dissolve into nothing.

Her breaths were heavy, and her hands trembled.

The water on her forehead was sweat. At least she thought it was.

No.

Hoped.

They were breaking down her door.

No. Knocking.

Was it them?

Would they send Leonardo? He'd show compassion.

Or would he? She had hurt him. She hadn't meant to. Would they at least send him? She at least knew him.

Not after the other night.

You're on your own.

But it was just Gabby.

Just Gabby.

She'd ruined everything for Gabby.

Solanis fumbled with the lock and let Gabby in, pulling her bewildered daughter into a hug and telling her that she loved her. She had messed up. She'd need to confess, tell the Higher Committee what she'd done, and throw herself at their mercy.

Would Gabby grow up as she had—alone?

The Klaxons that tore through the air came from her tablet.

Solanis screamed.

Gabby mimicked her.

"Sorry, sorry," she said, stroking the girl's hair as she shook. "I didn't mean to scare you. Everything is okay. See? It's just work? Everything's okay."

The Voice told her there was an emergency.

She shook her head. This was the last thing she needed to deal with today. But then she saw the note.

She grabbed her tablet and typed to the operator. There was no way she could manage a case tonight. She needed to think, figure out her next move.

Solanis typed the words "Give it to Winston," hoping she wouldn't regret this later.

The operator simply responded. "DA Winston, status MIA."

What? Where was he? The one time she needed him to be Mr. Perfect Free Republic.

She shook her head. There had to be someone else. But the operator flashed the name of the subject in question: Childre Underwood.

You have to be fucking kidding me.

Solanis tapped her nose and squared her jaw. This would be fast. She'd talk him out of his breakdown and come back home and figure out what was next. She told Gabby to go with her roommate and that she'd be back soon.

Gabby nodded and moved toward the door. But then she stopped and turned. "Mom?"

"Gabby?"

"The field trip?"

She frowned. "What?"

"Can I go on the field trip?" And then, "Please?"

She knew she should have thought about her answer more, but she'd responded too quickly. "Fine, fine, fine."

She needed time alone to think.

Gabby perked up and ran out of the room.

She grabbed a hair tie from her credenza and shakily tied her hair up into a bun. She called a cart and rushed into the hallway. But Gabby stood there with a smile on her face, gazing up at her mother.

Gabby motioned for Solanis to get down on her level. Solanis complied, sinking down on both knees. She reached over and gave her a hug. Solanis placed her hand on her back, feeling the rhythmic breathing of her daughter on her body.

They'd been in perfect sync once.

Gabby squeezed tight and then pulled back. "I love you, Mom." She kissed her cheek. "Thank you."

Solanis wanted to cry.

But she wouldn't.

She couldn't.

"I love you too, baby." She tussled Gabby's hair. "Now, be good. Mommy has to go to work. I'll be back soon, okay?"

Gabby nodded.

———

SOLANIS BUMPED INTO DIEGO, Katia's husband, who had been loitering near the entrance of her quadplex. Tatiana was with him.

He waved. Tati lit up when she saw Solanis.

She said hello without breaking her pace. "I'm sorry. I have a case."

"You're good. Luna wanted to play with Gabby."

"That's fine," she said, glancing at her tablet.

The Voice gave him access to her quadplex.

"I'll be back late. And I gave Gabby permission to go on the field trip. Just help her gather her things. Please."

He thanked her and pressed the button on the elevator.

———

LEONARDO WASN'T at the scene when she arrived. Instead, a woman wearing a deputy ambassador's badge stood observing Childre from afar, her arms folded. She shook Solanis's hand when she exited her cart and told Solanis she could manage the scene now.

"Thank you," Solanis said, distracted.

Childre sat on the shoulders of the statue in Worthington Commons, doing his best to hack Worthington's head off. The man rambled and moaned as he worked, his uniform stained with blood from his hands. His thick silver hair was matted and tangled, stained with sweat, dirt, and blood. Behind her, the blades of one of SPINE's drones grew louder as the debris from the ground spun around them.

"Please halt this unsocial behavior and come back to safety," the drone demanded.

But Childre ignored it. He hacked away at the statue, yelling how the Dome wasn't real, how Worthington had taken them all, and how he would remember if he could just get out.

This again. Propagation had failed.

Solanis gestured for the SPINE agents at the scene to stay directly behind her as she slid the Voice into her blazer. Would Leonardo come? The sound of grating metal punished her ears along with Childre's desperate whimpers.

"Childre," she said, holding her hands out at her sides in a friendly gesture. "What's this?"

"The solar system… Herself," he said slowly. "Hello, Solanis." He looked around, sadness covering his face. "Where is Gabby? She's usually with you."

"Field trip," she said.

Blood dripped from Childre's hands, where he held the saw upside down.

The Voice rang again in her ear.

Solanis answered. "Katia, I don't have time now please. I'm calling you back."

Solanis hung up, ignoring Katia's protests.

"Katia?" Childre asked. "Katia."

"She's my best friend." Solanis took a step forward. "But I'm focused on you. Childre, what are you doing? Again?"

He stared into space, repeating Katia's name. It was as if he was trying to break through a fog, but he couldn't quite make it. He looked down at his hands and then at Solanis, his eyes watering. He gave her a knowing look. "You need to listen to me. Everything about this place is wrong. It's all wrong. The notes explain everything."

He began hacking away at the statue again.

She frowned. No. That wasn't true. How did he know the one who called her Solar? He'd lost it. Unlucky Childre. He'd completely lost it. Would Propagating him again help? Or would Shamut insist on a Recycling?

She placed one hand on the base of the statue, preparing to climb up and get Childre herself, when the Voice alerted her that SPINE had arrived.

"Please be mindful as you continue your work. Ambassador Walkenshaw is leading the case."

Ambassador?

Another cart rolled up to the scene, and Leonardo stepped out and walked toward the two of them. Childre began hacking away again, ignoring the heavy drone above him that blew his hair and debris under its blades.

"We are done with this," Leonardo said as he and a few more agents approached the scene. They fanned out around him as he pulled off his glasses and approached her. "We can't afford to drag this out any longer. You can't anyway." He looked up at Childre and then at her. "We have two options, Solanis."

"Leonardo, wait," she said.

He shook his head. "You're not in charge here, Solanis."

An arrogance pulsed from him.

"We have two options," he said. "One, we shoot him and see what happens if he hits the ground. If he dies here, we don't have to Recycle him. Second, we use the smoke."

"We aren't killing him," she said.

"Then we use the smoke." He pointed to Childre. "Smoke authorization cleared." He looked toward her. "You'd better come back to the cart with me, or you'll be caught in this shit too." He turned and strode back to the cart. "Let's go, Solanis." He was stern.

She jogged to catch up to Leonardo as he stepped into his cart. He didn't bother holding the door for her. She climbed in and eased the cart's door closed behind her. She could see Childre from the display.

"What's going to happen?" she asked Leonardo. "And... ambassador?"

"Kruger's permission went through. Now, just watch. The smoke will make this easier."

The drone hovering above Childre fired a canister into the air that exploded over the statue. A thick purple smoke fell from the sky.

The flowers and grass around the Commons turned brown. Childre swatted at the smoke, trying to get the thick, purple vapor away from him, as it rained down around the statue. But his movements became heavy and labored.

"The smoke," Leonardo said, watching the monitor. "It's from our friends at Acer Labs. It slows down time. He's not going to be able to move as fast as he once could. See the muscles struggle?"

Solanis gawked out the window, watching all of this happen. "Fine, we'll Propagate him again."

He laughed. "Solanis, no. You're going to become an ambassador today."

"What?"

"Congratulations."

"Leonardo!" she hissed at him.

"It's all set. Your status has been cleared. And today, I just got you a Recycling." He crossed his arms as the cart rolled forward.

As she watched the display, the masked SPINE agents dragged Childre to another cart. "Hold on," she said.

"No, you hold on." He rolled his eyes. "This is what we've wanted. And if you don't do this, you won't get it. *We* won't get it. And then I would have threatened Anders for nothing."

"Who the fuck is Anders?"

"A happy guy right now by the look of things." He scowled and pulled out the Voice, typing away. "Childre is going to die whether you like it or not. And if you don't do it, I'm sure Winston can."

Solanis shook her head. It was foggy. This didn't make sense. "We can't just kill him. He's sick. He needs help."

Leonardo wouldn't hear of it. "You can't save him, you know."

"We can if we have more time."

He leaned forward in the cart, close to her. His breath smelled like peppermint. "You have time. This is your one chance. You want to be sitting around in your eighties, wishing you could have become ambassador?" He leaned back in his seat, glaring at her. "Why the fuck did you come in here?"

"Not to do this," she shot back. "Not to do this."

This was worse than arrogance.

"Then let someone else decide Gabby's future. Winston would be a great ambassador. He does what's required. He did what was required."

"Recycling old people isn't the same."

"We aren't just killing them," Leonardo said, louder now. "We are saving the rest of them." He pounded his armrest. "Solanis. Look at them. All of them." He gestured to the people on bikes outside the window. "They're here for one reason. Because they chose to build something greater than the hopelessness that was outside. The pain that's out there. The Haze, the darkness that is our life. You know why I'm here? Do you know why? Because there's purpose. You and me, Solanis. You and I are here because we chose purpose over selfishness. We chose to be here to protect *them*. To keep *them* safe." He shook his head. "You can't back out now. We've invested too much. Worthington has invested in us. It's the least we can do. The least we promised. You and me."

This was anger.

Solanis stared at him. Was she afraid?

Not because of what he was saying or the fact he pounded his chair like an angry god. He was right. This was her chance.

"It should be someone else." She wanted to cover her face. But she couldn't move. Her hands were stuck in her lap. All she could see was Gabby—her entire world wrapped up in one person.

"It's us or them," he said. "And us includes Gabby."

"Don't." She squared her jaw as the cart came to a stop in front of the Darkness.

"Do this, Solanis, and you'll go to the Fields. You can rest after climbing for so long. You will know you've secured Gabby's future. A safe future. For her."

The Voice vibrated again.

Katia.

She couldn't answer it.

She'd just start crying.

She was the needle.

And what was best for the mouse was the needle.

The Voice vibrated again.

———

CHILDRE WAS SHACKLED to a chair at the table, emitting a low moan as he tried and failed to fight back against the activating agent in the smoke.

Solanis and Leonardo sat across from him. Leonardo looked at her, nodded, and tapped his tablet. A needle poked out of the chair and jabbed Childre, and in an instant, the man moved at normal speed again.

He gasped for air and vomited all over himself.

"That's normal," the healer said from his perch in the corner. The healer's coat made him look like a gargoyle glaring from the top of a cathedral.

"Childre," Leonardo said, in a mocking tone, "you've caused some troubles, haven't you?"

Childre looked at him, his eyes wild.

The mouse had given the same look.

Leonardo was coming on too strong. Solanis had to do this. She owed it to him.

She grabbed Leonardo's hand, signaling he should stop. He jerked his hand away and leaned back.

"Childre," she said gently, "look at me, okay?"

The man's eyes floated lazily toward her. He smiled. "The solar system."

She nodded. "Yes. The stars. All of them."

What would her mother say right now, in this moment? Were there words from deep in the ground that could tell her what to do? She knew what her father would have said.

"Do you know why you're here?" she asked Childre.

"Do you know why *you're* here?" he asked and then sneezed violently. He tried to reach up to catch the sneeze, but he only managed to jerk his arms. He was still a prisoner.

She needed to get him to calm down or this could go bad. Very bad. "I want to know *your* story, Childre. Can you tell me?"

He pulled again. But the chair wasn't going to budge.

"Childre." She reached over to him, cupping the man's face. "Please look at me. Can you tell me why you are here?"

He sniffed hard through his nose. Then jerked as if an electrical charge was surging through him, like a puppet whose strings were too loose. "None of this..." He gaped for air. "None of this is real."

She nodded.

"You can see it, can't you?"

She motioned for him to continue.

"The details..." He laughed bitterly, rolling his head to the left and to the right. "No birds."

"Tell me more, Childre."

He looked up at the ceiling and then jerked his head back down. "You won't believe me." He shook violently, his veins straining and his eyes bulging. "You won't believe me. None of you do."

Solanis kept quiet. "Try me."

"Do you even remember how you got here?" He leaned so close to her that she could smell the seaweed on his breath. "What the world was like before all of this? Because I can't. I can't remember any of it. Nothing. It's just all darkness." A tear slipped down his face.

She stole a glance at Leonardo, who stared back at Childre.

He looked bored.

Insulted.

Childre rolled his head from side to side again, making a clicking noise with his teeth. "I woke up one day, and I was just here. And I didn't want to be here. So, I tried to go home. I tried to find a map, a GPS, or a compass. Anything. It got dark, so I looked at the stars. And they were wrong. So wrong." He shook his head again slowly. Deliberately. "The stars were wrong, Solanis. They weren't where they were supposed to be. And it came to me. There are no stars here. Not real ones anyway." His eyes drifted far from the white room they were in. "So, I started walking. I knew I wasn't from here. I had a feeling. I just knew. So, I kept walking. And walking. Until it had been forever and then past forever. I was hungry. So hungry. And tired. Until I did it. I reached the end. And there it was." Now, he wept. "The edge of the world. The great curve. I pounded on it, clawed at it. *I am not an animal!*" he snarled at Leonardo. "And yet I live in a cage, a box, a snow globe. They dragged me away." He pointed a finger at Leonardo. "And I was right back to when I started. But I know there has to be a way out. People disappear all the time around here." He tilted his head and looked straight at her as his words jumbled together. "You might not notice, but I did. I do. I woke up again and tried to stay quiet. I tried to. I did my job like everyone else. But I knew. I knew they knew. They had to know. And then I saw them. I knew them the moment I saw them. And now I need to go. *Please.* Just let me out. I don't belong here. If they can be out there, so can I. No one has to know. I don't have to tell them."

He wasn't making sense.

Solanis nodded. "What if I can get you out?"

Childre smiled. "Can you? Really?"

"Yes," she lied. Her voice was strong but quiet. "I can."

"I want that," he said. Fresh tears rolled down his face, gathering on his chin. "Please."

"How about right now?" she asked.

What would Gabby say if she knew what her mother was doing right now? She'd understand. Wouldn't she?

Stop. Focus.

Her mother would understand. Right?

Her father would. The mouse didn't know what was good for it.

"Please. I won't hurt anyone," Childre said. "Please, Solanis. Please."

She nodded and gestured for Leonardo to release him from the chair.

Leonardo gave her a hard look.

The moment Childre was free, he stood and rubbed at his wrists. There was some red on the chair from the needle that had brought him back home. He wobbled. A SPINE agent rushed forward and steadied him. Childre jerked at the touch but walked forward, meeting her at the end of the table where she stood.

He frowned and gave her a meaningful look. "I don't want to leave you." He wrung his hands. "You are important. I am here for a reason." He looked at his hands. "I just want to see them again."

"Who?"

"Them." He pulled the Voice from his pocket. "Them." He swiped a few times on the cracked screen and showed her an image.

Childre, a woman, and three children smiled back at her. The children all had silver hair, and the woman's was jet black. They all laughed as the fall leaves whirled around them, frozen in time. The photo was taken in a park that was unmistakably Des Moines, Iowa. Solanis knew these were just micropixels on the screen, emitting light so powerfully that her brain was flipping them around and telling her it was a photo of Childre's family. But they all looked so real as if she could scoop them up in her arms like a giant and give them a squeeze.

"They're all I have," he said, looking down at the tablet and grinning a silly grin. "At least I think so. I have hundreds of these photos on here, but I don't know them. Yet I feel the tug. A pull toward them.

Like gravity. If I can find them, I can know who I am. If I could just reach out there. Get out…"

There was sorrow in his laugh.

The healer, who had been hovering in the corner, pressed his hand on the wall. The tiles slid backward one after another, revealing the light, dark, and emerald green swirl of the recycler, which hummed quietly from behind the panel. There was a slight buzzing, and an electrical sensation around them. A vibration.

The room was silent as Solanis took Childre's hand.

He was calm.

It was time.

"Come with me," she said, walking him toward the wall.

He smiled and took a step forward. Then paused for a moment and stepped back toward her.

The SPINE agents all tightened their hands around their guns at that motion, but he merely reached around her and gave her a hug. She held up a hand to stop Leonardo from reacting.

Warm bubbles poured into the black hole inside her. But she knew it was too big to fill.

She blinked hard. "All you have to do is walk through that portal." She pointed to the hole in the wall, where electricity crackled and swirled. "And then…" Her voice caught. "You'll be gone."

He nodded and took a few steps forward.

Right when he was about to enter the recycler, he turned back around. "One day, when you're ready, you can come too. But don't look at the stars. They are not real. To be set free, you'll need to follow something else. And then you can come find me." He grinned. "Reach for me. I'll reach back."

He stopped.

He stared into her eyes.

His eyes were like the ocean right at the edge of the beach, where blue met crystal clear.

"He was right," he said. "They are beautiful. Pools of brilliant darkness."

Solanis gasped.

The man then turned, his face wet with tears, and stepped into the recycler.

He hovered there for a moment as his body tried to understand why it was being ripped apart atom by atom. The human mind could not comprehend pain at a level so small.

In a few heartbeats, all that was left was the swirling greens, and Childre Underwood was gone.

15

BLACKOUT

Manuel

Manuel's mother had her hair tied into a bun and looked like she hadn't eaten in several days. Sunken eyes, chapped lips, raspy voice. Her hair was going gray.

"I think I have about five minutes this time, mijo." Sylvia gave him a thin smile through Ronnie.

He tried to smile back, but he hadn't quite gotten it right even after eight years of speaking to his mother a few times a month in five-to-eight-minute increments. But Cassie had told him that keeping his spirits high would keep Sylvia's spirits up.

"Tell me about your week," his mother said as if he'd just gotten home from school and had math homework.

She coughed—heavy and wet.

"I have to vote in an hour." He looked at his watch. "But I don't think my bill is going to pass. I can't get the patriot wing of the caucus on my side. They're still insisting travel can't happen between us and you. They don't see the potential for normalized relations." He could feel the bitterness in his voice. "They call you snowmen. Frosty. They're monsters."

"Monsters?"

"Beasts forged under pressure, burning everything."

"Then find a phoenix," his mother said. "Something beautiful that can rise from the ash."

"Aren't I a phoenix?"

She smiled. "You're a politician. Politicians are dreamers."

"Dreamer?"

"Politicians are all dreamers." She sounded dismissive, disappointed. But he knew she was neither of these. She was tired.

"Your son is a politician," he teased, hoping his ribbing would bring energy back into his mother.

"Giants," Sylvia gave a smile. "You're giants with your heads in the clouds."

Manuel laughed.

His mother coughed again. She protectively raised her hand to her face, but he saw the small flecks of black that came up with her saliva. Her nails, painted with what looked like black highlighter, were chipped. "Careful, giants don't realize the dust they kick up at their feet are sandstorms for the rest of us."

"I'm coming to get you, Mom," he said. "If we get this bill passed…"

She smiled. She was better at faking it than he was. "We don't have a lot of time. Do you have a new filter for me?"

She carried her tablet to the other side of the room as she spoke. He caught glimpses of what was once a beautiful home. Now, there was dust everywhere, stains on the walls. Wires looped around the doorways, and dirty rags hung from a line, threaded through what could have been a clean, generous living room.

She kept looking over her head as if something or someone was upstairs.

Manuel nodded and looked at the model of a new water filter he'd been working on. The cylinder with three parts sat on his desk, waiting to be tested. Only it was difficult to test a device to filter out an unknown chemical compound when you didn't have the chemical. He had gone to his old job at the lab and managed to help his mother find strips that could test for trace amounts of the mystery compound Tomas Corporation had spilled into the waters of the Free Republic eight years earlier. They'd promised they'd put a dam in place to remove the chemical, but the notoriously gray water with a slight orange tint had been appearing throughout the Free Republic.

Not even his congressional inquiry could get another country to give up information. Even if the president refused to recognize their independence.

And the filters weren't working. He helped his mother refashion her filter to look like his. Sylvia poured the water through the top and watched it filter through the bottle and into a new bucket. She placed the test strip into the water, waiting for pink.

It came out blue.

Both sighed.

"Don't worry, Mom. I'll send over three more methods that might work." He pointed to his own model of the water filter. "This one has a special light inside that might help. The chemicals are small, and it's hard to get this light down there. But I can make it work." He shook his head and tried to reassure her with a smile. "Promise me you're not using your hands to scoop water."

She nodded. "You know I don't understand any of this. And besides, plastic buckets are my life now." She held up one of the bottles of murky water and glanced above her again. "This is as good as it gets for now."

"You should filter that again. Is everything okay? You keep looking around."

She looked up again and then smiled at the camera. "Just a few drones. They sound like ours." She looked at the bottle and shook her head. "That's the third time. It's not going to come out clear."

"Ours? You mean the Republic's?"

She ignored him and put down the water bottle. "Governor Mercedes says it's clean to drink. And it's all we have. I'm using the Iodine tablets at least."

"Yes. Keep using those. Two per bottle. Keep getting them." He frowned. "And you're not from there."

Sylvia nodded. "I know a guy. And, mijo, I'm your mother. I won't forget you."

That was not what he had meant.

She looked overhead again. "These drones sound different." She looked back at the camera. "But don't worry. We are far from the York Line. There's no fighting this far out."

"I'm worried," he said.

She smiled. "And I'm worried you look skinny."

"Mom, I'm serious."

"And I'm serious."

He watched as his mom spoke to someone outside her window. She handed out bottles of cloudy water with a packet of tablets attached to each bottle.

"Mom, those are for you," he insisted.

"They have children with them. They need them more than me."

"You have a child too," he said. Every week, he was reminded why his father looked at her the way he had. This selfless sacrifice was going to get her killed.

"Show me my beauty. We don't have much time." She flinched.

"Do you need to go, Mom?" he asked.

"No. We have alarms if something's going to happen. Now, show me. I want to see."

He nodded and stood. He walked across the dark green carpet in his office to the window with the monstera his mother had nurtured for years until she'd got caught between a war. The leaves were bigger now—white and green. The plant had wanted for nothing.

Sylvia smiled. "I have this dream, mijo."

He nodded.

She laughed to herself. "I have this dream that you will appear on that hill. The one out there. I wake up in the morning, and I look out and can see you. And you've come."

"I'm going to come get you," he said. "I'm not leaving you there. I'm going to fix this. I'm going to get you home."

She grinned at the camera. "I'm coming too."

"It's my job."

His mother looked above her for a moment, startled. There was a loud bang, and the connection ended. A moment later, the lights went out, and Ronnie went dead.

Manuel tapped Ronnie once to wake up the tablet. But it didn't respond. He tapped again.

Nothing.

He shook his head. What was this?

He looked around the room. The overhead lights were out, but the emergency lights were on. That was normal.

Ronnie not working alarmed him.

Manuel tapped it again. Nothing.

His heart was in his ears. Boiling water churned in his stomach. His insides were raw. His breath was too thin. There wasn't enough air coming into his—

Wait.

Manuel yelled for the office assistant, trying to shake the light-headedness.

His assistant stumbled into the room. "Sir, everything is out."

He stood and pushed the kid aside. He made his way to the door and out into the dark hallway. The assistant had left a flashlight on his desk, still lit.

"Ronnie!" Manuel yelled.

But the little tablet ignored him.

He shone the light down the dark hallway outside his office, where people stumbled in the dark and spoke in hushed tones. He suddenly felt too large for his suit as if the tie was choking him, squeezing the life from him.

He made a left to the stairs and shoved his way past the people who were shambling up, mammals searching for the light in the darkness. Was this another great earthquake? No, the ground wasn't moving. What had happened to his mother? Was she gone too? Did something happen here in Denver? In FROST?

Manuel exited the side door into the street and was instantly pulled backward as a cart smashed into a nearby parked truck. Fire bloomed from the vehicle as he fell to the ground.

All around him, the world had stopped, and in some cases had simply kept going. Cars were crashing; an airplane was flying danger-ously low in the distance—too low for the airport.

Manuel grabbed Ronnie again. "Call Sylvia. Find her."

But Ronnie stayed dark.

And then he saw Sebán. His father. Standing in the middle of the street. His hand was up at his waist, palm facing down, as he lowered it toward the ground. Manuel reached his hand out to his father. He needed to connect.

The world snapped back into cruel focus. He was a leader. He wasn't supposed to panic.

He needed to get to his mother.

No. He needed to get to the safe house. He was a member of Congress. There were protocols for moments like this.

Manuel oriented himself among the throngs of panicked citizens and ran.

———

CASSIE WAS WAITING for Manuel at the safe house. "You're okay?" she asked.

"I need to get to my mom," he said. "Any news from the Republic?"

She shook her head, frowning. "Manuel, are you okay?"

"I was just with her. I think a bomb went off. I need to know. Do they know?" His breathing sped up again; he couldn't control it. His hands were wet.

"I haven't been in yet. But give me a few moments so I can see if they have a briefing book for us."

"Fuck that."

A few other members looked his way with disgust. He closed his eyes, trying to center himself. He could count. People counted sometimes to calm themselves down. He could try that.

But all he could see was his mother looking up, stunned, and then Ronnie going black. What could he do? He had the power of the US government on his side, and they were busy hosting committee meetings and hiding in basements.

He shivered as the pain in his stomach churned. He bit his tongue and shook his head. But the volcano inside rumbled with restlessness. He looked around and then darted into a nearby restroom. He slammed the door shut behind him and glared at the single toilet that sat silently in the darkness, the emergency lights flashing off the porcelain.

He splashed water on his face.

He needed to calm down. Needed to think. He had to get to the Free Republic and find his mother.

A knock came from outside.

He opened the door.

Cassie had returned. "Nothing yet."

"Your friend," he said. "The one missing an eye. I need him. Now."

She shook her head. "Manuel, are you sure? He takes a price."

"Then we pay it. I have one job, and I can't change the world if she's dead. Call him, find him, whatever it takes. We are going to get my mother out."

He nodded to himself. He was certain. He was done waiting.

16

FIELDS

Solanis

Solanis was falling.

No, this wasn't falling. If she was falling, then she wouldn't feel pressure on both sides of her body, pushing in on her. Suffocating her.

No.

She was being pulled and pushed at the same time until something grabbed her and yanked her into the present, shattering the darkness.

Solanis gasped, opened her eyes, and watched the world materialize around her.

Crippling, bright, intense suns.

She shut her eyes. Green, blue, and red spots appeared where the light had been.

But the tug was insistent.

Her name echoed in her ears from someplace far away and then...

"Solanis!" Katia's voice jerked her fully awake.

Adrenaline shot through her body, filling her veins and pores with pure energy. The sheer surge of focus caused an explosion of pain as air filled her lungs, and her chest expanded to accommodate the intrusion of air. For a moment, she was in the airlock again.

Water overflowed from the tank she was in.

"Wake up," Katia demanded, pulling her up from the tank and over the edge. More water sloshed onto the floor as she tugged Solanis forward.

Solanis flailed her arms and grasped at the edge of the tank, trying to gain traction with her feet. *What is Katia doing here?*

"We need to go now," she said in her typical stern voice. "You are out of time."

"Out of time?" Solanis asked.

"Yes. Out of time. He's going to come for you."

She blinked, her breathing finally slowing.

Katia frowned. "You got the notes, didn't you?"

How did Katia know?

Was this a test?

Solanis's mind ran a kilometer before coming back to her. She was already an ambassador. She'd paid the toll to get this far. She had proven herself through sacrifice.

There were no tests.

Katia didn't budge. "Talk to me."

"I got the note. You're the one who sent it." It was a statement, not a question.

"What did you decide?"

"You sent it." She was stuck on a loop.

"What. Did. You. Decide?" Katia grabbed her shoulders, shaking her. "We don't have time for this."

She was quiet as she looked at Katia. Her wild bright blue eyes. The silver hair spread around her crown. This wasn't just the competitive rebellious woman from before.

Something was wrong.

Katia was sending her notes about the outside.

Treason.

"Who are you?" Solanis said.

"What did you decide?" The urgency in Katia's voice caused Solanis to shiver. "If you don't decide, we will decide for you."

We?

So, the message wasn't just from Katia. It was from *them*.

But Solanis wasn't about to leave Shamut. "Get away from me."

"You can do it. You've seen the evidence. Just make a decision. Make the right decision."

"Katia, I can't. You know I can't."

Katia rolled her eyes, her hands still gripping Solanis's wrists.

Why would Katia risk everything to leave? Were she and Diego having problems? That couldn't be it. Leaving didn't have anything to do with Solanis. Unless Katia wanted her to come outside with her so she didn't have to be alone.

That was understandable.

Solanis softened her tone. "Katia, you know I can't go with you. You're my best friend. This is our home. We chose this. My daughter is here." She spoke to Katia as she would with a child. She used all her skills gained over the decades to will Katia to reconsider the very actions that would cause her to die if discovered. "Our daughters are here."

But Katia simply gave a bitter laugh, harsher than anything Solanis had ever heard from her. "You're not safe here, Solanis," she said, and with a massive tug, she pulled the soaking wet Solanis from the tank.

Solanis fell onto the floor and slipped, trying to stand. Katia held her steady with a firm grip. Completely naked and wet, she steadied herself.

"Katia," she said quietly. "You don't have to do this. No one has to know about this." She attempted to pull gently against Katia's hand, but she refused to even loosen her grip. "I won't tell anyone."

"You aren't going to tell anyone about this anyway, Solanis."

"I won't. Wait." She paused. "Anyway?"

Katia shook her head. "I don't want to do this."

"You don't."

In one quick motion, Katia reached under her light green uniform and pulled out a gun.

Solanis stared at the weapon. Her stomach flipped. "We are safe here," she said. "You don't have to kill me. I need to stay here. Gabby is in school." She was rambling. She mentioned Tatiana. She mentioned her job. "Think about Diego. What will he say if he loses you? Katia, please. You're hurting me."

Katia's grip had tightened on her wrist.

"Please. No one has to know."

She stared Solanis dead in the eyes. "You know what the problem is with all of you refugees? It's your eyes." She leaned forward. The dark pits reflected in her face. "No one can tell if you're being sincere or not. Imagine the cold darkness people see before they die. Isn't that what you do over there in ComCen?"

This Katia was not the woman she had known before she'd entered the Fields. She knew why Leonardo was mad but Katia? Was it because she refused to leave? And why were her eyes the wrong color?

Katia didn't wait for Solanis to respond. She let go of her wrist and fumbled with the robe that had been hanging on the rack behind her. She tossed it to her. "Put it on. And then we are walking out of here."

Solanis, hardened now, glared at her former friend. "You're not going to get far. You know what I am."

"Do you know who I am?" Katia said, holding the gun steady. Her hand didn't shake. "Now, start walking and don't forget what this is."

She scowled and walked toward the door.

Solanis looked around for her tablet, but it was missing.

"I have your tablet," Katia said nodding her head toward the door again. She reached in her pocket and handed Solanis a pair of earplugs. "Put these in."

Solanis did. But the room didn't dampen. She simply felt like she had cotton in her ear.

Katia pressed the keypad, and the door slid open.

The soft music from the hallway wafted around as they began their slow walk down the corridor. The scent of evergreen trees, wood, and lavender floated around them. A cello played soft, long notes through hidden speakers in the walls as the two of them walked, one behind the other.

It wasn't lost on Solanis how odd the two of them must have looked. Solanis with her tight curls sticking to her forehead and water dripping down her skin as it dampened her bathrobe. Katia in her light green boxy spa uniform.

The grass under Solanis's bare feet crunched as she walked. Would she see Gabby again?

"We don't have to do this," she said quietly, her hands drifting upward. Her back kept wanting to cramp up because the gun was so close to her.

"Put your hands down," Katia hissed, looking and sounding calm —as if holding your friend hostage at gunpoint was an everyday occurrence.

She forced her hands to her sides and followed the bend of the corridor.

A healer walked by with one of the other spa attendants. They both nodded toward Solanis with a firmness that projected the utmost respect. Solanis would have to get used to that reverence as part of her status. People usually looked at her out of curiosity.

She fought the urge to scream, forcing her mind to not think about what would happen if she threw herself at the nearest healer and begged them for help.

Would Katia actually kill her?

The SPINE agent at the door that led to the interior forest of the Fields smiled and stood a bit straighter as they approached.

If they made it into the atrium, with the fields and forests, who knew what Katia was capable of? Maybe Solanis could get away, hide among the giant trees that scraped the sky. There were a few exits inside.

The gun was like ice on her back.

Solanis shivered for real.

"Afternoon, Ambassador," the agent greeted her.

She nodded stiffly and then, trying to act normal, said, "It's a rad day we're having."

The agent frowned. "Rad."

She squeezed her eyes shut, regretting this idea. How could she be so stupid? Fear did this, didn't it? "Yes, a code rad day."

The bullet killed the SPINE agent instantly. A hole appeared in his head, and the man slumped to the ground, his eyes still open. The blood on the wall behind him left the only evidence he had previously been standing.

Katia had moved so fast that she hadn't felt the cold weapon leave her back.

It was time to run.

Solanis dashed into the Fields.

The Fields were just like they were on the commercials—a wide open indoor forest with trees evenly spaced out for what looked like several football fields. Every ten yards or so, there were new massive oaks that jutted into the sky.

Solanis knew trees didn't really grow like this. But it didn't matter. It was peaceful.

Throughout the Fields were ponds and small lazy rivers where people could float and frolic during recovery. There was a massive human-made waterfall whose rushing water fed the lakes and streams inside the Dome within Shamut.

Solanis's robe fluttered behind her. The people who would be enjoying their experience would likely see all her intimate areas. But there was no time for modesty. She needed to get away. She needed to get to Gabby.

She made it to the first set of trees in the atrium and tried to zig her way into hiding.

But Katia was close behind. "You need to stop!" she yelled.

"Go away!" she yelled over her shoulder as she tried to zigzag her way through the trees. If she could avoid tripping, she'd be able to outrun Katia.

"Just let me go!" Solanis yelled back as she made a left and face-planted directly into a tree.

Katia leaned over her and roughly pulled her to her feet. "You get to decide how many people die today."

The cold was back.

The Klaxons sounded. Someone must have discovered the agent's body.

The ambient light in the Fields went from the soft glow of the sun and to a pulsing red.

Somewhere a speaker chirped saying, "All residents are advised to evacuate the Fields as soon as possible. Do not panic. Please go directly to the nearest exit and follow the direction of all SPINE personnel."

Katia pulled Solanis forward and quickened her pace. "We need to hurry."

Solanis ignored her and pulled back, dragging and kicking her feet as much as possible.

But despite skipping her workouts, Katia wasn't weak. She forced Solanis to move.

As they scurried forward, Katia pulled out a thin piece of glass the size of a keycard and pushed on it. In an instant, the glass card doubled in size, and she spoke directly to it. "I have Tailor, and we are a little early for extraction." She pulled Solanis down, so they were hidden behind some manufactured greenery.

Solanis shoved Katia and tried to flee, but Katia pulled her back.

"And we have SPINE on our tail. We need reinforcements now. They called a code red. Move to Plan B." She tucked the glass keycard back into her pocket and pulled Solanis backward. "Hold still," she said, yanking Solanis's bathrobe down over her shoulder.

"Bite glass," Solanis hissed.

"You're going to regret it if you don't follow directions."

"How can you do this to Gabby? She needs her mother."

Katia ignored her, pulled out a flat disc about the size of an earplug, and then pushed it into Solanis's shoulder. Solanis screamed as the little device burrowed into her flesh.

"This will keep us safe," Katia said, looking toward the enormous waterfall a few meters ahead. "We are going in that direction. Stay low so we can avoid the drone." She then tapped the side of her face, and it went completely blank. Her eyes were still there, but her nose, mouth, hair just became generic versions of themselves.

"What the—"

But she shoved Solanis forward as the drone's powerful blades chopped the air above them. The pair darted toward the next set of trees. Solanis clutched her shoulder.

"Comply, or we will deploy counter maneuvers," the heavy drone said.

SPINE was nearby.

Solanis's heart tried to claw out of her chest.

The booming intercom amplified the SPINE agents' voices from their suits. Solanis wanted nothing more than to throw herself to her knees, raise her hands, and surrender. But as the aggressiveness of the robotic tone slashed through her skull, shivers ran down her spine. The screeching horn that blared into the woods broke her vision, echoed inside her skull, and forced her to press both hands over her ears.

The earplugs did nothing to dampen the sound.

Solanis screamed in pain.

Katia wasn't fazed. She plowed forward, forcing Solanis ahead of her. Solanis staggered on like a wounded animal, clutching her ears.

The citizens around them panicked and scattered in different directions. One couple who were frolicking in the lazy river dove sideways and tried to get out of the way as the SPINE agents smashed into the rushing waters, their green suits contrasting the bright clear water that rushed around them. They acted as if the water wasn't there—not breaking their cadence, guns primed to fire. A civilian fell under the water, only to be pulled out and pushed to the rear. The agents passed him person to person until he was solidly out of the line of fire.

Fear. This was fear.

Katia stopped and looked back toward the agents rushing toward them. Some took positions in the rear while others crouched and walked forward at an aggressive pace. She looked down at the glass keycard, muttering how it was hard to see with this face, and then pointed toward the waterfall. "We need to climb."

Solanis hobbled forward, the horn still scratching in her skull.

But SPINE was relentless. They deployed smoke.

So, there was hope. They would be slowed down, and although it might be painful, the kidnapping would end. Solanis prepared herself to watch the world warp around her, every fiber of herself pulled backward as time worked against them. But as she ran through the waterfall's rushing torrents, nothing happened. The smoke gathered around their feet, killing the grass and slowing nothing.

The device in her shoulder clawed at her, digging deeper, as the smoke swirled ineffectively.

Solanis knew what was going to happen next. If the smoke failed to incapacitate them, SPINE would move to deadly force. They would try to flank them from the other side of the waterfall. There would be more agents coming in behind them. They would die inside the waterfall if Katia kept pushing them into a corner.

No. It would only be Katia's death.

But a new voice joined the chaos.

"Let her go."

Leonardo. He'd come for her.

Leonardo, in his uniform, was nuclear pasta, the remnants of a neutron star— strong, firm, and commanding. He cut through the swirl of the greens, the falls, and the debris as a spear would through the air.

He shone bright for her.

"Let the ambassador go now." His voice was hard, determined. "You cannot. You will not win."

Katia stole a glance at him and pulled her hood further over her blank face. She then pulled Solanis back, forcing her against the rocks, through the falls.

Solanis's nose scraped the rocks, burning on the wetness. She looked up in awe, watching the water arch overhead and cascade behind her. But she shook too; being this close to the rocks was dragging her mind back to the caves.

Katia pulled out a pair of black gloves and shoved them onto Solanis's fingers.

As she worked, Solanis said, "You need to let me go, Katia. I can leave now, and you can do whatever you have to do. I can't leave Gabby."

Katia mumbled something to herself, too softly to be heard over the waterfall. Then she demanded, "Climb."

Solanis flexed her fingers, clutched a gap in the rock, and pulled herself upward. The gloves helped her cling to the wet rock.

Katia fired a few shots past the waterfall and into the Fields.

A drone poked its head through the water, parting the falls like a shredded curtain. As Solanis climbed, SPINE hit the foot of the falls and began to climb after her.

"Solanis!" Leonardo yelled to her. "Jump! We'll catch you."

She looked back, but the fall was too far. She didn't want to die. Gabby didn't need her to die. She needed to live.

Parts of the waterfall began to move. The ground that made the mouth of the falls rose to meet the top. The earth shook as the water was dammed off.

The drone let out another siren. Solanis grabbed her head with her left hand, wobbled, and slipped. She tumbled down, smashing her side into the rock, and then fell backward toward the watery rocks below. She thought of the young woman Gabby would grow up to be. She thought of Greg.

Walter flicked across her mind.

This was the moment she would die.

Her leg nearly wrenched itself from her body as the drone yanked her upward, snatching her out of the air. Another siren split her skull.

The drone moved down slowly toward Leonardo, who was directing SPINE to keep climbing. Arms flailing, Solanis tried to spin around to see what was causing the distraction but only saw the bullets crash into the ground beneath her. She covered her face. The drone shuddered, and she fell faster—headfirst into Leonardo, who didn't fall. She bounced off him and smashed into the water, coughing and sputtering.

She clutched her head. He pulled her up, his massive hand gripping her arm.

"Get behind me," he demanded, his eyes fixated on the returning fire behind her.

The blaring siren forced her to grab her head in pain as she tried to regain her footing and scramble behind him. The rocks were so wet, the water still powerful.

She slipped. His hand was on her back, pushing her down, as he yelled for someone to come get her, to bring her back.

He yelled and fell backward on top of her. The others came down the waterfall, like spiders to their food, in full tactical gear. But unlike SPINE, their uniforms looked more flexible.

No. They weren't coming down the waterfall. They seemed to be *running down it*. As if the air was the ground, and they could break the laws that governed gravity.

Solanis tried to scramble to her feet, to get to the backlines and hide deeper in the Fields—only to feel someone tug her upward and back toward the closing mouth of the waterfall.

The mercenary who grabbed her came from behind. He was silent as he clutched her around the middle. She felt her stomach drop out from under her as he pulled her backward and up. Solanis flailed, kicked and screamed. Leonardo tried to grab her back but clutched his side as blood mixed with the water below.

She slammed against the waterfall as the mercenary said, "We have Tailor. Pushing through the falls now."

The man pressed a pad on his middle, and she was jerked upward and over the edge of the falls, where the two of them tumbled into a gap she'd never noticed before. The lights were dimming. The Fields were vanishing.

The waterfall gave a creak and sealed shut.

————

SOLANIS SCRAMBLED to her feet as the mercenary pulled down his face covering and shook the water from his face.

She screamed, as the adrenaline piled up in her very essence, and then lunged at the man. He just glared at her, shoved her backward, and grabbed a pack from his partner.

He unzipped the bag, and the world collapsed.

It was all she could do to pull the various bits of herself back together. Her skin was tearing open, her mind was screaming, and her hair wanted to fall out. The vibrations in her hands and knees forced her to the ground. The galaxy was tilting wrong. She struggled to breathe.

And then she was back.

"We need to move, ma'am," another one of the mercenaries said to Katia.

There were six of them and Katia.

But Katia wasn't listening. She walked straight to Solanis. She got on one knee and grabbed Solanis's face, cupping it gently in her hands. "Listen to me."

Solanis's head spun. She couldn't see Katia correctly. The pulsing red lights, the absence of the waterfall…

The lack of green.

"You need to tell me now," Katia said. "Are the dogs real?"

"I need to go back," Solanis said. "My daughter…"

"Are the dogs real, Solanis?"

Solanis helplessly looked back at the first mercenary, who just stared blankly at her. "Please. I have a daughter. Gabby. I need to go back. Please."

"Don't look at him," Katia said. "Look at me. Answer me. Are the dogs real?"

Solanis was back in the room. Present. There was no green in here.

"The dogs, Solanis. The dogs."

She shook her head. "Please?"

Shamut wouldn't use the dogs, would they? Leonardo had said they didn't work.

She struggled to slow her breathing. She forced herself to focus on what she knew.

The mercenaries around her were moving quickly, pulling equipment out of gear bags and exchanging tools. She paused her mind and breathed deep. Their uniforms were not white. They just glinted in the dim red lights that lit the corridor. They were somehow dark yet light at the same time. That was why they looked so green inside. They had adapted.

Katia nodded at Solanis. "So, they're real."

Solanis tried to keep her breathing calm, but if SPINE had sent the dogs, they would all be dead. Gabby would be left alone. Her breath began to come out ragged and quick. Through gritted teeth, she hissed, "Fuck you."

Katia rolled her eyes, stood upright, and stared at the caves in front of them. She reached under her chin and pulled off her mask. Her facial features returned. She then poked out her contacts. Her eyes were silver again. "The nanobots confuse the cameras." She glared around the cave and barked, "Stop looking at her pussy. Get her a suit."

The men in the room instantly sprang into action.

"They're coming, ma'am," a man said. His two partners faced the long tunnel on the opposite side, their guns trained on the pathway.

The other two mercenaries stood silently facing the waterfall as if Leonardo was going to approach from the closed door.

But the waterfall was still—sealed for the time being.

Click.

It was a faint sharp metallic sound. Sharp enough to echo off the walls of the caves and tunnels around them until it radiated in their ears. It was almost painful.

Click.

One of the men approached Solanis and handed her a package. The small square was about the size of her face. "It's a wet suit," he said, smiling, as she accepted it. "Put it on quickly. The dogs are coming."

The man turned his back to her as she stripped off the robe and deliberately stepped into the thin rubberlike suit that covered her body. The man pressed the circle on her chest, and the suit shrunk instantly to fit her.

"You can keep the gloves on," he said.

Katia didn't waste time. She grabbed Solanis and pushed her in front of her. "Let's go."

Click.

————

So, this was what Katia had meant when she'd said there were tunnels under Shamut. In their effort to escape the dogs and their rotating mouths, they traveled through ragged gaps in the rocks. Despite the warmth of the wet suit, Solanis shivered the more they walked.

As they moved downward, they found themselves crawling in single file. Other times, they could continue three people across. Around her, more paths led to endless ways to get lost.

Now wasn't the time to run. Solanis had an image of herself pinned down by a rock, the dogs ripping her to shreds.

The clicks were becoming more rapid.

After an hour, they were forced to stop. A dead end. In front of them was a still underwater lake.

Solanis began to breathe heavy again.

But the team didn't stop their work. Two of the mercenaries took positions at the rear as Katia plunged her hands beneath the lake's surface.

"Flooded," she said to the room.

One of the mercenaries pulled out several flat objects from her pack as two of the other soldiers began inserting rods into the cave.

"Wall getting started," the men said as they placed several small rods into the wall near the opening, where they'd just emerged.

Click.

But no one was panicking.

Everyone was calm.

They'd practiced.

"Wall's up," the mercenary said, squeezing a glass keycard. The tunnel shimmered like a wall of liquid glass. "Won't hold them too long. We gotta get out of here."

"Can they swim?" Katia asked Solanis.

She shrugged.

Two of the soldiers dove into the water as Katia approached her. She swept her silver hair to the side and gave her a stern look. There were small wrinkles in the corner of her eyes. The hint of dark circles. She'd been crying.

She handed Solanis what looked like a mouth guard.

Click.

"You're going to put this in your mouth so you can breathe, okay?" Katia demonstrated with her own device, pulling it in and out of her mouth. "You're breathing through your teeth."

Solanis stared at her.

"We need to go underwater." She gestured to the end of the tunnel, where the two men had vanished earlier.

The clicks were louder.

She grabbed Solanis and brought her to the edge of the water. She reached beneath the surface and pulled up a rope.

So, they had planned this.

"Just pull this. After fifty-two pulls, you'll be on the other side. I don't have goggles for you, so keep your eyes closed. Usually, it's dry, but the tide is moving."

Solanis nodded, her fingers tapping her thigh. It wasn't just the cold that made her shiver.

The clicks were louder.

"Solanis, don't worry," Katia said. "Just pull the rope, breathe through your mouth, and follow me."

Solanis nodded again but then stopped. "I don't know if—"

But she gave her that smile—the one where she looked down to her, not at her. A look she'd given her when they'd been friends. "You went through Haze. This should be easy."

Solanis nodded.

Click.

It occurred to Solanis that even if she wanted to go back, she couldn't. The guards, the dogs, everything was pushing her out of Shamut, away from Gabby. She stared at the black pool of still water and took a deep breath.

"You can do this," Katia said. "He said you'd be able to."

"Who?"

But she didn't answer. The shimmer in the tunnel exploded as a dog ran around the corner, its legs flying through the air—a victim of the bomb. A second dog rounded the corner and charged.

"You need to go now!" a mercenary yelled as the dog leaped toward them. He fired his gun, spraying shrapnel into the room.

Solanis felt the adrenaline spike underneath her gut. She took a deep breath, stuck the device in her mouth, and jumped down below.

The fall was a lot faster than she'd anticipated. All the air she had pulled into her lungs whooshed out of her. The device placed a seal between her and the water. The air rushing out produced bubbles that she felt but could not see. She'd closed her eyes.

She had forgotten to grab the rope.

She gasped, and the shock of the air that rushed in to fill her lungs forced open her eyes. She saw nothing but darkness.

Solanis's feet smashed into the ground, and her knees buckled to absorb the impact as her arms flailed desperately. Her right arm snagged on a thick, leathery rope, and she opened her mouth with joy, causing the inhaler to fall out and water to rush in.

Eyes stinging, she caught the mouthguard and pulled on the rope. It didn't move, but her body did. Around her, the tunnel grew narrower, the rocks rubbing against her skin and snagging her hair.

How many pulls was this supposed to be? Forty? Fifty? Surely she needed to pull until she got to the end of the line.

Solanis pulled hard, twisted her body, and kicked her feet in an effort to make the rope move faster.

Finally, after an eternity, she felt the rope curve upward, and she found herself heading up. She released the rope and kicked hard. The tension broke through the surface.

As she opened her eyes, she saw a bright white light in the sky and a boot near her face. A large arm pulled her up from the water and dragged her onto the dirt.

The air didn't come as expected. Solanis was going to die because she couldn't breathe.

Someone flipped her over.

Katia.

She reached down and pinched Solanis's cheek. The inhaler popped out of her mouth.

Air flooded in.

The world assaulted her. An aggressive screeching tore through her mind. The cold threatened to rip her face off, tear her in half, and blind her. Colors were too bright.

As a kid, her dad had taken her to a showroom to check out the newest monitors for their house. She had struggled to understand that what was on the screen wasn't real. She had asked her father, with such innocence, why the world looked so dull compared to the monitor that had been showing fish and other animals flowing past the screen.

"The world is real," her father had said. "That's just how we think it looks."

She shook. Her gloved hands scraped her face as she tried to cover her ears. She hated the noise. Her eyes snapped shut again and again, in an attempt to get that white light away from her retinas. But the arm that had pulled her out of the water held her firm, in a way that was familiar.

"It's okay," Walter said, shifting behind her and holding her still. She could feel him cutting away at her wet suit. "Breathe. Come on. In and out."

Someone said she was going into shock.

Someone else was yelling for someone or something to get back.

Walter pressed his cheek next to her, and she felt the soft hair on his face. It was comforting, familiar.

Someone was pulling off her gloves and adjusting her earplugs, muttering that they were fitted incorrectly.

They smelled like grapes. No. She was an adult now. Wine.

Behind her, she could hear the last two mercenaries appear from the pond.

Solanis faintly heard one of them yell to get down, and the ground shook.

The water exploded.

Her mind rushed back to her and told her that the white light, the one that glared at her from above, was the moon. And the screeching—crickets. The smell was the real grass, dirt, moss, rocks—the earth.

The birds. They chattered away in the moonlight.

The birds.

"Did you pull out the heart monitor?" a voice yelled. "The tracker?"

"Don't tell me what to do," Katia snapped, kneeling next to Solanis. She looked at Solanis, her silver hair glowing in the moonlight. "This is going to hurt."

"Wait!" Solanis yelled. "Wait!"

But she had already pulled out a small pen and was tracing it around Solanis's arm and navigating it up to her chest. Every place the pen went, her skin tingled. With a jolt, her heart skipped a beat, and she felt a tightening in her chest. She clawed for air.

"Got it," Katia said, pocketing the pen and nodding to Walter. "Can we get her to the boat?"

"Do you think you can stand?" Walter's voice was gentle. Deeper than she remembered.

"I don't know," Solanis said.

He rubbed her chest. "Let's try."

Arms helped her up as she took a few steps forward.

The gravel of the shore crunched beneath her wetsuit. She could taste the salt in the air. Birds circled overhead, silhouetting against the moon. The sound of the ocean was overpowering as the waves smashed into the coastline. Cliffs raised high above her.

Two mercenaries stood at a makeshift perimeter, eyes in the darkness watching them.

"Move along," one of them said to some of the huddled masses who watched them.

"What is all of this?" Solanis asked breathlessly as the wet suit fell to her waist, hanging limply around her hips. "It's too much."

"We need to move," someone said. "The drones will come."

Walter nodded and wrapped a towel around her, covering her bare chest.

The warmth was Boston.

She could smell the ocean. She could hear it. She could feel its power.

Solanis was eased back down, the stiff rocks and dirt stabbing her knees.

She winced.

Looking up, she saw the moon—the largest light in the sky. But most magnificent were the stars. There, underneath Orion was Sirius—the star Walter had promised would mirror in both of their minds.

Sirius was back.

Walter was back.

Her tears were salty.

Solanis hadn't known what she was giving up when she had retreated for Shamut. She didn't realize she had turned her back on the vibrant world that not only wanted to kill her but forced her to live. This assault from the planet that gave her life was a stiff reminder of something. But she didn't know quite what yet. What was the lesson here?

"It's okay." Walter was gentle. "You're back."

She felt his embrace again as she shook deep in his chest.

"You're home."

Sadness. Shame. Guilt perhaps?

But in the back of her mind, something that had been quiet for the past nine years sang. Something she hadn't felt since she was last gripping the earth beneath her feet, when her brother had first brought her back to Boston. And a memory long forgotten before.

She felt it in her soul.

Solanis was free.

17

BROKEN GIRLS

Katia

Katia tried her best to avoid looking at the sky as she prepared herself to get punched in the face. She hated the way the massive dark cloud that hung over Kansas just lingered. The massive mushroom plume was the side effect of the hole in the ground where the second Worthington Dome had stood days before it had collapsed. What had they called it? Shalina.

The Domes—those half snow globes the world had so eagerly embraced—were not an escape but a prison. They were an illusion—a shield for those who were too weak to face the harsh realities of the world. Haze was everywhere, but so was the flu. You couldn't hide forever.

Her mother was in one of those Domes. The note she'd left on the kitchen table hadn't been discovered for two days. Katia's husband, Diego, had handed it to her, concern on his face. He always looked concerned. Between budgeting, coaching the neighborhood kids, and obsessively washing his hands, he agonized over problems he could not solve. He didn't know it yet, but this would be one of them.

In her untidy scrawl, Katia's mother had written that she was freeing her daughter from the burden of caring for an old woman who couldn't quite establish a second career. "Children should not have to take care of their parents," her mother had written. "And living until you're over one hundred years isn't natural. I'll spend my days watching the fields and rolling hills before the Greens come to get me at one hundred."

Katia had stared at the last line of the note while Diego stood straight-backed. His hands weren't in his pockets; they constantly twitched—the manifestation of a compulsive need to act.

I will meet God as close to the finish line as possible, and then, He will carry me to the other side. Once there, when your time comes, I will reach back and guide you home.

Her mother's words were like falling down an elevator shaft. The pinpricks behind her eyes gave her a new option.

She could cry.

But crying was a choice, right? Just like death by Recycling was a choice.

She'd heard the rumors, how *in there* they'd convince people to step into the machines—the ones that tore you apart atom by atom. *In there*, the rules were different. Worthington's utopia was the inferno gates, obscured by a team of skilled makeup artists and perfumers. Skilled at shielding the masses from the pit of reality.

No. Crying wasn't an option here.

Her mother would disapprove.

This was the woman who'd taught her that tilting against wind-mills was practice for the real wars you would eventually fight. She'd even told Katia when she was scared she should count the turbines on the windmills.

One.

Two.

Three.

Four.

This was also the woman who had told her that her silver hair was not unique. Everyone else's was wrong.

So, no. Katia wouldn't cry.

Instead, she would get punched in the face so she could convince the right man to help her shatter all the Domes. They would fall, and she'd drag her mother back home.

———————

As KATIA PREPARED to execute her plan, the man on the other end of her earpiece informed her that her target was leaving the bar. She had been observing him for a month, learning his routines and his habits. He was the key to her mission.

"Dark brown hair, athletic build, odd walking shuffle," she repeated to herself a few times as she stared down at Ronnie. She'd just gotten the updated model and was pleased how easily she could tuck the device away. The tablets inside the Domes were fucking bricks compared to this.

Katia watched as a few people exited the canvas tent—each proof that a bottle could soothe or inflame—and began moving. The man exited the canteen, tucking away his badge, zipping up his puffy jacket, and flipping up his collar as he headed toward the taxi lot.

Katia would have loved to encounter him at the bar. A drink could do her some good. Diego wasn't happy with her as she'd been spending more time outside Shamut.

But she had a reason.

She was one of the few people Senator Aiesha Patterson, her boss, trusted with such matters. The rest of the world—the media, the lawmakers, the private and public police—had let her down profoundly. Besides, Katia preferred life out here. The air was thicker, easier to breathe. Well, easier to breathe when Haze or DarkLight wasn't swirling around, blanketing cities. It always took her a few days to adjust when she returned to Shamut. The air was too thin inside. The adjustment period made her feel weak and made morning exercises a bitch.

The man was on the move, still walking around the thick crowds of people, until he reached the taxi stand. A car automatically pulled up, and he tapped Ronnie on the door, which opened it. He climbed inside.

Katia rushed forward and grabbed the door. "I'm sorry," she said, grinning and pushing back her silver hair. "Do you mind if we share? There aren't many out here."

The man looked up at her and hesitated. His eyes had the color of dried leaves, late in the fall. Katia knew he'd say yes. Aiesha had chosen him for a reason.

"I'm headed downtown. You going the same place?" he asked.

"Yep." Katia climbed into the car and pressed the button to close the door behind her. "And I'll even let the car drop you off first. That way, you won't pay for any extra kilometers."

"Denver's paying for it anyway," he said, putting on his seat belt and telling the taxi to drop her off first.

She settled into the seat across from him. The taxi was designed so that the seats faced each other, like the taxis she'd seen in London when Charlie was still alive. Charlie had agonized over which seat he wanted to sit in before changing his mind halfway.

No.

Not today.

"It's shit, isn't it?" she said to the man.

He looked over at her. "Shit?"

"Yeah, that Dome thing. It imploded?"

"Oh." The man nodded and peered out the window. It had started raining. "Yeah. Nearly one million inside, I think. Fuck LTE."

"You think LTE can bring down a Dome?" she asked.

"That's what they said." He jutted his chin toward Ronnie. The tablet lay discarded on the seat next to him. "They hate the Denver guy. Can't blame them. People just"—he scratched his chin—"Leave."

Katia nodded. The image of her mother, clear as day at the kitchen table, watching the neighbors on the crowded street below, the wrinkles etched in her face. She had liked to sit, bathing in the sun. Her skin had glowed from the inside, the contagious color brightening the world around her.

Only the kitchen table was empty now. Dust collected where the clanking of plates and forks had been.

Katia let the silence hang in the air. Aiesha had told her that people would hang themselves in silence just because they didn't want to linger in a moment. She looked at the window, where the taxi gave them an ETA on when they'd get downtown.

At one hundred and ninety-five kilometers per hour, they had just about twenty minutes before they'd get to the man's hotel for the night. There'd be a hooker there for him, and they'd sleep together.

She leaned back in her chair and closed her eyes.

But she didn't sleep. She was at work.

After seventeen minutes, she let her tablet fall off her lap and slide across the floor to the man's feet. She knew what would happen next. The tablet would light up automatically in a few moments and show a photo of her and Solanis Tailor, sitting at a park bench inside of Shamut with Gabby and Tatiana at their feet.

Katia kept her eyes closed as she heard the man pick up the tablet. She didn't hear him put it in her seat—a good sign.

"Excuse me," the man said quietly.

She didn't move.

He cleared his throat, and she felt a gentle nudge on her shoulder.

Katia opened her eyes. She did her best to look confused.

"Where did you get this photo?"

The taxi was slowing down.

"Photo?" She acted confused.

"The one on your screen."

"What?" Katia looked down at the display where she and Solanis sat, frozen in time. "Oh, this?" She nodded as the taxi stopped. The door automatically opened into the rain outside, the warm Kansas City air fogging the windows. She tucked her tablet away and gave the man one last look, her hand on the handles that would help her out into the rain. "This is my best friend. Solanis." She stepped outside into the loud rain and the thunder that rumbled overhead and braced herself.

The fist that punched her in the jaw was not gentle.

Katia fell to the ground, making sure to roll on her shoulder. She didn't need to break something before she went back inside. Someone would get suspicious.

Another blow came from her right, the kick hitting her stomach. She gasped. It was a little too hard. She'd feel that one in the morning.

She looked up, the neon lights of downtown blurry because of the rain. Pedestrians scattered, determined to avoid sticking their noses in what could be a rival gang fight, a hit, or the business of one of the other organized crime factions that roamed most cities in the Midwest.

She watched the man exit the taxi and shove her first attacker, Lucas, backward. He was the one who'd promised he wouldn't break her jaw when he punched her.

She'd have to have a word with Chadwick, the man who had kicked her stomach.

The man from the canteen spun quickly and punched Chadwick in the face. The crunch of his jaw was audible, even in the rain. Her contacts had told her that he'd taken martial arts classes in the past and had done an extra year in the service. He was skilled.

He let out a fierce yell as he pushed Lucas again.

Right on cue, both men ran away quickly. Katia stayed on the ground, her clothes soaking wet. A shiver traced her spine, arms, and legs as the cold shower from above assaulted her.

"Are you okay?" The man knelt next to her, and his hand extended to help her up. "Come up. We're getting you up."

She stood dramatically, shaking and shivering. "I am so sorry. I didn't mean for you to get involved. I'm so sorry."

But the man looked concerned. "Where are you staying?"

"I'm just down the street. I think I can make it." Katia let go of his hand and started to walk down the wet road. She limped aggressively.

"No," the man said. "You won't make it."

"I think I will."

"No," he said firmly. "Come to my place upstairs. Get dry. We'll order you some clothes. I have warm tea. It's good enough."

She did a good job pretending to consider the options. "How do I know you won't hurt me?"

"I could get you your own room." He pointed to the neon Hilton hotel sign. "Just come inside."

"You'll stick me with the bill." She shook her head. "I'm not falling for this."

The man reached under his coat, pulled out his government ID card, and thrust it in her direction. "This is me," he said, water pooling on the badge, the neon reflecting off the laminate coating. "Walter.

Walter Mustafa. I work for HERA, but I'm on loan with disaster management. I can't do anything because you know who I am now."

Katia eyed the badge.

"I promise you. Come upstairs. You'll be safe there." He frowned. "And I think..." He looked down at the ground and wiped his hair back. "I think you know my ex-girlfriend."

Katia nodded and followed him into the hotel.

This was precisely how this was supposed to go.

Walter liked broken girls.

18

INTERSECTION

Solanis

They took her to a yacht, a few kilometers offshore. Solanis refused to acknowledge Walter when he entered the glass room on the upper deck.

He paused for a moment, studied her.

Before he could say anything, she stood, folded her arms, and demanded, "Take me back."

He shook his head. But he didn't say anything.

She wanted to yell, but her brain was a fog. She knew Gabby was with Diego and— fuck. She never should have said yes to the trip. But her daughter… She loved her, but holy shit, she could be a little glass-biter sometimes.

Wait… Was that today? No. It was…yesterday? When did Gabby go to the Fields?

Solanis couldn't make sense of the timeline. But had they been together…at one time? And safe.

She needed to get back to her.

Walter stared at Solanis as he took his seat at the long table bolted to the floor in the center of the massive room on the ship. She had expected a shitty military vessel—the death traps LTE had been known to use for missions. Instead, all around her were glass fixtures, sofas, and real wooden accents.

Would Gideon Voss walk in? Force her to make a choice?

Solanis pushed against the table. Maybe she could knock it over and make her escape back to Shamut. But it was bolted to the deck. She felt the grain. Real, polished wood. Not like the desks at home. Besides, they were too far out at sea for her to swim back. She couldn't even see the coastal lights.

Katia sat perpendicular to Solanis, her arms crossed and her silver hair in a ponytail. She gazed out the glass window to the waves outside. Solanis pointedly ignored her, boring her eyes into a portrait on the wall of a family that looked awfully familiar. The mother and father smiled proudly beside their two children—a daughter with blond hair and freckles and a son with brown hair and a goofy smile.

Gabby's smile wasn't goofy.

She missed her.

Solanis could feel Walter's gaze on the side of her face. But she couldn't bring herself to look back. She had loved this man once. But this was not the same man she'd known. The Walter of today walked with swagger; the slight shoulder rock as he entered the room would have steamrolled Barto. There was gray in his beard now—more wisdom than old age. He was larger than before, and his steps were heavier.

Maturity looked good on him.

Solanis sat.

She had written off this moment all those years ago. This reunion wasn't supposed to happen in this universe. She'd already said good-bye. And sure, there was a moment when she'd first entered Shamut, rocking Gabby to sleep as she sobbed into her daughter's face—depressed that the right decision, the one that had seemed so easy, still felt like irons on her wrists. Katia had cradled her in those moments—stroking her hair, wiping her face, and rubbing her back. But that had only reaffirmed that she'd done the right thing. Because being correct was difficult.

Was the woman who stroked her hair the real Katia?

Who was the real Katia?

And how the fuck did she know Walter?

Did Walter still love her?

Did she still love Walter?

Solanis pinched the bridge of her nose. *Stop.*

"I missed you." His voice hurt her. Because it was gentle.

She folded her arms and continued to look past him. Her chest stirred. Her heart sped up. *No. No. No.*

"Solar?"

Something inside her purred. *No. Stop melting. You're not weak.*

But the world was becoming blurry. She wiped her eyes and tried to stand, but her legs were too soft.

"Whoa, Ambassador..." Someone caught her from behind and eased her back into the chair.

"Stay with us, Solanis." One of the mercenaries placed a glass of water in front of her. "There's more oxygen out here. You'll need a moment to adjust. It's normal."

She nodded and resolved not to touch the water. The room was sharp again. She closed her eyes and focused.

Ah, that was it. She was angry.

"Don't speak," Walter said. "Sip the water."

"Don't tell me what to do," she snapped. But she picked up the water glass anyway.

Oh. She was angry at Walter.

Or was her anger for Katia just redirected?

The water tasted clear. There was something in it. Was she being drugged? No, Walter wouldn't drug her.

"Solar," Walter said, opening his hands.

Making eye contact with him was like sticking her finger in an electric socket.

"I didn't mean that." Solanis shook her head. "Why are you here doing?"

That didn't make sense.

She tried again. "What am I doing here?"

Walter nodded. "I am sorry we had to pull you out like that. But we ran out of time."

"Time?"

"We have a problem."

"We?" She sipped more water. Why was it so good? She felt as if she was waking up. "Stop." She held up a hand. "Walter, where is my daughter?"

"She's safe."

Katia cleared her throat. "We don't have time."

"No one is talking to you," Solanis said.

She shoved her hands into her pockets, leaning back in her chair.

Walter held up his hand. "Solar, I need you to listen to me."

"My daughter. Get me home, and then we can talk." Solanis felt more like herself now. It was like the water was hydrating long-dusty corners in her body, opening doors that had only been ajar for the last decade. Maybe with enough sips, she could flip the table.

He shot a dirty look in Katia's direction. "This isn't the best way to do this, Solar. We know. But I need you to listen to us. Katia—"

"I want nothing to do with her. Take me back to Gabby. Now."

Katia didn't react. This made Solanis even more angry.

He held up his hands. "Solanis, please. Just listen, and we'll take you back. Okay?"

So, it wasn't Solar anymore.

"You kidnapped me." Solanis glared at Katia and kicked her chair. Gabby would have done that.

"You do realize we are on the same team, right?" Katia said.

Why was she so calm?

Solanis scoffed. "We?" She pointed to herself and then to Katia. "Like us?"

"Walter and I," Katia said.

"Fine. I can hold both of you responsible for stealing me from my daughter."

She didn't react. She always reacted. She was dramatic. But right now, she was just...ice.

"They're going to take Tatiana from you," Solanis said. "They'll Propagate you when you go back in. You're fucked."

She didn't mind pushing harder, shattering the decade of friendship they'd enjoyed. Besides, she wasn't breaking anything. Katia and her gun had done that.

"You have to understand," Walter said, "Katia wasn't supposed to take you out like that." He held up his hands. "A lot has happened since you've been gone. Give me ten minutes, and after you hear me out, we will take you back."

"So, you are complicit?"

He looked like a kicked puppy. "This was the only way," he said. "But your daughter is safe." His voice cracked.

"How do I know that? How am I supposed to know that? She's in there, alone. I am out here, with you. Why are you here? What are you doing here? You had the option to be with me, you know. You had a choice, and you chose to stay. You chose to leave me. You left me. You didn't come with me."

"No, Solar. You left me. You abandoned me so you could go inside. You were selfish."

"Fuck off."

She tried to angle her body away from her ex but instead faced Katia. Finding that point of view equally unpleasant, she turned to the opposite side of the table where she now faced the young man who'd given her water.

"We are getting nowhere," Katia said.

Walter leaned forward in his chair. "Solanis, I'm asking you to just give us a little time."

"Please get me back inside," Solanis said.

"Ten minutes. That's all we need."

"Let me speak to Gabby first."

"Nothing can get in or out," he said. "Solar, please. Gabby is safe. One of ours is looking after her."

Solanis frowned. "One of ours?"

He nodded. "Katia isn't our only person on the inside."

Katia drummed her fingers on the table. "We don't have time for this."

He held up a hand, silencing her.

Solanis tugged her dark curls. Who was inside with her daughter? Katia wasn't the only one on the inside. That meant...

"Diego?" she asked Katia.

Katia smiled. "The water is doing you some good. It's cleaner out here."

"Solar," Walter said, "I am going to show you something. Watch it, and then we'll take you back if you disagree. But I need you to listen to me."

Solanis motioned for him to continue.

"Michael," he said to his colleague who hadn't stopped staring at her since she'd angled her body in his direction, "can you show her?"

Michael nodded, pulled out another glass keycard from his pocket, and unfolded it. His fingers hovered over it, searching for something.

"You're not safe," Walter said. "Let me explain, Solar. Let me tell you what's happening. And then I promise you'll have answers, and I'll take you home." He sighed. "But you won't want to go."

She studied him. He was stalling.

But he wasn't lying.

He had never lied to her.

"Michael, show her," he said.

Michael handed over the glass keycard to Solanis, who cradled it gently in her hands. This wasn't a keycard. This was Ronnie. The display was brighter and more realistic than anything she'd seen before. The foldable device had a screen that went edge to edge. But it was remarkable how fast it was moving. She tapped the screen a few times, and it was as if the device predicted where she was going to tap each time.

"Is this really Ronnie?" she asked, flipping the tablet over and seeing the familiar RealityLife phoenix on the back center.

Walter nodded. "Upgrades."

She nodded. Of course. The world hadn't stopped just because she'd gone inside. She instinctively reached her hand to her side pocket for the Voice. But she didn't have it when she left the Dome. When she was kidnapped.

On the display was an aerial view of Shalina, its half sphere embedded in the flat plains of the Midwest. Only something was wrong. Giant cracks and sparks sprang from the Dome's sphere. The glass was warped and bent.

The camera cut to the streets, where it was complete mayhem.

Solanis couldn't hear what was happening, but the videographer refocused the camera, getting as close as possible. A chunk of the Dome fell downward into the streets.

The crater it left would have destroyed the ComCen building.

The sky pixelated and went dark.

Solanis looked up, her heart pounding. "The sky isn't real?"

Walter motioned back to Ronnie. "Just watch."

The video feed cut to the streets where people desperately ran toward the tunnels to get out of Shalina. There were workers in green pushing forward at the massive doors they had used to come in, but they were now sealed.

A man turned his tablet to face himself and said to the camera, "They won't let us out. Why won't they let us out?"

The tablet fell to the ground as feet stomped around the screen. The frame shook as the Dome shuddered and rumbled.

Somewhere, a child cried.

A loud grinding noise filled the air.

Then the screen went black.

"That was Shalina," Katia said.

Solanis frowned and swiped up on the tablet, where Ronnie had additional news articles. She was surprised how quickly she was adjusting to the modern device. One article showed the vice president making a statement. Wait, no. She was the president now.

"She became president after the old one died," Katia said, seemingly noticing the confusion on Solanis's face.

Solanis felt sick. Solanis looked at Walter. "Gabby is still inside. We need to get her out now."

Katia and Walter both nodded.

"We have time," he said.

Solanis stood quickly, backing up against the wall in the swaying room. How were they so calm? Tatiana was inside too. "No. I need to get her out. If they aren't safe…"

She paused for a moment. They'd warned her about this. LTE would stop at nothing to corrupt them with nostalgia and the old ways.

"What about the first one? Dome one. Porciúncula. Was that the one?"

"Yeah, still standing," Walter said.

"For now," Katia added.

Solanis opened her mouth to respond, but something wasn't right. If the Domes were collapsing, wouldn't the oldest one collapse first? Walter had shown her the video for a reason. It wasn't just because he wanted her to come out. He could have gotten her and Gabby out easily if this was the purpose of this little criminal enterprise.

He wanted something else.

So, she stopped speaking. Let him hang himself.

"We need you to help us fix this. For both of you. For everyone." He leaned forward at the table and gestured that she should sit.

She ignored the gesture.

"We need your help."

"I didn't build these," she said. "Talk to Katia. She's in infrastructure."

Katia scowled.

Walter nodded. "We've been following the Domes for nearly five years now, and from what we have learned, they're all like this. Except Zenos. No one's heard from the fourth Dome since it went dark two years ago."

"Dark?"

"Yeah." Michael from the corner spoke up. "They turned their sky off."

"Look," Walter said, leaning over and swiping the tablet again. Blueprints and charts appeared on the screen. Evidence she would have read years ago for her job. "We've been following the data. The Domes all shake and bend. They all move with the earth. But over time, they shake too much. And they crack and fall."

She stared down at Ronnie, inspecting the data she knew she didn't understand.

"Shamut's safe for now. But it's going to happen," Katia said. "It takes time. I've inspected the foundation myself."

"If it happens at all," Solanis said, "LTE is great at spreading propaganda. And you're falling for it."

She scowled again.

But Walter nodded. "Regardless, people deserve to know what's going on. They deserve to know a Dome has fallen, so they can make a choice. They can choose to stay or go. If they feel safe, they can stay, and if they don't, they should be able to leave."

"No one leaves once they make the perfect sacrifice," Solanis said.

"Right. So, we need some way to get a message in. Get the evidence inside every single Dome."

She stared at Walter. "You're not part LTE? The creepy ones wearing red and holding the photos of people who went inside?"

"Creepy fucks," Katia said.

"No." He exchanged a glance with Katia. "We aren't."

Solanis scoffed. "You sure?"

"When have you known for me to stand quietly?" Katia said.

"This is the kind of shit people like LTE pull." Solanis looked down at Ronnie again, the charts still on the screen, the data animated. Shamut had warned them about antisocials—the ones who stubbornly clung to the earth. She searched for government inquiries, anything that could point to the Dome's collapse. "The government thinks it's terrorism." She pointed to an article.

"You really going to believe the government?" Walter asked.

"You're the government," she shot back.

"Not anymore." He sounded sad.

"You sure?"

"Solanis, we've done the work. More and more people outside are verifying this. It doesn't add up. There's a cover-up happening. Worthington is hiding something, and these Domes will fall."

She didn't break eye contact.

"Do you trust me?"

She felt her stomach flip. "So, you want me to go back and tell people Shamut's going to collapse? Because that's not how it works. And I don't think I believe this myself."

Katia spoke up. "No, that's not what we're asking for. I know you're not going to believe without seeing. You're not special. But we need to show the people inside, the Evergreens, that the Domes will fall. Let them decide. Let them choose to leave." She paused for a second, once again gazing out at the dark rumble and tumble of the ocean. "You know my mother is inside a Dome? She wanted to die. She's old." She laughed, now staring at Solanis, her silver eyes unblinking. "But I don't think this is what she had in mind. This choice was taken from her."

"You want me to just hand out copies of these videos?" Solanis said carefully. "And then what? I play Moses?"

"What?" Katia asked.

Walter shook his head. "No. We have another idea."

"Who is Moses?" she asked again.

"He's a Bible character," he said quickly.

Solanis shook her head. "I'm sorry, but you kidnapped me because you needed a public relations strategy? No one is going to convince a room of Evergreens that the Man from Denver has done anything wrong. Let alone that their home, Shamut, will fall. If anything, it'll confirm they need better security to stop LTE or whoever you are from kidnapping more people."

"I'm not LTE," Katia scowled.

"Have you heard of something called the BlackBox?" Walter asked.

She flashed back to Boston. The pulse. Omer. "Just BlackBox."

"We need to turn it off."

"Off?"

"So, we can communicate in."

"You're serious?" she said. "It's uncrackable unless you have a few centuries."

Somewhere, Omer would be proud.

Katia and Walter exchanged glances.

"What was that?" she demanded, pointing between the two of them.

He shifted uncomfortably in his seat. "We know someone who can." He looked down at his hands and back up at her. "Don't react."

"Walter, you kidnapped me and dragged me to a yacht off the coast. How much worse can it get? Who?"

Were they about to head off and kidnap Omer? Force him to crack the box?

"We need to speak to your brother," he said.

237

She blinked. "Excuse me?"

He raised a hand. "We need to speak to Greg."

"Bite glass." She stood. It was time to leave.

But Michael blocked her way out.

How could they? What kind of sick game were they playing here? Walter knew Greg was dead. He'd been there as she'd mourned. Katia knew he was dead.

What the fuck was happening?

"Solanis, I know how this sounds," Walter said.

"Do you?" she asked.

"We found the island."

She scoffed. "That was a story. A fairytale."

"Solar," he said, his voice hardly above a whisper. "We found it. It's real. All of it."

"Take me home. Now."

He extended his arms. "Come on, Solar."

"You said ten minutes. I've given you a solid fifteen. I want to go home."

"That's not home."

He put his hands on her shoulders. But they felt like irons. They didn't warm; they burned.

Solanis pulled away, turning her back to him and glaring at the gray wall. She spun back around. How could he do this to her? How could he ruin everything? Was he still so in fucking love that he was willing to fuck it all up? Something he and Leonardo had in common.

"This some sick joke to you?" she yelled at Walter.

But his face was stone.

"That was just a story. Right? A story you tell your depressed girlfriend while in camp." She laughed. "Barto was right about you. You like broken girls. So, what did you decide to do? Come in and break me?"

Barto had been right all along, and she just couldn't see it because she was too busy getting eaten out at sunrise. Walter had lost his mind, and Katia was mixed up in this somehow. She'd been lurking in the Dome for nearly a decade, waiting for this moment.

Only how had she known about Shalina collapsing?

The timeline didn't add up.

Katia's voice cut through her thoughts. "Show her the video. Show it to her."

The room went silent.

"Video?" Solanis's voice cracked. The knot in her stomach became unbearably tight.

"I have proof." Katia reached for Ronnie, and for the first time, Solanis noticed the woman's hands were shaking. She'd never seen Katia look so bothered. Her shoulders were slumped, and her right hand stroked her bun.

"Hold on," Walter said quietly. "You don't have to—"

"No," she said, thumbing the tablet. "You were right. She needs to see."

"You're not serious?" Solanis folded her arms. "Walter, Greg is dead."

Katia was on the screen. She didn't have the tattoo on her back. The camera followed close behind her, carried through the thick jungle.

Solanis had seen this green place before. It was the same jungle from the photo Walter had shown her his grandmother.

Katia tapped her leg over and over as she entered a clearing. She looked back at the camera and pointed.

"Charlie?" her voice was hardly a whisper, and yet it came from deep within her.

In the clearing was a teenage boy, knees in his hands. His arms made a tight seal around his face. He was afraid of something.

Charlie.

Charlie's hair was the same platinum silver as his mother's.

"Charlie," Katia said again, this time much softer. "Charlie. Charlie."

Charlie looked up, his eyes dark and hollow. One of them rolled to the left while the other stayed fixed on Katia. He opened his mouth and then closed it. Over and over. Smoke came out. Vapor. But the jungle should have been warm.

Solanis shivered.

Katia took a few rapid steps forward, her boots crunching the dirt and grass under her feet. The camera flickered a few times, trying to focus on her and readjusting for Charlie.

Charlie looked up.

"It's me. It's me. Charlie, it's your mother. Your mom. I'm here. Okay?"

He locked eyes with her, both of them focusing and staring at her. She reached him, and he grabbed her. He clutched her arm with such aggression that Solanis could see blood.

Katia cried, holding Charlie in her arms and seeming unbothered by the pain of his grip. The camera kept buzzing away, focusing and refocusing. Gathering data.

She cupped her son's face in her hands, looked at him, kissed him, and stroked him as the young man clung to her.

Solanis ripped her eyes away from the screen and stared at Katia, who had turned away from the room.

This wasn't real.

There was no way this was real.

Katia didn't have two children. She'd never had two children. She had Tatiana. She'd never mentioned Charlie.

This could not be real.

Solanis pointed a shaky finger at the screen. "That's not..." How were her knees weak again?

Katia was crying.

Solanis had never seen her cry before.

She'd never mentioned Charlie.

How, in a decade, had she never mentioned Charlie?

Solanis grabbed her chair and sat. Hard.

This was real.

"Walter," she gasped, her voice dry and cracked. She cleared her throat. "Walter, what is this?" Her arms were flailing, gesturing to the screen.

"That, Solar, is the intersection between here and whatever's there." He pointed to the display. "And that is where we need to go."

No.

"We need to go tomorrow. When you set foot on that island, the person you love the most will be waiting for you."

Now she knew what was happening.

"This is real?" she asked Walter. She needed to see it in his eyes.

But one look at the man told her what she needed to know.

She felt that familiar tingle in the back of her mind—the tingle that told her the mental architects from her past were starting to rebuild her future. She could reach into the ground and claw back a portion of her family. What she had lost.

She looked at her hands.

What do we know?

Walter wasn't lying to her. At least not about the island. She'd seen the photo. This video was real. Katia's emotional reaction was real. Walter's eyes were wide and unblinking. He was telling the truth.

Were the Domes actually going to collapse?

That didn't matter right now. She could see Greg again, speak to him.

Solanis found her way into the hallway of the yacht. She needed some air.

Maybe she could take Greg home with her.

She passed an open door as a sudden weightlessness overcame her. Among the waves, she heard the sounds of Greg in the other room, working on some project in the workshop as he hummed a tune with an abstract melody. She knew this wasn't real. He wasn't on the yacht.

He was on the island.

Which meant the grass outside Boston didn't have to be goodbye.

She could get Greg back and maybe, just maybe, rebuild a version of Boston in her own image.

Yes.

She'd get her Boston back.

19

LEONARDO'S MISSION

Leonardo

Ms. Cassandra Price looked just like Solanis Tailor. But he wouldn't tell her that. She was the only person close to the Shepherd. He had seen the Solanis Tailor lookalike when he'd been scrolling the news feeds late at night in the before. The woman never left Mr. Worthington's side. When the late-night pundits insisted that Ms. Price and Mr. Worthington had never actually fucked, Leonardo's balls ached at the idea.

How could you be around that and not at least try?

When he'd entered the plain white room, Ms. Price didn't greet him. She had simply continued working behind a desk that mimicked a tree that had grown from the ground and then birthed a flat top which she stroked with her fingers.

This was fine. Leonardo wasn't ready to speak yet. His escorted journey from the bottom floor, past the sculpture of Worthington wielding the charter that formed the Domes, and down the winding hallways to this room had been taxing on his shoulder. While the blue Acer pills they'd given him had closed the wound, they did little to quell the throbbing. He'd squeak like a pig if he spoke too quickly.

But Ms. Price didn't seem to want to speak to him. She kept reading whatever it was she looked at on the screen, her eyes moving back and forth with such speed it made him dizzy.

"Your arm?" she finally said.

"Ma'am." He tested his voice. It sounded strong enough. Regulating his breathing was working.

"They gave you the pills?"

"Yes, ma'am."

"They're a miracle, aren't they? They're new." She still hadn't looked up from the screen on her desk. "You need to do the physical therapy they give you. But we'll provide you more as you go."

He nodded, realized she wasn't looking at him, and said, "Yes, ma'am."

"You'll need to take the pills, or your arm will get worse. We need you healthy."

He frowned. She didn't bring him here to tell him he needed to take his medicine like a good boy.

Ms. Price looked up at him, folding her hands on the table. "Mr. Worthington has a job for you."

For a moment, his heart forgot how to work. But he recovered quickly.

"You're familiar with what happened to Ambassador Tailor." She wasn't asking.

"Yes, ma'am." He realized his breathing was slower than he wanted it to be. Mr. Worthington had a job for him specifically and had sent his confidant to discuss it. This was an honor above all honors. "We are going to—"

"Then you'll know how critical it is that we solve the problem that's fallen on our plates, Ambassador."

Leonardo's left eye twitched. This felt like being ignored. It was like the moment before the roller coaster went down. There had to be a name for that feeling.

Anticipation?

No, that wasn't right.

Solanis would have known. The Princess of Seaport always knew how to fuck with words. And his head.

"Did you recognize her?" Ms. Price asked.

Leonardo frowned. He hadn't recognized the kidnapper. "She was wearing some sort of mask," he said. "Her eyes were all that you could see. The rest of the face, blank."

"That tech doesn't exist in here." Ms. Price peered over the console. "Which means, whomever this was has help from out there."

Leonardo nodded. "They were blue?" He said helpfully.

"Our intel is telling us that whoever took Solanis Tailor out was a member of our Dome community." Ms. Price locked eyes with him. "And we need you to figure out who the leak was, if they had accomplices, and if there are others inside who will do this to someone else."

Leonardo nodded. "One of us?"

"No. None of us would pull a mother out of Shamut to score political points. This was clearly LTE or one of the various factions that exist out there." She sighed and gestured to the wall with a built-in display on his right. She pulled up a video where Solanis lay in the recovery tank in the Fields, arguing with the woman who had pulled her out of Shamut. "Here, you can see them. Only we can't see her face. Her mask is messing with our cameras. We can't focus on her. We get nearly six hundred thousand matches when we run this through the system." She waved her hand, and the display returned to the color of the window. "Whoever they sent knew Ambassador Tailor would be in the Fields and knew that was a space where she'd be vulnerable to extraction."

He nodded. "And there had to be accomplices. No one can map this out alone."

"Exactly." She nodded. "Find them. Figure out who they are, and we'll make sure this never happens again. The consequences could be devastating for us."

He nodded. "I can do this. If there's a network, we'll break it up."

Ms. Price nodded. "I'm not done."

She was rude.

"When Solanis Tailor comes back inside, you need to figure out what she knows and doesn't know. And then we'll have a decision to make."

"Decision?"

"We'll cross that bridge when we come to it. In the meantime, figure out who took her."

"I can do that."

"Great. I've asked the acting ambassador of the Communications Directorate to help you."

He frowned. "There's an acting ambassador?" He pulled out his tablet and quickly flipped through the menus. "I didn't see anything about an appointment."

"We didn't announce it. Acting Ambassador Lancaster will be taking her place while she is away."

Leonardo frowned.

"Is there a problem?"

"You know where he's from?"

"I know some of you have a hard time dealing with the descendants of the Free Republic, but it's Mr. Worthington's position that the sins of the father should not impact his children." Ms. Price shook her head. "You know the Founder's own mother lived in FROST? And yet his impact has changed the world. Heritage should not nullify his chance to lead."

His shoulder throbbed. "Of course. He's just not a big fan of me."

"No, he's not. But he'll work with you because if our beloved ambassador does not return, we'll need a replacement."

He hadn't considered Solanis might not come back. "We'll bring her in. She's not going to die out there."

Ms. Price didn't nod. She simply looked back down at the table where her hands tapped the glass screen. "Being outside isn't the only thing that can get you killed."

He turned to leave, but she looked up.

"Ambassador, do this for the Shepherd, and he'll thank you personally. He is in agreement that this cannot and will not happen again." She looked back down at her console. "That is all."

———

WINSTON WAS in the lobby with his fellow unicorns, speaking in hushed tones. Leonardo couldn't quite put his finger on it, but there was something off about the way ComCen officers carried themselves. They had hardly glanced his way when he'd entered the lobby, but when they made eye contact with him, their horns looked sharper.

They were gathered in a small circle in the lobby, gesturing at their tablets. One of them had a set of annoying bangles that clinked and clattered every time she moved her hands. How could anyone stand that? Were the unicorns ready for war or a press conference?

Leonardo's shoulder twinged. He needed another pill.

Winston had yet to notice him.

Leonardo cleared his throat.

The gaggle of hacks kept jabbering among themselves.

"Deputy Ambassador Winston," he said, a bit sharper than he intended.

Winston poked his head out of the circle and gave a quick nod in his direction. While they were similar size, he was certain Winston could go a few rounds with him in a scrimmage. But he looked tired.

"Apologies, Ambassador," Winston said with an unexpected humility. "About before. The elevator. It should be water under the bridge, okay? We have one objective now, and that's to get Tailor back."

"Did she tell you to apologize?" he demanded.

"She?"

"Ms. Price."

Winston frowned. "I don't know a Ms. Price."

Leonardo nodded and extended his hand. So, she had only spoken to him.

He shook.

"Who gave you your assignment?" Leonardo said. "I was told you have one."

"Supreme Ambassador Wick," he said with an intense formality. "He called me about an hour ago. That's what we were talking about. We have a problem on our hands." He pointed to the unicorns who still spoke among themselves.

Leonardo raised an eyebrow.

"People are hearing that Ambassador Tailor is missing," he said. "They're starting to ask questions."

"Ignore them."

"Not that simple."

"Oh?"

"My team has been reviewing the transcripts of conversations, and it looks like the people who were in the Fields during the kidnapping went home and told their friends what they saw. Turns out you can't drag someone outside without rumors flying." Winston nodded as he spoke. Leonardo was certain he was doing this on purpose, as if doing so would get him to believe what he was saying. Magic. "They then told others about the kidnapping, and now we have a virus on our hands."

"Virus?"

"People asking questions."

"Is anyone not surprised by the kidnapping?"

Winston paused. "What do you mean?"

"Anyone hear the news and aren't surprised by what they hear? Anyone who might be in on it?"

"That's really not the point—"

"Then make it the point."

Shock crossed Winston's face, but he quickly covered it up. He turned, approached his colleagues, and spoke to them quickly. One of them held out a tablet and pushed some data over to Winston, who looked down at it and then returned back to Leonardo.

"There are nearly two million people inside Shamut," Winston said. "We can classify over one hundred and twenty thousand people as antisocial. Divide those up by people who are likely to kidnap an ambassador and are female. That leaves one hundred and forty-six people on our list."

"I'm sorry. Likely to kidnap'?"

"An ambassador," he said. "These are people who have been reassigned or who just don't like the policies of the ambassador committee. People who might have lost custody battles in the past. I'm not sure how the nerds figure this out, but they build a profile. The point is, Leonardo, all these people are likely to be involved. And they're not going to just tell us they're working for LTE."

"I'm not asking if they are antisocial. Who are the ones who heard she was missing and didn't sound surprised?"

"We need time to figure that one out."

Leonardo frowned. "Take time."

"But that's not my job."

"I thought you were helping find the kidnapper?"

Winston shook his head. "No, Leonardo—"

"Ambassador."

"I've been told to find a way to mitigate the damage from Ambassador Tailor's vanishing. To stop the spread before it causes problems."

So, Winston had been instructed to do the most unicorn job possible—create a marketing campaign to make people feel better about Solanis going missing. Useless.

"We're building a campaign that will make Ambassador Tailor a hero, should she return," Winston said.

Leonardo frowned. "A hero?"

He got a look in his eyes and puffed out his chest. He pressed his tablet a few times and then held it up for Leonardo to see. An image of Solanis Tailor, looking optimistically out onto an invisible horizon line, in a frame appeared on the screen. Beneath her were the words *Bring Our Ambassador Home*. The aesthetics reminded Leonardo of a campaign poster he'd seen when Alderman Hunter had run for reelection. What had his second father called it? *Dreamily optimistic*?

"Rumors, like nostalgia, are poison," Winston said. "But they're normal whenever something traumatic happens to a society. Right? Insecurity will corrode the core faster than simple instability. That's why we've built a campaign that will turn Ambassador Tailor into an icon. A rallying point for Shamut. I'm too young to remember, but I know some of you recall when the lights went out after the great earthquake. How everyone banded together. We can create a moment like that here." He spread his arms. "We tell people she's been kidnapped, that the dangerous forces outside have taken one of our own because they're trying to hurt us. We inspire the people inside to rally for her support. They'll rally, and we'll unite. Morale will go up. And if she returns, we can celebrate."

Leonardo found himself nodding along. He was right. He'd seen how groupthink could destroy the purity of a crowd. It was how he'd ended up here when they'd turned on him.

"How will you know if this is working?" Leonardo asked. "What if it just makes things worse?"

"We track everything said inside of most of this place. Besides the ambassador residences and a few dead spots, we can hear and see nearly everything."

"I know how it works." Had Supreme Ambassador Wick really told Winston to build a public affairs campaign? It could keep things calm for the short term, but it did nothing to help find out how she'd been kidnapped to begin with. He frowned. "Wait. You can measure how people feel? Sentiment?"

"Yes."

"Then can you look for keywords? Like phrases. If someone before the kidnapping mentions kidnapping Solanis?"

Winston raised an eyebrow. "Ambassador..."

"Winston..."

"We can. But I'll have to get the nerds working. It'll take some time. It's not as simple as that."

Leonardo shrugged. "I really don't care. Figure it out. And before you tell me Wick hasn't told you to do it, I outrank you."

"I'm gonna do it," Winston replied. "Wick said you're in charge. We'll get you your data. Updates will be sent to your tablet." He took a step forward and lowered his voice. "One more thing. I've been told Katia doesn't yet know Solanis is missing. I was going to send someone to tell her, but maybe it makes sense for you to deliver the news. You're friends?"

He almost laughed. "Yeah, I'll speak to her. Should probably go in person."

Winston shook his hand, vanished into the throng of unicorns, and left the building.

———

LEONARDO COULDN'T FIND KATIA.

She wouldn't answer his calls.

But he could leave that for later. First, he'd need to check out Solanis's quadplex to see if there were any clues to why she would have been the one taken. People kept secrets in plain sight in their homes, generally without even realizing it. Seek's mother had kept the hammer she used to kill Seek's father on her credenza.

In Solanis's apartment, among the SPINE and ComCen officers, was Gabby.

"Have you seen my mom?" Gabby asked. She gripped his shoulders the same way Solanis had tugged at him in the Fields, right before she was taken.

"No." He gave her shoulder a light squeeze. He'd handed his rifle to another agent who'd been stationed near the door. "But we are going to find her, you know. She'll be back." His stomach was a rock. He'd said that before, in another life.

But Gabby nodded and said that a lot of people seemed to go missing. "Childre wasn't near the fountain either. We used to sit and play with the fish."

He didn't respond. He simply patted her on the head, promised he would keep looking, and handed her off to one of his other agents who were milling around the living room, taking photos for their investigation.

Leonardo walked into Solanis's bedroom.

He hated to admit it, but he had imagined what it might be like to enter this room under different circumstances. While he didn't expect the place where Solanis slept to be filled with pink sheets and pillows —everything inside of Shamut was green—her bedroom lacked any sort of personality. It looked exactly like the model homes he'd seen in one of those Shamut preview centers. There was the portrait of Worthington near the door, the self-watering plant he still couldn't remember the name of, and a small desk with a display attached to it.

Solanis hadn't decorated.

Maybe she had been planning to leave all along.

No, that wasn't possible. She'd never leave Gabby behind. Besides, she had been scared. He'd seen the look of terror on her face when the terrorist pointed the gun at her. Maybe she just didn't like decorating. Or she was simply distracted.

Leonardo kicked himself silently as he joined the other officers looking into drawers, closets, and underneath the sink in the bathroom. Kruger had warned him about this—entering a crime scene with an idea of what he might find. He was supposed to be a blank slate and absorb information, but he'd come with an agenda.

Leonardo slid open Solanis's underwear drawer and quickly closed it.

Don't be a dog.

"Ambassador?" a voice came from behind him.

He turned and saw one of his investigators enter the room, holding an evidence bag. She was like a meerkat, standing straight on her legs with her chin parallel to the floor.

"I am sorry to hear about Ambassador Tailor," she said quickly and loudly. "I know you two were close."

Leonardo nodded. "Can I help you?"

"The team did a search of the room. We found something." She handed over an evidence bag containing three tiles with a squiggle bouncing off the edges.

"This is electric paper."

"Indeed." She paused and then took a step forward. "Do you remember when you asked me to keep track of Katia Delgado?"

He frowned. "It was you?"

"No, sir," she said quickly. "Another investigator had the assignment, but he passed it down to me." She shifted on the spot. "It's not an ideal assignment, sir."

"Never mind. What are you thinking?"

"These tiles match the other tiles I've been collecting from Katia's place."

"The other tiles?"

She stepped forward and lowered her voice. "Sir, if I tell you what I found, I need some assurances."

Leonardo rolled his eyes. "I'm waiting."

"Sir, please. I need to know—"

"You'll be fine. You have my word. What did you find?" He tapped his foot.

"Sir, Katia has been delivering these to Ambassador Tailor." The woman glanced at the tiles in his hands. "We intercepted most of them. But don't worry, sir. She doesn't know. I promise."

He took a step forward. "How many did you intercept?"

"Six of them, sir. But we couldn't... I couldn't read them, sir." She looked nervous. "I didn't have the full paper, so I can't activate the puzzle. But, sir, these three complete the set. We're certain of it."

"Where are the other tiles?"

"Cold storage."

"Who has access?"

She looked scared. "Sir, they are labeled personal. So, just you and myself, sir."

"Good work," he said. He stuffed the tiles in his pocket.

"Sir..." She paused. "Does this have anything to do with Ambassador Tailor's disappearance?"

"Doubtful," he lied, the gears in the back of his mind turning.

"Sir, I just—"

"What do you want?" he snapped.

"Please. I don't want to get in trouble."

"You won't," he said. "You have my word. I'm seeing the Shepherd soon."

The woman perked up.

"I will tell him you helped me during my investigation. He rewards those who help."

She nodded. "I hope to meet him someday."

"We all do," he said, leaving the room.

His mind was a blaze. He'd nearly forgotten the tiles and the assignment he'd handed out. Part of him was praying that this was nothing. That the instinctual reaction to the electric paper was just his hatred for Katia manifesting into criticism of everything she did. But when he reached his office, turned on the privacy filter, and thanked one of the many investigators for handing him the box from cold storage, he realized he might not be so lucky.

The paper quickly snapped together. As he watched, the black snakes swirled and combined to form letters, then words, and then full sentences. The electric paper formed the words he wished he had seen before. Not just phrases but entire diagrams and chapters. Propaganda from LTE insisting Shamut was going to collapse.

The letter begged Solanis to help them expose the truth and told her she should expect a visitor.

He focused on the last line.

I will send for you, and you will know it's me. I will call you by the name you share with all the stars.

Only it wasn't signed *Katia*.

Instead it was signed *Walter*.

Who was Walter?

20

GREG

Solanis

The captain of the yacht showed Solanis how the life rafts worked. The patient old man, deep in the throes of his second career, patiently taught her how to tie the knots that ensure the boat wouldn't float away in the tide. He walked her through how to use the beacon to navigate the craft once it was in the water.

"You know," the captain said, the scent of chewing tobacco filling her nose. "You won't need to worry about any of this. That crew down there is pretty good at what they do."

She nodded. "How long have you traveled with them?"

He shrugged. "I go wherever my boss tells me. I just like the open water. It's safer."

"Safer?" she asked.

"You might not have been alive during the shake." The captain squinted into the late-day sun. "What was it? Forty years ago? You know, the one that created the edge." He pointed to the darkness back near the shore. "But the ocean doesn't swallow you unless you really mess up."

She looked hesitantly toward the thick, dark waters.

"But Aiesha gives me the time I need to do my thing, and I make sure her vessel gets where it needs to be." He patted Solanis on the shoulder. "You're a smart lady." He picked up the raft they'd been inspecting and handed it to her. It was about the size of a brick and would grow into an emergency boat large enough for eight people to sit inside if needed. "Always have a way to protect yourself. Only you're responsible for keeping yourself safe. You never know when the seas might turn. Anyway, help yourself." He pointed to the supply closet and mumbled to himself as he turned his attention back to the massive displays on the deck.

She nodded, inspected the closet, and grabbed what she needed.

Walter had given her a tablet on which she could learn about the nearly unrecognizable world she'd left behind. There were more news feeds now. The moon was carved up between different nations. Worthington was opening his seventh Dome project and had several more planned around the world. Australia was debating the relocation of all its citizens into two massive Dome-like habitats that looked rectangular and would span the continent. New designs, she guessed.

A new drug on the market called Acer was said to be a miracle, and the president was considering pardoning former FROST President Franjola-Ricardo.

Skinny jeans were back in fashion. As she read some of the style news feeds, she now knew why Katia's hair always looked off. Bangs were back.

She pulled her hair over her forehead a little bit. Then pushed it back.

Boston was dead.

Haze had crept its way up the coast, devastating Concord, New Hampshire. Bangor and what was left of Ellsworth, Maine were cordoned off as HERA declared much of the northeast uninhabitable. Videos showed Canadian and American relief workers urging the fleeing civilians to move quickly and abandon their homes before the dark particles set in.

Los Angeles had been dark for a year. Authorities called it Dark-Light—a version of Haze that didn't have as many fine particles but still blocked out the sun. The new, massive fan projects on the coast were trying to move the storm with no success. Someone had recommended dropping more chemicals into the air to try and make the particles heavier, forcing the air to clear. They'd vanished a few months later.

Solanis flipped the display in time to see a ship, torn and broken and beached, as its navigation system had failed during a particularly bad Haze. She glanced over at the captain, who was lost in space. She'd keep that one to herself.

LTE had its own news feed—scrolling photos of the people who had decided to live inside the Domes around the United States. They were all there, clad in red and staring into the distance. They had gathered outside of the second Dome after it had collapsed—staring, holding photos. Gideon Voss was rallying a small crowd, the banner on his podium proclaimed, 'If you died today, who would thrive?" Another news feed called him a radical. There was a warrant for his arrest. There were more LTE members than a decade ago, demonstrating in malls and town meetings. The less radical, like Aiesha had made it to Congress.

Solanis tucked Ronnie away, overwhelmed at how the world gave her the harsh reminder that she'd abandoned it and, like an ex, was fine without her. Only the earth hadn't gone to the gym and listened to self-improvement news feeds. This version of the planet was... depressed. The fact that Earth hadn't hit pause made her feel small, insignificant.

She'd been dead. And then just back.

Would Greg feel this way?

And then there was Walter 2.0. The way the hints of the version of him from a decade ago peeked through the larger, almost arrogant human who was her new and improved ex-boyfriend. The old version —the one holding the book, grazing a hand over her elbow, kissing her chest—was still there. But the shell around him made it harder to see.

Time had made its modifications with no regard to her feelings.

Would the old Walter have kidnapped her?

No. You couldn't kidnap what was already yours.

———

THE CAPTAIN ESCORTED Solanis to the side of the yacht so she could prepare to go ashore. They found Walter waiting, a backpack slung over his shoulder.

He gave her a nod as the captain wandered off. Even his nods reeked of authority, his chin giving a confirming, rigid fall.

There was something deep inside her that tightened at this version of Walter.

She couldn't bring herself to nod back.

"I'm sorry, Solar," Walter said quietly. "Katia was supposed to wait."

Solanis didn't respond. She didn't want to be so rigid but couldn't help it.

He brushed his hand against her elbow. "I am sorry."

The shiver ran from her elbow to her chin, the ripples flowing through her body. He was telling the truth.

"You know, I looked up every night. When there weren't clouds."

Solanis nodded.

"Did you look up?"

She shifted on her feet. "Yes."

"And what did you see?"

His eyes were the same eyes from before. The same soft brown eyes. Too much cream.

"Nothing," Solanis said. "Orion was there… But, you know, the sky wasn't real."

"I didn't know that when you went in."

"Neither did I."

His hand was right next to hers.

She wasn't ready for that. But she let him touch her though because she didn't want to close the door completely.

"I need you to do me a favor, Walter," she said.

His finger stopped roaming.

"When we get to the island, I want to go alone. Give me time to say goodbye to my brother."

He nodded. "Yes. Of course."

She let his pinky link with her own and linger.

It was the least she could do.

She would betray him.

———

THE MOMENT SOLANIS stepped onto the island, she felt death.

A deep fear welled up inside her as she waited, expecting the Haze to plunge inside her and squeeze her lungs. She would feel the harsh, rainy particles cut the sides of her throat and slowly attempt to suffocate her. Her entire body had frozen the moment her boot splashed into the water and made contact with the red and tan silt.

Breathe, Solanis.

It was the high-pitched whistle of the birds that propelled her forward.

She lifted her boot and took one step and another and another until it was as if an autopilot was moving her forward.

There was something on this island. A presence, a heaviness she couldn't shake. Sure, the thick underbrush looked like she expected any old underbrush to look. The trees that arched high above her looked correct. But everything around her, even the air, felt heavy.

Solanis wanted to cry.

But she kept moving forward, the invisible hand on her back pushing her steadily in the direction she needed to go. It was a forceful, weighted push that gave her no choice but to move, all while the feeling of profound, dark loss hung in the air. Her eyes itched again, the world slightly dark. This island had a dark presence.

Did she see a firefly?

It felt like Greg.

She ducked under a clump of branches and stepped over nature's natural conquest of the island floor. The animals ignored her as she traveled, sometimes blocking her way as they grazed on the greenery around her. At one point, she had to bypass a large animal that looked like a horse with great arcing horns on its head. The animal, a rich tan, stood proudly and hardly glanced at her as she passed.

Solanis stopped. She knew this place. This was where Katia had seen the person she had loved the most—the person she had wept over.

She took a step forward and entered the clearing.

The world was heavy here.

And standing there, with his back toward her, was Greg.

At least, it was a version of him she'd seen before. The last time she'd seen him, his arm had been mutilated by bones jutting from his body. This time, there were no bones. His eyes weren't black. He looked younger than he did before the Boston Haze.

This wasn't reality. This was how she had wanted to remember him.

"Greg," she said gently to her brother.

His head shot up and slowly pivoted toward her. Once his neck had reached breaking point, his shoulders, torso, and body followed.

He frowned in her direction as one eye darted from her to the ground, left to right, jerking back and forth. His eyes were cameras trying to focus on too many things at once.

"Greg," she said again, a bit louder. She took a step toward the man.

He didn't move. Just stared.

She took a few more steps. She needed to touch him, feel him, smell him—burnt plastic, coconut. Every bit of her soul ached to see him make that clever smile one more time.

Solanis collided with his chest as she wrapped him into a hug.

He didn't smell like anything.

There was no usual reciprocation in her tightness. His arms were limp as she squeezed him. She looked up at her brother, holding both hands and surveying his face. There were no cuts or marks. But all of him was there. He looked healthy, well. He was alive.

"Greg," she said, tears spilling from her eyes. "It's me. I'm here. I am here." More tears fell. "I'm back. I'm okay. I made it out. Okay? I'm here. Okay?" Her mouth tasted like salt.

Greg looked down at her as if something had registered. "Solanis?"

"Yes. It's me. Solanis. Your sister." She held his face, trying to get him to focus.

"Where..."

"An island. Pennsylvania or something. Off the coast. I got you back. It's okay. You're with me."

He trained both eyes on her. "I..."

"It's okay. Don't say anything. It's okay. We need to move."

He ignored her. "It wasn't just dark," he said, looking at her. "It was heavy."

She pulled off her backpack and took out a T-shirt, pair of pants, and boots. "Here. You need to put these on."

"There was this...pulling." He held the bundle of clothes as she swung the backpack onto her shoulders. "Down here." He gestured to his navel. He sat, naked on the grass. "I'm so tired."

She grabbed the pants from him and began maneuvering them up his legs. "We don't have much time, okay? I need to get you out of here. They're coming."

Greg nodded, focus hitting him. His eyes had stopped darting around like cameras and now worked in unison.

She helped him put on the shirt and grabbed his hand. "Come on. We need to go." She ushered him out of the clearing.

Greg struggled, dragging his feet until the process of walking came back to him.

He stumbled over the boots she had given him for the first fifteen minutes of the walk. By the end of the first half hour, he finally got the hang of the thing and seemed to match her cadence.

His voice grew more confident too. He stopped talking about the tugging in his belly button and began asking where he was. The last thing he remembered was getting in the car to head to safety. He had no memory of the black bag, the refugee camp, or the soldiers.

"I feel like I've been in darkness for so long. And now, I'm here." He shook his head as if trying to clear a hangover. "It's a fog. I can't shake it. Did I die?"

Solanis tried to listen, but she needed to keep her eyes on Ronnie to lead them toward the edge of the island. She urged him forward, but he kept stopping, saying he was tired.

She guessed being dead for nearly a decade played havoc with his cardiovascular system.

As they moved expeditiously, she filled Greg in on what had happened while he had been gone. She spoke to him about Walter, visiting the sick, Shamut, and how she'd decided to enter.

"You didn't lock yourself away because of me, did you?" Greg asked.

Why did his voice sound lower than usual? Had she remembered it wrong?

They were running out of time.

"No," she said impatiently. "I left because there was nothing to go back to."

"You said the compound was still there."

"It is, but Boston's off limits."

"Off limits?"

She glanced back at her tablet. "You can't live there." A message had popped up from Walter, saying he was on his way to her now so they could get what they needed from Greg.

They had to move faster.

"You said it's been almost ten years," Greg said.

"Almost ten, yes."

"And it's taken them that long to rebuild?"

Solanis frowned. The shore should have been just up ahead. "The Haze destroyed everything. It left its permanence."

"I wish you hadn't gone into a Dome," he said.

The surf roared on the coast.

She shook her head, throwing down her backpack and grabbing the bright orange square that was the raft.

"The Domes are not safe," Greg said. He spoke in that flat, monotone voice she'd remembered.

"I know," she said. "Which is why we are going to fix it."

"Fix it?" He shook his head. "What do you mean fix it?"

She tossed a packet into the water, holding the bright blue chord in her right hand. The moment the packet hit the water, it expanded into a boat and bobbed on the ocean's ripples. She used her tools to stake the rope into the ground.

"Solanis?" he asked. "What do you mean, fix it?"

"You worked for Worthington. You can fix it."

261

He laughed for the first time in nearly a decade. "You're joking, right?"

"Come on!" She splashed into the water and waded toward the boat. "We need to get off this island before—"

Solanis stopped. She suddenly had that crippling feeling of being alone. Greg was gone.

She turned and saw him standing back on the beach, looking sadly at her.

She waded back to shore. "Greg, we need to go."

"Tell me you're not planning on staying in the Dome."

"After you fix it. Now, come on. We have to go before—"

But the trees shifted, and Walter, Katia, and Michael all exited the forest, their black tactical suits striking a stark contrast to the dark evergreen trees and the gritty red and tan, glass-like sand.

Michael was pointing his gun directly at Solanis.

Walter let his rifle dangle over his shoulder as he approached Greg and Solanis on the beach's edge. He showed his teeth in an attempt at a smile, but it came out as more of a grimace.

"Solanis," Michael said, walking up to Greg and looking past him. "What's the deal?"

Solanis got quiet.

"Seems like you forgot to ping us when you reached the meetup point."

Greg stiffened and angled his body to block her from Michael, who still had his gun trained on her.

"People forget things all the time though, you know?" Michael said.

She stared at the gun, her face hot and her heart pounding. This was the second time in twenty-four hours she'd been at the wrong end of a gun. She didn't like this.

"But now that we are here," Walter said, "we might as well get those questions answered." He was pointedly ignoring her obvious attempt to leave the island without them.

"Greg..." Solanis stood up straight, ignoring the gun. Her voice was tight. "Get in the boat."

Greg didn't move. He kept his eyes trained on Michael, who still hadn't put down his gun.

"Greg," she said again. "Please. The boat."

"I can't."

She shook her head, the fire boiling in her chest. Her breathing quickened. "Please. Greg. I need you to get in the boat."

Michael cocked his head to the side and gave a little grin. "She doesn't know he can't."

"What do you mean?" Solanis was speaking quicker as she ran out of air. "Greg. Get in the boat. We can leave. It's time to go. We need to go."

Katia spoke up from Walter's right. "No, she doesn't."

Michael was still pointing his gun at her.

Why did Walter look so sad?

Greg turned to Solanis. "I can't get in the boat."

She looked wildly around. "You don't have to listen to him." She gestured to Michael. "You can get in the boat. Just take a few steps and get in the boat. Just get in the fucking boat!" She was yelling now.

She pulled Greg hard, causing her to lose her balance.

As she fell, Greg dissolved into the air as if someone had simply blown him away. The water didn't even register that he'd been in it. She dropped under the water, the waves covering her.

An arm grabbed her. As she resurfaced, coughing and sputtering, she heard Walter's low, solid voice.

"He's not going anywhere, Solar. He can't."

She stared back at the spot where Greg stood, somehow rematerialized. The sun was beginning to set behind them, the day exhausting its energy.

"What do you..." She couldn't find the last word.

Walter looked back at her as he guided her back to the beach. "No one's leaving here who didn't come here, Solar."

"Don't call me that."

She looked at Greg. But she saw it. Somehow, he'd known too.

"But we were supposed to..." she stuttered. "We were supposed to go back together. We were supposed to fix Shamut so we could go back together. You're alive. I can't just leave you here. Come back with me."

She shook her head, the plan in her mind crumbling at its first test. All the work she'd done on board. Talking to the captain. Learning how to work the boat while it cut through the waves overnight. Planning how she was going to get back into Shamut. None of this would work without Greg.

"How could you do this to me?" Her world crumbled as she charged Walter, sand stirring in her wake. "You should have told me. You should have told me. *You should have told me.*" She pounded his chest as the rest of the beach stayed silent.

"I didn't think you thought you could actually bring him back," Walter said.

She felt stupid.

She sat. Hard.

"We are running out of time," he said. "We need to talk to Greg so we can save those people."

"Those people!" she cried out in exhaustion. "What about my people? What am I supposed to do now? I've seen him. I can't go back knowing that…knowing that…" She closed her eyes and shook her head. "That this is it. The last thing. He's alive. Look at him."

"It's hard," Michael said.

"What the fuck do you know?" she screeched in his direction.

"Solanis," Katia said, "you have been given an opportunity here."

"I wish I'd never come here. I wish I'd never seen you. You dangle him in front of me only to…" She sniffed hard and looked back at Greg, who stood silent, his shadow elongating over the beach as the sun continued its race away from the moon. "To steal him back from me."

Katia crouched next to her. "You get to say goodbye today."

She looked up at Katia. "What?"

"No one is lucky enough to know when they'll go, but today, you can say goodbye."

"We have half an hour," Michael said.

Solanis's heart skipped a beat, and she looked back at Greg. "I can't watch you die again." She was still crying. "I can't watch you die again. I will not let you die again."

Walter's hand was on her back, but she jerked away from him.

264

"He's not alive, Solar," he said and nodded toward Michael, who slung his rifle back over his shoulder.

"No," she said. "You're on your own. I'm not fucking doing it."

"Solar?" Greg asked suddenly. His voice almost sounded normal. "Are you…" He pointed one shaky finger toward Walter. "Are you Walter?"

Everyone looked up in surprise.

"Solanis told you about me." Walter's response was a statement.

Greg went silent.

He looked at Solanis. "And yes. You will help us."

She positioned herself in front of Greg. She could barely look at him, knowing he'd be gone soon. "No, I won't. Fuck you. Find another broken woman."

Michael spoke up. "Walter, this isn't going to work."

But something in Walter's voice had alarmed her. There was an edge to it. It was almost pleading. "I really think you want to help save those people."

She, locked in at this point, shook her head. "I don't know this version of you. I don't recognize you. Bite glass."

Michael spoke up again. "Plan B?"

Walter held up a hand. "Hold on a second. We aren't there yet."

He rolled his eyes and glanced at Katia, who nodded. "I think we are."

"Do your fucking worst," Solanis said. "I'm going back in, and you can find another way."

He ignored her and gestured toward Katia. "Show her the tablet."

"Just wait a second!" Walter yelled.

But Katia opened a pocket on her bodysuit and tossed a tablet to Solanis.

She caught the tablet. On the screen was a list—her daughter's daily schedule. She scrolled through Ronnie and could see Gabby's movements for the past two years. Mealtimes. Playdates. Even medical visits.

"Walter?" Solanis felt weak.

Walter took two steps toward her. "Solanis, look at me."

She stared at Ronnie. Of course Katia had her daughter's schedule. She picked her up from school sometimes.

What was the point?

She looked from Katia to Walter. "What are you—"

The world came into sharp focus. She was suddenly aware of how far away from Gabby she was.

Michael's gun was out again.

She looked up at Walter. "No."

Her heart skipped a beat.

Walter stood between her and Michael. "We don't need to do this."

Katia spoke up. "I'm sorry, Solanis. We are wasting time. We don't have time."

He shook his head. "We agreed we wouldn't do this."

Greg frowned at the tablet from over Solanis's shoulder.

But Katia tossed back her silver hair and scoffed. "*You* said we wouldn't do it. My mother's not dying early because of her selfishness."

Solanis looked back at the schedule. She never should have assembled the tiles. She should have just tossed them out and reported them to SPINE. Why did her life seem filled with regret?

"Guys, let's talk about this," Walter said to the mercenaries.

"No." Michael kept the gun on her. "If you don't help us, you're not seeing your daughter again. It's that simple. Don't try to get off this island either. I'll shoot you before you take three steps."

"Michael!" Walter yelled. "We said we wouldn't."

"Don't be a little bitch."

"Walter, stop them," Solanis said.

Greg cleared his throat. "Wait, Star. Wait. I'll do whatever you want. No one has to get hurt. Don't take this any further."

Michael jutted his chin toward Katia. "Katia, debrief Greg. I don't know how much time we have." He glanced at the sky. "Can't tell if those are stars or satellites." He then glared at Solanis. "Don't think of moving. We know where your daughter is."

Solanis looked from Walter to Michael. Walter's face had hardened as he positioned himself between Michael and Solanis, blocking the barrel of his gun. He looked as if he was trapped in the middle of a bar fight, trying to decide whether it was worth interfering or not.

"You have a daughter too!" Solanis yelled at Katia, who proceeded to escort Greg a distance away. "You're a mom."

But Katia ignored her. She pulled out Ronnie and began to speak with Greg in hushed tones.

"Walter," Solanis pleaded. "Stop them. Please."

Walter looked around at his crew. "They're doing what they're trained to do, Solar. I can't."

"Aren't they *your* team?"

"It's more complicated than that," he said.

"Then un-fucking-complicate it."

"Please. There are checks and balances. I don't want this any more than you do. If you'd just—"

The rage boiled over, replacing the panic. *"But she's your daughter."*

He took a step away, his back accidentally pushing himself into the barrel of Michael's gun.

"You would just let your daughter die? You'd let them kill her?"

He blinked.

"You wouldn't dare." She felt the bile in the back of her throat—a bitter, thick sludge.

Walter stumbled. "She's what?"

She glared at him.

"She's mine?" He was stuttering.

"Ours." She turned her nose up at the man.

"I didn't… Why didn't—"

"Don't be fucking stupid," she said cooly, her time on the offense. "Nothing goes in and out. You know that."

"Solar, I didn't know." Walter's eyes softened. Then he gave a sheepish grin with a slight laugh. "She's mine."

Solanis gave a cruel, bitter laugh. "You didn't know? Yet you knew when to pull me out? Bullshit."

He frowned. "We don't know everything."

"Katia didn't tell you?"

"You didn't tell *her*." He kicked the sand. "She said she didn't know."

He wasn't wrong; Solanis had avoided the subject.

"You'd still kill a child," Solanis said.

"It's not like that."

"Protect her."

Walter turned back to Greg and Katia, who were still deep in conversation.

"Don't even think about it," Michael said. "I can take two shots. I'll kill her first. Give you a memory that will last long enough for you to know what you did before you blank out."

He frowned. "No. I don't like that." He looked back at Solanis. "Can you tell me about her?"

Solanis ignored him, crossing her arms.

Katia pocketed her tablet, and turned back to the group. "We're done."

Greg stood and brushed the dirt off his pants. He walked over to Solanis and gave that weary smile she recognized from when they were kids. The smile that dared her to believe the lie that everything was going to be okay. But this time, there was no foundation to make the lie convincing.

She knew what was going to happen next.

It was time to go.

"I can't..." Solanis said. There was an ache in her chest again. Her heartbeat was slow and dense, pushing against her rib cage with rings of fire pulsing. "I can't just leave you here. I'm not leaving you again."

"You didn't leave me the first time." He tapped his forehead. "Trust me. I can't remember much, but that much I know."

She stood close to him. "If we had left earlier..." She could smell him again. He was coming back. Salt, dirt, sweat, burnt plastic, and coconut. Not pleasant. Familiar.

"No," he said. "No. It's just the way it was supposed to be."

The sun was just about set now. The stars were coming out.

"You don't have much time, Solanis," Walter said.

Michael still had his rifle trained on them.

Greg grabbed Solanis's hands and clutched them tightly. "Star, I know you're mad at them, but you need to trust me. You need to do this for them. The Domes aren't safe."

She shook her head. "You don't understand. It's not safe out here either. Haze is out here. It's all over the place. After they get what they want, they mights still hurt Gabby. And then I'll be left with nothing. Gabby needs to be safe."

Greg stroked her cheek, smearing her tears. "It's hard. I know. What do I always say?"

"No," she said. "No."

He gave her a hard look. "Star, what do you know?"

"Can you just stay a little longer?"

"Listen to me," he said. "You don't have to leave if you don't believe them."

"Please?" She shook her head.

It was all too much. She wanted to go home to Gabby.

Truth was wedged somewhere between the gray of her kidnapping and this moment.

How had she gotten here? Why couldn't she have taken Gabby before she was kidnapped? They could have come back to the island, the two of them. Gabby could have met her uncle. They could have all hidden together. So much time wasted.

"I told them exactly how to build the tool that turns off BlackBox," Greg said. "Help them deactivate it and get them off your back. Let the Evergreens decide for themselves." He rubbed his temple. "I feel like I'm missing something. I know I am. Pieces of my life keep coming back into my mind like..." He closed his eyes. "Stop hiding, Star." He pulled her into a tight hug. "Nothing gets out of a snow globe. You're a strong, fantastic woman who can have the world bend at her will. You know that, right?"

She shook her head. "I'm coming back for you."

He gave her that crooked smile. "When you were adopted, that was the greatest day of my life. You know I had prayed, right? For some- one? I hated being alone."

A tear rolled down his face.

She cupped the side of his face in her hand. The tear was real.

"And they brought you home." He laughed. "And Mom said she'd..." He looked up. "She said she'd plucked you from the stars." He grinned, still looking up. "Look. You can see them now."

Solanis looked up.

The sea of stars, scattered over the earth, shined at them. Light from millions of years ago winking among the fireflies.

Oh, the fireflies.

"I asked her which one," he said softly.

"And she said all of them," she finished.

Greg did not make a sound when he disappeared.

21

COLLATERAL

Leonardo

Leonardo had Katia. He finally had her. He'd need to send officers to arrest her right now. Pull her from her job in the tunnels and throw her in a cell someplace. His fingers twitched at the thought of marching her out of her office and into the SPINE cart.

But the tightening in his chest, the dimming room, and his spinning head told him he was missing something.

He popped a peppermint in his mouth. An easy way to relieve stress.

Why had Katia sent a note to Solanis from Walter asking her to leave? There were probably two thousand people named Walter in Shamut. And they'd all been trained to see through the bullshit LTE had peddled for the past decade. Mr. Worthington had been clear— LTE would stop at nothing to see Shamut and his domes fall. They weren't willing to make the perfect sacrifice.

Was Walter an LTE leader? His name didn't come up in the Voice as a recognized antisocial. In fact, his name didn't come up at all.

Clearly, Katia was working for LTE.

But turning her in wasn't that simple.

He was compromised.

Yes, he was the one who had ordered his team to intercept the tiles, even if he didn't know what he was intercepting. But it was also he who had ignored the evidence.

Evidence he didn't know existed.

Fuck.

He could go to Kruger with his findings, only to be reminded that he ignored evidence because he was worried about being blackmailed. Would she kick him out of Shamut. No... you don't leave once you're in. But he'd be propagated, humiliated. But even worse. He would have broken his promise. He would have let Mr. Worthington down. Failures aren't useful. They don't redeem bloodlines.

My little lion. How did Katia know?

There wasn't time to sit around and feel sorry for himself. He'd had a reason at the time. He didn't want Solanis to know he'd killed a child, put a gun to James's head. But he had a good reason for it. He'd done it to save the others. The gun wasn't supposed to work.

Leonardo wasn't stupid. He knew if Solanis knew, she'd never let him near Gabby again. She was one of those *keep my daughter safe at all costs* kind of mothers whose kids grew up to be picked last on the playground.

Leonardo shook his head.

It was all for nothing.

Solanis had rejected him.

The door was closed.

Or was it?

He stared at the tiles. If he could bring her back home... No. He wasn't going outside of Shamut. Was it possible she was mixed up in an LTE conspiracy without even knowing it? She had, after all, not gotten the notes. She was bad at tech. She couldn't possibly know what Katia was doing.

But no one would know that.

Winston was right. People would assume the easiest timeline. They'd think she'd been complicit.

This wasn't her fault. Even Shamut was like Boston. She'd never be equal to inherited, generational elitism, even with her princess status.

But damn Katia. What kind of friend would risk putting her confidant in danger like this, mixing her up into conspiracies? And how was Katia getting notes from the outside? They always said nothing could get in or out.

Ms. Cassandra Price lived outside of Shamut, and yet she'd managed to give him a mission just fine. What was it Katia complained about all the time—the tunnels under Shamut being too small?

Was it possible she'd been going in and out? That would explain her missing her morning workouts.

But why would she want Solanis out?

Leonardo laughed to himself. It was obvious. If LTE had an ambassador on their side, they'd be able to deal a blow to Mr. Worthington. A massive blow.

So, for the past decade, Katia had been telling hard lies. The kind of lies that would get people killed.

His shoulder ached at the thought. He should take another pill.

These lies would get Solanis killed.

He needed to get to Katia before anyone else did. Before she could use her knowledge of Leonardo against him.

He would have to save Solanis Tailor from the one person she didn't expect to be saved from. And then she'd thank him. And maybe, just maybe...

No.

That was all.

———————

WHEN DIEGO OPENED the door to the quadplex, he took one look at Leonardo and Winston and scowled.

"What?" he demanded.

Leonardo faked a smile. "We need to chat, Diego."

Diego looked like a college professor. Earth-toned jacket, elbow pads, and shifty hands. He even wore glasses—not just for fashion but because he refused to get corrective surgery. Was he always worried, or were the lines on his brow because of his wife's vanishing?

"The girls are napping," Diego said.

"Girls?" Winston asked.

"Gabby? Luna?" he shot back.

"We'll keep it down," Leonardo said, shoving the door open wider and pushing past Diego.

The shared kitchen was filled with toys, food, and potted plants from well-wishers around Shamut. One of the plants had a note written on it, telling Gabby they'd be praying for her mother.

Diego reached over Leonardo and clipped the leaf of the plant that contained the note. "We don't want to scare her." He tossed the leaf into the recycler. "I don't think Gabby knows she's missing." He glared daggers at Winston. "Not sure why you decided to launch a marketing campaign right now."

Winston shrugged. "It's working."

"*Bring back our ambassador*? What the fuck? Who do you think you're speaking to? Solanis is outside. She's not coming back."

"Back off," Leonardo said, holding up a hand between the two of them.

Diego scowled and retreated further into the quadplex.

Like most living rooms in Shamut, there were plenty of plants growing in the windows, soaking up the golden light of the sun cascading in. On the far wall, there was a display that was currently off, and beside the stacks of cookies, cakes, and fruit, the room looked normal. Only the lights were all off.

Depressed people, Leonardo guessed.

Leonardo just came out with it. "We need to speak to Katia."

Diego looked from Winston to Leonardo. "Work."

"No. Try again. She didn't show for her shift today."

He gave an aggressive shrug. "She gets these migraines sometimes. Did you try the Fields?"

"Did she come home last night?" Winston asked quickly. He seemed to have picked up on Leonardo's triggers. "I know she and Solanis are close."

"Ambassador," Leonardo said quickly.

But Diego angled himself with his back to Leonardo. "When I came to bed, she was asleep." He gestured down the hall. "I took the girls to dinner. You know, when I heard."

Leonardo tried to ignore the messiness of Diego's passive-aggressiveness and simply nodded. He looked down the hallway. "Mind if I take a look around?"

"I do, yes. I don't need SPINE scaring the kids."

"But you said they're asleep."

"And I'd like it to stay that way until it's time for them to wake up."

"We can wait."

Diego folded his arms. "It'll be a while."

He looked at Winston, who noticed and gave an amicable smile.

"Diego." Winston pulled out the Voice. "Let's retrace Katia's movements." He angled his body close to Diego and hunched over the tablet. Diego fell for the human instinct to mimic and looked down.

Leonardo took his chance. He moved quickly down the hall toward Diego's bedroom. The floor squeaked as he moved. Diego's protests faded out as Leonardo focused on the doors down the hallway. Which room were the girls in? The essential oil diffuser that sprayed the scent of the ocean made the hallway feel artificial. He'd never been to the ocean himself, but he hoped it didn't smell like this.

He paused. A small snore drifted down the hallway.

One person.

He pushed open the door.

Tatiana had been standing near the door and jumped backward when he entered the room. Gabby was asleep in the bed against the wall. There was a cot set up next to Tatiana's bed, but given how the sheets and blankets were positioned, Tatiana and Gabby had obviously shared the same bed. A mountain of stuffed animals covered the plain wooden flooring.

"Are you lost?" Tatiana asked, peeking out at him from under her platinum hair.

Everything about Tatiana mimicked her mother, including her rude comment. She even put her left hand on her hip—a confusing gesture from a child. Her chin was softer like her father's. There was a photo of Tatiana as a baby with Diego and Katia around her hanging on the wall, broad grins on their faces as the fall leaves fell around them. There were several other photos around, including one that looked like

Katia's cousins—a mix of silver and black-haired people. This looked like the photo Childre had shown Solanis outside of the recycler.

"Who are those people?" Leonardo asked Tatiana, kneeling in front of her and pointing at the photo. "Do you know them?"

She stared at him. "My mom said not to trust cops."

"Me?" he said. "I doubt that. We're friends."

He had feared this might happen. Of course Katia's rebelliousness rubbed off on her daughter.

He smiled. "I'm Gabby's friend too."

Gabby stirred from her position in the bed and opened her eyes. She sat up and grinned when she saw him. "Leonardo!" She stood and walked over to the pair.

He patted Gabby on the head. She looked silly with her green hoodie coming down to her knees, the ComCen logo in the center. "How are you, Gabby?"

"I'm fine." She looked around the room. "Is my mom with you?"

He shook his head. "She's probably at work."

"Doesn't she work with you?"

He faked a laugh. "Sometimes she does." He pointed back to the wall and then looked at Tatiana again. "Tatiana, who are those people?"

Tatiana stared at him. He could almost see the gears moving in her little head. He positioned himself so he was kneeling right next to Gabby, who had one hand on his knee.

Tatiana nodded, as if coming to a decision, and walked over to the photo. "That's Uncle Childre and his family." She gestured to the silver-haired clan of people. "He's my mom's brother."

Leonardo nodded. This was a version of the photo that had broken Childre's mind. He'd need to go back and take a look at the picture when he left. There had to be something here that their techs had missed.

He could hear Diego yelling from the hallway; Winston had used up his goodwill.

"Did you see your mother last night?" he said.

Tatiana looked up at the ceiling. "I don't know."

"Try and remember." He looked at Gabby for support. "How about you, Gabby? Did you see her?"

"My mom wasn't home," Gabby said.

"No. Katia." He pointed to Tatiana. "Her mom."

The two girls looked at each other.

"Yes," Tatiana lied.

"No." Gabby shook her head.

Leonardo nodded and stood as the door swung open. Diego had thundered down the hallway.

"They're kids," Diego said. "Leave them alone."

He gave Diego a cold stare and told the Voice to station two officers outside of the quadplex. In full view of Diego, he told the Voice that the officers were not to leave Diego's side until Katia was found and that he was going to recommend Gabby be put into the care of another guardian while Solanis was missing.

"What are you doing?" Diego invaded his space.

Winston tried to push his hand between the two of them, but Leonardo grabbed the rifle off his back and used it as a barrier.

The girls screamed.

"Look, professor…" Leonardo gave a wide, dangerous smile, the condescending nature of the nickname dripping from his mouth. "Step the fuck up if you think you can handle the pain. I'm not the guy to mess with today."

Diego didn't step back, but he narrowed his eyes.

Leonardo almost wished the little man would try something. He'd love someone to punch. Someone to take out the energy that could not be spent outside looking for Solanis. He'd love to jam a fist into Diego's teeth, shattering them so the man would have to drink his burgers through a straw.

But that wasn't the point of today. Getting Diego fitted with dentures would be satisfying, but it wouldn't find Katia. It would not save Solanis Tailor.

There would be time for pain later.

———

Still no Katia.

The weights behind Leonardo's eyes threatened to drop them to his chest. He'd snuck a few hours on the cot in his office, but that only led to him becoming disoriented. He'd never been the type to take a nap and then wake up refreshed. Instead it was as if he'd spent the hour wrestling with his demons. He also suspected the reason he was so disoriented was the lack of windows here in the bowels of SPINE. The artificial light only did so much.

The fatigue was also because he was failing in his efforts to find who kidnapped Solanis Tailor.

Had Gideon Voss and his gang of LTE thugs been torturing her for the past forty-eight hours? Did they keep her up at night, demanding she tell them everything? And what was everything? Solanis was a new ambassador. She only knew so much. But there had to be a connection.

Katia, LTE, Solanis.

When trying to solve a complicated problem, he would often review his case notes before bed, talking out the crime with Ronnie and going back-and-forth with the whirring, chirping tablet.

As a kid, he'd seen the detective news feeds where the lead detective in his trench coat and flat-brimmed hat would build collages on the wall, full of clues, while violently mumbling to himself until he had a eureka moment. That was a chaotic way to solve a robbery. What would the detectives of yesterday say if they knew he just spoke to a computer to do what they did to a wall?

Leonardo stood, the cot creaking with relief, as he heaved himself toward the display. There was something he was missing—something that existed to bridge the gap between Solanis and Katia. He pulled up the case files again. Katia had been missing for the past twenty-four hours. She hadn't gone to work, and she hadn't been home. The girls had told her that much. Diego was lying to him.

Did Diego kill Katia? Wives were murdered all the time outside. But he wasn't the type. He loved her enough to lie.

Was Leonardo even sure she was still inside Shamut?

But how could she get out? She wasn't Mr. Worthington.

Leonardo moved tiles around on the screen, switching between his own notes and those from his team. His agents had interviewed Katia's office, and they'd all said the same thing. They hadn't seen her in the past two days.

He drew a line on the screen. On the top he wrote *Solanis*, and on the bottom he wrote *Katia*. He began to try and map out a timeline.

Solanis had gone missing forty-eight hours ago. Katia was last seen at her shift thirty-six hours ago. But for her shift the day before, she'd been sick. Leonardo traced Solanis's movements from the tank to the waterfall. He tried to zoom in on the face of the woman who had kidnapped her.

Nothing.

Ms. Price had been right.

It was as if she just didn't have a lower face. Everything about her was just erased. Well, not quite erased. Blurry. Pixelated. It also didn't help that the Field's uniforms were these horrible boxy robes.

Leonardo checked another report. SPINE had analyzed the foot traffic outside of Katia's quadplex. She hadn't been home the night Solanis had disappeared either.

He looked back through the footage again. The woman's face was still shrouded in a blur. He skipped over to the part where Solanis managed to smash her face into a tree and bounce onto the ground.

The woman with the blurred face pulled her up.

He zoomed in. The pixels were all fuzzy around the terrorist. He moved the footage forward some more. Solanis was yelling at the woman now as the woman prodded her forward with her gun.

Leonardo looked back at the slow-moving Solanis Tailor who was now creeping across the monitor toward the waterfall.

He looked back at the Voice. "Do you know where Solanis Tailor might be?"

The Voice returned with no answers.

It was worth a try.

Solanis was covering her ears now as the blast from the drone rippled across the screen. With her eyes closed, he could hardly tell she had black eyes.

He watched as the woman pulled a glass slate from her pocket and fiddled with it. She looked intently at the device, and the screen glinted. He had never seen anything like it. It looked like a keycard that you'd use to get into secure buildings where the Voice wasn't giving you access. He knew there were places in the Dome where you could only get access by swiping a card. The room that held BlackBox was one of them. Only the ambassadors had keys.

But this slate the woman had in her hand was different. She pulled it apart, and it doubled in size. The camera rippled slightly as he watched data appear on the tiny screen.

Leonardo pinched the screen, seeing if he could read the data. The focus wasn't sharp enough, but he caught a glimpse of something else.

On the screen was a reflection. The reflection of the silver hair.

Leonardo looked closer.

He was so close. His mind urged him to stretch beyond the screen.

And then he had an idea.

Leonardo told the Voice to isolate every single time the kidnapper's reflection appeared on the footage. The Voice beeped affirmatively and began sending back frames where the kidnappers reflection was visible. Thirty-two images came back. They combined and gave him the answer that both filled him with vindication and a deep sadness.

Katia's photo appeared on the screen, rebuilt by the reflections in the water, the slate, and other reflective surfaces. The anger inside of him grew. She was a fucking traitor. She came in here and stole Solanis from them. She had to be more than a mule. She had moved throughout Shamut with operational efficiency. Blackmailing him. Using him.

Does this mean Solanis Tailor was in on it?

She and Katia were best friends. Friends didn't hold each other at gunpoint.

Only sometimes they did.

Leonardo looked back at the screen where Solanis was frozen in time, a panicked look on her face. No, she was a victim here.

Unless she wasn't.

It could all be an act.

It was her eyes. They were different.

He'd tried to get past them, but the truth was always in the eyes.

Leonardo told the Voice to call Kruger. But it told him that Solanis Tailor had just reentered the Dome.

She was home.

And so was Katia.

The woman who had betrayed them all.

22

WEEDS

Solanis

The fireflies were back.

Which meant Solanis's eyes were deteriorating again.

She'd need to get back to Shamut before she went blind.

She studied her reflection in the mirror of the little cabin Michael had dumped her into when they'd returned to the yacht. Her dark eyes —the ones that had defined her existence for the past decade—were normal now. She could remember a time when her eyes had been a dark, impressive brown.

People used to compliment them.

After her adoptive parents had died, and Solanis had entered the foster home in Denver, the first thing the woman in charge had said was, "Wow. What pretty eyes you have." She'd then lectured Solanis that foster care wasn't going to be just like home and gave her a squeaky bunk bed in the corner of the room. When Solanis asked what to expect, the woman barked, "Predictability is unpredictability."

She'd been right.

The group and foster homes *were* unpredictable. Predictably cruel.

There, she wasn't Solanis. She was a number. Just one stat out of many. A dollar amount on a spreadsheet.

She'd watch as her caretakers received their monthly payments, gave her side looks, and treated her like a burden. One of the women who managed kids Solanis's age—Granny—had complained that since now Solanis was thirteen, she would only receive half of her usual money.

"The other half goes into your account. Fuck Denver. Stealing from the taxpayers." The squat woman spoke from her perch in front of the display. She had been peering at Solanis, her sloped toadlike shoulders rounding her back. "Maybe you should start paying rent now that you have dollars in your wallet."

Granny always smelled like pickles.

Solanis stood up for herself, the way her mother had taught her, telling the woman she couldn't spend the money on rent. It was against the law. But that had only made Granny madder.

Granny. A strange, soft nickname for a monster from Denver.

She told Solanis that if the world revolved around her then she could spin like the sun to prove it.

Solanis, puzzled, just stood there.

But the toadlike woman with yellow nails placed one of her fat feet into her flip-flops, stood, and creaked her way over to the girl. "Spin around," she demanded. "You're the sun, aren't you? Then spin for me. Like the sun does."

Solanis turned around once.

"No," Granny demanded, the floor creaking as she shifted on her feet. "Faster."

Solanis knew the sun rotated about two kilometers a second. She wasn't going to match that speed. But as she spun around in circles to please the sadistic toadlike woman, she knew what was happening.

The woman didn't care about the sun. She wanted control.

Solanis spun until Granny got bored and told her to go away. She stumbled down the hall, the corridor around her leaping to the left every few seconds as the earth moved too fast. The other kids in the home helped her outside, where she vomited in the yard and clutched the grass for dear life.

She knew Earth moved at millions of kilometers per second, and yet people didn't feel a thing.

But she felt the rotation. In the grass in front of the old creaky apartment building, she felt every movement.

She had retreated into herself, spending her nights staring at a hand-drawn photo of her parents. The man at the bodega had drawn her a photo based on the one she'd shown him on her phone. He'd used the fancy pens he kept under lock and key and drawn the four of them together—Greg, Mom, Dad, Solanis. She liked to look at them and pretend they would be together again soon.

Only Granny had found out. Solanis had been under her covers, using the light of her tablet to gaze at her parents, when the covers were ripped off the bed, and she was called ungrateful. The other kids in the shared room had sat quietly and watched as the woman ripped up the drawing. It had been on paper back then.

They didn't use paper now.

No. Instead, they were all addicted to Ronnie. Just like Solanis was addicted to her daughter.

Which was why Solanis trembled, alone in her cabin. She needed to be with her daughter. She'd been away for too long.

She swatted another firefly in front of her face. Of course, it ignored her.

Katia had lied to her—a lie that hurt deep inside into her bones.

Katia's rebellion hadn't just been a personality trait designed to give Solanis an outlet for her own freedom. No. She had been some sort of double agent—working her, using her for her own status. Katia had lied to her, manipulated her. And for what? So she could betray Shamut?

And Walter.

What had he done?

He'd worked with Katia, planned how to get her out, and knew that if she didn't comply, they could threaten Gabby.

He was willing to sacrifice a child to get what he wanted.

Men always had the audacity.

What would have happened if she hadn't done the Recycling and become an ambassador? Was there someone else Katia had been working on? Would Leonardo or Winston have been pulled from the Dome at gunpoint and whisked to the island?

On the island that shouldn't exist.

She could smell Greg.

The familiar.

There might not have been a Plan B. Sure, Leonardo had a brother. But did he love him hard enough for him to appear on the island? An island where the dead came back to life and meddled in her affairs.

Solanis clutched the flat disk around her neck to steady herself.

Leonardo also didn't have a daughter to threaten. But he could be threatened. Katia had evidently done so a few days ago.

Solanis looked up as she heard the sliding door to the bedroom unlatch and open.

"You okay?" Walter asked, staring at her from the doorway.

"I'm alive," she said.

He ducked and stepped into the room. He closed the door behind him and settled himself next to the desk in the corner. "I was wondering if you could..." He grabbed the back of his neck and squeezed. "Well, I thought it might be nice to learn more about..." He paused and caught Solanis's eyes. "God, your eyes have always been so beautiful."

Why did it hurt so much when he did that?

"What do you want?" she asked.

"I want to know more about my daughter."

"Our daughter."

He nodded. "Our daughter."

She didn't move. This man didn't deserve to know more about Gabby. He didn't deserve to know that she had a rebellious streak. He didn't deserve to know that whenever she got upset, she pinched the bridge of her nose—like her mother. Only when Gabby did it, it looked funny because kids shouldn't be stressed out.

How Gabby tested her.

How Gabby's face held the solid echo of Walter.

"Walter?" Solanis asked. "Why are you here?"

He stroked his facial hair. "I came back for you, Solar."

She rolled her eyes. "Why did they come with you? Michael. Katia."

"I saw an opportunity and took it."

285

Solanis leaned against the opposite wall.

He continued. "When you left, and I went to Denver, it took a few years. But the second Dome imploded, and I went to the site and did some work there with the cleanup. I had to determine whether people were ready to go to the refugee camps or not. You know, reintegration duty. Evergreens really do believe in Worthington, and you have to break their conditioning to get them to function outside. You know most of them are Vitamin D deficient? The kids are shorter. They have a hard time in wide open spaces."

Solanis folded her arms, half listening.

"I arrived at the site, and the hole was unlike anything..." His voice trailed off. "The worst part was that people were vaporized. It wasn't like Boston or Maine, where there were bodies. I mean, there were some, but many were just vaporized because of the heat and the explosion. In the first week, we dug a man out of the rubble. He was wearing one of those leaves, tilted to the side. Turns out he was an ambassador. You're one of those. Right?"

She nodded.

"But when we dug him out, he told us that the Dome was defective. Said that this wasn't an accident. They knew it was going to happen. I remembered escorting him to the medical tent as he was kicking and screaming and sobbing the whole way. Couldn't really blame him. There were all these cameras on him, and he'd been drinking rainwater without food for a week. Rainwater can kill you, you know?

"When we got him to the medical tent, he started freaking out again. He refused to be put under. He said he wanted to speak to the influencers. But he was weak. He needed help. But somehow, he figured it out. Used Ronnie to call an influencer over, and then media tried to get into the camp. We told them they had to wait outside.

"But then Worthington showed up. He landed in the field outside of the camp with his Evergreens and walked right inside. It was an experience. Like one of those mega church services. All those people reaching for him, crying out to him to save them. Haze sucks. It's hard to breathe sometimes. They really think these Domes are the way. There's a fucking waiting list.

"Anyway, he went right to the tent where that ambassador was. I was in the tent when he walked in, and you would have thought Worthington had killed someone. The ambassador started screaming, begging him to leave and telling the doctors in the room that he didn't want to see him. The ambassador was still too weak to travel. Worthington sat there and let him curse at him. The things he was saying… *You knew. The world will know.* It was a lot.

"But on my way home, Katia showed me a picture of you. An impossible photo. Of you. Inside. You were on a bench, speaking to Katia. You looked healthy. Alive." Walter paused, as if remembering. "And I knew I should have never let you go."

"Let?"

He shook his head. "Solanis. Not like that."

She shrugged.

"But that was when I met Katia. She showed me what we've shown you. The schematics, the plans, and the failure that's waiting to happen. And that was when I knew I should have tried harder to get you to stay." He let the words hang. "And because I fucked up at that, I will now do everything to get you out." He paused. "And now that I know Gabby is mine, we need to do this."

"Ours."

"Ours." He nodded.

"I thought Katia was my friend."

"She is."

Solanis stayed quiet.

"*She is,*" he said. "She got me because without you, LTE will kill every single person in that Dome."

She frowned. "I thought they wanted to get their families out."

"Different factions." He shook his head. "There's reasonable, and there's radical. Aiesha and Gideon Voss."

"Aiesha?"

"Doesn't matter," he said. "We'll go in, turn off the box, and then get back out. Katia is working to draw up the plans now, to make that device your brother was speaking about."

"If Shamut is going to collapse, why are there pilgrims huddled outside? Trying to get in?"

Walter sighed, looking up. "There will always be people who hope, ignore the truth."

"Why do you need to go back in?"

"Because I have to keep you safe."

Solanis shook her head. "That's not your job."

"As a father, I need to keep you *and* Gabby safe."

She flinched. "That's...not your job."

"Yes, it is."

"No, it's not."

"Yes, it is, Solar."

"Since when?"

His volume ramped up. "Since you decided for the both of us to lock yourself away in that cult."

Solanis recoiled. She had never heard him yell before. "You knew I was going. We decided."

"No, there was no *we*," he said. "You decided for the both of us. You just left."

"Walter..." She pinched the bridge of her nose.

"No, Solar. That's the truth."

He hadn't stood or anything. She wished he had. It would have given her something to complain about. But he just sat still at the desk, both feet planted firmly on the ground. His hands were folded neatly, but she could see it in the way his eye twitched. The way his ear wiggled when he spoke.

He was angry.

Or was he upset?

Frustrated maybe.

With her.

Solanis didn't like how that felt.

"Did you think what it would mean for me?" he asked. He didn't break eye contact. Most people would have by now. "You vanishing inside of that Dome."

"We had the conversation—"

"You had a conversation *at* me." His ear wiggled again. "I loved you. When you walked out the door that morning, it hurt."

288

"I did it when you were asleep," she said. "I thought if you didn't have to watch me leave, it would be easier."

"I heard you. The door jammed. The tug woke me up."

Silence.

"Do you know what you did to me?" he asked. He looked down at his hands and gave that heavy, hibernating sigh. "And now I discover that Gabby is mine... Ours."

Solanis stepped forward. "Don't bring her into this."

"She's in it regardless."

"Whose fault is that?"

"I didn't know she was mine."

She locked eyes with him. "That's what made the difference?"

He raised an eyebrow.

"You were willing to kill a child, Walter. *Kill a child*." She wanted him to feel those words. Let them sink in.

"It's not like that, Solanis."

"What is it like, Walter? What are you going to say to get me to ignore the red fucking banners from heaven?"

"It wasn't supposed to come to that. It would be a last resort. A long shot if we couldn't convince you to do the right thing."

She stared back at him. When he was upset, he always rambled on. He didn't disappoint.

"I didn't think it would come to that. I took a risk." He cleared his throat. "But you thought about yourself first, right? Like you always do."

"I begged you."

"You made that decision on your own."

She shook her head at the revisionist history dripping from his mouth. "You didn't fight it."

"No..." He maintained eye contact. "I didn't. You know what's funny? When you have all the information you need, you should make good decisions. But we don't all think correctly, do we? I should have fought harder. But I knew you were hurt. Bad. I didn't know what to do. I was too young. I'm different now." His boot squeaked as he leaned his foot forward. "If you tried that today, you would not leave."

"Excuse me?"

"I would have told you no."

"Told me?" She could hear him clearly. "Who the fuck do you think you are?"

"No, Solar. Not like that," he said. "I'm not that guy."

"You sure?" Solanis looked him up and down. "I hardly recognize you."

"Ten years will do that, Solanis." He held up a hand. "I'm not that guy. I would tell you that if you left, if you vanished inside of that Dome, I'd never recover. And I didn't. I still haven't. You hurt me." He touched his chest. "I don't know how you did it. But you broke something I had to rebuild. Solar, you are selfish and predictable. Most people are. It's not a bad thing." He raised his voice slightly, countering her protests. "But that was then. We have a new mission now. We knew you'd do whatever it took to become an ambassador. We knew you'd only think of yourself once you were inside. Explains why you would think you could take Greg home. That's normal. We're all here for selfish reasons. Katia for her mother. Michael for his kids. Me for you."

"Childre wasn't..." she started.

But he closed his eyes. His sigh felt different. The bear wasn't sleeping. "I don't want to talk about that."

A darkness brewed inside her. There it was again. That accusation that she was predictable. But was it such a terrible thing, considering the world teetered on such a fine point?

Walter knew her every move.

Had he told the mercenaries that he fucked around with Solanis Tailor, the ambassador inside of Shamut, when she was just a private citizen in a refugee camp? He probably told them all about their most intimate secrets. He was the one person on this planet, besides Katia, who knew her.

What was he expecting her to do next?

She had the sudden urge to do the opposite out of spite.

But Gabby held her attention, even from far away. Solanis needed to go back, hold her, and recenter herself. Walter had a mission, she had hers.

She could smell him; the sandalwood was stronger.

"Solar, I would never... I could never hurt her." His breath was warm against her cheek.

Solanis wanted to ignore him, to block the memories that came rushing back to her when he stroked her forearm. His calloused hands were a rare kind of welcome interloper. Strange yet familiar. It was as if his body was speaking a slightly different version of English. A dialect from long ago. The language nearly forgotten but familiar. He gently stroked her arm. Why couldn't she pull back?

"I can't let you go back in there without a plan to get you out."

Solanis closed her eyes. His hand encased hers in its rough warmth as he gave her a gentle squeeze.

She couldn't stop him.

His hair smelled damp.

"You're not leaving me again," he said.

She squeezed his hand. "She has your eyes. They're the same."

He looked at her. "I wish she had yours."

"My pools of darkness."

He gripped her, his breathing matching hers and his body signaling that they should be in sync again. She let the moment envelop her, carry her away

But Greg tugged her back to Earth.

Star, what do you know?

Her brother was dead. For real this time.

What do you know?

Walter and his people, regardless of their intent, had threatened her daughter if she didn't break BlackBox. Or was it Katia and her people? Solanis wanted to shake her head, but she was so deep in Walter's gravity well.

What do you know?

LTE would do anything to destroy the Domes.

What do you know?

Walter defended her on the beach.

Solanis shivered. She was cold. For real.

No, not cold. Walter had stopped touching her.

But she needed to focus.

Somehow, he was the key to this.

He'd come for *her*. On the beach, her gambit had worked. He wanted to meet Gabby. *His* daughter.

Solanis forced herself not to pinch the bridge of her nose. There was something there. Something she knew.

What do you know?

Walter hadn't left her side since the beach.

Solanis's fingers tingled. Gabby had a hold over him. He would not leave them. She was the perfect weapon.

Solanis was aware of the irony of using Gabby as a pawn, considering how she'd just slapped him for doing the same. She didn't like the idea. But no one liked the lengths they had to go to keep the people they loved safe.

She would need her ex-boyfriend on her side, and Gabby would just have to endure the discomfort. Safety came first.

She'd invite him into Shamut, she'd tell them she'd play ball, and then the Tailor women would do what they did best—bend the world to their will. There were bound to be other spies inside Shamut.

She'd try to mend things with Leonardo. He'd come around.

Solanis forced a smile at Walter who had been staring at her intently.

There it was.

A plan.

———

KATIA GLARED at Solanis when the group came together for one last meeting before returning to Shamut.

"They're going to lock you in the Darkness for a few weeks when we get back," Katia said. "The Evergreens are a suspicious bunch. They'll want to make sure you're still on their side. They'll let you out eventually, and that's when you need to get this done."

Solanis nodded, her mind elsewhere. How would she neutralize Katia? She couldn't just tell Leonardo. Katia had been escaping Shamut for a decade.

"You have your story, right?" Katia asked her as she opened a pouch and inspected her transparent mask.

"I was dragged onto a boat and held at sea for a few days." She waved her hand over her face in an attempt to swat another firefly.

"What are you doing?" Walter asked.

"Just...fireflies," she said. "We need to get back inside. I need my meds."

"You take—"

"They put it in my food every day. For my eyes." She pointed to Katia, who was still fiddling with the mask. "Do I need one of those?"

"You cry too much," Katia said dismissively. "Your salty tears will fuck it up. You'll burn yourself." She then turned to the captain, who was lounging in a nearby chair. "It's not raining, right?"

He shook his head.

She turned back to Solanis. "Just make sure you convince Leonardo that you're okay. He's going to be the most suspicious."

"Leonardo?" Walter asked.

"Did you not read your briefing materials? He's the other ambassador. The one who likes her. He'd probably die for her."

He stood. "I still think we should attack ComCen by force. Just overrun it."

"Stop, Walter. I'm done hearing you on this." She held up a hand. "We aren't an invading army. We are a strategic operation, minimal death. Aiesha was clear: *give them a choice, or LTE will choose for you.* We'd don't want that."

"Minimal death. Yet you want to kill Gabby?" Solanis spat.

"You need to get over that." The look Katia gave her caused her to wince.

"I'd kill one person to save millions," Michael said from the corner.

She looked away. Another firefly.

He cleared his throat. "I'll be in your apartment. In case you forget again."

"Forget?"

"Your job."

Solanis looked at Walter. "You're going to let him—"

"He doesn't get a say," Michael said. "He lost that chance when it turned out he was sleeping with you." He glared at Walter.

"That was a long time ago," Walter said.

She flinched. "I'm right here."

"You have a child with the bitch," Michael said.

"Still here," she growled.

But he ignored her. "You should have told Aiesha."

Katia glanced at Solanis. For a second, it looked like she had sympathy in her eyes. Maybe it was just the lights dimming.

"You should have told me," Walter said to Katia.

"I never told her," Solanis said. "I can't believe I'm defending you."

Katia looked away.

Walter took a step toward Solanis.

"No." Solanis held up a hand. "I'm fine. Back up. I said I'll help you," she said to the room—mostly to Michael. "But if you hurt Gabby, I'm done. It's simple."

Michael held up a finger. "You think you're in control? You're not special. There are other girls in other Domes."

She flipped her hair back. "I will be special," she said. "You'll be on my turf. And you'll need me to unlock the box."

He opened his mouth.

But Solanis didn't stop. "I'm not special, right?" she said in mock sympathy. "You can go find someone else, right? Other daughters to murder? Other ambassadors you can threaten to kill? So, if I don't work out, you can always go with someone else? Right?"

"Who the fuck do you—"

She took a few steps toward Michael. "You're a big guy. Find another woman."

"Your daughter is depending on you." He glared back. He tried to step backward but collided with the glass.

She glared at him.

These eyes could still bully someone.

———

RONNIE TOLD them it was time to get into the small boat that would take them to shore. Solanis followed the group to the boat, staying close to Walter. She needed him to feel her gravity. He squeezed her shoulder and handed her back the Voice. It felt so heavy compared to Ronnie. She tucked it into her side pocket.

She stood near the front of the boat, next to Walter. Her hand clutched the rope as they plowed through the waves to shore. She was glad she'd kept up with her morning workouts, otherwise she'd look pretty stupid falling overboard.

She chuckled to herself. At least now she knew where Katia had gone when she vanished for a week at a time. Out here with her ex. Just hanging out.

Walter stared ahead into the darkness, the fireflies surrounding his head. The lights of his contacts cast a warm glow. Solanis squatted, one hand still on the rope, and let her wet bag dip into the water. Once the bag was full, she closed it, sealing the water inside. She tucked the small bag into her blazer and straightened back up. She fought the urge to look around to see if she had been spotted.

That was how you got caught.

Once the group reached land, they hiked in the darkness, past the pilgrims who were huddled outside Shamut. Solanis thought she could see the massive half sphere that was the Dome glowing in the distance. But it was hard to tell.

Once in the tunnels, they hiked for a few hours until they reached a rope.

"Climb," Katia said. "And be ready to hide."

Walter went first, climbing up into Shamut. Solanis followed, Michael close behind her.

Her heart was so loud in her ears. Gabby was close.

It was a strange sensation, climbing from under a manhole cover and into the brightly lit side streets that were the outer edges of Shamut.

She looked up.

There were no stars here.

The Voice vibrated happily as it reconnected to the network.

Any second now.

Katia climbed into the street.

Solanis heard the drone before she saw it, the heavy chopper blades cutting through the air as the Klaxons sounded. Worthington's voice urged citizens to stay calm.

Michael pulled out his gun.

Walter took a step backward.

Now. Solanis ran toward Katia, startling the woman.

"Get down!" Katia yelled, her arms up in a waving motion. She probably thought Solanis was some panicked little girl, running frantically and searching for protection.

Confusion was good for what Solanis needed to do next.

Solanis pulled the swollen wet bag from under her blazer and thrust the salt water into Katia's face. The effect was instantaneous. The transparent shield instantly short-circuited. A loud hissing filled the air, and the crackle of electricity gave way to the smell of burning flesh as Katia's face flickered off and back on several times. She dropped her gun in shock, her hands smashing at her face and trying to claw the mask off.

Solanis punched her in the jaw, the dull thud barely audible among the noise of the combat waging around them.

Katia screamed, clawing at her face as the hydrophobic miniature robots bore into her skin and panicking as the water severed the mesh connections that held them together. Solanis didn't have time to see if the entire mask would be neutralized, but she'd seen enough.

She spun back around and grabbed Walter's shoulder hard. "We need to go."

He gaped at Katia and then at her as if he was seeing her for the first time. He took a step toward Katia, almost on instinct. But Solanis held his shoulder firm.

"You want to meet Gabby?" she asked.

He nodded.

"Then go." She pushed him forward. "Now."

He broke into a jog, still holding his weapon on the approaching SPINE agents who were appearing up and around the street. He shielded her from the blast of the drone, their earplugs softening most of the blow that would have otherwise forced them to the ground.

With a few bursts of his gun, the first drone hurtled toward the earth. Its blades spun dangerously close to Katia and Michael, who dragged her backward from the center of the street.

Solanis kept up with Walter, her gait staying as close to his shadow as possible. She ran, nestled into him, and used him as a shield. They fit perfectly, like dancers in perfect sync, her running and him shielding her from the falling embers around them.

She focused hard, typing a few words into the Voice as she moved toward the sidewalk. After a moment, the Voice confirmed her message had been sent. *Shivery.* They reached the nearest house, and both Solanis and Walter crouched behind a rack where four bikes hummed on their charging pads.

She watched Walter as he scanned the horizon, his broad frame crouched between her and the oncoming agents. She could almost see the gears moving as he seemed to map out the pathways in his mind to get them to safety. He was going to tell her they needed to take the backyards because the drones would be focused on the streets. But she knew the two of them couldn't stay together for long.

They'd need to split up.

"Walter," she said calmly. "You need to go. Now."

He fired his gun a few times and ducked back down, his back to the bikes facing her. He had a cut on his cheek. "I'm not leaving you," he said.

"You aren't leaving me." She grabbed his face, feeling the scruff of his beard and his clenched jaw. "But you need to go. SPINE is going to be here, and they will kill you when they catch you."

He stared at her, his hand off the trigger of the gun as it rested on his shoulder. "I'll come back for you."

She shook her head. "Not this time."

"I will," he insisted as he pushed her to the ground. Gunfire exploded over their heads. He returned fire.

"No," she said. "My point is I'll find you."

"What?"

She nodded. "Two weeks. I'll find you."

"How will you know where I am?"

"I have a plan. Stay hidden, stay low, stay quiet."

He looked confused.

She reached up and covered his mouth. "You can't say a word, so don't speak. They track our voices. In two weeks, say my daughter's name. Loud and clear. And then hide. And I'll find you."

He nodded.

"Trust me," she said.

He nodded.

Solanis pushed him back. "You need to go!"

But he refused to move.

Instead, he pulled her toward his gravity. Their lips met. As the drones cut through the air above them, Walter grabbed her hard, demanding everything from her. She let her eyes close as she felt the wind of the drone and heard the clatter of the rounds smashing into the bike rack in front of them. He held her tight, and she gripped his forearms with such passion that she almost forgot the reality of where and what they were.

They were out of time.

She pushed him away. "Go!"

But he didn't move yet. He reached forward, tapped her chest three times with his index finger, and mouthed the words, *I. LOVE. YOU.*

God he was Boston.

Walter took a step backward, his finger over the trigger of his gun. His eyes moved wildly, focusing on the surrounding area. He spun around and headed toward the row of backyards where the drones couldn't see behind the homes—not yet anyway. She watched him as he moved—his jacket kicking up in the dirt and his hair doing that thing where it messily spun in the air, illuminated by the roaming searchlights. He had only gone about ten meters before he turned his head back around, met her gaze, and grinned before vanishing into the darkness.

The universe purred inside her again.

As she threw her hands up in the air and walked toward the green chaos in the center of the cul-de-sac, she could still feel his arms around her, his body shielding her from the bullets, the sirens, and the shrapnel from the street.

No, she was not invincible—the tingle on her lips from his kiss was a haunting reminder of that.

No.

She was in control again.

Complete control.

23

THE GREAT MIRACLE

Manuel

Manuel tried to focus on his footsteps as Cassie, his guide, and he made their way closer to where they thought is mother would be. But Manuel was distracted. In the homes pushed far back from the side roads, were bodies. When the government had cut off FROST's sources of energy, people had died. They starved in their homes during the cold winter, pinned inside during the bombardment. By design, there was no place to run.

Manuel remembered his colleagues in Congress, demanding that these people, victims of a prolonged war, not be forgotten. It was a failed request. They had been forgotten. There were no long lists of names of the dead in the Free Republic, no memorials in their honor.

What if his mother had forgotten him?

What if Sylvia didn't recognize him? Would she look at him, say in her charming, clever voice, "I'm sorry, sir. I'm waiting for my son," and then turn back to her tablet and try to message him?

Manuel shook his head.

That wasn't going to happen.

She knows what you look like.

He shook his head again and tapped his temple.

Stop thinking like that.

Maybe he could show her the monstera? Show her how her single plant from a quarter of a century ago was now five separate growing thriving plants. How it had brought life to his office, to his home, to Cassie's home, and to the local library. That her green thumb had brought joy to so many others. To him.

He chuckled to himself. He was going to tell her about a fucking plant when he saw her. No. That wasn't what he was going to say.

He'd tell his mother that he loved her. Tell her that over the past twenty-six years, he'd never stopped thinking about her. That when his father was alive, he had never stopped writing to secure her release.

What would Sebán say in this moment? Would it be okay to be overcome with emotion when seeing your mother for the first time in a long time? Did his mother count as a confidant? What was the protocol? Was he supposed to just pick her up and carry her back to the jeep and get her back to Denver where she belonged?

Manuel froze.

What if she was dead?

The last time he saw her, she had been hit by the drones. What if they arrived at the location, and she was also abandoned—suspended in permanent sleep?

Manuel felt a nudge on his left. It was Cassie, encouraging him to keep moving. But he was stuck. He didn't want his mother to be hurt. He'd have no way of fixing her. All he had was a fucking water filter.

An untested filter to purify water she'd already been drinking for two decades.

Water didn't do anything for the dead.

Manuel grabbed Cassie's hand and continued forward.

His stomach was in knots as he tried to remember what she looked like, what she smelled like. He wished he could have practiced his movements in the mirror before he arrived and made a fool of himself.

The trio stopped, and their guide pulled off his hat, approaching Manuel.

"It's just beyond that hill. The farmhouse. I'll be right behind you, but I figured you'd want to do this yourself."

Manuel looked at Cassie, who nodded to him.

"I'll be behind you," she said.

He climbed.

There was a sprawling ranch nestled in the valley. Behind him, the sun forced his shadow over the fields below. A river lazily drifted by on his left, the murky black and orange staining the grass and rocks around it.

There were children in the field, their multicolored scarves blowing in the wind as they played. Adults with the emblem of the Red Cross on their backs handed out food and water and issued medical care.

One of the children ran to another, tapped them on the back, and ran away, giggling.

They were playing tag.

In the center of all of it, Manuel could see Sebán. His father had his hand straight out, palm down, making a lowering gesture.

Stay calm, Manuel.

He reached for his father. But one of the scarves drifted by, and he was gone.

Manuel took a few steps down the hill, each bootstep heavier than the last. He moved carefully around the swirl of children who ran around laughing, coughing, and giggling as they played their morning games. There was something medicinal in the air as he wove his way around the relief workers who ignored him.

A child bumped into him, falling. He helped the kid up as the kid hastily pulled the scarf back up over his face.

"Tag," the kid said.

Manuel ruffled the kid's hair. The kid gave a wheezy cough and a giggle and ran after his friends.

Up close, the ranch was held together by prayers and good intentions. The once white exterior was gray with cracked and bent siding. There wasn't a single unbroken window. The sloped front porch was filled with nails, rusty daggers poking through the peeling boards.

Should he knock on the door? Would a splinter give him some incurable disease? There were diseases here. Maybe he should just walk in. What was the protocol in a place when you arrived at your destiny?

Manuel decided to knock. But before he could, the door swung open. An old woman with a baseball cap on her head peered up at him.

"Your eyes are green." It wasn't a question. Just a statement. The old woman held up her forearm to shield herself from the sun behind him.

"I'm looking for my mother," he said. "Sylvia."

Behind him, Cassie's steps caused the porch to creak.

"Your mother said your eyes were like the leaves," the woman said. "She was wrong. They're like"—she coughed into the air— "emeralds. Pure emeralds." She looked down at the cracked and warped porch. "We're all mothers here. At least now we are." She gestured to the roaming children in the front yard. "There aren't many fathers left."

The children's laughter evolved into echoes.

The sun had moved higher.

"But you are someone's son, are you not?" The old woman reached up and touched his face. Her hand was cold, clammy, and calloused. "You look just like her. She always said, 'My son, he's a man from Denver. He will come for me.'" She pulled the door wider. "Be careful. The damage is extensive."

The entire back of the farmhouse's roof had been sheared off. Plastic sheeting did its best to cover the hole in the ceiling, but there were spots of mildew where the water had seeped in. Manuel could hear something in the air, like notes lost on their way to a melody. But he couldn't be sure.

Around him, in the corners of each room, women worked. They scrubbed clothing and counted food. Others had children in their laps, reading to them near the broken taped glass of once windows. Through one door, he could see a man leaning on a crutch as he pointed to a whiteboard at the front, three teenagers watching him intently.

The old woman moved quickly for her age. But her confident steps were as silent as a church mouse avoiding the exterminator.

The door at the end of his journey had been red at one time. Now, the paint had stripped away, and the knob was missing in action. But a hint of crimson trim—deep fire, like a sunset—still whispered along the door's edges.

"Go," the old woman said, stepping to the side. "You'll have to wake her." She smiled. "She said you'd come. Sylvia did. You look just like Sylvia."

Manuel pushed open the door.

Sylvia's black hair was tied into a bun. She lay on her side on a dark green couch, one hand resting on her chest, as she took shallow, ragged breaths. Her nails—still chipped but clean—were painted a dark green. A cup, forgotten, lay by her arm.

Plants filled the room, their vines snaking around the couch, the chair, and her arms and legs. She had fallen asleep while holding a pot, the dirt sprinkled on her chest.

He moved quickly. He needed to smell her, make sure this was really her and make sure she was all there.

But he stopped. There was something wrong.

Her left arm was missing.

He jerked his head up so he couldn't see the damage, feel the pain.

"Mom," he said quietly. "Mom? What did they do to you?"

Sylvia's voice rasped. "I saw you on the hill. I have this dream. Are you that dream?"

He kneeled beside his mother, his knee catching the edge of a stray nail. He ignored the wobble that jolted through his kneecap.

His mother was still alive. She was here. With him. *Right here.*

"No," Manuel said softly. "No... I'm not. This is real. This is absolutely real. I am real." He was convincing himself.

The light streamed in from the morning sun, reflecting through the window and making the leaves look so green. The dust in the air swirled as if they were fireflies. The room didn't look real.

But the woman smelled like his mother.

Sylvia smiled. "I fear I've fallen asleep, Manuel." She closed her eyes and then opened them back up. "I saw you on the hill. Like in my dreams. You reached for me, didn't you?"

The fire behind his eyes echoed the burning in his soul. The heaviness. "Yes, I was. For you. I told you I'd be back. I told you I'd come for you."

She reached her one good arm up and wiped a loose tear from his cheek. What would Sebán say if he knew he'd cried in front of his mother? What would Sebán say if he was here? Surely, he'd be proud of him.

Everything had led to this moment.

His mother reached down and adjusted the scarf around her neck. But it fell, revealing a hole in her throat. It was as if her neck had been slowly worn away, like a cheese grater from the inside. Smooth, not rough. Each time she swallowed, he could see the neck move inside.

She was burning up. Her forehead was clammy, her skin cold to the touch.

They had done this to her.

The earth had done this to her.

"Mother?" Manuel stared at the gaping hole. "They hurt you?"

"They're politicians. They dream in the sky, too far from the ground." She coughed, the echo feeling heavier now that her throat was exposed.

Cassie was by Manuel's side, tucking the scarf back around her neck and preserving Sylvia's dignity.

"I'm a politician." He clutched her hands.

"There's nothing wrong with dreaming," his mother said. She coughed again. "The water, Manuel. It's not good."

He nodded. His voice dropped to a whisper. "It's okay. I can fix it. I figured it out. I can help you."

She gave a little smile and breathed deeper.

She laughed.

"It's a bit late for that, don't you think?" she asked. "Help them." Her finger pointed toward the window, to the children outside.

"No," he said too loudly. And then, quieter. "No. I'm here for you."

"What about thereafter?" she asked. "This is only then."

Manuel took off his backpack. "Look," he said, rustling through the bag. "See…" He pulled out the wet bag and tried to undo the buckles. But his fingers were too fat, too clumsy. He couldn't squeeze the buckles to get it open. "This is it. The filter. The one that's going to change my world. It's in here. It'll save you. Them."

Sylvia breathed deep again and placed her hand on his. "Tranquilo, Manuel," she said gently. "How's my beauty?"

"Your plants are alive. They are thriving." Tears made lines down his face.

She gave a small laugh. "No. You're my beauty. Manuel, it's always been you." She stared at him, grinning. "You were and always will be my thereafter."

He tried to stop the tears. But they kept coming.

"Sit with me, Manuel," his mother said, her hand on his cheek. The tips of her nails nestled the back of his neck. "Stay here until it's time."

"How much time?" he asked.

She closed her eyes as if thinking. She opened them again, her dark eyes shining wet with tears. "Enough," she said. "It's enough time."

So, he stayed, his head resting on his mother's chest and feeling her breathe in and out—each time just a little less deep. He stayed until her breathing became shallow, and the light departed from her.

———

MANUEL WAS ALL CRIED OUT. Done.

He stood, unclipped the wet bag, and pulled out the filter. He looked at his mother for a moment, grabbed the cup from the floor, and then turned around. Screwing the filter together, he left the house. Cassie followed close behind.

The children ran around him, the scarves around their necks and faces wafting in the wind as they danced and sang. The tune was a playful dirge.

It was the scarves. The damage. War left scars.

This nightmare wouldn't end, would it?

Manuel approached the stream and waded in. His boots and socks filled. He took one look at the filter and dipped it into the black-amber mess.

Maybe he could die here too? With his mother. There was nothing else to do. She was gone.

He flipped the filter over until the liquid drained out into the bottom. He poured the remaining filtered water into the cup attached to his waist and studied it for a moment.

He hadn't had time to test the filter.

He hadn't had enough time his entire life.

Time had never worked for him.

But that didn't matter.

His mother was dead.

Fuck it.

Manuel drank.

The water was cool. Fresh. Crisp. It flowed clear from his cup.

Manuel, who had been living on lukewarm bottled water since he had arrived in the Free Republic, offered his cup to a child sitting on the side of the river. The child tentatively took the cup and stared at him, suspicion shading his face.

"It's okay," Manuel said. "It's clean." He gave a soft smile. "Drink."

The kid sipped the water and looked up at him in shock. He greedily drained the cup, held it out for more, and then ran back to shore with the liquid gold balanced between his hands. He handed the cup to another child and then ran around, jabbering excitedly.

Manuel didn't hear what the kid said. He simply added more water to the filter as another child came, holding out his hands in demand.

He complied.

More kids were in the water, joining the moment. They jumped in after him and took turns drinking. They brought cups, pots, pans, their hands. Their parents joined. The people surrounded him, their arms reaching and their hands pulling him back. For hours, he poured poison into the filter and out came cold, clear, safe water.

He was exactly where he needed to be. As if everything had led to this moment. He didn't care about the drone that buzzed overhead, or the people who cried on the shore, watching, reaching, and pulling.

In that moment, in the final years of the Free Republic of South Texas, there was a miracle.

PART III

THEREAFTER

24

PRISONER

Solanis

Fireflies in the snow, Solanis determined. That was what this room reminded her of.

No, this wasn't a room. This was a prison.

This white bed, the crisp duvet and pillows neatly aligned at the head of her mattress, were just lies. The table was bolted to the floor. The mirror that spanned the length of her cell wasn't a mirror. She had checked. Her thumb perfectly kissed its reflection when she pressed up against it.

It was a window.

They were watching her.

They still hadn't brought back her daughter. She had alternated between begging and demanding. One moment holding her chin high and barking orders as she'd seen Wick do, the next pleading and sobbing at the window. There was this constant ache in her chest, a fog that clouded her vision, and a chronic pain that crept through her body —a throbbing that made her wish for death. If she could just see Gabby and wrap her arms around her, she'd never let go. But this cell wasn't a pharmacy.

The window had remained silent.

So, Solanis did the second thing she did when she felt like her body needed a reminder of who was in charge. She made her way toward the resistance bands that were attached to the wall and tugged through a workout. The platform on the floor enabled her to run, and the corner would mirror the outdoors, showing her lush forests and Shamut's acceptable imitation of Boston as it mimicked her cadence.

Walter had been right; her workout was more challenging than usual. The air inside Shamut was thinner than the air outside.

After her workout, she dressed in all green and asked again for her daughter.

Nothing.

Ronnie—no, the Voice, insisted she read the guides that would tell her about her role as an ambassador. The books told her about her responsibility to check BlackBox monthly to ensure it was in working order, how she needed to report to the Higher Committee, and where she could find the access codes to her new accommodations. She'd been given her own private home. If she got out of here, there would be no more co-op living for her. Instead, she would have privacy, room service, and unlimited cart access.

But not Gabby.

The sliding door opened, and for a moment, she was hopeful that Gabby would run inside to see her. But it was just a healer—an older woman.

"Miss. Please. My daughter?" Solanis asked.

The older woman gave a warm smile. "I'm sorry, Madam Ambassador, but we can't yet. We need to run some tests. There are diseases out there that don't exist in here. We need to make sure you can't get anyone sick."

"What about you?" she asked. "Won't you get sick?"

The healer's smile was warm and forgiving. "We get inoculated, just like you will. Now, take your blazer off. I need to look at you."

"Hold on. I told SPINE that she's—"

"She's in danger. We know." The healer gestured to the chair. "Please let me do my job so we can get you to her quicker."

The healer was gentle as she looked Solanis over, asking before she touched and speaking in soft tones as she dictated her notes to the

Voice. The healer noted the lacerations on her feet, the slight infection in one of her ears, and the crowding in her vision. The healer took several blood samples and swabbed the inside of her mouth.

"Did you notice your haze scleral hyperpigmentation has gotten worse?" the healer asked as the Voice silently took notes next to her.

"There are more fireflies," Solanis replied coldly.

"We'll need to get you back on the pills," the healer said. "Your vision should clear up pretty quickly, including the fireflies." She handed Solanis two blue pills.

"What are these?"

"Your meds."

Solanis frowned. This should have been integrated with her food. This was a regression.

"New format. New drugs. Works better." The healer handed Solanis a cup and gave her a warm smile as she studied the pills. They had *ACER* printed on the outside in black with bright blue liquid inside. "Go on," the healer urged. "If you don't take them, you'll go blind. It'll take forty-eight hours maybe. That pill is holding back the worst effects of Haze. And not taking your pills while in captivity only made this worse." The healer held up her hand as Solanis tried to protest. "Most people in your position out there are blind. You don't want that. Once you're blind, you're blind." The healer smiled. "Take the pills please."

Solanis scowled and dry swallowed the pills. She looked back up. "Why does this keep happening? The fireflies?"

"You can see a bit more of the light spectrum than most people." The healer pulled off her gloves. "We aren't sure why or what it means. We think it's more of a nuance than anything. Either way, it doesn't last long. You'll just go blind." She collected her things. "Your pills will arrive in the morning each day. Don't forget to take them."

She left the room, and Solanis retreated to her tablet.

———

LEONARDO CAME AROUND NOON. He lurked near the door, his eyes flicking up and down Solanis's body. His presence should have been enough to give her some sort of relief, but his stiff reluctance to detach himself from the wall gave her pause.

"Don't worry," he said. "Gabby is safe."

She tried to give a curt nod, matching his standoffish energy, but she couldn't quite conjure it. She just stared at the snow-white table. If she said anything, the waterworks would come back.

So instead, she hardened herself and asked, "When can I see her?"

He moved to the other side of the table, directly across from her, and leaned forward, his palms resting on the flat surface. He winced and quickly stood straight up instead. "I read the medical report. Your feet, your eyes. What happened?"

She shoved a smile onto her face. "Nothing I couldn't handle." She reached out to him, to grab his hands, but he had crossed his arms.

Supreme Ambassador Wick swooped into the room and hovered over her, his manufactured green eyes peering deep into her. "Praise to Worthington." His voice wavered. "You're safe now, Ambassador." He beamed in her direction. "You're safe now."

"It's good to be home." Solanis's eyes never left Leonardo, who simply stared at her. Her chest was throbbing. "I need to see Gabby. Please."

Wick's smile vanished.

Leonardo pulled out a chair and sat. Wick walked around the table and pulled one out for Solanis. Neither of them spoke.

She felt cold. "What happened to her? Is she okay? I told the agents in the cart over here that she was in danger. Did you—"

Leonardo cut her off. "Solanis, I said she's safe. Earlier. You heard me, right?"

She crossed her arms. He was being rude.

"We have her. But the healers said you have to stay here for a while before she can come in."

"No," she said, refusing the chair that Wick gestured to again. "I need to see her now."

"She's okay. I promise," Leonardo said firmly. "Please sit."

"Leonardo..." What was he doing?

"Sit," he said firmly. He wasn't asking.

She stiffened.

He gestured to the chair again. "Please."

She shook her head.

He took a few steps toward her. "Hey." He lowered his voice. "The healers have said there are bacteria and diseases we need to be mindful of. We've been inside here for a decade. Safe. Healthy. We don't know what viruses have mutated out there. Please just sit down. We need to talk. The healers are checking. They'll have her here as soon as it's safe. My team has her. Okay?"

The throbbing in her chest threatened to break her. But there was nothing she could do.

So, she sat.

Like a dog.

At his order.

Leonardo returned to his chair, placing the Voice on the table, and yawned. He didn't cover his mouth. Both men looked tired.

"We need to ask you a few questions, Solanis," he said. "You up for that?"

She frowned.

Wick was nodding.

"Yes?" She didn't mean for it to sound like a question, but the walls were bending in on her. The room felt smaller. Like she was the one who had done something wrong.

Leonardo was still on her side, right?

But he ignored the upward note at the end of her sentence and looked down at the Voice. "I need you to tell me what happened when you finished Childre's Recycling."

She glared at him for a moment, wondering what would happen if she just didn't tell him anything. If she just held out until the healers finished their tests, and Gabby was brought back to her. But she wasn't stupid. They'd just wait her out. You could always outwait an addict.

She reached back in her mind to Childre's death. But everything was blank. She remembered Childre stepping into the swirls of the recycler. How he had been ripped apart. She closed her eyes, rubbing her sternum.

The ache in her chest was unbearable.

"Give us what you can remember first," Leonardo said.

"Katia pulled me out of the Fields. She had a gun. Told me I had to go with her." She looked at Wick. "I didn't want to leave, you know. I begged her to let me stay. I'd never leave Gabby."

Wick nodded, but Leonardo simply motioned for her to continue.

"She made me climb the waterfall. And I fell, and that's when I think you saw me, right? You told her to stop." She nodded at Leonardo, remembering how he'd been a beacon of strength before the jaws of the waterfall slammed shut. "They took me outside. On a large ship, a yacht. Told me they were going to hold me hostage. You know the only reason I couldn't come back was because you sent those stupid dogs after me." She glared at Leonardo.

Leonardo cleared his throat. "It wasn't my choice," he said. "Unlike some people, I'd never hurt you on purpose."

She gave a slow nod. Was that a dig at her? Or was he talking about Katia. But she just continued. "They threatened to kill Gabby. That's why I had to stay with them."

Wick nodded. "Do you remember who was on the boat?"

"It was a yacht."

Leonardo rolled his eyes.

"I think there were like six to eight of them. If you include the captain. He kept mentioning someone called Aiesha, who was paying for this." She gestured to the wall. "For the yacht."

He exchanged a glance with Wick. "The senator?"

"Go on," Wick said. "Who else? Was Katia their leader?"

"I think so," Solanis said. "They all seemed to listen to her."

He nodded.

Leonardo tapped the table. "So, Katia, the captain. Who else?"

She squinted and pinched her nose. "I need to see Gabby."

"We've had this conversation already," he said quickly. "Who else was on the boat?"

"I don't remember anything else."

"How did they take out your heart monitor?"

"They seemed to know a lot of things." She pointed out that they'd blackmailed her to get her to do what they wanted. She didn't mention the island or Greg, and she tiptoed around Walter.

"Was there any indication this would happen?" Leonardo asked.

She scoffed. "You're not serious."

"We just want to know what happened, Solar," he shot back.

"Don't call me that!" Solanis yelled.

"Why?"

"You don't have the right."

"Who does? Walter?"

Solanis fell silent. Did he know?

But Wick squirmed in the silence and spoke. "Ambassador." He was gentle. "I know this isn't ideal, but we're trying to protect you. If you were getting notes or indications that someone was trying to get you to go outside, it would be helpful as we figure out who the spies are."

Leonardo glared at Wick.

"Oh yeah." Solanis rolled her eyes. "Katia said there were spies, but she's a liar. So, I don't know what to do with that information. She gave me a message to deliver too."

"Did she give you a hint of who?" Leonardo asked. "Is it Walter?"

She shook her head and lied. "I don't know a Walter."

"You sure?"

Silence.

"How many?"

"No, Leonardo." She tightened her arms across her chest. "Do I need a lawyer? Or is my daughter in a cell someplace else?"

"Solanis, we are trying to help," Wick said, the calm never leaving his voice.

"We just want to know if there were any indications that this was going to happen. We are interviewing lots of people," Leonardo said.

"The kidnapping was a surprise," she said. "I didn't kidnap myself."

"Right," he said quietly.

"How did they get me out?" She pointed a finger accusingly at him.

"That's what we're trying to figure out." Leonardo didn't break eye contact. "You said they gave you a message. A task. Wanted you to do something."

"Shamut is going to collapse."

His eyebrow shot up to his forehead. Wick went pale.

"Really?" He looked at Wick, who scowled.

"Shamut is perfectly safe," Wick said. "Don't be dense."

"So she is lying?" Solanis asked.

"Katia lies about a lot of things," Leonardo said. "Evidence?"

"Documents, blueprints. They showed me a video of the second Dome—Shalina. They showed me the collapse."

Leonardo looked at Wick, who shook his head and rubbed his temples.

"Supreme Ambassador…" Leonardo said quietly.

"One second, Ambassador Walkenshaw."

The formality must have shocked Leonardo because he frowned and put his hands in his lap.

"Just tell her," Wick said finally. "She probably hasn't read the guides yet."

Leonardo nodded and pulled out the Voice. "You know they only told you half of the truth, right? The kidnappers."

She tried to keep her face neutral.

He continued. "Shalina did collapse, but it wasn't because of anything we did wrong." He nudged the Voice over toward her. The documents on the screen were too long for her to devour in one sitting. But there were highlights. "You know LTE have always hated what we stand for. Our mission is to save the planet." He swiped up to images of the people in red, holding their massive portraits and standing silently outside on the streets. "Those people in the portraits? The ones they hold. They chose to go inside, Solanis. And these"—he searched the room, looking for a word—"terrorists vowed to destroy what we are trying to do here. They are disregarding their families' wishes, Solanis. You know that, right? You understand?"

She nodded.

"Do you?"

"I haven't lied yet." Saying yes sounded like giving up.

He held up his hands. "I'm not the enemy."

"Just tell me what happened to the second Dome. It's dead, right?"

Wick cut in. "Hurry up, Ambassador."

Leonardo shook his head and then nodded quickly.

"The video's real, right?" she asked.

318

"Video?"

"The video they showed me. It's real, yes?"

"Walter?"

"Katia, Leonardo"

"It's real, Solanis," Leonardo glared at her.

"Why did it fall? Why did it collapse?"

"LTE destroyed it," he said, pulling the Voice back toward him. "I was trying to explain."

"You suck at communicating."

"I'm not a unicorn."

Solanis laughed for real this time.

His face relaxed.

"Katia said there were cracks in Shamut. How did LTE cause the cracks?"

"That's the thing. Every Dome has cracks. It's the natural give-and-take with the earth. Infrastructure deals with all of that. But if you're a bad actor, you can exploit these things. Anyone can knock over a house of cards."

"We're living in a house of cards?"

"Solanis…"

She sighed. "I want to see Gabby. She's in danger. There are people inside here who want to kill her. I keep telling you, but you just sit here asking me questions."

"I know, I know. It's hard to understand. I get it. They were brain-washing you. Trying to. We are fine, okay? You're safe, Solanis. Do you understand?"

But she couldn't believe him.

Leonardo glanced at the large window and then back at Solanis. "Do you want to speak to Ronan, the head of infrastructure? He can walk you through the truth. They usually give the ambassadors the tour anyway."

Solanis looked down at her hands. If seeing Ronan would get her back to her daughter, then fine. But she couldn't help but wonder how Leonardo and Walter's story danced so well together. How both had reasonable explanations for Shalina's collapse. Reasonable or convenient?

"Fine. And then can you bring me Gabby?" she asked.

"Ronan is a good guy. He's a little intense though." Leonardo tapped the Voice a few times, refusing to answer her question. "I asked Kruger to make the request. He'll come knocking quicker that way."

"And when do you intend to let me out of prison?"

He extended his arms. "You're here for your own safety."

That was a lie.

———

THE SLIDING door to Solanis's cell opened, and in walked a man who was so aggressively narrow that she was surprised to learn he was the infrastructure ambassador. She had expected a thicker man with a hard hat who looked like he'd spent some time catcalling women on the corner. But Ronan, with his angular chin, multiple rings on his fingers, and dangly earring, looked more at home at a communications gala than a construction site.

"Ambassador Solanis Tailor." He gave a deep nod in her direction, the golden bangles on his wrists clinking together. "I was so relieved to hear of your rescue. I assure you we were hoping to Worthington for your safe return."

The man swooped over to the table and inspected the chair next to Leonardo, who rolled his eyes. After giving it a once-over, he determined it was suitable and eased himself down.

"Ambassador Walkenshaw tells me that you have questions about Shamut," he said. "How the infrastructure team has been mitigating the natural fissures that appear in the structure of the building."

Solanis opened her mouth to respond, but he plowed forward, his rehearsed monologue manifesting as monotone.

"As you know, Shamut isn't just a snow globe cut in half and placed on top of a city—despite the name of the Founder's company." There was a slight bitterness in his voice as he criticized the name. "The exterior is built of a number of shingle-like flats that are on top of each other and give the appearance of a half sphere. Together, they are designed to hold incredible weight both in and outside of Shamut. A plane can smash into Alpine—our seventh project—and we are certain there won't be issues."

"Is LTE flying planes into the Domes?" she asked.

Ronan ignored her and just smiled, revealing an emerald embedded in his canine.

Would that have hurt?

"As you should be familiar," he droned on, "there is some give-and-take with Shamut's Dome and the earth. Earth is constantly rotating at a million kilometers an hour, and as a result, we must mold ourselves to that movement, and sometimes, we get cracks."

She frowned. "That's not right."

He cast a disapproving look toward her from over his nose. "Excuse me?"

"The Earth. It's not rotating at a million kilometers an hour. It's closer to a thousand and a half."

He stared blankly at her. "Irrelevant, Ambassador."

"If you don't know how fast Earth is moving, how do you know how fast it breathes or the pressure it exerts on the Dome?"

"Aren't you ComCen?" he asked. "You're hardly the person who should be lecturing me on the way things work."

"My parents were scientists."

"*Were.* And from what I understand, they're not inside Shamut, not a part of our community. Maybe you should cede your childhood fantasies of being a rock collector to the people who have the expertise."

"They're dead," Solanis said.

"A tragedy." He deadpanned.

This was the wrong approach. "Ambassador." She looked at Ronan, layering her voice with softness and manifesting the heaviness of burden. "Please understand. This is hard to accept after seeing the video they showed me."

He scoffed. "You're willing to lend your time and attention to an enemy who seeks to destroy the very foundation that Worthington built?"

"Katia helped build this place. She's the one who told me that all of this was going to fail. She's the one who threatened my daughter. I just want to make sure Gabby is safe. It's why I came straight to you when I returned."

"She wants reassurance," Leonardo said to Ronan.

Ronan shook his head. "Faith in the Founder should be enough. Why you would trust an employee who hardly shows up to work…"

She nodded. "What do we know?"

He rolled his eyes. "We know that you've been safe for a decade. Let that verifiable truth be enough. Don't let LTE set the agenda."

She stayed quiet.

He narrowed his eyes at Leonardo. He stood and pushed in his chair. "Visit the underground. Meet the barracks beetles who keep the sky up at night. Give you a better appreciation for their hard work."

Ronan looked at her expectantly, as if he expected her to nod along with his casual, erudite racism. But she just frowned. She didn't dare look Leonardo's way.

Ronan laughed at her. "You're not better than us, you know, princess." The dark lines creased his face as he hardened. "The earth doesn't kill the Domes, Ambassador," he said. "Doubt, nostalgia, self-ishness—those are killers."

He didn't look back when he exited the room.

"After you see that this is all fine, you'll stop. Right?" Leonardo asked.

"Stop?"

"Stop the antisocial bullshit."

Solanis snorted. What had gotten into him? "I'm not the one being antisocial. I was kidnapped from the Fields, and you couldn't protect me. You fucked up. What was I supposed to think?"

His laugh came from his chest. "You still called me to protect Gabby."

"Like I had a choice."

"There is always a choice," he growled. His left eye squinted into a wink as he stared directly at her. "We thought we had lost you."

Solanis opened her mouth, but he held up a hand.

"I'm not done."

She fell quiet.

"I know you can't see it through the sludge that's staining your eyes, but we did everything we could to get you back. I did every-thing." He pounded the table, winced, and then stepped into her face. "For the nearly three days that you were gone, I moved concrete to bring you home. I'd think someone who would want to reintegrate would be a little more grateful."

Solanis was taken aback. She'd never seen him like this before. Who was this angry ambassador who lashed out? He wasn't the victim here. She was. She was the one who had been dragged outside and faced with a horrible choice.

"You're different," she said. "This is about Dirt, isn't it? That's why you're being like this."

He clenched his jaw and shook his head. "No. I'm treating you like everyone else. That's what feels different." Leonardo paused, then said, "Don't throw this away."

Solanis tried to grab his hand. "I'm sorry. I didn't mean that. I'm just..." She searched for the right word, studying him as she did. "I'm scared. Please. You need to help me. Make sure they don't get Gabby."

"You know why he called you princess?" He took a step back. "You know that's what they call you, right?"

She was silent.

"The guys at work. The princess. *The Princess of Seaport.*"

She crossed her arms, her chin raised in defiance. Katia would have done this.

He walked to the door. "Come on. We have another stop to make today."

"Where are we going?"

"We need to talk to Katia."

"I don't want to see her."

"You will if you want to see your daughter again." He vanished through the door.

25

TORTURE

Solanis

The bots hadn't been kind to Katia. The left side of her face was hollow and lifeless compared to the right. It was as if it had melted. She still had most of her platinum silver hair, which did a decent job covering the scars Solanis had left for her.

Solanis had no sympathy for Katia. While unsettling to the eye, Katia still had a boldness to her that met the moment—even in a room smaller than her college dorm. The shock collar around her neck could have been made of diamonds the way Katia emulated the straight-backed queens of a long distant past.

When Solanis sat across from her, Katia slowly tilted the bad side of her face toward her as if she was intent on showing the scars and the robotic flickering that glinted from her cheek to her eye.

From the corner of the room, Leonardo asked, "You ready to give up names?"

Katia wouldn't stop staring at Solanis.

"*Katia.*" He raised his voice. "It's only going to get worse if you don't cooperate."

Her voice was strained as if she hadn't had water in several days.

There was a robotic reverb behind it as if it was filtered through a machine. "They're keeping Gabby from you."

Solanis didn't speak. She hated this woman.

"It's what they do, you know? To keep you in line." Katia coughed and leaned forward, her hair falling over her face. She flipped her head back up, and the hair fell back. "I bet they've told you it's normal."

Leonardo sat next to Solanis. "You can't keep lying to her, Katia. She's back now. She has the truth. LTE won't win."

But she ignored him. "Why did you do it?"

Solanis raised an eyebrow.

Katia scoffed, using one hand to gesture to her face. "This. Why did you do it?"

Solanis clenched her fists under the table. "You know why."

"I want to hear you say it." The robots in her voice were louder.

"You threatened to kill her."

She nodded. "And what are *they* doing?" She tilted her head toward Leonardo.

Solanis clenched her jaw.

"They're keeping her from you." And then, looking directly at Leonardo, she purred, "Isn't that right, my little lion?"

He shook his head. "Watch yourself. It can get a lot worse."

"Can it?" She coughed out a laugh. "I bet you've been waiting for this moment. To have me tied up in here at your mercy." She nodded toward Solanis. "But it's her you wanted. Right?"

Solanis frowned.

"You still watch her, don't you?" She lowered her chin, sighing. "Even after she laughed at you at Dirt. Does that happen to you a lot? The laughter?" She examined Solanis up and down. "*Don't look at Leo.* He can't help you. You're on your own. You know what? I underestimated the ever-predictable Solanis Tailor. Never thought you'd do this." She gestured to her face. "But then again, after you killed my brother, everything was fair game. I should have known you had more in you." She coughed. Drool fell down her chin; she didn't attempt to wipe it.

Hold on a second. "I didn't kill your brother," Solanis said.

Katia coughed. "Yes, you did." She held up her chin, her breathing a little faster. "You did. It was how you became an ambassador."

"Katia, this isn't why we're here," Leonardo cut in.

"Shut up, Leo," she snapped. "You know why I can do that, right? You think you still have a chance. You're on your best behavior. Still."

Solanis bristled. What was she talking about? Katia was spouting nonsense, holding whatever it was she had over Leonardo and suggesting she had killed her brother. That wasn't true. Was it? Childre wasn't her brother. He was just sick. A sick man she'd Recycled.

"Katia, Childre wasn't..." Solanis pinched the bridge of her nose, trying to solve the enigma that was Katia. *Give it a moment.*

Katia was a walking box of secrets. She didn't have a son—until she did. She didn't have a brother—until she did.

"Childre wasn't your brother," Solanis said, trying to convince herself Katia was lying.

But what reason would Katia have to lie right now?

Katia wanted to hurt her.

Lying would hurt her.

"I called you, you know," Katia said. "It was a moment of weakness. I know I broke the plan. I thought if I begged you, you wouldn't do it. You wouldn't kill him. But he was right. You'd do anything to get what you want." Her grin vanished. The edge was back in her voice, the darkness embedded in her words. "You ignored me."

Solanis pinched her nose, hoping. "You don't have a brother."

Katia looked down at her hands, her silver hair falling over what was left of her face. "You don't listen," she said. "Childre."

Leonardo waved a hand. "We are getting off track."

"Shut up, or I'll tell her what you did to that boy!" she screeched.

Solanis stood, nearly tripping over the chair as she backed up. Nighttime had crept into the cell.

In the corner of the room, she saw Childre—a vision, just like Greg. He stared at her, his body pulled apart and reassembled over and over as an invisible recycler tugged his atoms. His platinum silver hair waved in the nonexistent breeze.

No one else moved. They couldn't see him.

"What boy?" Solanis asked. "Childre Underwood?"

Katia glared at her. "There it is. Connect the fucking dots."

"No." Solanis shook her head as the Earth spun faster. She was on a scale, trying to balance between her feet. She refused to believe. She didn't want to believe. She'd never seen him with Katia before. They didn't even...

Hold on.

Wait a second.

It was the silver hair. Katia, Tatiana...and Childre.

"The silver hair," Solanis said.

Katia seemed to deflate. She stared at the wall behind Solanis, her back still straight and her hands resting in her lap.

Their silver hair, the way both of their faces curved in that half-diamond shape. Childre was much taller than the pint-sized revolutionary in front of Solanis, but if she had seen them together, she would have noticed the resemblance. She should have noticed the— wait. She *had* seen them together.

When Gabby had gone missing.

"You didn't say anything," Solanis said. "When you were with him. When Childre found Gabby. Was that on purpose?"

"He didn't kidnap her. Childre's sweet. He was sick. He's one of ours," Katia said. "Couldn't acknowledge him with the Greens nearby though. We had jobs to do."

"He's LTE?"

"None of us are LTE."

"But your last name," Solanis said in hopeless justification. "It's not right."

"Katia Anya Underwood Delgado," Katia said proudly, tossing back her hair again with a flick of her neck. "Marriage changes things." She winced, and the collar rattled.

Solanis was sick.

Childre still stood in the corner, torn apart and reassembled over and over.

"Walter had warned us," Katia said. "He said you would do anything to get what you wanted. He told us you'd want to be an ambassador, so you could be in control of everything. And you'd eliminate anything in your path. I guess it makes sense. Childre was in the way. We should have known better."

She'd killed Katia's brother.

She looked at Leonardo for guidance. "Is this real?"

"Who is Walter?" Leonardo demanded.

Katia looked away.

"It's our duty to Recycle." Solanis said stubbornly.

How had she let herself get to this moment? How had she decided she could be complicit in the process of recycling? They Recycled because it was good—for the community, for the ecosystem. It was their duty. But suddenly… suddenly, it hurt. The Recycling hurt more than it should have.

"I didn't know…" Solanis looked back at Katia, who seemed to glow under the light of the room. She shook her head as her breathing sped up. Her chest couldn't expand fast enough. She was in the water again, at the bottom, fighting to get out of Shamut so she could breathe. "There was no way of knowing. It was my job. I didn't know."

Katia mocked her in a robotic singsong voice. "*It was my job.*"

She was suddenly very aware that she was alive—her erratic heartbeat was proof of that. But she wasn't sure if she was okay. She was dizzy. She needed to go outside, ground herself, dig her toes in the dirt, and recalibrate her universe.

Childre wouldn't stop staring, his sad face breaking and reassembling.

She pinched the bridge of her nose. "Had I known…" She stumbled over her words.

"Sure," Katia said, checking her nails in mock defiance. "And that determines whether you'll murder someone? If you know them or not?"

"It's not—" Why couldn't she breathe properly?

"It's funny," Katia said. "You can do all the shit you do, but until it impacts you, you don't give it a second thought." She folded her hands and winced. More drool fell down her cheek. "People are like that."

"I'm sorry," she said. "I—"

"An apology isn't what we've asked of you."

She pressed on the space between her eyes. "I can fix this."

"Can you?" Katia asked darkly. "Or are you still lying to yourself?

You're their little killing machine, safe in a snow globe. I can tell. You believe them because it's easy."

"They didn't threaten to kill Gabby."

"Not all threats make noise. You're going to have to get over that."

"How can I?"

"Because it was our last option. We didn't want to do it. But he was right. He knew you'd do anything to keep Gabby safe. You're predictable." She threw up her hands. "God, we're speaking in circles."

Leonardo held up a hand. "Katia, you do understand if anything happens to Ambassador Tailor's daughter, you're in the next recycler."

"Nothing can happen to her." Solanis scowled.

Katia leaned back in the chair. "Solanis will never let anything happen to Gabby. Besides, I'm dead soon anyway." She looked around the room as if she was touring an apartment. "I don't have much time left. I know that much." She cracked her neck. "But there's still enough time for you to do the right thing."

Leonardo stood. "Katia, this isn't an LTE recruitment video. Just stop. Who else inside Shamut is a spy? Tell us, and we won't turn the bots back on. It's thanks to us they're not still eating you alive."

"You still think I'm LTE." Katia shook her head and laughed. "The reds have put fear inside of you. And that's why we'll win. Even in isolation, in this snow globe you fear what Aiesha, Gideon Voss and any rational person stands for. We are a million little embers in a million places. Little fires everywhere." She gestured to her face. "And about this? I kind of like how it looks. Pretty metal if you ask me. I don't think my daughter will like it very much."

"They'll eat the rest of your face," he said, motioning for Solanis to stand.

She didn't move.

Katia raised an eyebrow. "I sometimes envy you."

"How can you do this to Tatiana? If you die, she'll be all alone."

"Because the Domes will still be here even if just this one falls. I don't want her wandering in one of these death traps one day if she gets scared. You know, like you did." She folded her arms.

When had she become so cruel?

"He would die for you, you know," she said. "Walter. Be careful with that."

"You're going to abandon Tatiana when you die," Solanis said.

Katia opened her mouth to respond but closed it quickly.

"You can't be there for her if you're dead."

She shook her head. "My life was built for Tatiana. I'll reach out. Every second of my life is for her."

"If every second of your life includes what you did for Charlie, it's no wonder he's dead."

Solanis instantly knew she shouldn't have said it. She shouldn't have pressed that button.

Katia jumped across the table and tackled Solanis. Her wet, crusty cheek brushed against Solanis's face as she felt Katia's warm breath on her hair. Solanis flailed her arms, trying to push her off her.

"Go underground," Katia hissed, the urgency forced through the robots in her neck. "Talk to Heidi. Tell her the stars aren't real."

Katia howled in pain as the collar shocked her.

Leonardo pulled her away, punched her in the jaw, and then shoved her in the corner. Two more SPINE agents rushed into the room and pulled Solanis out into the waiting area as she struggled against them.

After a moment, he walked into the waiting room. "Are you okay?" he asked, looking over her for injury.

"I'm fine," Solanis said. She was breathing hard. She looked up at him. "Gabby. I need her."

"You know they showed you a version of the world they want to believe. LTE doesn't care if the planet dies. They think this is the natural order of things. Don't throw this away, Solanis."

"Leonardo, Gabby," she demanded.

He pushed on. "Katia wants to destroy this place because her mother abandoned her and left to live in Jericho. She's not doing it for the greater good. Even she's being selfish. We have to respect her mother's wishes. And everyone else who chose this. Your choice." He grabbed Solanis's arms. "Are you telling me everything?"

She tried to get out of his grip, but he held her. Her heart was going to pump out of her chest. His hands were firm. "Everything?"

"Everything, Solanis." He looked sad as if he was delivering more bad news. His ears almost seemed to droop, like a puppy who'd found out its master had to work late. "Are you telling me everything?"

Solanis heard it.

Me.

The conversation wasn't about the Dome. It had become about him. Her lying to him. He'd been different after Dirt.

Solanis shook her head and then nodded. "I've told you everything, Leonardo." She tried a small smile, the corners of her mouth dragging upward, held by fishhooks. "You need to trust me, okay?"

He didn't move. "Are you sure?" His hands hurt her. "Katia will lie, she will say anything to corrupt you. That's what LTE does."

"Please. I just want to see Gabby."

He let go.

"When can I see her? You can't keep holding me hostage."

He strode toward the door. "Go home, Solanis. You were never a prisoner." The sliding door opened, and Leonardo vanished into a long white corridor.

———

THEY SENT Gabby into the room right after Leonardo left. Her hair had been tamed into a single braid that fell neatly on the back of the small blazer they'd given her. The uniform made her look like she'd just come from an important board meeting.

For a second, as she stood in the doorway and stared, Solanis worried she was sick and might pass on viruses and bacteria that would hurt her daughter.

What was the last thing she'd said to her? Was it the apology for scaring her? Did she kiss her goodbye before she'd headed to the Fields? She'd said *I love you.* Right?

Gabby plunged herself into Solanis's arms, shaking as she tried to crush Solanis. She gripped as hard as she could. Solanis was going to break her, squeeze the air out of Gabby, until she stopped moving.

"I'm sorry," Solanis said, suddenly realizing how tall Gabby was.

Somehow, she'd forgotten. She'd dreamed of picking her up, holding her. "I didn't forget you. I missed you." She squeezed harder.

Gabby clutched her mother, refusing to let go.

"We can go home now," she said. "I'm not trapped in the box anymore." She pushed Gabby back and grabbed her face, inspecting her. Gabby didn't look hurt; she looked okay. "You're safe now. You're safe now that we're together. Okay?"

Solanis wiped the tears that streaked down her daughter's face.

She held onto Gabby and stared at the sliding door that had remained open. Any moment, she would be expected to walk through that door. Crossing that threshold meant she was one step closer to making the decision—the choice she'd been avoiding since she'd gotten back into Shamut. Could she just forget everything that had happened over the past few weeks?

No.

Walter was here.

She needed to find him. Then she had to go underground and investigate for herself. She'd learn what work needed to be done to fix her home. Then she could plan for the future.

A future where Gabby would never have to know what Haze was.

A future where Gabby would never wonder if she would have to pack up and live in a refugee camp.

And Walter would be a part of that future. She'd bend him to her will, her daughter as the mold.

A future made in her image.

A predictable one.

26

CEREAL

Solanis

The day after her parents died, Solanis had woken up in a bed that wasn't hers, in a city that wasn't Boston. The light patterns of the Virginia sun had felt similar to Boston's. She was in the same body as the day before, albeit a little achy and dehydrated, but when she wandered around the hotel, she felt like an impostor in another world.

She wandered in a dream.

This was how her new home felt.

Solanis leaned against the counter and told the Voice to open a private session. She hadn't even considered the transparency when she was DA, though there was probably some poor officer reading her messages back then. She tapped the screen a few times, pulled up the voice recognition program, fed it Walter's voice, and typed in her daughter's name.

The tablet gave a happy beep and then returned several close matches. There was a young man near Ruggles who had been speaking about her. Solanis pulled up the voiceprint. It wasn't Walter. Just a sympathetic man wishing her daughter well during a small group meeting.

She scrolled further down. Another match at ninety-eight percent. She listened closely.

It was Walter.

She tracked him and his actions over the past two weeks. The Voice showed that he had used the backyards to flee the drones that had chased him, that he'd hugged the backyard walls until he'd entered an empty quadplex and stayed for the past week. Remarkably, he'd only left once, to say Gabby's name.

He'd listened to her. He'd done exactly as she'd instructed.

Solanis tapped the tablet a few more times and then dispatched a drone to drop a message off at the quadplex. She set the tablet down on the counter.

She could feel Gabby watching her.

Gabby stood near the kitchen, lingering near the arch that led to the seating area. But she wasn't looking at Solanis; she was just tapping her tablet over and over, the menus static.

She watched Gabby from the corner of her eye for a few more moments and then cleared her throat. "You want dinner?"

Gabby looked up and frowned. It was like looking into her own past.

Gabby looked just like her.

"I'm fine," Gabby said.

"I'm going to grab some food." Why did this conversation feel so stupid? "Walk with me?"

She looked up quickly. "You can't order in?"

"I can." Solanis cleared her throat. "If that's what you want?"

She shrugged.

Solanis told Ronnie—no, the Voice—to bring them food.

Solanis moved to the living room, switching on the display and settling on the couch. Shamut was still gossiping about her resurrection from the outside, and the posters with her AI-generated side angles were still up. She cringed each time she saw them. A host said with glee that Worthington would be coming for Shamut's tenth birthday.

Gabby didn't need this.

Solanis didn't need this.

Solanis changed to a live feed of the Fields but decided she hated the forest. The memories stung. Her middle ached, remembering how she was tugged upward into the sky and pulled through the waterfall. Gabby would probably love to gaze at the massive trees climbing into the fake sky. She doubted her daughter knew the sky wasn't real. Should she tell her?

Walter had been right about that one. When she hadn't known they could turn the sky off, it had felt real.

Now, it just felt... She didn't want to think too deeply about it. She'd avoided looking up. Dreams crumbled when you realized they were simple orchestrations—your mind conducting an uncanny score.

Solanis focused on her tablet, tapping it a few times and pretending to do something, until Gabby wandered over. The girl slumped on the couch and stared at the display on the wall.

"The trees were really cool." Gabby pointed to the feed of the Fields, where the great oaks climbed into the sky. "We saw them on the field trip."

"Yes?" she said quietly. "You had fun?"

"I did. They said many of them are dead out there." Gabby angled herself so she was looking directly at Solanis. "Did you see any?"

"No. But I used to play in the forests as a kid sometimes. When we went down south."

Walter's hand gestured to her to keep up.

The rocks crunching under her boots right before they shared that kiss.

The smell of evergreen.

The scent of him.

The display faded into an overhead view of the fountain. The fish swam just under the water, darting to the left and right as they searched for food.

"They're cute." Gabby pointed to the display. "The way they swim in circles. Do you think they know they're in a fountain?"

"Probably not. Their world is small for us, but to them, it's massive. They probably don't even realize food doesn't come from the sky in real life."

She nodded. She'd kicked off her house slippers, unconsciously moving her feet in circles. "Thank you," she said, her head falling onto Solanis's shoulder.

"It's my job to keep you safe. Keep us together. You know that, right? That's what I am supposed to do. "

"No," Gabby said, grabbing her mother around the middle. She squeezed hard and pushed her face into Solanis's chest. "For coming back."

———

GREEN SUITED WALTER WELL. His beard was longer than it had been a week ago, and he was in desperate need of a haircut. His newly acquired pants were a little too large but politely buttoned over a tucked, green-collared shirt that would have made Wick's tops envious. He sweated under the coat that trailed his shoulders, the dark green making him look like a healer. He said he'd chosen the dark green because the people who wore it were creepy and usually left alone.

Fair.

"Thought you said you'd never be caught dead wearing green," Solanis said from her desk in her home office. She'd shut him inside the room when he'd arrived; she didn't want Gabby seeing him.

Walter didn't smile. He just pointed to the leaf on his lapel. "I had to borrow this."

This all looked familiar.

He put a cube on Solanis's desk. "You place this on the box. It calibrates, shuts it off, and we're done." He slid the cube toward her.

The cube was heavier than she had expected, weighted in the wrong places. Long ago, she would have sent this back to Omer to even out. Consumers hated uneven tech.

"We also have an interference device," Walter said, pulling a small flat disk from his pocket. "You press the center, and everything goes fuzzy. Cameras, listening devices. Use it when you go anywhere so they can't track your movements." He straightened back up. "And you need to use it when you get to the box. Otherwise, they'll drop it."

"Drop it?" She played with the device in her hands.

"The box," he said. "If they think the box is in danger of being shut off, they'll drop it into the vault below. But if we use this, they can't trigger the signal. Buys us time."

"Why don't they just drop it now?"

"It's a bitch to restart."

She nodded slowly.

"You're going to turn it off, right?" he asked.

She shook her head. "Stop."

"Solar…"

"Walter, why don't I have a nickname for you?"

He gave her a confused look.

"It didn't have to happen this way," she said.

Walter stayed quiet.

"You could've just come with me. Walked in the door. There's a Sprouting every month."

"It's not that simple."

"You could have just asked me to help. Katia didn't have to threaten Gabby. You didn't have to threaten her."

He sat on the edge of the desk.

She pushed. "You should have just sent me a note. You managed to tell me to come outside."

"We did."

"Did?"

"Sent you a note."

"You didn't."

"No, Solar. We did," he said. "We sent you two notes. Piece by piece. Had to smuggle them in. You should have seen Katia, running back and forth. The first one explained what was happening. The second was the final call for you to come outside. I think you didn't get the first one."

Solanis didn't say anything.

"I know you think we are some high-tech group of revolutionaries or that we are like the LTE leaders, but we're not."

"You're not LTE?"

"LTE isn't one organization. They're—" He tugged at his earlobe. "They are the loudest. Makes sense? And people use them. We use them. But they're violent. Gideon Voss, he has a list, you know? Of people they want to kill. Ambassadors. Supreme ambassadors. Worthington." He shook his head. "It doesn't matter. We have to work with what we have. And we don't have a lot."

"You said you would kill Gabby," Solanis said.

"They, not me." Walter insisted." He rubbed his chin and scrunched his forehead. "That was never supposed to come to that. Katia was supposed to approach you after you'd gotten the second full note and put it together. The one that told you to come outside. She was supposed to meet you in the Fields during one of those long thinking walks they make the ambassadors go on and bring you outside. Gently. And then we'd speak. We have to be careful. Some of the pilgrims are outside, the ones hanging around the Dome. They're waiting for someone like you to come out."

"Why?"

"Because killing an ambassador is a victory."

Solanis frowned. "Why didn't you follow the plan?"

"Why didn't *Katia* follow the plan?" he corrected.

"Walter."

"It's because when you killed Childre, she snapped."

Solanis tried to shake the ice from her veins, but her body refused to warm itself.

"She was upset."

The rickety chair was back.

He held up his hands. "I know you didn't know. But that's why you can't stay here. Any place that will make you murder someone is dangerous."

"It's dangerous out there too, Walter. I was just there. You saw—"

"Solar, come on. You have to see it, right? What they're doing."

"What are they doing?" Solanis felt the stubbornness return.

"Dome, Shamut, or whatever you call it is a fucking experiment. Worthington doesn't care about you any more than he cares about the planet. If he did, he'd tell you this place is going to collapse."

Solanis didn't say anything. She highly doubted Worthington

would spend his fortune on a temporary structure. Walter had been brainwashed by LTE, the mob outside salivating at the chance to drag her body down the street.

Walter threw his hands up. "This is a cage."

"We trade for safety," she said firmly. "We sacrifice for safety."

"But there are no birds here, Solanis. No stars—real ones anyway. This isn't real." He tapped the desk. "If we can't save everyone, LTE will do what they do best."

"How are they going to get in, Walter? Are you letting them in?"

"I'd never hurt you."

"But they would if I go out there. I have to keep Gabby safe. I know. It's predictable. I know I'm fucking predictable. I get it. But when you have kids, you'll understand."

He raised an eyebrow. "I have one."

"We."

"Ours."

Solanis walked to the other side of the desk. "Stay with me. Please. I'm going down there tomorrow. To below, where they work on the infrastructure of this place. I'll see for myself. And you'll see that we are fine." She grabbed his hands. They were cold. "Stay with us. We can try this. Again. We can try and make it work."

"It's dangerous everywhere, Solanis. But it's more dangerous in here. Out there, we live with Haze, but we are adapting. Most people don't live in Domes you know? There are places where Haze hasn't been like…" He paused.

Solanis knew the word *Denver* was on the tip of his tongue.

"Des Moines."

"We are staying in here."

Walter looked at his feet and then back at her. "I will not lose you again. You'll see. I know you. You have to see to believe."

She pushed aside the arrogance and let him hug her. He placed his chin on her head.

The nuzzling of his chin felt familiar. Correct.

But his arrogance worried her. He was so certain she'd leave with him, certain she'd risk everything to turn off the box.

But she had one more move to buy herself some time.

339

Solanis tugged him toward the hall, toward the heavier gravitational pull of her daughter. She put her finger to her lips in a shushing motion, guiding him past the closed doors and blank walls. Inside the room with a green night-light, Gabby slept, light snores filling the room. Walter leaned against the doorframe and tightly grabbed her hand as if she was going to just float away.

He wiped the corner of his eye. And then the other one.

Solanis looked away, almost embarrassed to see the man in such an emotional state. No. This wasn't embarrassment. She felt like she'd walked in on a private moment; it was uncomfortable for her. Guilt lingered somewhere inside.

And there was Childre, still dissolving and reappearing in the dark emerald of the night.

———

WALTER AND SOLANIS were at the table when Gabby entered the kitchen. Gabby, still under the influence of sleep, paused and considered them both.

In perfect Gabby fashion, she asked, "Who is that?"

Solanis forced herself to smile. Of course, her daughter had an attitude.

"Why don't you have a seat?" Solanis gestured toward the empty chair at the table.

Gabby made her way across the room, still gazing at Walter, before she settled down in front of her bowl of grains. Solanis had coached him on what to do, to pour the milk for her. He poured some for Solanis and then asked Gabby how much milk she wanted with her breakfast.

Gabby considered Walter for a moment and then looked back at Solanis. Solanis nodded in encouragement.

"This is Walter," Solanis said. "And he's important to us. He's important to me."

Gabby examined him.

Gabby must be able to see that her hair was similar to Walter's, that their noses echoed one another, and that her cheekbones followed the same slight protrusions of him. Was there some sort of instant connection that should have formed between the two of them when they met? Some biological, cosmic bond?

She looked back at her bowl and then at him. "Just a little. Please."

He poured her some milk. "How..." He cleared his throat. "How was that?"

She looked down at her bowl approvingly. There was hardly an inch of milk in the bowl; the grains were still piled on top. "That's enough," she said.

He nodded and added an inch of milk into his bowl. "I've always liked my breakfast like this." He pointed to his bowl—a direct imitation of hers.

She pointed toward Solanis's bowl. "Hers is always so soggy."

Solanis looked down at her cereal. Her grains were swimming in milk. "I don't want it to be dry."

"And I don't think saturated is right either," he said.

Gabby looked at him, who was peering down at her with a slight look of amusement on his face. "*Saturated*?"

He nodded and pointed to Solanis's bowl. "You see how her cereal is soggy because there's too much milk?"

She nodded.

"That's saturated."

"*Saturated*," she said again. She looked at Solanis, who gave her a smile, and then switched back to Walter. "I don't like saturated."

Walter leaned forward, grinning. "Neither do I. But between you and me, I like your mother anyway."

She snorted and began crunching away on the grains. He grinned at Solanis and did the same.

The knock on the door was harsh.

Walter grabbed his bowl from the table and tucked himself neatly behind the kitchen counter. Gabby stood, alarmed. He held up his finger, urging her to stay silent and seated.

She quickly sat back down at the table. Her hand shook as she tried to eat her breakfast.

Solanis did a quick scan around the room, confirming that a cursory investigation would reveal the room was for two. The couch and table looked correct. Her bedroom might not look right though. She had let him stay in there. Trust and warmth were interchangeable.

More knocking.

She started toward the door, but a whirring noise came from the handle, and before she knew it, the door burst open.

Michael shoved himself inside.

She jumped backward, the door just missing her.

"You didn't hear me knock?" he demanded. He tossed an envelope onto the floor and growled, "There's a letter."

"What do you want?" Solanis asked.

"Don't be rude." He stepped past her into the living room. He limped, clutching his arm, in his all-green jumpsuit, a jacket draped over his shoulders. "Where is he?" he asked as she quickly shut the door.

"Who?"

"You've never been stupid."

Walter stood from his hiding place in the kitchen and took three steps to the left. Solanis scanned the room, but she didn't see Gabby.

"Where the fuck were you?" Michael yelled.

Walter didn't answer.

"You went with her?" He jabbed his thumb toward Solanis. "You saw what she did to Katia."

"You should lower your voice," Solanis said, her hand raised in a lowering motion.

"She even moves like the Man from Denver," Michael spat in her direction. He sniffed hard and coughed. "Now, shut the fuck up. Adults are talking."

She studied him—his sweaty forehead, his shaking leg, and the coughing. He was sick.

Walter leaned backward, his left hand behind him.

Michael turned back to Walter. "The bots ate her face, Walter. *She* did that. Your whore did that." Another cough. "And you still went with her? We had a plan. We have days maybe. *Days* before they come in. And you're what? Playing house?"

"She's going to do it," he said. "She'll turn off the box. She just needs time."

"She's had time." Michael shook his head, pushing his temple with his left hand. He rounded on Solanis. "Why haven't you done it yet? What is taking so long?"

Walter crept slowly toward the hallway, his hand behind him, shielding Gabby from Michael's view. Gabby clutched Walter's belt as the pair moved to the left.

Solanis locked eyes with Michael. "You're sick. You need help."

"You can help by turning off the box." Michael took a threatening step toward her. "You should have the key by now, right? Go to the Communications Directorate and turn the box off. Walter and I can get Katia out of holding, and we can still get out."

She backed up, hoping he would take a step forward. If she could keep him engaged, it might lead him farther away from Walter and Gabby, who were still trying to get to the hallway.

But he didn't move. He kept pounding his head with his left hand, his right still under the coat.

"It's not that simple."

"We don't have options." he said. "Aiesha struck a deal. Either the box goes off or LTE comes in. And if we fail, LTE kills all of you. All. Of. You." He shivered and grabbed his arm again. "Your fucking bots ate her face. They almost ate my hand too, but I shorted them out. *But they ate her face.*"

"I need more time."

Walter and Gabby had almost made it to the hallway. But they'd stopped. She had gotten caught on something, and he was trying to shield her as she tried to untangle her shirt from the obstacle.

Solanis looked back at Michael.

But he frowned.

Then spun.

Walter charged forward.

But Michael pulled his damaged arm from under his jacket and pointed a gun directly at him.

Solanis tried to run to the other side of the weapon, to shield Gabby, but Walter had frozen, stopping a moment from the barrel. Gabby ran down the hall and vanished into one of the rooms.

Michael's hand had been eaten nearly to the bone. Solanis was surprised he could still move it.

"I would blow your head off, Walter, if I hadn't promised Aiesha I wouldn't."

"Put it down, Michael," Walter said. "We still have time."

Michael glared at him. "Three days. Aiesha bought us three days. And after that, they'll come in. Or sooner if we can't get this to work." He didn't lower his gun, but he gave him a hard look. "You can't trust Solanis. She's not gonna do it, is she?"

"I'm going underground today," Solanis said, her hands up. "To see if we can fix this. No one has to die."

Michael gave her an incredulous look. "Did you not just hear me?" He tapped his forehead with the gun and began pacing the floor. "They will come in and kill you."

"You can't get in without—"

"How the fuck do you think we got in here?"

"They'll close the entrance—"

"The tunnels, bitch. The tunnels. We know the tunnels better than Worthington. And the train, the one your fucking god-king takes to get in." He threw up his hands. "Jesus Christ. She showed you everything. Katia gave you everything you needed. The blueprints, the videos, the statements, the lies. You've seen it all, and you still need more?"

"Hold on—"

"Jesus fucking Christ. You do. You want more." He pointed his gun back at her. "I should just kill you. You're not going to do it. They said you had to see to believe, and they were wrong. We showed you."

She didn't flinch. "You realize if you kill me, no one will be able to open the box."

Michael shivered and coughed. He shook his head but didn't put the gun down. Instead, he swung it toward Walter. "You said she'd listen to us. You said this would work. You told me she was predictable."

Walter nodded. "She will do the right thing."

"No!" He shook. "You wanted to get your dick wet. You wanted this? The girl. Where is the little girl? She's the bargaining chip, right?"

Walter shook his head. "I told you, that's not going to work."

"Only it will, right? It's working for you. You're here, aren't you? We don't have time, man. They're gonna die if she doesn't turn off the box." Michael let his arm fall to the side as he lumbered toward Solanis. "Please, Solanis. I'm begging you. Just turn it off. They're going to die if you don't. You're going to die. They can't die like this." He coughed again. "My kids. They can't die."

Solanis stared at him. "Suddenly you care about children?" She pushed back her hair.

He walked to the bar in the center of the room and leaned on the granite, still holding the gun. "I have kids," he said. "I'm sorry." He began to shake and cry. "But they can't die. They can't die. I'm a fucking lobbyist out there." He gestured to one of the massive windows in the living room. "You realize if we can't do this, they'll kill all of you. It's only a matter of time before Jericho is hit." He picked up Gabby's bowl from the table, held it to his mouth, tipped it, and drained the cereal. "Why the fuck isn't there any milk in here?"

"You can't stay here." She pointed to the door.

He plunged his hand into Solanis's bowl. "There's too much milk in here." He tossed it into the sink, where it shattered.

She moved toward the kitchen, planting herself in his face. "You need to leave."

He shook his head and stepped away from her. "I'll get caught. And I'll tell them to come here. And you're all fucked." He thumbed his finger at Walter. "They'll take him too. They'll kill us."

She blinked hard. He wasn't wrong. But he couldn't stay.

He looked down the hallway where Gabby was hiding and then walked to the living room and sat on the couch. "Yeah, I'm staying here. Call it an incentive."

Walter grunted for Solanis to follow him into the hallway.

"Get him out of here," she whispered.

Would Gabby be smart enough to stay hidden?

"He goes out there," Walter said, "and he can get us killed."

"You watch him," Solanis said. "I'll send for meds. They'll send one of everything. Antibiotics, inhalers, steroids. They make everyone sleepy. After you give him the meds, watch him. Don't go outside. They can still track your voice."

"Wait. Right now?" He looked around.

"No. In here, you're fine. Out there, no." She patted him on the chest. "I'm going underground. They'll know how to fix this place."

"Fix— Solanis!" He glared at her.

"Walter, not the time."

"He just—"

"And you trust him?"

He fell silent.

She called down the hall to Gabby, who appeared and tentatively made her way toward them. She positioned herself behind Walter and peeked up at her.

The ache was back. Why was she standing behind Walter? She didn't know him. How had this happened so fast? But something else was behind the ache, a pulsing burn, like a torn ligament or muscle. Her entire life had changed and now, even in this most unpredictable of moments, she knew she needed to evolve too.

"You're going to school," Solanis nodded to Gabby. "Pack your backpack and don't tell anyone what happened here, okay?" Gabby would be safer around other kids, where SPINE could see her. Leonardo wouldn't let anything happen to Gabby, even if her relationship with him had soured.

"Will Tati be there?" Gabby asked.

"Gabby, you can't tell her anything." Solanis didn't mean to snap. But this was urgent.

Gabby took the hint and simply nodded. She still held Walter's arm.

As Solanis walked back to the living room, Walter and Gabby in tow, she wondered what her next move needed to be. Michael, who sat shivering on the couch, thought she was weak. Maiming Katia hadn't done much to gain his fear. He thought that was an anomaly.

She needed to make him fear.

Solanis squared her jaw and carefully kneeled in front of Michael and in one swift movement, grabbed his skeleton fingers, causing him to cry out in pain. She pried the gun from his hands and handed it to Walter. She pulled Michael toward her, her nails digging into his neck. "I will destroy you if you try anything."

Michael snarled, mucus bubbling from under his nose. "If you don't turn off the box, they will rip this place apart. And they'll start with you. You're on the list."

Solanis stared at him and make sure this pathetic man on the couch could sense the heat from the burns inside her. "You may not fear me now, but you will learn."

Michael's whimper was ice to her burns.

27

UNDERGROUND

Solanis

Solanis closed her eyes, focusing on her breathing, as the elevator carried her deep into the earth. The same earth that had shook, cracked, and killed her parents in Virginia.

She was sick. She wanted to hide.

The Evergreens upstairs told her it was a fifteen-minute elevator ride, but the clanging steel box might have been traveling for an eternity. She should have brought Walter down with her.

Solanis had to use her back to pry the elevator doors open once the box stopped with a grinding halt. The doors were similar to the airlock in her old home, just more rusted and warped. After a few good pushes, she managed to get them fully open, and she entered the bowels of Shamut.

The familiar tingle brushed past Solanis as she moved forward, squinting through the dim light underneath Shamut's infrastructure. This organic warehouse seemed to go on forever, merging the limits of her eyesight with the curve of the earth.

"You Solanis?" a short woman in a stained green jumpsuit with a red light and a helmet on her head asked.

"Sorry. I didn't see you there." Solanis extended her hand. "Solanis."

"Right." The woman handed her a pair of new boots. "These are for you. I'm Heidi."

She shifted in her tennis shoes but grabbed the boots. She stowed hers in a box near the elevator. Behind her, she heard the elevator doors grind shut and the box clang its way back to the surface.

Solanis turned back to Heidi and said, "The stars aren't real." She felt stupid.

But Heidi simply nodded and led her forward as the sleeping gods beneath them stirred.

Solanis tried to concentrate on the action around her, but her focus was drawn two hundred meters ahead to the flat wall that held the edges of the Dome firmly in place, the glass and silicone slats held together by the natural elements gorged from the earth. Like the rest of the cave around her, the wall was a deep cascading white-red-gray color wheel of rock. The Voice in her earpiece told her this was a mix of elements—sunstone, halite, and chromite—fused together to build the mighty foundation of Shamut. While she could not see it at this distance, she knew that fused within that rock were the giant tiles of glass and machinery that made up the massive curve of their home. The wall in front of her stretched left and right as far as she could see, following the natural curve of the Dome above.

Heidi nudged Solanis forward toward a nearby cart, where a man stood waiting. His dark green hard hat shined a red light in her face.

"Tailor." He pointed to Solanis.

Heidi nodded. "Ambassador Solanis, Salazar. Salazar, Ambassador Solanis." She spoke to Salazar directly. "She's good."

He nodded, ducked into the cart, and pulled out a dented, dark green hard hat. He thrust the helmet toward Solanis, who accepted it.

"You gotta put it on," he said, grabbing the helmet from her and placing it over her curls. He tugged the straps on the side of the hat a few times and, with a twist of the knob in the back, tightened it around her head.

"Thank you," Solanis said.

He paused, gave her a suspicious look, and coughed. His hand

349

lazily wandered toward his salt-and-pepper mustache but never made it. The scent of tobacco assaulted her. But he nodded and said, "Keep it on, Tailor. Rocks aim to kill. Here, let me look at you."

He took a step back, inspecting her with his sharp gaze. The knots in her stomach tightened. But he simply narrowed his eyes, sizing her up. She tried to look unbothered.

He stopped at her boots. "Are these new?"

She looked down.

"They're new," he confirmed. He took his foot, kicked the dark red clay onto the green of the boot, and rubbed the edge of his own worn boot onto them. The green was now a muddy yellowish brown. "There. Safer this way. Ronan has clean boots."

Had Solanis not been cognizant that she was a guest in Salazar's home, she would have reminded him who she was. But the indifferent authority radiating from the man forced her to take him seriously.

Satisfied, he pointed to the cart next to him.

Unlike the carts above, this cart was thicker with rubber bumpers around the edges. It looked like someone had added armor and rubber to a cart.

"Designed to keep us safe if the whole thing comes down. The doors can pop off," he said.

"It's not coming down, right?" She tried to sound casual.

He laughed. "You made a good first impression, Ambassador. Don't ruin it this early. You ever ride a WorthyCart?"

She shook her head.

"You might know it as a Worthington Tumbler. WorthyCart if you don't print money for a living. At least not in here anyway. Strong versatile cart. Door come off in a pinch, real pedal, backup gas tank." He lowered himself into the cart and pointed to the other doors where she and Heidi were to enter. "And we don't have time."

Solanis quickly entered the cart, crouching into the front seat. Unlike the carts above, the Voice didn't drive the vehicle forward. Salazar simply jammed his foot on the gas, and a great weight leaned on her chest.

Heidi popped between Salazar and Solanis from the backseat. She pulled the strap in the middle of the console. "Can we show her the panel that fell this morning?"

"Which one?" He laughed and gave Solanis a side-eye. "You been down here before?"

Solanis shook her head, holding the strap on the roll bar by her head. There were straps everywhere in this tumbler. "Not here. But I've been in caves."

He nodded curtly. "Stay close, Tailor. The earth breathes deep. Sometimes, it cracks."

"I know."

He stopped the cart and motioned for Solanis to follow as he exited.

Closer to the wall, every detail was clear. The panels she'd read about were so close she could touch them. But she didn't want to. These massive curved pieces of technology about twenty meters across and ten meters high mimicked the world around them. Had she not been this close, she would not have been able to tell these were the elements that made up the Dome's inner and outer shell. But looking around, it was clear that several of them were cracked and broken.

The panel closest to her flickered as it struggled to match the color of the earth tones around it. There was a screeching sound of metal in the air. The panels continued to bend and buckle as the Dome's tension pushed downward. Heidi gestured for Solanis to follow her as the three of them wove in and out between the members of the infrastructure team. They were running and dashing in different directions, yelling orders and operating heavy machinery.

About twenty people were clustered around one particular section of the wall, where around ten panels were cracked and warped from the middle. The Evergreens had a machine that was holding a gap of three panels open while another team hung from a beam, trying to push a panel into place to seal the gap.

Solanis pulled out the Voice and zoomed in on the space the team was trying to cover. Behind the hole the slat had left behind were leaking wires, pipes, and rocks. A man yelled for the team to stay steady as the crane nearby slowly lowered the new slat toward the wall. As the slat got closer, it became clear it would not fit.

"Shit," Salazar said, squinting.

"What's that mean?" She stared at the structure in front of her with confusion.

"It's the wrong size," Heidi said.

"Did they cut it wrong?"

Salazar snorted. "No. The holes keep changing."

"Changing?"

He nodded as if he'd just explained that the Earth was round to a child. "The tension, it's all over the place. Look." He gestured toward the panels closest to the workers who were trying to reconfigure the slat while it was in the air. "You see the edges of the panels? They can be cut to size once they are up there. But they all used to be that size. Now, they warp and shift faster than we can cut."

Sparks rained down to the ground as the workers sliced through the panel. One of them tossed down a tool and caught another device from his partner. The lights on their hard hats danced around the cave wall.

Salazar gestured that Solanis should follow him. She did. Quickly.

He pointed to more bent and warped panels. "They shouldn't be cracking. They should be flexible to the tension. They are supposed to breathe with the Dome. They're not. They lie about a lot of things. We fix it."

Solanis stared up in awe of the work being done above her. She couldn't see how high this part of the Dome went. Was it because it was simply too tall and too dark? Or was it because there was a layer of rock between them and the surface? Where were the tunnels they had used to get outside? Were they below or above those?

"We have a new panel we've developed that breathes," Salazar said. "But we can't produce enough of them. That's impossible."

He pointed to another set of panels shifting in front of her eyes. As she watched, the panel tilted slightly to the left, as if pushed. The panels around it all flickered off one by one until Salazar cried out.

"Panel!"

He pushed her backward several meters as the panel shifted again, groaned, and cracked in half. Silicone, glass, and a brightly colored liquid raced toward them from the side of the wall as the panel exploded. The other workers ducked for cover and scattered to avoid debris.

The impact caused the techs around her to fall. She grabbed Heidi to stabilize herself. Salazar cursed, spat, and ordered them back to the cart. The flustered team drove a construction robot toward the fallen panel while another group scurried around the gap toward the wall.

Once inside the cart, Heidi leaned over Solanis and pointed up toward the fallen slat. The construction robot wheeled it away. "That's the same design they use in Dome one, Dome two, Dome three, and this one," she said as Salazar drove close to the wall.

The knot hadn't left Solanis's stomach, yet both Heidi and Salazar seemed unfazed.

Seeing her face, Heidi nodded. "Don't worry. We'll be fine. For now." She stopped the cart at a gaping hole in the Dome, where a man with a hard hat stood in deep conversation with another worker. They both wore their overalls open, their compression monitors visible and strapped across their chests.

"Heidi." The man grinned at her and wiped his forehead. The lights dimmed on his hard hat. "Back so soon? Didn't think you'd come back down here." He shook her hand and then turned to Solanis. "Who is this?"

"That's the one who went outside. We saw the posters and stuff."

The other worker gawked at Solanis. "And you came back, huh?" She extended her hand. "I'm Majoria."

"She didn't know this place was going to shit." The man laughed. His name tag said *Frank*.

"Get out of it." Salazar shook his head. "We got new panels. We'll fix them, and the uppers can sleep easy at night."

"You mean like her?" Frank jutted his chin toward Solanis.

"She's good," Salazar jutted his chin toward her boots.

"How does an upper like you have mileage on their boots?" Majoria gestured toward Solanis's scuffed footwear.

Solanis made a mental note to thank Salazar later.

Frank chuckled. "You see the last time Ronan came down here?"

Majoria pranced around in an imitation of the man, her hand

shaking as she imitated the bangles on her boss's arm. "Oh, dear me. Are these rocks?"

Solanis laughed. "That was good."

She got a serious look on her face. "You see anyone outside? My son is still…"

Salazar cleared his throat and shook his head.

She stopped.

Solanis offered a warm smile. "I spent most of my time on a yacht. I wish I could help."

Frank squinted at her. "Your kidnappers wealthy?"

"Has it always been like this?" she asked.

"This?"

"The cracking, the warping, the failures."

He scratched his chin. "Not really. Started a few years ago."

Majoria nodded. "I started two weeks ago. I don't know what the fuck I'm doing. They only teach you how to do the shit they need outside. Build Haze fans and the like. Frank's showing me the ropes though. Says the falls are normal. Nothing to panic about."

"Not until Ronan came prancing down here."

Salazar spoke up. "He looked scared. About two years ago. Said we needed a new design."

"But this was always going to need work. We knew that already. Supposed to replace these panels every ten years."

"But Shamut hasn't been around for ten yet." Majoria tapped the panel closest to them. It flickered in response. "Almost but not ten."

Salazar nodded and pointed twenty meters down, where several workers were replacing a panel at ground level. "Our curved baby always needs work. See those guys? They replace about ten panels a day."

The men drilled the new panel in place while another was holding a massive tablet that powered up the screen. They pushed hard on the display as the drill finished its work and watched it light up, flicker, and then die.

"Gonna have to push double shifts if we can't get more people in." He shook his head in disgust. "The only thing that's happening—and this comes with age—is we've had more panels die. Whatever fucking idiot decided to integrate the panels and infrastructure into one system deserves death."

Frank nodded. "Or make them come down and fix this shit. For a smart man, the Man from Denver isn't very smart."

"Ahh," Majoria said, summoning another impression. "The man who raised the seas and fucked the greens."

The group laughed.

But Solanis was stuck. The panels and infrastructure were integrated into one system. Why was that a bad idea? Seemed like a logical way to keep things streamlined. She frowned. "You said the structure was integrated. What does that mean?"

Salazar placed his hand on the small of her back and guided her, so she was standing right in front of the hole in the rock. He placed his chest directly onto the rock in front of them and pointed up. "Notice how there's about three feet between the rock and the panels?"

But she couldn't nod. She shook as she felt the earth tremble under her chest. She'd been buried once. The rocks had felt just like this as she lay entombed in the earth, her father's dead body centimeters from hers, his blood dripping into her open mouth. He'd promised her that they'd be safe as long as they were together.

But Salazar either didn't notice her shaking, or he didn't care. He must've determined she wasn't close enough and pushed her closer to the wall. Small rocks and debris fell into her face, hair, and uniform.

She didn't want to gain a reputation like Ronan, even though her mind kept flashing back to the darkness, the distant bark of the rescue dog and the cold wetness of the deep, dark earth. But she was feared now. So, she tolerated his brashness. It would be over soon.

"Look there," he said.

She forced herself to look up. The intense vibrations shook her. She shivered but didn't move away.

"The walls of this place are made up of three layers," he said. "The outer panel looking out reflects what's inside. It's how the world can *see* what's going on in here. But that shit's fake. It keeps the military off our backs. The middle is the pipes, power, infrastructure, cooling." He took her hand and pushed it on the panel. "See how it's warmer here than there? Gotta keep it the right temperature. So, you've got the air gaps, water, power. And then you have the inner panel. Gotta keep the sky on."

She nodded.

This was how you turned off the sky.

"Only that means you get these junction panels. This might have worked on Mars and the moon. But ain't gravity a bitch?" Salazar pointed up to the panel that hung above them. "Panels have to do everything. So when they break, they cause a chain reaction. The cooling for the entire section stops working. Electricity, stabilizers." He let go of her and pulled her back toward the cart. He didn't apologize for her uniform. "So, now you've got ten panels that don't do anything." He gestured to the space around them. "We gotta replace them fast."

Heidi nodded. "Without working stabilizers, the panels can't shift with the earth's movements either." She pointed to a cracked panel a few meters down from them. "That's what happens. The weight is pressing down on all of this. And these cracks are just on the top panels. They go deep. They impact the water, and they spread. If the center can't hold, the rest of the Dome is compromised."

Salazar took over. "Luckily, we've got the best team in the world here. But fucking shit, we need more. Ronan shows up once a month with a new idea. But he's chewing glass." He pointed to a set of panels that had gone dark and protruded from the wall. "See how all ten of those panels are dark, and three of them are bent? We're gonna have to get that done tonight."

He walked away from the group and began tapping away on his tablet.

"Wait a second." Solanis caught up with him.

He stopped. "Yes?"

"You said you were behind," she said. "How far behind?"

"We are behind. But they're sending more people, and they should have a new design for us too. They're not all qualified. Most are coming from the barracks. But they learn fast. Eager to work. It's dark out there." Salazar gestured around him. "We got this."

"No." She stepped in front of him, prompting him to look her up and down. "Like with the current crew you have. How long till too many of these panels break, and this all fails?"

He scratched his chin. "Tailor, if we only have this crew, we're dead in a few weeks, tops. It's a shitty design. But like I said, that's not going to happen. They're sending in new tiles, new designs, and new panels." He pointed to the cart. "Take that back to the elevator. I've got work to do."

But when he reached to shake her hand, he pulled her forward and began checking the back of her helmet. She could hear him, speaking urgently in her ear.

"Heidi says you're going to get out of here. Take me with you. Please. I have a brother. Out there." He cleared his throat. "I didn't realize I'd miss him like this. I knew I'd miss him but not like this." He let go and walked away. "Heidi, take her back. It's dangerous down here."

Heidi climbed into the driver's seat of the cart. Solanis, shaken, followed.

"They're sending in more people?" Solanis asked Heidi.

"Most newcomers are assigned to this team." She grimaced. "The barracks, prisons, immigrants. But they're not sending new designs, Solanis." She drove the cart forward. "Good workers like Salazar, Majoria, Frank... They think they are. But you can't replace an entire Dome worth of broken panels."

The earth shuddered again under her.

"You know second careers weren't always a thing, right?" The cart bumped as it rolled back toward the elevators. "You'd work till you were seventy and then retire. But when we started living longer—a hundred, a hundred and forty—things changed. You can't just not work for sixty years while living off the first sixty. So, we shifted to second careers. Suddenly, executives got older, and some companies stopped hiring people under sixty to work in the C-Suite. But what's funny is when you go to the doctor when you are in your second career, they're just in maintenance mode. Sure, they fix broken bones. But they're not solving problems. They're just gluing you back together, fixing symptoms of what will eventually be death. Band-Aids."

Solanis squeezed the bridge of her nose. "Band-Aids."

"Until the inevitable."

She ran her trembling hand through her hair. The walls around the cart seemed so heavy. "So, this is the job?"

Heidi nodded.

"This is inevitable." She grabbed her knees. She felt woozy. Sand slipping through their fingers.

She looked at Heidi, who had stopped the cart. "There's no way. They can't fix it."

Heidi nodded. "Band-Aids."

The earth shook under her again as she pushed open the door and fell to her knees. She didn't care that she skinned them in the dirt. The pain meant she was still alive. For now.

How wrong she'd been.

The two of them stood a few meters away from the elevator that had returned, its doors propped open and its ominous orange-and-red light leaking into the dimly lit space.

Her soul ached. A false hope that burned deep and dark inside of her. The hopelessness of someone trapped in a black hole, searching desperately for the event horizon as gravity stole light away from everyone—even the gods. The gods that rumbled the earth beneath them. She knew this cause, her plan, was lost. Could you be feared if you were afraid?

"They're all going to die," she said.

Heidi nodded. She placed her hand on Solanis's shoulder and leaned against her. "Yes, they are."

"It's real," she said, her voice hollow.

"They weren't lying to you."

Walter hadn't lied to her.

Solanis cleared her throat and steadied herself. Another panel fell from the wall. The workers and machine techs rushed around the floor to stabilize the other panels that would no doubt crack and warp throughout the night.

The panels that spelled death—not just to her plan but to the people above her.

Walter had been right.

Her life in the Dome was dead.

What was it he'd said? That she needed to see to understand.

The guilt inside her was predictably cruel.

28

GRAVITY

Solanis

Solanis couldn't help but look suspiciously up at the sky to see if she could spot the panels that made up the red and pinks of the setting sun. Would one of them fall? Could you even call this blend of manufactured colors a sunset?

But their invisibility mocked her. It was all just brilliant colors, fake hues of red and pink. And the fake stars. Everything about this place was designed. Manufactured. The burden of knowledge weighed on her, creating a fatigue, a wandering helplessness she couldn't shake.

Walter blocked the door as she entered the apartment, his hands up in front of him in a calming motion.

"Walter, what..." She followed his eyeline and landed on Michael standing in the center of her open living room. He was pointing a gun at Gabby's head.

"Don't move," he said to Solanis.

She darted forward. But Walter swung his arm out, stopping her.

Michael was soaking with sweat, eyes bloodshot. "You need to do it tonight!" he yelled, his hand around Gabby's neck as the girl sobbed. Shudders traveled up and down his body. *"Tonight.* We can't wait. *Did you hear what happened?"*

360

She frowned. "Michael, put down the gun. What are you doing? What happened?" How had Walter fucked up so badly?

"How did you not hear?"

Gabby winced in pain as he squeezed harder.

"Stop!" Solanis yelled. "You're hurting her."

"Porciúncula collapsed," he spat out. "It's gone."

"How do you—"

"We have people. They know."

Gabby whimpered.

"You're hurting her!" Solanis yelled. She turned to Walter. "Help her! Please just stop this. Please!"

Sweat poured from Michael's forehead as he pushed the gun harder into Gabby's cheek. Her daughter clawed for her.

"It's going to be okay." Solanis tried to be gentle. "Just don't move. Just stay—can you stop jamming the gun in her face?"

"Why haven't you done it yet?" Michael ignored her. "Why haven't you turned off BlackBox? Ronnie still doesn't work in here. I found out the news from a courier. A RUNNER. I know you haven't done it. Don't lie to me."

"You're sick, Michael," Walter said. "You need to calm down. You're sick. You're going to hurt someone." He tried to move toward Gabby.

Michael narrowed his eyes. "Your fucking meds were going to kill me. Step again, and I will kill her."

"Then you'll lose all your leverage," he said. "Come on. We had a plan."

Michael laughed, shaking the sweat off his forehead. "Yeah. Before you started playing house. I'll kill you after the girl." He nodded toward Solanis. "She cares about you. I know it."

Gabby sobbed, shaking as she tried to get out of Michael's grasp. But he held firm.

"This isn't the plan," Walter said.

Michael nodded. "Yes, it is. Katia has plans. She always has plans. And this is what was supposed to happen if Solanis didn't do what we told her to do." He shook his head harder as if trying to dispel a bad dream. "You said she needed to see. Well, she saw, and it's still on." He glared at Solanis from his spot in the rising light that imitated the moon. "You need motivation, I guess. An incentive. Walk to your bedroom."

Solanis didn't move.

"Go to your fucking bedroom. You Evergreens understand English. Don't fuck around."

She moved backward, keeping her eyes on Gabby. The floors creaked as the group moved toward the dark hallway, Walter focused on Michael. She didn't turn on the lights as she walked down the corridor, thinking it would somehow give her an advantage. But the spotlight of the fake moon didn't let up.

Could she call Leonardo? Get him to help?

But he hadn't been kind to her. He'd been gone for a while. Suspiciously gone.

He'd only kill Walter.

Solanis walked backward into her bedroom.

"Get in your bed," Michael said. "And take your clothes off."

"Come on," Walter said, a heaviness behind his voice.

But Michael shook his head. "Not like that. I need security. So, take them off. Now. Your clothes."

Gabby sounded like the mouse.

Solanis glared at him as she pulled her dress over her head. She kicked off her boots, dirt falling onto the floor.

"All of them," he said.

Gabby whimpered under his grasp.

"Gabby, it's going to be okay." She nodded toward her as she pulled her sports bra over her head. "Just close your eyes. You don't need to watch."

"Your underwear," he said. "Everything." He sneezed.

"I'm moving," she said. "Just calm down."

Walter glared at him, his breathing heavy, nostrils flaring. Gabby continued to cry, but she'd stopped moving and stared at Solanis as she revealed herself.

Solanis stood, defiantly naked now, in the fake moonlight of the Dome. She refused to cover herself. She would not look weak. Not now. "Now what, Michael? It's your show. Got a good look?"

"I'm married," Michael said. "Get into bed."

She blinked.

"Get into bed."

Gabby closed her eyes.

Solanis pulled back the blankets and climbed into her bed. "It's going to be okay, Gabby."

It was strange, entering her cozy bed, her place of peace and serenity, while her body was amped up on fear. But she climbed under the covers and stared at Michael. Surely, he wasn't demanding she get a good night's sleep before she turned off BlackBox.

"Tuck her in," he demanded Walter. "Tightly. Like a burrito."

Walter hesitated.

"Or I will kill the girl."

Gabby screamed and began sobbing again.

Solanis wanted to die.

Walter walked over to her and began tucking the covers under her, swaddling her in her bed until she couldn't move a centimeter.

Michael motioned for Walter to stand in the center of the room. "She's coming with me," he said, gesturing to Gabby. "If the box isn't off by tonight, I'm drilling a bullet into her head." He coughed—backbreaking and wet. "Walter, follow me." He pulled Gabby into the hallway.

Solanis strained against the sheets. She couldn't let them take Gabby. This would not be the last time she saw her.

"Wait!" she yelled.

Michael stopped.

"You're a father. Right? Then please take her medication." She tilted her head to the bathrooms. "She has asthma."

He frowned. "Asthma?"

"It's a respiratory disease found in children. Chronic. Many kids have it because of Haze."

Gabby frowned.

He squinted at her.

"She needs her inhaler," she said. "All this crying and kicking and screaming. She gets too worked up and might die. Please don't let my baby die." Solanis pointed to Gabby, who was breathing hard. "She's panicking."

"That's in your control. Just turn off the box."

"If she dies before I can get downtown, you're not getting anything."

He considered it for a moment. Then nodded.

He dragged Gabby into the bathroom. She could hear him rummaging around. After a few moments, he returned. Gabby held the little red device in her hands, still breathing heavy.

She'd need to calm down if they were going to sell this.

"This it?" Michael asked.

"Yes," Solanis said. She looked directly at Gabby. "Don't lose that, baby. Okay? Keep it with you. So you can be safe. Control your breathing."

Gabby nodded, her breathing slowing. Solanis was about to tell her what she'd been told all these years, that they would be safe as long as they were together. But that was no longer true.

"You're going to be okay? Gabby? You understand me?" she said. "You're going to be okay. I am counting on you. You will be okay."

Gabby nodded.

Michael demanded Walter follow him to the living room as he dragged Gabby backward.

There was a yell, her daughter's scream, and a thud. The front door opened and slammed shut.

Solanis was trapped.

Alone.

She screamed.

The darkness didn't scream back.

———

SOLANIS STRUGGLED UNDER THE COVERS. Why had Walter wrapped her up so tight? She yelled his name a few times but no response. After half an eternity, she heard him stand and then his footsteps as he stumbled into the room.

He ripped the sheets off her. "I'm sorry," he said, holding his head. "I didn't want them to—"

"I know, I know," she said, quickly running to the closet. She pulled out a pair of pants and stepped into them. "It's fine." She grabbed a dress shirt and quickly began to button it up. "We need to get her back. How do we do that?" She closed her eyes, trying to keep her grip on the earth. But after all this time, she'd failed. She had thrown herself in front of the cart, but Gabby had still been taken. She grabbed the extra tablet on her desk. "Walter, find her. The inhaler has a tracker in it. Find the dot."

She shook her head. Hard.

He would find her, but what good would it do? They could just kill her daughter the moment he arrived anywhere close to her. No matter how hard he tried, he would never be faster than a bullet.

Her mind ran through the scenarios and came to one conclusion.

She was trapped in the cave again, shivering.

She needed to get Gabby back.

But how?

Solanis closed her eyes, pinching the bridge of her nose.

Something dark swelled in the back of her mind.

She opened her eyes. "Walter? Wait." She held up a finger, closing her eyes again. This entire time, the other side had backups for their backups. They'd known how she'd react to everything. She'd been predictable. They'd known her every move.

Why couldn't she do the same? She was an executive. She was the chief communications officer, an ambassador. She made plans for a living. But what would her plan be now? Turn off the box, right? Go straight to the room and turn the box off.

But what if that failed?

Then Gabby was dead.

She shook her head and paced the room.

She needed to know why Michael did what he did. No, she needed to know who controlled it all.

It wasn't Walter. It was Katia. He'd said so himself. Well, it was Aiesha, out there anyway.

In here, Katia was the puppet master. What did she care about more than anything in the world?

Oh.

There it was.

More darkness grew inside.

She needed Katia to fear her too.

"Walter?"

He stared at her.

"There are spies in here, right?"

"We have spies everywhere."

"Who do you have in SPINE?"

He paused. "I'll make a call. I can get their name. What do you need?"

She wasn't ready to say yet. "Get them on the line."

Why did she feel so calm all of a sudden?

She walked to the mirror and fixed her hair. She couldn't look wrong when she walked into ComCen. She should have put on a bra. She looked like she was headed for a hookup. Never mind. She grabbed a blazer and a scarf.

She picked up a pin from the basket near the counter and pocketed it, along with the key cube and the interference device.

Heidi's voice came from Walter's tablet. Solanis leaned over the screen just in time to see her messy hair and squinted eyes. Heidi'd been sleeping.

"Who is your contact inside SPINE?" Solanis yelled over Walter. She tapped her own tablet, calling two carts to come to her apartment.

Walter held up a hand as he spoke to Heidi. "We have two of them in SPINE," he said. "What do you need?"

"Access to Katia."

He blinked. "Katia?"

"Heidi," Solanis said over him, "I need access to Katia. Who will give me access?"

Heidi looked at Walter.

He nodded.

She looked off camera. "The name is in Walter's inbox."

Walter jammed his finger on the tablet.

Jessie SaToya answered on the first ring.

"Evening, Madam Ambassador." Jessie sounded so young.

"I need access to Katia's cell in half an hour," Solanis said.

"Ma'am, it's after visiting hours—"

"You don't give me access, and you'll be working in the underground for the next fifty years of your life. You'll break big rocks into smaller rocks until your arms fall off. And then you can use your forehead."

Walter took a step back.

Jessie nodded.

A notification appeared on the screen. Access granted.

"Walter..." Solanis headed toward her bedroom again. Her mind was moving quickly, the gears turning and shifting as she rearranged the next few hours.

A firefly wandered past.

Walter trailed her.

"Gabby's location will be on here with her inhaler." She stopped, refusing to let go of the tablet. Something nagged at her.

"What?" He frowned. "I can get Gabby,"

"*No, no, no, no, no.*" She stared at him as the darkness completed its takeover of her mind. She knew what she had to do, and for some reason, it felt so easy. Her ex-boyfriend, despite everything he'd done, looked incredibly innocent with the subterfuge moonlight highlighting his brown hair, reflecting in his caffeinated eyes. "I need them not to kill her."

He nodded. "Right. I'll go get her."

"Michael, even though he's sick, is listening to Katia. Not you." She closed her eyes again. "You can't talk him down. He's looked at you differently ever since the island."

"Solanis?"

"All Katia cares about is Tatiana. She won't lose another child."

"Solar?" He gave her a strange look.

"I am going to turn off the box. But if I can't get it off, I am going to find Katia and demand she release Gabby. But she's going to say no. I need leverage. I need a needle. And for that, I need you to find Tatiana." She looked down at the Voice, where the small green dot

367

blinked silently. It hovered over Katia's quadplex. Tatiana would be there; Katia had said so herself. "Find Tatiana first. The girls will probably be together. Michael doesn't strike me as someone with an imagination. And when you find her..." She paused and tilted her head slightly to the right, prepared to say what she needed to make him fear her too. "You need to call me. Make sure when you call me, your gun is pointed to her head. You must be ready to pull the trigger."

Walter took a step back. "She's a child."

"So is *your* daughter." She pushed the tablet into his hand. "We don't have a lot of time." The Voice dinged. Her cart was here. "I will be at the Darkness in an hour. You *need* to have Tatiana in an hour. You *need* to have *our* daughter in an hour."

"Hold on." His eyes were wide. "Solanis, I'm not—"

"Walter, you once said you loved me. Prove it."

"Solar..."

She could see his mind moving. "Both girls, Walter. Point the gun at her head."

Katia had said it herself.

He would die for you.

My life was built for Tatiana.

Every second of my life is for her.

And Walter would do anything for Gabby.

Predictability wasn't a one-way street.

"Solanis," he said, "this isn't you."

"No one is this person until they are." Solanis shook her head. Everything was so incredibly clear. "This is how you keep Gabby safe. Get her for me. Do this for me. And then we can leave together." She wanted to smile, but her mouth didn't work properly.

"This isn't you," he said. He had taken a step back, into the shadows. The moonlight was empty in front of him.

She let out a bitter laugh and took three steps forward. She stared directly at him. "I'm not the broken girl you dragged out of here." She gritted her teeth and braced herself.

She needed him to do this.

If there was anyone in this world who would always come back to her, it was him. He'd come this far. Abandoning her would never be an option.

She needed him to not fight her.

And to do that, she needed to hurt him. "Love me, Walter. Love me."

She shoved him. Hard.

He stared at her as if she were a stranger—a look that almost broke her.

But after a moment, he simply nodded twice, turned, and sprinted out of the home.

Katia had been right.

He'd forgive her.

He'd have no choice.

Nothing can escape gravity.

29

BROKEN

Walter

There were five people inside the home. Three bigger figures huddled in what looked like the main seating area, and two smaller figures were together in the back room. That would be Gabby and... What had the other kid's name been?

Walter shook his head.

He was sleep deprived. Aiesha had said to expect that the air was thin inside Shamut. He needed to go easy on the stimulants too, but the last few weeks of huddling in the dark quadplex, with every creak and outdoor movement keeping him alert, had exhausted him. His coach would have told him to take a deep breath and center himself.

Walter did just that. He shifted his feet. Leaning on his left leg too much had made it tingly. He tapped the leg a few times and checked his watch. He still had time. Solanis had said he had, what, an hour? He tested the strength of his left leg and found things pretty stable. He didn't want to limp his way into the house. Limping was a good way to get yourself noticed by the wrong person—or drone.

It was like how he'd noticed the changes in Solanis Tailor. And not for the better. There had been something inside of Walter Mustafa that had hoped she'd be exactly the same—that she would have only grown *slightly* older, *slightly* wiser after being locked up for a decade. But his optimism was misplaced. While the Solanis Tailor of today was still filled with the anxiety of yesterday, there was a rage inside her, like an animal trying to escape a cage. An animal that would hurt itself and others trying to get free. That was when animals became monsters.

He blinked rapidly, switching his contacts from heat to night mode. The home, as clear as day in front of him, looked normal enough. Most homes with hostages inside of them looked normal from the outside. The intelligence in his tablet would scan the building and give him the best route to get the girls out. He would bring the human element— common sense—to the problem. Intelligence was a tool, not a solution. During training, he'd learned how quickly the intelligence would simply suggest he eliminate someone who it felt was in the way. Even a friendly.

Like Solanis had just done with him.

Did she really expect him to kill a child?

And why was he considering it?

The tablet told Walter the quickest way in was through the side window, which would lead him to the second floor where the girls were, and he could go out the same way. For a moment, he had imagined what it would be like to take both his hands and wring them around Michael's neck. Ever since the beach, he'd stopped seeing Michael as a brother-in-arms. And ever since the kidnapping of his newfound daughter, he would be happy to hear bones snap. One quick motion was all it would take. Like snapping pasta if you were a psychopath.

But using his hands would feel good and personal.

He moved quickly to the side of the house, where he spotted the window. There was a steel trellis attached to the side of the building, claimed by vines years ago. He grabbed the edge of the lattice beam and pulled himself up, rung by rung. The trellis groaned under his weight. It held though. Overengineering and a one-size-fits-all approach to design would do that.

Walter leaned over and pushed hard on the window. It slid right open.

He pulled himself into the room. Cardboard boxes, clay pots, and wooden folding chairs cluttered the space. He landed quietly, scanning. His contacts labeled the clutter around him, warning him the room was monitored by a microphone. He'd need to be quiet.

He sniffed. Something foul lingered.

In the center were two small cots, where Gabby and Tatiana were sleeping. His earpiece picked up the noise from downstairs.

"...isn't going to do it. You know that, right? She's in it for herself. I told her Solanis is one of them. She's no victim."

It was Michael.

He coughed a few times, the wheeze forcing him to stop. Glass shattered. "I'm not fucking thirsty. This should have been done tonight. Can we do this ourselves?"

Another voice, a woman's, spoke up. "Katia said the door is biometric. Only Tailor can..."

The rest of her words were muffled.

"Then cut off her hand," he demanded. "LTE has an entire army waiting outside. They've been there for months, waiting for us to fuck this up. Take the hand to the communications center and press the keypad and cut that thing down. We have the key."

"Michael," the woman said calmly. "It's not that simple. Anyone but her, and the box falls into the vault."

"We jam the signal."

There was an overlap of voices and then something pounding.

"Sir." Another man's voice. There was a forced calm to it. "Are you sure you're all right? Maybe you need to take the pills they gave you."

"Fuck that!" Michael yelled.

Walter's earpiece automatically modulated the audio as needed, otherwise it would have deafened him.

"They are trying to kill me. I'm not dying until I see them again. She promised me. Fucking Walter chasing that fucking pussy. Why haven't we killed him?"

"He's the senator's favorite," the woman said. There was no bitterness in her voice. It was just a factual statement. "You heard Aiesha. You come back without him, and you're not getting anywhere near Jericho."

Walter shook his head and focused on the task at hand.

He crept to the cots and tapped Gabby on the shoulder. She'd be easier to start with; she had taken a liking to him since he'd walked into the Dome. She'd clung to him, asked him questions. He had seen the disappointment in Solanis's eyes each time she had asked him for anything. But there was nothing he could do about that. He had missed so much time with her.

Gabby blinked at him a few times. God, she looked just like her mother. He suddenly felt too small, like he needed to go to the gym to get bigger, faster, and stronger. He was inadequate, weak. He wasn't prepared.

He was a zombie around his daughter. An NPC moving toward a set objective. Just a passenger in his mind's journey.

Walter hadn't wanted to say yes to this unauthorized mission. But he didn't have a choice, did he? Everything Solanis said was water to a man wandering the desert. And ever since he'd met his daughter, he'd been flooded with a drug that had changed him. The work that poured out of him was in service to Gabby. For her.

Walter put one finger over his mouth, urging her to stay silent. He reached over and tapped Tatiana lightly on the shoulder. The girl stirred but didn't wake.

He tried again, ready to put his hand over her mouth to silence her.

Gabby reached over and shook Tatiana. Katia's daughter opened her eyes, blinked, and saw Gabby. She blinked again, the helmet of silver falling over her face.

When she saw Walter, she screamed.

He jerked forward, quickly muffling her mouth with his hands, but it was too late. The voices from downstairs went silent.

The light in the hallway flipped on.

"Get behind me," he hissed to both girls, jerking Tatiana up from the cot.

Gabby grabbed the back of his jacket, but Tatiana pulled against Walter.

"I'm here to help," he said. It was hard, maybe impossible, to hold the gun and muffle Tatiana at the same time while trying to rally both girls.

Could they make it to the window?

Yes.

But the girls were not going to survive a two-story fall.

They'd need to cling to his back.

And that would slow him down.

Tatiana bit Walter.

He simply adjusted his hand and refocused his mind. Pain was temporary.

She bit him again.

They couldn't jump.

They'd need to go to the door.

Hide behind the door.

The footsteps were at the upstairs landing.

He moved quickly and positioned them behind the door's hinges, where he knew the wide swing of the entrance would give them cover when it opened. They would be concealed for mere moments, but he could drill a bullet in the right place and then push the girls down the hall.

There would be more people to encounter. Michael would be easy. He'd lost his mind, and he was always weak without a gun. In training, his hand-to-hand combat resulted in all of them running more laps. But he hadn't recognized the second male voice or the woman.

Of course, Aiesha hadn't told him everything. Senators were like that, heads too far in the clouds.

Walter put his finger next to the trigger. He didn't want to kill someone in front of Gabby, but Aiesha's voice nagged at him.

What matters the most?

Not this.

The door swung open, and the lights in the room faded up, pushing out the moonlight. Walter's contacts automatically adjusted; he wouldn't be stunned by the unfortunate incursion of natural light. But he'd miscalculated. He should have left the girls in the cot. It would have bought them more time. The second the man entered the room, he saw the beds were empty, and yelled.

But Walter was fast.

He bounded forward, clasping one hand over the man's mouth and grabbing his right hand that had gone for his gun. He swept his leg under the man, driving him to the ground with a thud. The man howled in pain, mimicking Tatiana's squeal from behind him. The man kicked his other legs back to try and reorient himself from the floor, but he pulled his wrist hard, forcing the man to almost roll over. There was a popping sound as the man's wrist broke, or maybe his elbow dislocated.

No, it was his shoulder.

The man tried to wiggle out of his grasp.

The man kicked his leg, connecting with Walter's ankle. Unlike the Evergreens who were smaller and wispy versions of their outside cousins, this man was trained. He pushed back hard, forcing Walter to stumble backward.

He stood, limping as he pressed his earpiece. Walter moved quickly, jumping and tackling him to the ground. The thudding noise would alert the others to what had happened. He'd run out of time. He slammed the man's head onto the hardwood floor, his right ear clipping the side of the cot.

Blood leaked from his head.

A look of surprise crossed the man's face.

But Walter wasn't here to counsel those who sat in death's waiting room. He had seconds and could still lose this fight.

Walter reached back with his left hand, his right holding the man down on the ground, and shoved his gun into his ribs, just under the vest. He fired twice. The jacket muffled the gunshots, but the man still shuddered. The smell of burning and gunpowder filled the air—a stronger version of the smell in the hallway.

He didn't die right away.

Instead, he jerked a few times, coughing and spluttering as he drowned in the blood pooling in his lungs. His hand tried to grab Walter's arm but just flopped around uselessly. He gurgled a few times and then jerked again. Finally, he stopped moving.

Tatiana screamed again.

Two more kills, and he'd be out of the house.

Walter pulled both girls into the hallway, his contacts pointing down the narrow passage and to the steps being his optimal route to get out of the house.

He could take anyone who came upstairs one by one. He was a

good shot, and the people downstairs were scared, irrational. They were like Michael—emotional.

"Stay behind me," he demanded, his left hand pushing the girls toward the wall and his right using the gun to guide them. His earpiece lit up.

Tell them we failed, Michael said. *Kill them all. Kill them all.*

The front door opened and closed.

Walter reached the top of the steps and paused. If he walked to the bottom now, the girls would be sitting ducks, open targets. They'd need to stay at the top of the stairs. But there was risk in this plan. What if they wandered off? What if the other person was on their way around the house, through the back? He tightened his grip on his gun. He'd need to risk it.

"Stay here until I call you," he urged the girls.

Tatiana nodded, sobbing. Gabby hadn't cried yet. Instead, her wide eyes focused on him. She nodded.

He headed down the steps, his back to the railing and his left shoulder using the wall as a guide. When he reached the first landing, he faced the open floor. Michael stood alone, shivering in the dark green jacket. His hair, matted and creased, stuck to his forehead. His gun, as expected, was pointed directly at Walter.

"Where's the other one?" Walter asked.

"Doing her job." He then gestured toward Walter's gun. "You're not going to use that."

Walter raised the gun and aimed at the center of Michael's chest. "Let us out, and you won't have to die."

"Do you hear yourself?" He coughed. "What the fuck happened to you?"

Walter reached the bottom of the stairs. He looked back at the landing. The girls were still there. There were several ways into the room.

He caught that revolting smell again. Stronger now.

"No, what happened to you?" Walter said calmly. His shot wouldn't pierce Michael's bulletproof vest. But hold on. There was a way. "We never agreed to kill any kids."

Michael rolled his eyes. "You're a fucking idiot. Whipped." He shivered hard but kept the gun in his hand. "You knew the plan going into this. You knew everything was on the table."

He shook his head. "I told you we shouldn't let it get that far."

"And you knew it could. You agreed to everything. Solanis needs to turn off the fucking box. And she didn't agree. So, now we force her to. And if that doesn't work, then we let them come in here and collapse this one too."

"Katia jumped the gun—"

"Katia's more of a warrior than you are. She's an emotional cunt, sure. But she was here for ten years doing what needed to be done. And you?" Michael laughed. "You've been simping all over the place. You let her lead. You let her tell you what to do. And now look at you." He coughed hard. "Look at you. Getting what you wanted. Boston-eyed pussy. Leaving the rest of us to fight for ourselves."

Walter raised his gun higher. His arm had been drooping. "I'm done. Back up. We're leaving."

"You are not going anywhere. You're not finished."

"Michael!"

"Don't be selfish Walter!" Michael shook his head in disgust.

Walter frowned. No he wasn't. He'd risked everything to get inside Shamut. He risked dying. He'd given up his job at HERA. He'd hunkered down in that quadplex alone, just to get Solanis out. He was the picture of selfless devotion.

"Oh…" Michael smiled, blood staining the lines between his teeth like caulk. "You thought you were different?" He laughed—a loud, sarcastic laugh. "You thought you were some hero, didn't you?" He coughed again. "The moment you got what you wanted, the moment you got her, you stopped trying for the rest of us."

He realized his gun had dipped slightly, so he raised it higher. He didn't care if Michael was right. He needed to get them out.

"You know what I miss, Walter? When we were all fighting in the war together. You're too young to remember. You don't know what real sacrifice is, what it means to have *real* brothers. Not by blood—brothers by circumstance. We all fight wars. Personal, physical, global… we all need victories. The senator was right though. You need plans within plans because everyone has their own agenda."

Walter blinked a few times. "Michael, just let us go. Please. You don't have to hurt the girls."

Michael laughed, a fleeting giggle. "See, you're still doing it. Thinking of yourself. My wife took everything from me. When she moved into the Domes. Everything. My kids are in Jericho with her. She was just gone one day. And they are going to die if you do this. You understand that though." He shook his head over and over. "Doesn't matter. LTE is on their way. Their private army. Backups for backups, plans within plans."

"Wait…" He frowned. "Tell me you didn't. They'll burn this place to the ground."

"Does it look like I care?" Michael said again, tilting his head to the side.

"But they'll kill everyone. Including the innocents."

"That's what happens when you fuck around."

"How do you expect to get to your daughters if you're dead?"

"They won't kill me."

"LTE only protects their own."

"I am LTE, you dumbass. I'm not here for Aiesha. I'm here for them. For Gideon Voss. *If you died today, who would thrive?* Those people in here need to die for the earth to thrive. Now that Solanis has failed, my people—the true saviors of the world— will take real action, not the shortcut, half-measures Worthington takes. You two will die tonight when they break this Dome. We've gotten good at it. Shalina was easy. Shamut should be easy."

Walter narrowed his eyes. Michael had aligned himself with a radical.

Michael rolled his eyes. "Fuck it," he said, raising his gun again. "I've said too much."

He tilted his head to the left and then right and fired.

The first bullet missed Walter.

Walter fired three times, all three shots landing in Michael's chest. The impact pushed him backward, stunning him. But he didn't fall. He took four steps back in shock.

Walter moved fast. He tackled Michael, knocking him off his feet and to the ground.

Michael, in his weakened and crazed state, was too tired to push back against Walter's face as he squeezed both hands around the man's neck.

"Will you stop?" Walter demanded. "Will you stop?"

Michael couldn't respond.

But he didn't let up. "Tell me you'll stop, and I'll stop!"

He was aware of his left side aching as he squeezed, the edges of his vision pulsing a deep burgundy as he pushed the life from Michael. The dying man kicked and writhed—each jerking motion weaker than the last, until the light was gone.

Walter stood and turned to tell the girls to come down.

But standing at the foot of the stairs was Gabby, her mouth open. She stared at the scene in front of her. And her eyes were as dark as her mother's.

"Gabby," he said softly.

But she just stared at him. He was a stranger to her.

He shook his head, pocketing Michael's gun. He then grabbed both girls and pulled them toward the door. As he moved, he searched the room for a cloth, something to cover the girls' eyes with.

He was different, right? They weren't going to actually kill Tatiana if Katia didn't do what they needed her to do. Right? Michael and he were not the same.

He wasn't selfish.

Walter spotted a bundle of curtains by the door and yanked at them, finding the source of the smell. Wrapped in the curtains was Diego's body.

Tatiana screamed before Walter could push her back. "Daddy!" she yelled, sobbing. "Daddy!"

Walter pulled her back, ignoring the emotional acid flooding his stomach, and tore the curtain free. He hustled both girls from the home and out the front door.

Once outside, Walter pulled the girls onto a dirt road, behind another row of homes, and huddled underneath the fake light of the Dome. He couldn't breathe. He'd been moving too fast. Everything was coming too fast. He took a deep breath, refocused his mind. Centered himself.

How would he do this?

He tore the curtain down the middle. "I need you to put this on," he said to Tatiana, who moaned in the dark. "Over your eyes."

"What happened to my dad?" the girl wailed. "What happened?"

"I don't know." He tried to keep his voice steady. Something inside him felt wrong. A faint tugging, like a rip inside him.

They needed to move quickly. If Michael had actually been LTE, it meant he'd lied to him all these years. It meant their entire mission would be compromised. It meant the people who wore red and held the portraits would spill all their blood today.

"I want my mom," Tatiana cried, her eyes searching their environment.

He looked at Gabby, who cowered behind Tatiana. He reached toward her.

Gabby screamed and took a few steps back.

Oh.

A thousand needles drilled into his chest.

His stomach ached.

His mind throbbed.

"Please you have to," he said. "Please."

Tatiana crossed her arms—as Gabby took the cloth and tied it over her eyes, her hands shaking—wincing as she did so. "I want my mom."

"Just put this on please," Walter said, holding out the other strip to Tatiana.

But she refused.

He grabbed her and held her still as he tied the cloth around her eyes. She screamed and kicked, her tiny frame bucking in his arms. But he was stronger. She'd never win. As soon as she was blind, she fought harder.

He pulled Tatiana onto his lap as Gabby screamed and cried from her spot on the ground.

This was wrong.

So wrong.

"Please. Be quiet," he said.

But they only got louder.

"Stop!" he yelled. "You need to stop. Please."

The girls fell silent.

He looked up at the Dome, the fake stars staring down at him. Solanis had been right. There were no stars here. Not real ones anyway.

He closed his eyes and focused.

The pain in his side tore at him.

Oh, he'd been shot.

He could still move, so it wasn't urgent.

He'd have to deal with it later.

Could he do this?

Was he really so different from Michael? From Katia?

Was he different from Solar?

Selfish.

And why had he let himself become a passenger in his own mind? An autopilot activated by whatever Solanis had over him?

It was because she had asked him to. Solanis Tailor, the woman from Boston, could bend his world to her will. And she'd taken him into her gravity.

She would never let him go.

No. He was trapped by his own doing.

But those pools of darkness were poison.

For the first time, they scared him.

This place was rotting.

Walter held the squirming, kicking Tatiana hard as she shook. He was supposed to be helping her, and yet...he had promised to pull the trigger.

Could he?

For her?

Would this be where he'd lose his soul?

Walter pulled out his gun, testing the weight in his hands. "Keep your blindfold on," he said. "And cover your ears."

Both girls complied.

They shook.

They whimpered.

The pain in his side, his mind. Everywhere ached.

"Please don't hurt us," Gabby whimpered, her voice heavy with tears.

No, he couldn't.

But he needed to.

Walter fumbled with the Voice in his left hand, propping it up on a nearby rock. He called Solanis.

Then he pointed the gun at Tatiana's head.

30

MONSTERS

Katia

It was getting harder to keep an unimpressed, bored expression on her face the more it itched.

Maybe Solanis had some moisturizer in her pocket, Katia thought. Not like she'd ask her.

Solanis just sat across from her, glaring.

She blamed herself for having half a melted face. Had she not gotten so…emotional after her brother's death, maybe Solanis would have been easier to break. She should have let them take her outside gently, avoided the whole nonsense in the Fields.

Maybe, maybe, maybe.

Solanis looked down at her tablet and then back at Katia. "I need you to let Gabby go," she said. Her voice was harder than it usually was as if she'd been yelling too much. There was this underlying husk to it.

Different voice. Same stubbornness.

Katia made a thin line with her lips. She would need some lip balm at some point; the dryness was getting to her. "You know how to get her back," she said. Fuck, did everything have to hurt? "Turn off the box, and Michael will let her go."

383

Solanis leaned toward her. "Come on, Katia. Just let her go."

She had never noticed there was this thin dark line where the blacks of her sclera and pupils met. It was remarkable to see up close, hints of the past breaking through.

She raised an eyebrow. "You turn that box off yet?"

"Come on," Solanis insisted.

Was that a wobble at the end of her voice?

A hint of emotion?

Katia dug in. "You can have Gabby back when you turn off the box. It's in the other room, right? The box? Just go in there and turn it off. Then you get Gabby back. This is simple."

She leaned back in the chair, sadness crossing her face. "I'm not sorry for this," she said, sliding the Voice across the table. "Don't think I am."

Katia looked down at the chunky tablet and saw the dark night of the Dome through the display.

Walter held a gun to her daughter's head.

Tatiana was crying.

Katia blinked. *Solanis Tailor. What did you do?*

Katia fought the urge to cry out as her body twisted itself into knots.

Luna was in danger.

Walter wouldn't hurt her, right?

Katia almost frowned. He would do anything for her.

She counted to four in her head and forced her voice to come out even. "What am I looking at?"

Solanis's mouth twitched. But when she spoke, her voice was a perfect monotone that Katia had never heard from her before. "Stupidity doesn't look good on you."

She almost laughed. Solanis sounded like Michael.

She shouldn't have looked back down at the tablet.

Her face hurt.

She'd been clenching her jaw, forcing the scarred tissue on her mangled face to tense and stress. Pinpricks welled up behind her eyes.

One.

Two.

Three.

If Walter was with Tatiana, where was Michael?

Tatiana struggled in Walter's grasp, the blindfold sparing her the worst of the moment.

Katia could not lose two children.

She needed to stop looking at the display. Her daughter's tiny face framed with too much hair. Her entire world was in danger.

One.

Two.

She couldn't demand Solanis to let Tatiana go. That wasn't part of the plan. Besides, Solanis would just insist on a trade, a daughter for a daughter was fair game. But if she gave Solanis back her daughter, she would have no incentive to stay and more innocent people, like her mother, would die. That was what Solanis was counting on.

One.

Two.

Three.

Okay. This was salvageable.

Solanis would bend eventually. She'd have to see. She always had to see to believe.

"Stalemate." Katia shoved the tablet back toward Solanis—a slight reprieve from her pain. "Michael's not letting Gabby go. You and I both know that."

"I don't need Gabby to be let go," Solanis said. "You're going to stop hunting my daughter."

Katia frowned. "Why would I do that?"

She pushed the tablet back toward her. Walter had tilted the screen.

Gabby was with him too.

Which meant Michael was dead. So, Walter had killed him. And the only reason Walter would have killed Michael would be because Solanis had told him too. Which meant...

Katia met Solanis's gaze.

She didn't.

But she did.

"You actually did it." Katia laughed in amazement. "You ruined him. You actually did it."

Solanis shook her head. "What are you talking about?"

She looked up at the ceiling as her options narrowed. "He's never going to forgive you, you know. This is what happens when you hang around glass. You get cut."

Katia knew this could happen. That Solanis would do anything to get what she wanted, even by hurting the people closest to her. This was her pattern of behavior. Greg when they didn't flee from Haze. Childre to get the promotion. Leonardo at Dirt. Herself upon reentry. And now Walter.

Katia chuckled.

Hang in there, Luna. I just need a few more moments.

She had a mission.

"You told Walter to do this, right? I wonder how Gabby's gonna feel about this." Katia tapped her fingers on the table. She needed to count, or she'd get lost in the fear. "You know she'll never look at him the same ever again, right? You've ruined him, Solanis." She clapped her hands three times in a mockery of her mission. "Welcome to the game, the war. I'd be impressed if I weren't so angry."

"This is a game to you?"

She held up a hand. "All games are war. We're just proxies. I admit you've won here. But I need a second." She tapped the table. She needed to move. She, for the first time since her captivity, felt truly trapped. "You have the interference device on, right?" She gestured to Solanis's pocket. Even this evolved monster was predictable.

Solanis nodded.

She gestured to the room. "The reason I came in here was because my mother told me, my brother, and my husband that she wanted to die. She's old-fashioned like that. She thinks it's unnatural to live until a hundred and forty or whatever. Can't blame her. But that's her choice to make. Right? My old boss, Worthington, promised the world that he built hope for the planet. Fuck climate mitigation or whatever. The Earth is doomed regardless. But she went into that Dome, knowing she had a certain amount of time left, and he's going to steal that away from her because he can't build a fucking snow globe.

"But that's just her. What about the others? The ones who moved in thinking they were doing the right thing to save the world? They sold everything, gave him everything, and locked themselves away so their children's children could inherit the earth. Only it's just genocide, right? I'm not telling you Worthington should be stopped." She shook her head. "I'm not inside this Dome because Senator Aiesha Patterson thinks the Man from Denver *can* be stopped. You can't stop gods from roaming the planet. He's too wealthy. I'm here because people should be given a choice. An honest choice to take the risk or not. You deserved that much when you came here. Would you have made the same decision to go in had you known?"

Katia held out her hands. "Pass me the tablet. I'll send out the word to my people that your daughter is not to be touched."

Solanis picked up the tablet and placed it in her hands. She went to work, sending out a message. She wasn't sure how many there were— a few thousand out of the two million maybe. LTE had people here too —sleeper agents waiting to burn this place to the ground, those who would not hesitate if she and Aiesha failed.

"Shame we couldn't turn off the box," she said, the blatant sarcasm dripping through her voice. "I guess we'll all die now. LTE will kill all of us. There." She slid the tablet back over the table. "You're free."

Solanis glared at her. "You made me do this."

She chuckled again. "No, Solanis. Every decision you have ever made has been yours. Predictability doesn't make you a slave to well planned activism."

"It doesn't feel like it," Solanis said, turning to leave the room.

"Wait," she said.

Solanis turned back around.

She frowned. She should warn her. "If Michael is dead, be careful. I don't control LTE. And if he was able to call them before he died, they will kill everyone. Especially you. You're an ambassador, a target on their list."

Solanis rolled her eyes, a gesture Katia instantly recognized. Her eyes simply shimmered as they moved, a blatant sign of anger reduced to a whisper of emotion. "You can't help it, can you?"

She raised a painful eyebrow.

"Even when you've lost, you still have to lie. You can't just apologize."

"Solanis, I..." Katia stopped. "I just want us to get out."

Solanis scoffed and left the room.

And in the silence, Katia realized that she'd failed. She'd never actually failed at much in real life, especially something as critical as this. Failure meant her mother would die under glass rain, in fear. And Tatiana...

Well, her daughter would be fine, for now. Solanis wouldn't leave her behind. She wouldn't do that.

Katia closed her eyes, considering what version of Solanis Tailor had come from the crucible of the past few weeks. The woman in front of her, the one with all the arrogance, was she the phoenix or the monster?

Monsters destroy the people they love, and she'd destroyed the one man who had loved her. It wasn't hard to admire her for choosing blood over chosen connections.

Yeah, it was the monster. A version of Solanis Tailor found so deep that it left destruction in its wake. A monster that could still stumble and do her bidding.

Katia sighed heavy and tried to relax.

How much longer would they keep her alive before they let her die? At least in death, she could still do her part.

31

ERASE

Leonardo

Katia's cell stunk.

But it didn't matter.

This would be the last time he'd be down here.

Leonardo pulled out a chair and sat. She stared past him. People like her always thought they were better than him.

She'd regret that, if she could remember.

A healer entered the room and set up a tablet on the table. He slowly turned the tablet so the screen faced her and then took a seat next to Leonardo. There was a wet spot on the tablet, where the healer had handled the Voice.

Gross.

"We're going to let you go, Katia," Leonardo said, searching her face for a reaction. But as usual, there was none. "But first, we need to give you a shot." He gestured to the healer, who had placed a case on the table and was putting together an injection. "We'll explain how this works in a moment."

"You're not going to turn the bots back on, are you?" Katia asked.

"No," he said. "But we always can if you get out of line."

The healer injected the serum and disposed of the needle in the wall unit. He then sat, watching Katia.

He smiled. "Do you want to show our friend Katia a little presentation you've put together?"

The healer nodded, his eyes never once leaving Katia. There was a hunger in them.

He tapped the tablet. On the screen, three patients sat, staring into empty space and giving the same glazed look Childre had given just weeks ago.

"These are people who received the same injection as you, ma'am," the healer said, breathing quickly. "They are in a controlled zone to ensure accuracy. But we turned off the zone, and this is what happened."

She frowned. "What am I looking at?"

"You are looking at three people who have lost their minds. Like Childre did," Leonardo said.

"What?"

"Yes." The healer grinned as if the horrors of modern science were exciting. "Their brains forgot just about everything."

"Why are you showing me this?" Katia asked.

Was that fear in her eyes? God, he hoped so.

"Well…" The healer stared at the screen, his eyes shining in the reflection. "The Shepherd asked if there were ways to keep the antisocials in line." He spoke deliberately, each word enunciated. "There was the idea that we were building a community here, that everyone plays a role in the cycle that is the Dome. So, to make that work, everyone does their part. Willingly or unwillingly. It doesn't matter. A cog is a cog. This breakthrough proves that we can do this. If any of them leave the zone—in this case, the room we had them in—they will"—his voice elongated as he searched for the right words—"experience memory deterioration."

"They forget everything." Leonardo couldn't help himself. The healer was being too fancy with this.

Leonardo watched Katia's face. He wanted to see it when she realized he had her.

"Of course, it's not everything," the healer said. "They'll remember how to eat, breathe, speak… They generally remember how to use the bathroom. They'll retain the basics. But everything else—their family, children, lovers—is lost." The healer seemed to scoot to the edge of his chair in excitement. "We got the idea from the people who got Domesick. We've been using this technology in the Fields to help people forget traumatic events. Solanis Tailor has probably forgotten her breakdown after she Recycled Childre."

Leonardo watched as Katia realized what was happening.

"So, I can't leave this room?" she asked.

He stood and leaned forward. "You're going home today. But if you leave Shamut, that is your future." He pointed a finger to the tablet, where one of the patients was huddled in the corner of the room, staring at the wall and mumbling to himself.

"Wait a second." She shook her head. "You didn't really…"

The healer was breathing loudly though his nose.

"Test it out," Leonardo said, a smile breaking out onto his face. "Go ahead. Leave again. Go out there and destroy everything we've built. Everything we've sacrificed for." He leaned so close he could smell the rot on her face. "Only you can't now. Can you? If you go outside, you'll forget everything. Your daughter. Solanis. Everything."

She stared at him and squinted.

She then headbutted him, forcing him to fall backward in shock.

But he didn't mind.

He'd won.

Leonardo laughed and wiped his mouth, tasting blood. "I am here to protect Shamut. I am here to keep everyone safe." He snapped his fingers, and the healer stood.

Two SPINE agents entered the room and began unchaining her from the chair.

"Oh, and one more thing." He turned to face her from the sliding door.

She was fighting against the agents, yelling insults and straining under their grip.

"If you decide to leave, and your daughter becomes an orphan because her mother has lost her mind, I'll personally make sure she's taken right back into Shamut or any other Dome Mr. Worthington builds. Maybe I'll even make sure she's the infrastructure ambassador. You know, make her mother proud."

The doors slid closed behind Leonardo.

He could hear Katia sobbing, even in the outer hallway. The wail from her was delicious.

Now, it was time to focus on Solanis Tailor.

He'd been watching her, and it was time to stop her.

32

REACH

Solanis

Walter glared at Solanis from his space in the empty living room of the quadplex they'd taken for the night. They wouldn't return home.

"How dare you?" His voice sounded hurt.

But she was too tired to care. The contradictions pounded her mind, forcing her vision to swim. She was so over this routine. He had been willing to sit by and let a child die if it met Aiesha's goals. She wasn't going to extend sympathy his way. At least now he'd know how she felt.

She crossed her arms.

How was it that both Walter and Katia coaxed the same emotion from her?

"Are the girls okay?" she said.

"She looks at me like I'm a monster." Walter's voice caught.

She picked at the lint on her pants in an attempt to look unbothered. "Regrettable."

"Don't be a dick. You were supposed to—"

"Supposed to what, Walter?" she yelled. "Go ahead. Tell me what I'm supposed to do. And while you're at it, tell me what I'm *not* supposed to do. Everyone has been telling me for the past few weeks

393

what I am *supposed* to do. Because I'm the all-predictable Solanis Tailor. Don't you see what's happening?"

"This is different. You knew what you were doing. You knew I wouldn't say no."

She snorted. "You're strong, Walter."

"Solanis, stop." He looped his fingers together, twisting them back and forth. "I get it. You're mad. But how could you do that to me? You made me hurt her." He gestured to the other room, where Tatiana and Gabby were still huddled together, the shock from earlier still weighing on them. "I just met her. And I've hurt her. I'm not that guy. I'm not a monster." His head fell into his hands, and his shoulders shook.

"But you are that guy!" Solanis yelled at him. "You literally show back up after what—nine, ten years—and tell me that my home is going to collapse. And to get me to help you, you tell me you're going to kill my daughter."

"Solanis—"

"Shut the fuck up!" she yelled. "You. Know. What. You. Did."

The room next door went quiet, her vision tinted red.

The fireflies were excited.

"Yet when I ask you to save her, my little girl—when I ask you to do one thing for me, to save your daughter—you complain because it's dangerous? Because it makes you look bad?" she asked. "You're her father Walter, not her friend."

"It has nothing to do with danger. Breaking in here was dangerous. Finding you was dangerous. Being here is dangerous." Walter shook his head and threw his hands up. "I was never going to hurt Gabby. It was something I had to go along with to get in here because—"

"—you would do anything for me. I know. We all know. You're an echo."

He glared at her.

"Think about it, Walter. Did you mean it?"

He stared at her.

"Did you mean it?"

"Mean it?"

"When you said you'd do anything for me?"

He looked shocked for a moment but quickly recovered. "I've never lied to you, Solanis."

"Then drop it. We're even now. We put this behind us."

"Even?"

"Yes." Solanis stepped toward him, determined to finish this argument. "Even." She tried to give him a smile, to remind him that he was hers.

But he jerked back, stung. "Don't." His voice cloaked in an icy tremble. He stood, holding himself in his arms. He looked down at the ground and then up at the ceiling. "I thought you'd get it. You know, out there in the real world, it's a fight to survive. You have to meet monsters, play with monsters, and sleep with monsters to fight other monsters." He shook his head. "But if everyone's a monster, aren't we all just... I didn't want to join Aiesha. I only joined her—Katia—to get you."

"It's the same thing—"

"It's not, Solanis. You don't live out there. You don't have an excuse to be a monster. You knew I wouldn't be able to say no. You were counting on it when you made me do that terrible thing. You know what it felt like, knowing if you ordered me to, if you gave the word, that I could?"

She frowned. "Could?"

"Pull the trigger." He closed his eyes. "I can't say no. Couldn't say no. When you looked at me with those eyes. Those"—he shook his head and shuddered—"pits."

Solanis shivered.

The whimper that came from him startled her. He leaned into the corner of the room as the pinkish red rays of the fake sunrise peeked in on them. It was as if he was afraid of the light, hiding in the shadows. "Do you remember the first time we met, Solanis? The first thing you said to me?"

She tried to blink away the fireflies.

"You asked me if I was going to take your order. You didn't ask my name, how I was, or even say *excuse me*. You *wanted* something from me. You take."

She shook her head, realizing too late that the feeling inside was failure. He wasn't coming back to her. He was falling away. She grabbed for him. "Walter, no. Walter. Hold on."

He pulled away and winced.

For the first time, Solanis could see he was hurt. A bandage, tainted red was wrapped around his side, right where the ribs met the waist.

"Walter, you're —"

"Solanis no."

"Walter?"

This wasn't supposed to happen. He was supposed to accept that they were even, agree that he needed to be with her because he was trapped in her gravity. Instead, he'd reached back and rewrote the story of them, the story of how they had met. If he could rewrite their past, he could erase their future.

He kept wringing his hands, shaking his shoulders.

You broke him, didn't you?

"Katia tricked me, you know," he said. "I know she did. I expect that from her. Pretending to need my help. She got me to tell her all about you so we could come in and rescue you." He nodded slowly. "And you know the funny thing? I thought that if I came in here, that if I told you people were going to die, that you'd… Like I knew you'd need to see it; you've always needed to see to believe. That's what the boat was for, right?" He stared out the window.

"Walter, hold on." She was so cold. Her joints, bones, hands felt like ice. "You can't sit here and feel sorry for yourself. Let me explain."

"No need." He closed his eyes, the corners of his mouth pulled by gravity. "There was a time when I craved your heart in my arms. I think that time is over."

The earth tilted sideways, and the bottom fell from under her. She was too warm, sweating. Her heart was too loud.

You broke him, didn't you?

"Walter," she demanded. "Stop."

But he stepped around her and headed toward the living room. "They're waiting for us."

He left.

Solanis didn't follow. She shouldn't reward this sort of double standard.

396

She shouldn't, but she suddenly felt like a chunk of her had been ripped off, stolen from her. She walked to the corner of the room where he had been hugging himself and stared at the space where the corners kissed.

Her chest burned.

She hadn't been breathing.

Wait. She couldn't breathe.

She smashed her fist into her chest. Her lungs unlocked, and she sucked in air.

What was happening?

She hadn't expected him to lash out at her as if she was the bad guy. His anger because she did exactly what she was supposed to do baffled her. How could he stand there and suggest that she was the bad guy when he'd done the exact same thing to her earlier?

She shook her head to clear the confusion, but she found herself gasping for air again. She rested one hand on the corner of the wall and could have sworn if she got close enough, she could smell a hint of him. A lingering memory that he had once been in the room.

You broke him, didn't you?

Solanis wiped her eyes, the fatigue getting to her. She should go to bed. Should sleep. She needed her pills. These fireflies kept roaming in and out of her vision.

She needed to get out of this fucking Dome.

So what if Walter wasn't going to come with her? Fine. It didn't matter. She and Gabby could figure things out. She'd been great at keeping her safe the last decade. She could repeat that victory.

She'd keep doing it.

Forever.

But her mind played cruel games. All she could see was the hopeful look Gabby kept giving him whenever he was in the room. The way she'd hidden behind him when Michael had forced himself in the room. The way she'd looked to *him* for safety. The way they both ate dry cereal.

Solanis closed her eyes, blocking out the intensity of the purples and pinks that reached through the room. The sunrises were always so spectacular inside this Dome. She remembered them looking magical outside too. Gabby would like to see the sunrise and the fish out there. They could do this together.

Just the two of them.

But that isn't right either, is it?

It couldn't be the two of them. It was all wrong. She'd been at this crossroads before, believing she had no choice but to hide away in a Dome. It hadn't been hiding back then, it had been the right decision— or as Worthington would have called it, the perfect sacrifice.

Solanis couldn't take Walter from Gabby. It was cruel.

But she couldn't figure out how to get him back.

They'd just have to adjust.

Besides, she'd been a bad mother. How the fuck had she let Walter become more important than she? How did she let him replace her in her daughter's eyes? He should have been a stranger. He should have stayed a stranger.

Gabby deserved someone who would sacrifice for her, be there for her—always. Solanis was that person, that mother.

Then why now, as Solanis slid on the floor, did she press her face against the wall just to trap another moment of him inside her?

Why then did this hurt so much?

The last time she'd left Walter, it had felt like this, like her heart had been torn in two.

And now.

The pain was the same.

Only worse.

———

"Solanis?"

Katia stood in front of her among the swirl of fireflies. She held an envelope in her hand, Tatiana clinging to her arm. She tugged at her hair, swaying back and forth on the balls of her feet. There was something different about her. She looked exhausted.

"No." Solanis shook her head. "You're not here. Go away."

She raised an eyebrow, wincing as she did so. "What does he want?"

Solanis turned her head away from her. "I have nothing to say to you."

She held out the letter from earlier. "No. Worthington. What does he want? It's from his office." She handed Solanis the card.

"What does it matter?"

Katia shrugged and wobbled to the left. Tatiana caught her before she fell.

Was Katia drunk? No, she didn't drink like that. But if half of your face was melted, drinking wouldn't seem unusual.

"I'm getting out of here," Solanis said.

"We're not getting out of here," Katia said sadly.

Tatiana looked up. "What?"

She smiled at Tatiana. "Don't worry. You'll be fine."

What did she mean?

"Never mind. The tunnels. There are tunnels. We can take the tunnels, not the same one where we dragged you out, but there are plenty of them."

The voices in the other room were arguing. Walter and what sounded like Heidi.

"Why did they let you go?" Solanis asked, suddenly suspicious.

"Because they were done with me." Katia folded her arms. "Like you seem to be done with *him*."

She looked up.

"Oh, don't be like that," Katia said as Tatiana helped her onto one of the nearby sofas in the room, Katia's left leg struggling to keep up with her cadence. "We all know what happened. How you destroyed him."

Tatiana settled on the sofa and lay down, placing her head in her mother's lap.

"Stop." Solanis shook her head.

Katia sighed with relief, holding up her hands and beaconing for Solanis to come closer. "I'm not blaming you, Solanis. I did the same thing to him. You know his weakness, right?"

"It's me," she said.

"I mean, yes," Katia said, her voice hardly above a whisper. "Yes. It's you. But it's not you exactly. It's what you represent."

"Black girls?"

"It's not a fetish, Solanis." She frowned. "One of our spies studied him after you left the camp. He didn't date much after, but he found this woman whose kids had died in one of those Haze storms. Waited on her, helped her for years until she left him for someone else. He tends to do that. Go after women who are broken."

Solanis felt the stabbing of debris in her gut.

Katia leaned forward. "He likes broken girls, Solanis. It's who he is. It's not bad. He likes to help. Means well. And don't get all offended. Most of us are broken. He gets his pick of the litter."

"I'm not broken."

"You're the most broken out of all of us. Dead parents, dead adoptive parents, dead brother, and scarred by Haze." Katia tilted her head to the left and winced. "Dictionary definition."

"You're a bitch." It was time to leave.

"But just because you're broken, doesn't mean you can't make it a win for Gabby," Katia said loudly.

Tatiana stirred in her lap.

Solanis stopped and turned. "What?"

"A win for Gabby. It's what you want," Katia said. "I know you. You're not going to want to yank her father from her life. You can see it in her eyes. The way she looks at him, the realization deep inside her that there's a connection there. You hate it. It scares you."

"I'm not predictable—"

"We all are if you study long enough."

She wasn't wrong.

"You know what I'm talking about," Katia said. She gazed down at Tatiana, who lay on her lap. "It's the same one I have with Luna, the connection." She stroked her hair. "I would do anything for her. Even die. I would die for her."

Solanis nodded. "Why do you call her Luna?"

"Her hair looks like the light of the moon."

"Why would you want to leave her here? Dying doesn't solve anything. It doesn't keep her safe."

"It's not my job to *just* keep her safe. I could do that, and then when I'm gone, she would've learned nothing. She'd learned to rely on someone else to protect her. No. I am here to teach her how to survive *after* I am gone. We aren't perpetual, despite how hard we try. One day, Tatiana and Gabby will have to go out there and figure out how to do what we did. How to do what *you* did."

"What did we do?"

"We survived." Katia nodded toward the sofa next to her. "You should sit."

Solanis didn't move. The fireflies faded in and out around Katia, sparks framing her face.

"Solanis, you're exhausted. Sit."

She sat. The relief felt good on her back.

"How did you survive all this?" Katia gestured around. "All of this. The Fields, the Haze, the caves where your parents died? Have you really thought about *how* you got here?"

She stared at Tatiana, who clutched her mother in her sleep. She was too old to act so needy. "My brother. You know what he always said."

"We are safe as long as we are together. And?"

She couldn't hold back the stupid grin. "He would always say *what do you know*?" She chuckled. "Greg said it. Those two things."

"And so do you. I've heard you. You told that to her when she was born." Katia gestured toward the door, where Gabby stood, her hair matted and the extra large ComCen sweater hanging to her knees.

Her daughter curled up next to Solanis, one arm clutching hers.

"Your brother reaches out. He reaches beyond, even now, to help you. *That's* the job as a mother. To teach her now, so I can reach beyond when I'm gone and help her. She will get hurt as much as I hate it. But she needs to. Even if I forget her, I will reach out." Katia looked down at Tatiana, stroking the silver mess of hair. "I've lost one already. That's pain, Solanis. Unbearable pain. But what's worse is realizing that you might set them up for failure.

"You need as many people as possible to reach forward, reach out to guide them when we're gone. Because we will be gone one day. That connection. The one that reaches through the earth..." She was whispering again. "Denying that connection only hurts them."

"How am I supposed to get it back?" Solanis shook her head. "How? If I've hurt him so much."

She shrugged. "Become him."

"Katia."

"Seriously. Fix something," she said. "He fixes broken girls. His obsessive need to fix things is because he is broken too. Fix him."

"I'm not a therapist; there's no time for that."

Katia closed her eyes and slowly opened them. "You don't believe that."

Solanis shook her head. "Excuse me."

"You don't believe there's no time." She nodded to the letter Solanis had abandoned on the sofa. "Read it."

The invitation was a heavy card stock, the perfect shade of green with official looking font that read:

The Honorable Manuel Worthington
requests the honor of the presence of
Ambassador Solanis N. Tailor
in the
Executive Offices of the Higher Committee at
8 a.m. DST
Dress Code: Ambassadorial

The clock said five past seven.

"If he's still here, it means this place isn't falling yet," Katia said.

"How did you know—?"

"I used to work for him, Solanis." She shrugged. "They're obsessed with living forever. I guess once you see above the clouds…"

"We should just leave," Solanis said. "It doesn't make sense to stay here if we know the inevitable."

"You can't leave yet," Heidi said from the door. Walter was lurking behind her, a fresh bandage on his side. This new bandage looked better wrapped. Fireflies dotted the space around them.

"Heidi?" Solanis said.

"Michael sent a runner. He hit the panic button. LTE is coming in."

"Fuck!" Katia said.

Tatiana woke up.

"They're coming to destroy," Walter said.

"Solanis is on the list," Heidi said.

"Then we have to leave now," Solanis said.

"It's too late for that. The tunnels will be filled. You'll be easy to pick off." Katia tapped her forehead. "Can we get our people ready? There's, what, a few thousand? Can they clear a path?"

"It'll take hours," Heidi said. "But they can get on it."

"Hold on," Walter said. "So, we can't leave because LTE is on their way in. And we can't turn off the box because the key doesn't work. So, we're stuck?" He looked at the ceiling. "When does this place collapse again?"

"The key didn't work?" Katia asked, sounding alarmed and looking at Solanis.

"No, it didn't. Nothing happened," Solanis said.

"Fuck."

"The *first* key didn't work," Heidi corrected. "But we have another key. I have it. Hold on."

"Wait," Solanis said. "I can't go back there if the key's not going to work. I can't avoid getting killed by the reds only to be killed by SPINE. I don't like that trade."

Her stomach wanted to explode. How was it that she was sitting here negotiating her death options with a traitor, a disillusioned boyfriend, and a woman from the underground? What had her life become?

She looked at Walter. Maybe he would know what to do.

But he simply looked at the wall behind her. And in that instant, she knew what she wanted more than anything was to restore that connection.

What did it feel like for Gabby to have that, the genuine relationship of biology, one that wasn't chosen but preordained? Surely it felt like this, like fire pouring into her soul? Like the first time she and Walter met, the familiar sensation? Or was it stronger because it was forged by the universe?

What was the fix that Walter needed from her?

"Okay." Solanis stood, Gabby with her. "LTE is on their way in, so

403

we can't go out. Our people—your people"—she gestured toward Katia—"are going to work to clear a path out. And meanwhile, you have a new key that you're certain will drop the box?"

Heidi nodded, holding out the cube.

"Then we have to go see Worthington." She took the cube. This one was more level in weight. "I have to go see him."

Katia nodded.

Walter's eyes shifted just enough so she could tell he could see her.

"What was it you said, Katia?" Solanis said. "Aiesha doesn't want to destroy these things, the Domes? She thinks people need to be given a choice? She's not wrong. The people in here are good people. They're just like me. They ran because they were scared. They don't deserve to be killed for making a choice. Worthington can fix that. He can just do what Aiesha wants, right? He can give them a choice. Let people leave if they want too. Right? That will get LTE to stop?"

Katia nodded slowly. Her face didn't betray her inner thoughts. She was frozen.

"I'm going to ask him to tell me the truth." She patted her hair a few times, trying to get it back to manageable. A failed attempt at control.

"He's going to lie to you," Heidi said.

"I know when people are lying," she said. "And if he lies, I'll go for the box. But..." She held up her hand. "If it fails this time, you're getting us out of here. You'll find a way around LTE. We aren't staying."

Heidi nodded.

Walter stared at her from the other side of the room. He didn't nod or blink, but his eyes were less narrow.

That was a start.

This was the fix.

Solanis shook her head, trying to get the fireflies away from her face. "And I need pills. Heidi, can you see if you can get me some of those little blue pills? The ones I use for my eyes?"

Heidi nodded. "I'll meet you outside of ComCen after your meeting with Worthington. Check your tablet."

"Where can we put Gabby and Tatiana, so they are safe?"

404

Heidi motioned that Gabby and Tatiana should come with her. "I have a place."

Solanis reached down and hugged Gabby.

In her sleepy state, Gabby's grip was weak. But she said, "I love you."

"I'll be back," she said. She looked at Walter. "Watch her. Please."

He nodded.

"Do this for her. Okay? I know you don't like me. I get it. Don't do it for me. Do it for Gabby. For her."

He nodded.

This time, he didn't look through her.

33

THEREAFTER

Manuel

"You want to find a way to save the planet?" Tiberian rubbed the edge of the chair he'd settled in without even nodding toward Manuel. "Real wood, huh?"

Manuel didn't respond. Tiberian was peacocking. Flexing.

"We're sitting on dead trees, and *you* want to save the planet?" He cackled. "Do you know how to save the world? Because it needs saving."

"You look at the research?" Manuel gestured to the wall display in his office, the edges of the projection blurry as the sun threatened to blind the screen while it assaulted the shade that covered the balcony. "There are several designs that can be considered. Machines that take the carbon from the air. Shields we can deploy in space to redirect sunlight. Policy reforms. They're all in there."

Tiberian flicked through Ronnie. "These have no chance of success. All tired and old ideas. You want to save us? Tell Russia to stop digging to the core. China too. They won't find energy down there. Just death."

Manuel shook his head. "There's one idea. One I think we are ready for."

406

"Don't be dramatic."

"A dome."

"A dome."

Manuel stood and walked to the other side of his desk, to his child-hood snow globe. He waved the snow globe in the man's face. "Right now, we are hurting more than we are helping. And we need to give the planet a break. A time for it to heal. We are going to build a city inside of a dome. The largest dome you can imagine. It'll be tempera-ture-controlled, all waste and thermal output regulated inside. Imagine one million people whose impact is no longer felt on the planet." He leaned forward and stared into Tiberian's good eye. "It will be like they never existed. Like they were never there. That will give the planet time to heal. It will give our children a fighting chance."

"You don't have children," Tiberian growled. He looked at his tablet. "And if we proceed with this dome idea of yours, how long would it take?"

"To build? I can have the first one done in less than a decade."

"No. To heal the planet."

"Centuries."

Tiberian snorted. "Too long."

"Not for a planet that measures time in millennias."

"You can't do this on your own. There's no way Kinder will let you build a new country inside of his country."

"Yes, he will," Manuel said. "I'm going to tell him I will not run for president. He can have the White House. Politicians will do anything to keep power. I'll take myself off the board."

"What if I want you to be president?"

He shook his head. "You don't. You can find another way to use me. I already got you StarLight. We are even."

"I mean after I fund this project of yours. Your dome. And we are not even. Not yet."

He waved a hand. "You don't get to sit on a favor forever. You'll be dead by a hundred and twenty if you play your cards absolutely perfect. And seeing you're already missing an eye, I doubt you'll make it."

"Don't start writing my eulogy yet. You're not the only one I'm working with. There are more people who want to change this world and the next. You want me to pay for this?"

"Yes. And I will pay you back. After tomorrow, people will pay me for a chance to live inside. They'll give me everything. And I believe we will get people who will take the chance. I've hired consultants who have already told me how to build a circular trade economy inside. I have engineers who are planning how to build the dome, and I have an inbox filled with evangelists who are begging me to do something more."

"So, you're the most powerful man in the world." Tiberian shook his head. "Even Samson fell at the hands of a woman. Like time, power is relative."

Manuel frowned. "Samson?"

"Read a Bible," he growled. "He was a strong man. She killed him." He made scissors with his fingers. "His hair was his weakness. Quick short cuts."

"I don't intend to fail."

"No one does. So, you think this will work?"

"We have no choice." Manuel held up his chin. "Tomorrow, I will tell the world that while I saved the Union, we still have work to do. And then I will tell them that hope is here. That we have a chance to turn back the clock. That we can regain the earth's trust."

Tiberian considered him. "You can't defeat death. But you actually believe everything you just said."

"The science agrees with me. And this is what we need to do."

"It was a statement, Manuel. You politicians can't stop talking. Telling your stories."

Both men fell silent.

Manuel walked over to the window. Outside, thousands had gathered, laying gifts, flowers, and candles to wish him well. He'd gained a following since returning from the Free Republic. "These people are hurt. Just like I was. And for the first time, I have something to offer them. A way they can do something for themselves that can help everyone. Tomorrow, I will ask each of them to make a choice. One that is so easy, they cannot help but make the right decision."

Tiberian scowled. "People will never make decisions that help others—"

"Which is why I am going to ask them to save themselves. And in the process, they'll save us all."

He nodded. "I'll give you the funds. My accountant will build you a corporation. You'll have full control. I want the data though." He patted Manuel on his shoulder. "I want all the data that you get from the people living in your dome. We can learn about them, and it might just help with a few other projects I'm working on. Like I said, you're not the only one trying to change the world." He walked to the door of the office, yanked it open, and turned back toward Manuel. "You know what's funny? When I first heard of you, Cassandra said that this Man from Denver had a great story. Cassie said this candidate for Congress had a way with words. People flocked to his rallies and speeches to hear him talk about their families stuck across the York Line. They said you were different. You meant it. I sat in the back of one of your speeches. The one you held in City Park. And the people cried." He nodded to himself. "You *are* different, Manuel. And I think you know it. But you're also just a man. Do not forget that the end of the day comes. And most men do not go gentle into the good night. They cry, kick, scream, moan. Don't get your head too stuck in the clouds, when you walk, the dust at your feet are sandstorms for ordinary people. And when it's your turn, when your light dims, you have a spot in history. You've dented the world, Manuel, not moved it. You can shake the earth, but it turns at its own pace. Remember who helped you do that. You will always be mine. I can be your Delilah if you forget."

Tiberian vanished into the hallway.

Manuel shrugged and walked to the balcony, hardly aware that Cassandra Price was standing in the shadows of the room behind him. He pushed open the doors and looked down. The throngs of pilgrims had all copied his style, each wearing variations of green. The men, women, and children grew quiet at his appearance as the sun eased itself into the west.

He could see Sebán reminding him.

Tranquilo, Manuel.

His arm making that smooth downward motion.

His mother's smell, her smile, and her warmth was somewhere.

Manuel leaned forward over the balcony and swept his hand over his people. He closed his eyes. He could feel them—their presence, their yearning, their pain, and their sorrow. He lowered his hand gently—to reassure them, as his father had once done for him.

When he opened his eyes, all the men and women in green below were silently staring up at him, their candles casting a warm glow.

His eye twitched.

This was going to be the start of his purpose.

He would set them free from the chains of their fate.

For Manuel Worthington, these people—his people—would be his purpose. They would be his thereafter.

34

THE MAN FROM DENVER

Solanis

The Man from Denver sat cross-legged on the floor under a bright light, tending to a plant that was a mix of dark green and pale white. He didn't look up when Solanis entered the room. Instead, he peered down at the pale brown mass of wires—the exposed roots of the plant.

"Have you ever seen an albino monstera before, Ms. Tailor?" His voice was quiet from underneath his carefully combed mass of hair. As if he'd wake the plant if he was too loud.

She shook her head. She hadn't thought she'd seen one before. Not even in the Fields.

"They are rare." He stroked the bottom of the plant, looked satisfied, and then picked up the entire plant and stuck it in the white pot sitting near him on the floor. "Do you mind?" he asked, gesturing toward the monstera.

She stiffly walked over and kneeled on the ground next to Worthington. He smelled like old coffee, wine, and wet soil. Or was that the plant?

"Hold it steady." He guided her hand to the plant's thin stalk while he picked up a trowel and began scooping dirt into the pot around it.

"We put lava rocks on the bottom to help with drainage. A special blend of soil around the plant that allows the roots to grow without being constricted. But they'll grow out of a waste container if they had to."

Solanis nodded. For some reason, she didn't want to make eye contact with him.

"Yes, these plants are rare." The man continued scooping. "And you know why? It's because to get the albino leaf, you need a genetic mutation. Somewhere in the cells that were rapidly dividing and building the structures that made life, they forgot to add enough chlorophyll. The cells that make the plant green. As a result, wide swaths of the plant are green, and the other half will be white. But this variegated monstera is all white. Years of selected breeding. Years of following the formula the biologist Gregor Mendel laid out for us. I dedicated myself to creating this beauty. Only you and I both know that this delicate and beautiful white albino plant in front of us will never survive on its own. Its beauty is because it's so delicate. It's why it's rare. It's why it brings us a rare kind of joy. Underneath the white shell is a plant that is dreadfully unprepared to fight Mother Nature. They don't live very long without our intervention."

"You can let go." Worthington put down the trowel. "This plant is a descendant of the one my mother gave me many years ago. She used to keep it in a terrarium in our apartment in Denver. She was so proud of it. Called it her beauty. But when she was taken from me, because the United States didn't do anything to fix the planet, it was left for me to do something. I was left to care for this plant. I think I have about ten versions of my mother's monstera. Ten versions of the life that first sprouted nearly a century ago."

Solanis let go and sat back on her bottom to give her knees some rest. The monstera stood upright by itself, its three white leaves standing proudly in the center of the room. Worthington reached for a spray bottle and gave the plant a few sprays.

"We'll let it sit for a while," he said, wiping his hands on a green towel. He handed it to Solanis. "You need this?"

She declined.

She wasn't sure what to make of this old man gardening attitude. Was she expecting a prelude to him expressing sympathy for her kidnapping? Was she expecting to be scolded for being friends with Katia? There was no way he didn't know what she was up to. Her heart was beating faster than usual, but that was perfectly normal when meeting the gods who wandered among the earth.

Worthington shrugged and settled into one of the armchairs. He crossed his legs as he got comfortable and motioned that she should sit too. She did.

"You're one of the few people who have left the Dome after coming in. Besides the Higher Committee and the spies who infiltrate our home, not many go in and out." He fiddled with the leaf in his lapel. "But you did."

"I didn't leave on purpose." She surprised herself with her response. She hadn't planned to say anything.

"Sure," he said. "And you intend to destroy this place." It wasn't a question.

Had he been listening to her all along? Watching her? Did he know what was in her pocket—the key that was supposed to break the box that hung deep within the ComCen compound?

She tried to keep her face blank, but he seemed unbothered.

"And what have you decided?" He continued to stare at her.

She sat quietly. His frankness was surprising.

Was this something that usually worked?

Solanis pushed back. "Why did Shalina collapse?"

He smiled. He didn't have emeralds in his teeth. Those were for poor people. "I think you know why."

"No." She shook her head. "I want to know why it fell. The real reason."

He stroked his chin for a second, studying her. "What did they tell you?"

"I've heard two stories."

He gestured that she should continue. He was playing with her. But she had time. She could play.

"Shoddy construction," she said. "LTE."

He nodded. "LTE played a role. They've been trying to knock down my gift of salvation for a long time now. Aiesha Patterson hasn't been helping either. We've learned a lot since building the first few projects." He smiled. "Porciúncula, Shalina, Jericho, Zenos, Shamut…" He let his voice trail off.

Solanis watched him. He seemed lost in his own world.

But she wasn't going to break the silence.

And he was fine basking in it, holding his smile.

"Ambassador," he finally said, "my team always says I tell too many stories. But if you'll indulge me for a moment. Growing up, my mother, Sylvia, used to tell me a story. After my mother went missing, he was obsessed with stories. Fictions from eras ago."

Solanis had the unsettling image of a small boy clad in all green listening to bedtime stories.

"It is a love story. I think my father's mother told it to him or something like that. I can't be sure. Stories, like rumors, have a way of cascading down throughout the generations, shedding context, vocabulary, and language until they spin into something almost unrecognizable. But Ambassador Tailor, I think you and I can both agree that even though much is lost in the passing down of stories, there is one element that is always consistent. Meaning."

He leaned forward in his armchair. In person, his eyes were strikingly green.

He continued. "The way the story goes, a brave warrior and a beautiful princess fell in love. The man, honorable, was drafted into a great war. This was one of those wars that could end civilization. Not like our civil war. That was a small skirmish compared to this. And he promised the king that he would defend the homeland whenever the time came. The king said that if he served, when he returned home, he could have the princess for his own. He would bless their union. Before the man left, the princess gave him a necklace with a square turquoise gemstone on it.

"But there were rivals in town who didn't want the marriage to happen. They wanted the princess to marry someone of noble blood. So, as the man went off to war and fought with honor, they told the princess that he had died in battle.

"They showed her his turquoise necklace—the one she had given him when he'd left for war. But the plan backfired. Upon hearing the news, the princess wandered the countryside until she died from a broken heart. When the man returned and found the princess dead, he took her body, carried it to the top of the mountain, and sat with her.

"For a month, he kept watch over her body, dreaming of the future they might have had together. Telling her the stories of their kids, of the castles they would have built in the sky. He died next to her. There are two mountains in Mexico named for these two souls as reminders of the sacrifice. Do you know what the sacrifice was, Solanis?"

"He wanted to be with her, so he died with her," Solanis said.

What was his point?

"Almost."

He was toying with her.

Or was he stalling before SPINE would enter and drag her to the Darkness.

Worthington kneeled in front of the monstera, stroking one of the leaves with his hand. "His leaving. That was the sacrifice." He looked at her. "When the king told him he needed to go to war, the man stopped what he was doing and left the one person he loved behind to make sure she would be safe. He would do anything to protect the king's kingdom if it meant that she would stay alive. Even if the king had not promised him her hand in marriage, he would have gone anyway. When you love someone so much, you will sacrifice anything to protect them, even yourself. I think you know that, Solanis. It's why when Ambassador Wick interviewed you for your position inside of Shamut, he told you about the ambassador job. We knew you would do anything to keep yourself safe. And now that you're inside Shamut, both of us know you'd do anything to keep your daughter safe. That's you, isn't it? A woman who craves safety."

Solanis's hand jerked as she tried to squeeze the bridge of her nose and hold her hand in her lap at the same time. Why did it seem like she hadn't had a single shred of free will over the last decade? Had she really been handpicked? Selected because Worthington thought she was—

"I'm not predictable," she said.

"We all are." He stood and brushed the dirt off his pants from the floor. "You made the perfect sacrifice. You didn't come here because you love the planet. And that's okay. You came here because you thought it was safe."

"How is a Dome collapsing—"

"Safer than outside." He raised his voice. "You've seen Haze, the murky amber and black rivers. You gave up everything to keep yourself safe, and you proved to everyone here that you are willing to do what it takes to keep your daughter and the people around you safe. And I am willing to bet you'd make the same choice again. You know, people only want the monstera at the end. The bright, white, beautiful albino plant. But they aren't willing to accept that the insides might not all be what they expected. So, we Propagate. We Recycle. We refine our process. We build new Domes so the earth may have one more chance." He sat again, staring deep into her eyes. "So, if 1.7 million people have to die so we can ensure the survival of eleven billion, that's a perfect sacrifice. We don't get to the final white leaf without sacrificing something." He paused for a moment. "My parents were torn apart by the war. My dad was killed because the planet tried to kill all of us. And my mother..." He grimaced. "She was killed drinking the water. The poisoned water of the Free Republic. Surely, you can see the earth is running out of patience?" He nodded as he spoke. "You can see it has been warning us. Yet people still ignore its warnings. Warnings always turn to demands eventually."

Solanis kept her hands still, refusing to swat the fireflies in her vision.

So, he was mad.

He was going to build new Domes, and people were going to move into them. The Domes would collapse, and they'd all die.

This wasn't sacrifice. This was murder.

"What if they had a choice?" Solanis asked.

"They all have a choice, Solanis. They chose to be set free."

"No. It's not a choice if they don't know they're choosing to die if this Dome fails."

"They're choosing to die if they stay outside."

"But what if we gave them the facts? Let them choose for themselves. Show them what all of us know. Then they could choose to make the sacrifice." She scooted forward in her chair, getting as close to him as possible. "What do we *know*, sir? In your story, if the princess had known her boyfriend was still alive, she would have stayed and waited for him. Nothing anyone did would have caused her to stray from him. She was loyal. But we also know he was loyal. Had he known she'd be dead upon his return, from natural causes or otherwise, he still would have defended his country. He would have fought because he'd rather she had one more day alive without him than no days at all. Like you said, he was an honorable man, and that's what honorable men do. The planet is obviously dying. Why not appeal to people to help solve the problem? Give them the option of joining the grand experiment so others may live?"

Worthington drummed his fingers on the edge of his chair as if studying her. She wished her eyes were normal.

She stared back, unblinking.

"We're so close," he said, his eye twitching. Was that sorrow on his face, or just weary conviction? "Caer and Thessala look promising. We have a new panel formula that's designed for our gravity. We only got it through learning from these first batches of Domes."

"I'm talking about now," she said. "They deserve to know now."

He didn't respond.

There was a soft boom from far away.

"What was that?" she asked.

But he didn't seem bothered. "If anything's wrong, my team will come for me."

She continued. "You keep telling people you want them to make the perfect sacrifice, but if people don't know what they're sacrificing, does it really count?"

He shook his head. "You're not the first person who has tried to kill a box."

She froze.

"We turned off the box in Zenos, and they just went back to their old ways. It's not a sustainable solution. Humans become drones when nostalgia is let into this environment. When given a choice, they choose themselves. Not us. They are selfish."

Solanis thought back to Walter. He'd sacrificed a lot for her. Even his soul. "They might surprise you."

Worthington shook his head. "No, I don't think so." He scratched his chin. "How about this? If someone were to learn the truth, I will not stop them from leaving. SPINE won't do a memory wipe, and they can go out into the world and try to live with themselves."

"Try?" she asked.

"People think we are a crazy bunch of tree-hugging radicals anyway. When Porciúncula collapsed, Haze attacked Austin, Texas, and we filled up our ninth project the next day. I don't think you understand how desperate people are for hope. Something to believe in."

She stood. "Swear on it."

"If I do, will you give up your crusade?"

"Crusade?"

He wagged his finger. "Stupidity looks bad on you, Solanis. I know what you want to do with BlackBox. But you should know, based on your background, that the box is uncrackable. Everyone else at your level, every other ambassador, is willing to make the perfect sacrifice. We all are willing to do what it takes to ensure this planet is still here for our descendants. Solanis, don't you want your sacrifice to mean something too? For Gabby?" He took a step forward. "Trust me, Solanis. The world will die if we do not meet our goals. People remember their ancestors and the damage they've caused. Ask former President Franjola-Ricardo, she was stuck cleaning up, begging on behalf of the Free Republic. So, ask yourself. You're forty-five years old. Is another seventy-five years worth it when you have to spend the time stumbling around in darkness only for the earth to wither and die under your feet? Is knowing you were selfish and that you hid from the real war all worth it?"

Solanis waved her hand in front of her face. The fireflies were unavoidable.

He broke into a smile. "Ah, the Haze is coming back. You need your pills, don't you?"

There was a pounding of feet outside the door. Raised voices. A scuffle.

He continued. "You know we're the only ones who make those pills? The ones that keep your eyes clean? And I don't need to tell you what you have to do to get them." He smiled at her. "Which sacrifice are you willing to make, Solanis Navreet Tailor? The one for the greater good or the one that's no sacrifice at all?" He took her hand and shook. "I promise I will not stop you from taking the easy way out. I have a simple solution for you. Just tell Ambassador Leonardo Walkenshaw that you want to leave, and you'll wake up outside. You'll have your house back. You'll have the memories of Shamut. Gabby's education will be paid for. You'll even get the money you hid from us when you first entered Shamut. You'll remember us. I'd never steal your service from you. You will go blind. But you'll live. Live in the dark, knowing you did exactly what *they* expected you to do. What the cowards who hide outside and do nothing to protect the planet that brought our ancestors life expected you to do. You can betray your ambassadorial oath, and I will not stop you. But we will live, we will thrive." Worthington laughed. "For a second there, I sounded like Gideon Voss."

Worthington shook his head, turned and walked to the door. He leaned forward and listened. The noises grew louder. But he didn't seem to care.

She narrowed her eyes. She'd seen this before. Men like Worthington, who had infinite resources, never cared about the things that mattered to most people.

"Keep the plant, Solanis," he said. "I doubt we'll meet again. I'm okay with that. You are indeed a fantastic woman. Your brother told me as much." The Shepherd smiled. "I miss him. He was a lot like you. Challenging us at meetings. He was the one who told me about you. He didn't know it, but he was the reason we recruited you. We tried to save him. It's too bad the pills had side effects…"

His voice wandered off as he gave a heavy sigh, and he looked at the display that showed a crowd of people swaying and singing to the collective music of Shamut in Worthington Park. The Green Monster teemed with life as people excitedly chatted. New Evergreens, excited to be home.

"I knew bringing you here was the best decision we could make. It might have also been the worst." His hand lingered above the touch pad next to the door.

But before he could say anything else, he jumped back.

The door burst open, and in barged four people in black suits.

There was a loud grinding and rumbling.

The lights flickered out.

35

ASH

Solanis

"Sir, we need to leave," one of the men in black said, his voice elevated as the emergency lights strobed red and white.

Had the sky fallen in?

Solanis couldn't make out Worthington's response over the bang and shouts from the corridor, nor could she focus as the building rumbled and vibrated.

No, the sky hadn't fallen in yet.

She tried to take a step toward Worthington. She'd be safest next to the man who crowned himself the god-king of the Dome. But one of the security forces held out his arm, stopping her. She tried to steady herself but wobbled. Another one of the agents pulled her back and spun her firmly toward the door.

One of the men in black shoved the albino monstera into her arms.

"He said that was for you."

They ushered her into the hallway.

These men were too efficient to be SPINE. They seemed to travel as one unit, like sets of twins who were too close for comfort. Their guns were at the ready, they spoke in low voices, but most of all, they wove her through the chaos that was the Higher Committee offices.

The common areas of the Higher Committee building were pandemonium. Evergreens had abandoned their desks, fleeing for safety. An announcement, in Worthington's voice, urged people to safety. The agents in black did not spare any of her colleagues, trampling over them as they moved down the hallway and ignoring their pleas for help or questions about safety.

More booms in the distance.

What was happening? Was this it? Was Shamut collapsing? Had she waited too long?

No, that couldn't be it. When the second Dome had collapsed, it was quick. They'd hardly had time to leave.

Her tablet vibrated.

The men in black had hustled her to the staircase and were holding the door. Solanis checked the Voice, colliding with the man in front of her. She dropped the monstera, the pot shattering.

A message from Heidi. *Lobby, statue, duck.*

What the fuck was that supposed to mean?

"We're moving," the agent behind her said, urging her forward.

Without thinking, Solanis pulled the top half of the white monstera's stalk off and tucked it away. The agents moved her down the cold concrete steps.

She tucked her tablet away and continued forward.

The lights were dim in the staircase. There hadn't been any attention to design in the emergency exits of the opulently decorated interior of the Higher Committee building. But as more booms and rapid gunfire echoed outdoors, the agents around her mumbled to each other.

When they reached the bottom of the staircase, a man greeted them with a vest in his hand. He instructed her to pull off her jacket as he helped her pull the vest over her head. "LTE has infiltrated Shamut," he said as she tugged on the straps. "We're pushing them back. They're unorganized, guerrillas. We'll be fine."

He kicked on the door three times with his foot, and she pulled her blazer back on over the vest. It fit too tight in the chest.

"We're moving you to the safe house," the man said.

"What about my daughter?" She tried to get comfortable, but she could hardly move her arms in the bulky one-size-fits-all vest.

He hesitated.

"I will not leave without her," she said.

"We are trying to locate her, ma'am." He tapped his chest. "Stay low and keep moving."

The earth shuddered.

She pinched the bridge of her nose and closed her eyes. She was back in the cave again, underground, the cooler over her head. Her father buried behind her.

No. She forced herself to come back.

"Move," the man said.

The world crashed back in harsh focus, and the door sprang open. They hurried into the lobby, the fireflies scurrying around her. The man shoved her forward from behind as the two agents in front of her swept the chaos in the lobby. Her men in black were roaming sentinels, emitting quick bursts from their weapons, while SPINE waged war against others in green. Bodies littered the floor among the shattered marble chunks of the front desk. The once-proud statue of Worthington was missing an arm. The model of the Dome he once proudly held, lay in the center of the room, the marble cracked and broken where it had fallen.

"Don't slow down." The agent behind her pushed harder on her back.

Their train wove to the left but then stopped as one of the agents in front suffered a head injury and collapsed to the side. But as quickly as he was gunned down, the agent from behind Solanis took his place and pulled her to the right, dodging a chunk of marble that shattered behind them.

Around her, in the cold, dark lobby, people pushed, pulled, fought, and screamed as they tried to overcome one another. The leg of the statue exploded as a rocket smashed into it. The agent in front of her shielded her from shrapnel.

A buzzing on the back of her neck yanked the world into focus.

Wait.

The statue.

Solanis threw herself to the ground as a loud whooshing noise and crushing bang overcame them. Bullets exploded overhead as she covered herself. The cave was collapsing again, and it was all she could do to keep breathing as the world shook, and the room crumbled.

The light was fading. The fireflies brighter than ever.

So, this was how she would die.

Away from Gabby.

Just her and the fireflies.

No.

Her body jerked upward. Light exploded around her.

Walter's voice came loud and clear in her ear. "We're moving," he said, pulling her toward the shattered doors.

There was no more noise in the lobby as the world sharpened into focus. The statue of Worthington was gone, as was the grand staircase that led to the second-floor atrium. Her entourage was missing. Her mouth tasted like iron.

A buzzing tingled her skin.

"Wait!" she yelled, pulling Walter backward and to the left.

They collapsed under the slight overhang in the lobby as the pillar near the door smashed to the ground, right where they had been.

He made a grunt, seeming too tired to speak as war raged around them. She kicked herself back up as the two scrambled down the side of the steps of the building.

She stopped. In front of her, she saw the proud avenue that led to the ComCen building, but that wasn't what gave her pause. The black smoke that rose over Shamut reminded her of Haze. It lingered over the Dome, creating an ominous black cloud hovering in wait. The massive displays on the skyscrapers flashed one consistent message in dark green: *STAY INSIDE.*

Walter pulled her hard as the two scrambled behind an abandoned WorthyCart. She panted, catching her breath with both hands on the manicured lawn. The echo of something collapsing caused her to cover her ears.

"Where are you, Katia?" he yelled into his tablet. "LTE isn't fucking around. We need to get out." He reached over and adjusted Solanis's vest.

"Where is—"

"Gabby's fine," he said. "She's with Heidi and Tatiana. They're getting her out."

She nodded and grabbed her tablet. "Good. How can we get there?" She nodded across the firefly filled boulevard toward ComCen. The streets were clear closest to them, but further down, LTE and SPINE fought. Somewhere above, a drone hovered—the heavy whipping of its blades overwhelming her senses. But when she looked up, she saw nothing.

"What?" He shook his head. "No. We need to go."

"No," she said. "We need to drop the box."

He stared at her, the brown held in the demitasse that were his eyes. What was he thinking? "No. Don't do that for me."

The wall next to them exploded. He pulled her back toward the other side of the truck, which was rolling forward into the street.

He nudged her forward, putting them in cadence with the cart. They had to break into a quick jog to keep pace with the armored vehicle. Bullets were slamming into the cart from the other side of the street, where people in red charged their way up the boulevard while battling SPINE, who were in their classic green uniforms.

A bullet missed Solanis and embedded itself into the rubber wheel of the cart. The cart began to slow.

Where was that drone? Why was it so loud?

"Fuck, fuck, fuck." Walter pulled at the doors of the cart, but they refused to open. "Fuck!" More bullets pounded the side of the cart. He shoved Solanis so she was in front of the rolling Worthycart, and he began laying down cover fire down the boulevard. "We need to get out of the street, Solar!" he yelled. He reached into his kit and tossed her a gun. "We can't stay here." Then to his collar, "Katia, where the fuck are you?"

Solanis weighed the gun in her hands. Was it a good idea to fire a weapon when her vision was fading? How much time would she have left before she went completely blind? It should be hours, not moments. A firefly stubbornly hovered in front of her face.

"Move." Walter shoved her forward. He fired toward the opposite end of the street, where another cart was picking up speed and rumbling in their direction.

This new cart wasn't stopping.

Solanis dragged Walter backward as the newest cart crashed into the cart they'd been trailing.

A loud screeching from the cart smashed into Solanis's ears. Fireflies bloomed from the vehicle, escaping the dented front end, cracked glass and the bent door.

From the wreckage came an injured Katia.

"Sorry. It wouldn't stop," she stuttered, wincing and grabbing her scarred face as she climbed out.

"Can you still drive it?" Walter asked.

Katia climbed back in the cart, inspecting the dash.

"We need to get out," he said. "You can fix it?"

"I just need time."

"We don't have time."

Bullets pounded the side of the cart. The people in red seemed to be winning. They needed to get out of the—

"No!" Solanis yelled. She grabbed his shoulders as the two crouched in front of the grill, Katia tinkering at the wires under the dash. "He's not going to. Worthington's not going to stop until he gets it right. Millions more are going to die. She might end up as one of those even if we get out. Gabby might get trapped. And..." She pushed her palm into his chest. "We need to do this now."

"Solar..."

"Walter!" Katia yelled, gesturing toward LTE, who were again advancing down the boulevard.

"No," Solanis said, both hands cupping his face. She pulled him closer to her.

His cheeks were rough.

"You were right. And I'm not scared. I mean, I am. But I'm not running."

"Solar, don't do this for me," he said.

She shook her head. "You're not that special. I'm doing it for her."

He blinked, squinted, tilted his head to the left, and then stood. "Katia, we need to get to the communications center. Now!"

"The battery's dead." Katia hopped from the cart, crouching as she joined the two of them.

Bullets pounded the side of the cart.

"The doors!" Solanis yelled, remembering Salazar. "They come off."

He nodded and got to work, peeling the doors from the cart. She got to work on the back door, the memory of dividing and conquering with her brother triggering a sadness at the base of her skull. The cart doors were easy to pry off; all it took was a simple flip of the side fasteners and yanking hard. The door was heavy, but she could manage.

She blinked rapidly as the fireflies gathered around the cart, creating fiery outlines around them.

Walter shook his head. "Give Katia your door," he said. "You're half blind."

Katia pulled the door from her, and Solanis checked the gun. "Should she have that if she'd blind?" she sneered.

"I'm not completely blind," Solanis complained.

"Yet."

Walter crossed to the other side of Solanis. "Solar, you're in the middle. Cross and up the steps."

Solanis nodded. "Don't drop the door, Katia."

"Bite glass," Katia shot back.

The three of them began to cross the street.

Advancing in the sloth-like second line proved more difficult than it should have been. Each time a bullet pounded the side of the door, Katia or Walter would push back, their bodies shoving Solanis to either side. She found herself pushing back so they didn't get off course. LTE warred with SPINE as they tried to make their way up the street where the banners blew, at least what was left of them.

There was some revelation in the back of Solanis's mind she had yet to unpack, an epiphany that could explain why SPINE wouldn't just let LTE kill them. She figured Worthington should know by now that she was going after the box. Or maybe she was being ignored, underestimated. A perk of being a proxy in the war of Worthington versus Aiesha.

Or maybe, Worthington was the god men claimed him to be, so

high on the throne that her insignificance didn't even register. Republics had fallen when gods abandoned the people.

Solanis, Katia, and Walter managed to reach the steps without holes in their body, and they began to make their way up. Climbing wasn't difficult. At one point, she needed to lean hard on Katia who was pushing her to the right as they began to list to the edge of the steps. But she kept them on track.

A SPINE green came bolting down the steps toward her, his gun drawn. She fired twice, the second bullet clipping the man's neck.

He fell, gurgling on the marble steps.

Walter leaned on her again as another agent came from his side. The doors were in sight.

Four more dead agents.

Katia had better aim than she.

She jammed her shoulder against him, correcting his positioning. He was pushing back too hard as bullets pelted them from the side.

"We need to go faster!" he yelled unfairly. How could a man who was at least eighty-five kilos of lean mass tell all one and a half meters of Solanis Tailor that she had to keep up? But he kept moving.

She tripped on the steps, pitching forward. She rolled to avoid smashing her face but jammed her hands on the steps. Pain radiated up her elbow and into the side of her chin.

"Get up!" Katia yelled, crouching and using the door as more cover. She fired ahead of them as more of SPINE ran down toward them. She grabbed Solanis's shoulder and pulled her up.

Solanis covered her ears as the drone assaulted them again, its massive blades and siren cutting through her ears.

Somewhere, a rocket made contact.

The drone exploded.

Katia yelled that they should make a run for it.

Walter shoved Solanis forward, and they sprinted up the steps.

Everything hurt.

She couldn't keep moving like this.

But she didn't have to. They'd reached the doors. A woman in green had her gun pointed at them. Death could come quick.

But when she saw Solanis, she broke into a smile. "Finally," she said, pulling Solanis forward into the busted atrium.

Walter and Katia filed in behind her, stepping over the broken glass of the door.

Four Evergreens, obviously spies, lunged toward the door and began firing down onto the marble steps.

ComCen hadn't fared any better than the Higher Committee building. The lobby was utterly destroyed, the marble shattered and the screens filled with static. The grunts of combat echoed around them. Worthington's statue was chipped and cracked; the arm was gone. The mini war being waged in ComCen spanned the second-floor balcony, where SPINE shot down into a mix of LTE and what had to be Katia's spies.

They huddled behind the massive help desk that was splintered and broken. On the balcony above, three SPINE agents shot down in their direction, cracking the marble floor. Solanis peeked over the desk toward the elevators on the far side of the room. Katia and Walter settled in across from her.

"We need to get to the elevators," Katia said to Walter, who nodded.

Solanis frowned, very much aware that she could hear Katia, as clear as if she was sitting next to her, even though she was about three meters away.

"We're going to knock down the staircase!" the woman who'd met them at the door yelled to Katia. "That'll be the distraction we need. And then you run. Cross the room."

Solanis nodded. "How will we know when to run?"

Katia frowned at her.

Walter held his hand to his ear. "What?"

"When will we know?" Solanis slid across the floor, leaning against the help desk. It vibrated as bullets pelted the other side. "When will we know?"

"I'll give a signal," he said in her ear. He was too loud.

The fireflies danced around the room, covering nearly every surface.

He patted her leg. "You good?"

"I am," she said. She blinked a few times. The fireflies winked out.

"It's not too late to—"

"Walter, stop."

"I'm just saying you don't have to prove yourself. Or die. Gabby needs you."

"I have no intention of dying, Walter. She needs me to reach out when the time is right," Solanis said, very much aware that she'd just quoted Katia.

He nodded, one eyebrow raised, leaned past her and spoke to their guide. "When?"

"About twelve seconds," the guide said. "Use the elevator shaft, don't get in the elevator."

"I'm not stupid," Katia rolled her eyes.

"Are you sure they won't drop the box?" Solanis yelled over the noise.

Katia spoke at a normal tone. "We jammed it, remember? It's paralyzed. Can't move."

The room was aggressively loud. More bullets slammed into the desk.

"Now!" Walter yelled.

They scuttled forward toward the elevators, staying low. The world exploded around them. Solanis pulled him by his vest, leading him, as he fired bursts upward. He kept pace with her, Katia bringing up the rear.

Smoke from the rocket-propelled grenade thickened as the floor rolled and bucked underneath them. Flecks of marble skinned their shins and knees as they ran through the shrapnel. Fire burned around them.

If she squinted, Solanis could see the mouth of the elevator opening in front of her, the panels hopelessly warped and bent. It was like the screams in Shalina. The whooshing of a still functional elevator as it traveled downward, deep into the building, stood out among the atrium's thunder.

How were they supposed to avoid getting crushed? Surely someone would turn it off.

She heard a click, and a soft chime directly behind her. She stopped, turned, and instantly reached for Walter, pulling him down. Something whizzed over their heads, and her face burned before she registered the fireball. Her right hand, cut by broken marble, split open.

The elevator shaft exploded in front of them.

"The right, the right one!" Katia yelled, already on her feet and leading the charge.

Solanis grabbed Walter's hand as he helped her up.

Solanis could hardly see as they closed the gap between them and the elevator shaft. Her face was in pain, her hand cut, leg throbbing. The room pounded against her skull.

When they reached the darkness of the shaft, they grabbed the rungs that made up the wall of the long service elevator shaft, and they climbed.

———

IGNORING her injury proved to be impossible even if Solanis wanted to. Each time she grabbed a rung of the ladder, her elbow pulsed, and her leg struggled to command itself. She was going to fall. At least then, she wouldn't have to worry about becoming blind. Or maybe she'd just be crushed by the elevator. She could hear the sounds of the magnets tugging at the elevator's edges below.

"Is the elevator working?" Walter asked from above her.

"Yes," she said. "I can hear it down there. We should hurry."

"How the fuck do you hear an elevator?" Walter demanded.

Moving her mind to other things helped with the physical pain. Thinking of how Manuel Worthington had made sense was mental pain.

Worthington always had to have a good reason to build his beloved Domes. He'd spent the better half of her life convincing the world they needed to make sacrifices. The Man from Denver who ended the war and raised the fucking seas. People had just nodded and accepted he had to be right. He was like a religion that had always been there, his disciples converting the masses.

You didn't need to believe in God to appreciate the cathedrals built in the Lord's honor, even if understanding came in parables, obscurity, and contradiction. In the Bible, the dead walked again. That couldn't happen. Only, it *almost* could. Greg had *almost* been back.

Almost.

But what do you know?

Katia had tried to kill Gabby, or had been willing too. Solanis couldn't let that go.

But she also knew Worthington was simply wrong, and even though he spoke with the poetic staccato of her mother, he didn't have the right.

But why hadn't her brother told her that the Domes were going to collapse? All he did was die. Though he had been coming back when they'd been together. Recovering from death, let alone a marathon, was hard. Did he buy into his employers ideas? An employer who had experimented on him. And killed him.

That's what Worthington had said, right? The regret at the end of their conversation?

Would she die today?

Would she get back in time to *see* Gabby?

See Gabby before the darkness rolls in.

Solanis swatted away more fireflies. It would be nice if they left. Around her, the shadows had begun to come to life, growing and darkening in front of her eyes. A hidden world of aureate brilliance unfolded before her.

Walter's eyes glowed orange. Katia's pockets glowed. The Voice glowed. Solanis was tempted to lose herself in the sea of fireflies and glowing embers. Just drift in the field of nothing. Heavy bass pulsed around them.

Would this new world be her reality?

Walter stopped ahead of her. "This is the floor." He pointed to the darkness. The wires around him began to glow a bright orange. The fireflies swirled and danced. "Give me a sec to get them open."

"Elevator is moving," Katia said, a slight panic in her voice.

"We're moving," he grunted back.

"What's with the music?" Solanis frowned.

Walter grunted, and the doors above them eased open. Solanis almost fell as she covered her ears. The pulsing bass swelled. But she used her legs to push herself up behind him and hopped into the room.

Unlike the last time she had stumbled into this room, there was no attendant, no security. Just windowless. Just light green and white lights pulsing from the walls. There was a scattering of fireflies in the corners of the room. Deep in the center of the room would be the glass drop-off point, where one wrong step would lead to a ten-story fall. It was where they would drop the box.

Why was the music so loud?

"Where's the panel to control this place?" Solanis yelled to Katia.

"On the far wall!" Katia yelled back.

The elevator whooshed past them in the shaft, still traveling upward.

Solanis took a tentative step forward, searching for the panel. It was too dark; she could hardly see.

But something felt wrong.

Katia took a sip of water from her canteen and breathed out. Walter was also breathing steadily, but there was another sound beneath the bass—the sound of faster breathing.

And the smell of peppermint.

The elevator whooshed back down the open gap they'd left.

"Walter," Solanis said. "I think—"

From the shadows, Leonardo pulled the trigger. Katia stumbled backward, hit, but groped for her weapon. It was no use. He fired again. The impact pushed her backward.

Katia seemed to hover briefly, her silver hair flung in front of her face, as gravity decided what it would do next.

And then it was decided.

Her fall into the dark was like ash, burdened by rain.

36

THE PERFECT SACRIFICE

Leonardo

Walter reached for his gun, but Leonardo was faster.

"Touch the weapon, and it'll be the last thing you do," Leonardo said, his gun already pointed at him.

He lowered his arms.

"Come here," Leonardo demanded.

He moved slowly across the room. Leonardo grabbed the gun from his holster and tucked the spare gun into his back pocket.

It had worked. Killing all the electronics in the room and pumping in loud music so Solanis couldn't hear him. The healer had been right. She was effectively blind. They'd stopped her meds.

She looked different. Not physically. It was more like how she carried herself. Her back was straighter, and she didn't look worried. She also stared at him like he was a stranger. Or did she stare through him?

It was Walter, wasn't it? The man from outside who had come back with her. The man who had sent her the notes. The man who was putty in her hands.

How dare she love someone so weak?

434

"Do I have to tell you to drop your gun, Solanis?" Leonardo asked. The same stubbornness.

She dropped her weapon.

"Kick it over to me."

She complied.

He placed his foot on the gun and picked it up, sliding it into his holster. "What are you doing here?" he asked.

Walter opened his mouth, but Leonardo didn't want to hear from him.

"You speak, and I'll kill her." He shifted his gun, so it was on her. He wouldn't move if the bullet could beat him to its target. "And don't lie to me," he said to her. "I'll know. I know you." He jutted his head toward Walter.

Solanis didn't speak.

"What are you doing here?"

"There's a war outside, Leonardo." She took a step forward.

"Do you want to see what you look like with a hole in your head?" he demanded.

She stopped moving. "Leonardo, I'm here because—"

But he cut her off. "Don't lie to me. I'm not stupid. You think I'm stupid."

"You're not."

"I know I'm not."

Yet her tone mocked him.

Ever since she'd come back inside Shamut, she'd been like this. She lied to him during her reintegration, she'd avoided him, and she'd visited the underground while spouting all that nonsense about Shamut collapsing. Why hadn't she taken his word for anything as she had in the past? Why was she suddenly so quick to undermine him? They were supposed to be friends. Partners. *Ambassador or bust*, they'd said. A decade of friendship just vanished because LTE had come in and brainwashed her.

Because Katia had brainwashed her.

"Why, Solanis?" he demanded. "Why did you believe everything they say?"

Solanis closed her eyes.

435

"Solanis," he said.

"What?"

"Pay attention to me."

"I am."

"Then why did you lie to me?" he asked. *"To me?"*

Solanis glanced at Walter.

It was him, wasn't it?

Leonardo should just kill Walter too, like he'd done Katia. Was that what she needed to be tugged back to him? Walter had been the one giving her notes, pulling her outside. It was why she'd said no at Dirt.

It was why she had laughed at him.

Once she was back with him, he could remind her why they were in Shamut. Their purpose.

The way Worthington had wanted.

Solanis shook her head. "I had to."

"Had to?"

"Yes. I lied because"—she looked at the floor—"I didn't know what to do. But now I know, right? I know now."

"Know what?"

"These people don't deserve to die."

He laughed. It tasted awful. "No one is going to die."

"I know you think that, but I've seen it. I've seen all of it. You just have to see it too." She jerked her neck and waved her hands around. "Sorry. Don't shoot," she said. "Fireflies."

He glared at her. He wasn't going to get distracted. "What didn't you get about the things we showed you? The things infrastructure showed you. We are here for a reason. We all have jobs to do. The people down there? They work. We lead. We were chosen to lead."

"You've been down there, Leonardo. You've felt the way the walls rumble and the earth shakes?"

"We all have our part to play—"

But she didn't stop. "I know what it's like when the earth crumbles around you, and it's not pretty. You know that's how my parents died, right? In front of me. Buried in the earth. It's why I was sent to Denver. You don't want that to happen here. Trust me. You don't want that."

"They keep the sky up." He seethed. "I keep it safe, and you make

436

sure our people stay in line. We fight nostalgia. We're the tip of the spear."

She hadn't blinked yet.

He tightened his grip on his gun. Those eyes would not manipulate him.

"But what if they weren't doing their jobs?" Solanis asked.

"Are they?"

"The best they can." Solanis dug her foot into the floor, shifting uncomfortably. "Leonardo, you should see them. For every panel the workers in the below fix, ten more break."

"This is a system built on trust." He squinted. "You have so little faith in the system that you let LTE play you. I've been down there. Those people you look down on, they're *my* people. They're from the barracks. I know you think you're better than them—"

"I don't think—"

"Don't cut me off!" He clenched his jaw. "You're not better than them. They're not afraid of hard work."

"Leonardo, I'm from the barracks," Walter said softly.

"Do you want a trophy?" Leonardo snapped.

Yes, I should kill Walter next.

"Why can't you trust them, Solanis? As they trust you?"

"Because they know," she said. "And they're lying to you."

———

WORTHINGTON, from behind his desk in the busy Higher Committee offices, had warned Leonardo's encounter with Solanis would be difficult. His colleagues swirled around him, speaking in hushed tones, while others seemed to be dismantling various devices and cables from within the walls. Yet despite the flurry of activity, Mr. Worthington was fully engaged with his sleeves rolled up and his blazer hanging over the edge of his chair.

"Sir," Leonardo said, bowing his head slightly and grasping the man's hand with both of his own.

Mr. Worthington's hands were strong, calloused, and rough. "Please sit." He gestured to the chair in front of his desk.

Leonardo took a seat on the edge of the chair. He wanted to look ready.

The Shepherd waved his hands, his colleagues left the room, and it was just the two of them. "Cassandra Price tells me you've done excellent work," he said. His voice was like a cello—strong, smooth. "I can't thank you enough for discovering who was responsible for taking one of our ambassadors outside."

Leonardo's cheeks were warm as he accepted the praise. How he'd longed to hear these words—just any words—from the man who had saved them.

"Sir." Leonardo bowed his head again. "I'm just doing what you asked of me."

"Of course you are." The Shepherd tilted his head down so he was looking directly at him. "But I find that when you're doing a good job, someone should recognize it. I know how stiff Kruger can be sometimes."

He blushed. "Not at all, sir. She's—"

The Shepherd held up a hand. "I hired her. She's a cold condom."

He snorted.

Mr. Worthington leaned back in his chair, smiling, and sighed. "I have another job for you, if you're willing."

He nodded quickly. "Of course, sir."

"It will test you. I won't lie to you about that. But it's a test I know you will pass. I will not give you more than you can bear."

Leonardo nodded. He'd heard that line someplace before. Echoes from the elders in the barracks—the ones who told stories of a pre-war nation. "Sir," he said confidently, "I'm here to protect your beauty. What can I do?"

The Shepherd had nodded and leaned forward, steepling his fingers. "I need your help with Ambassador Tailor."

———

"You always know better, don't you?" Leonardo snarled at Solanis.

He tapped his temple, trying to stay calm. The anger inside was rooted deeper than he expected, poking through the rational surface of his investigative persona. The adrenaline he'd felt after killing Katia had worn off, and now it was just an uneasy anticipation.

Solanis waved her hand in front of her face. He realized, in his anger, that he'd forgotten to check to make sure she didn't have any other weapons on her.

That was stupid.

He took two steps forward, closing the distance between them. Just as he'd done in Dirt. "Don't try anything." He wiggled the gun. He could feel Walter's eyes drilling into him, but it didn't matter. His finger could move faster than anything Walter could do.

Leonardo started at her shoulders and traced her sternum down to her chest. She hadn't bothered to wear a bra. He checked under her arms, tracing his hand from her lower back to her pockets.

There was a small cube inside her pocket. He dumped it out onto the ground and then crushed it under his heel. He yanked off her necklace and tossed it to the side. She'd feel vulnerable without it.

He made her turn around, checking her butt with the back of his hand. He could be respectful, even if he was angry.

The fact she had no weapons was little vindication for him. People died for less.

She turned back around and glared at him, her eyes shimmering. She glanced at the cube and then back to him.

"What was that?" he asked. "It's important to you."

"It's nothing," she said. She waved her right hand again.

"Why do you keep waving your hands?"

She crossed them and didn't respond.

He knew the answer. She was going blind. Her vision was decaying. Just another lie, even if by omission.

Why did she keep lying to him? All he'd done was try and protect her and her daughter. He'd helped her become ambassador, and this is how she repaid him? She should be thanking him. Why couldn't things go back to the way they'd been before? Before Katia had poisoned her with LTE's lies.

Wait.

Katia.

"She told you, didn't she?" he asked.

439

———

"SOLANIS... Ambassador Tailor. It's not her fault," Worthington had said. "LTE dragged her outside. They showed her footage of Shalina. And then they told her a story. Stories have a way of warping themselves over time." He gestured to the massive wall that had morphed into a display. "This is what they showed her." He pointed to the display as Shalina imploded.

Leonardo tried to show no emotion, act as if this was just a great feat of cinema. But it was difficult to watch what looked like his home collapse.

The Shepherd waved his hand, and charts and reports took over the screen. "This is the Supreme Committee's findings." He pointed to a report. "This shows the truth. Thirty-five members of LTE broke into my Shalina and sabotaged the panels. All ordered by Gideon Voss." He pulled up footage of a few LTE members, clear as day in the underground, speaking to the workers. Another photo showed death. Bodies in the underground. "When they couldn't do what was required, Shalina died."

"Wait. How did they—"

"We were betrayed," the Shepherd said stiffly. "Ambassador Tailor was sold a selective story. Yes, the Dome was faulty, but they were fixing it. But this was sabotage." Mr. Worthington had shrugged his shoulders. "The worst part, Leonardo, is that she lied. She lied to you. Without prompting. About everything."

———

SOLANIS LOOKED PUZZLED.

"About the boy."

"Leonardo—"

He cut her off. She was about to lie again. He wasn't going to let her.

"It wasn't my fault, you know." He shook his head a little too hard. It was throbbing at this point. "It could happen to anyone."

She stared at him. Each time he and those dark pits connected, the nail drilled an inch deeper.

"You know kids in the barracks can print guns. His second father was a piece of shit. The kid had enough one day and had shot him. And when I got the call, I went in and found him holding the gun."

He shook his head again.

He'd entered the room, and the kid had pointed the gun at him. The kid's finger had twitched, and he had known it was him or the child. He didn't want to shoot the kid. There was a vulnerable mother in the house. He'd tried to help. The medical drones could have saved the kid if they'd just let him apply the med kit. But his mother, wailing and screaming, entered the room. Shoved him away. She dragged her son outside to the courtyard. They ambushed him. Grabbed his service weapon, stripped his uniform, and beat him. He'd fought back, tried too anyway...but the will was gone.

"You don't know what it's like to make that choice," Leonardo said. He could feel the frown lines deepen on his face. "To choose between yourself and someone else."

"Leonardo..." Solanis's voice was soft.

"But despite what Katia told you," he spat, "I'd never hurt Gabby, you know. I'd never hurt her. There's no reason to be afraid of me."

"Then don't," she said, both of her hands in front of her, palms out. "Listen to me. It's not too late, Leonardo. We can save them."

He scoffed.

She was lying again.

He checked to make sure Walter hadn't moved. Walter was still in the same position as before, unblinking. His eyes were a tepid brew.

———

WORTHINGTON HAD WARNED Leonardo that Solanis would lie. As she'd done for a while.

"And you can't fall for it," Worthington said.

Leonardo nodded. "I'm used to dealing with liars."

"No, you're not." He dimmed the displays with a wave of his hand. Without the lights from the screens, it was just the two of them, sitting alone, in the room. "She's not a liar because she believes. Nothing more dangerous."

"Sir, I can do it. Let me try. For you."

Mr. Worthington had stared, his brilliant green eyes boring into his soul. He was like a lion, studying its prey right before it pounced. Leonardo had seen videos of the great cat lying on rocks in the African plains. Lounging, not a care in the world. Only it was usually the lionesses that hunted. So, what would the Shepherd be?

A wise gorilla? He'd seen one of them rip a man's face off on a news feed.

Panther, maybe?

No.

Worthington was human.

Deadly. Intelligent.

Human.

———

"ARE YOU SERIOUSLY CHOOSING THEM?" Leonardo demanded. "They took you away from us. Your family, your people. Katia wrapped you up in this entire conspiracy and plot to bring this place down." He shook his head. "No, no, no, no, *no*. You have to decide. Katia turned you into this…" He searched for the word. What was it? "*Revolutionary* against the very thing you swore to protect. You promised. We promised to protect this place. We promised to be a part of something bigger than ourselves. You know what's happening out there, Solanis? They are dying. My brother died in a ditch. But he…" He laughed. "He brought us here. The Man from Denver brought us here. He promised redemption."

Solanis shook her head. "No, you ran."

Don't say it.

"You're running from the kid," she said, her eyes wide. "The one you killed."

"You don't get to say that!" His voice was a harsh, rough bellow, the edges scratching his throat. "You don't get to say that." The rage was uncontrollable. "You could never understand. You're the Princess of Seaport." He grunted out a laugh. His arm was heavy, his shoulder shook. Why was his next move suddenly so easy? "Do you remember what they told us the first time we entered Shamut? What Mr. Worthington said?"

"Leonardo..." She took another step toward him. She looked at Walter.

"Why are you moving?" Leonardo yelled.

She was doing this on purpose. She was used to breaking the rules.

He could just pull the trigger.

But it wasn't time.

He didn't want to.

Solanis froze.

"Mr. Worthington said we had to make the perfect sacrifice." He closed his eyes, remembering the moment—the way the Shepherd had raised his hand toward all of them, blessing them where they stood. "He said it would be hard. That there would be a test. That each of us would have to pass that test at some point. That each of us would be challenged so we could earn our place in history. It was easy choosing the Dome. The barracks are dark. They're cruel. This was safe. It still is safe. But I bet for you, the Woman Who Went Outside... I bet coming in here was the hard part."

"No," Solanis said softly. "It was too easy." She looked at the ground. Her left arm jerked, but she didn't raise it. "I was running away." She looked up. "And by the looks of things, so were you."

He scowled.

He hadn't run.

"You killed that kid," she said.

"Solanis..." he warned.

"No, Leonardo. No. Listen. I don't know what happened. I won't ever know the full story. But I know you came in here for a second chance. Okay? I get that. I really do. I came in here because..." Her mouth turned down as some invisible burden shifted to her shoulders. "We are not so different. I killed someone too. Did you know I killed my brother? Greg. I refused to let us leave in time. I refused to listen to him. I came in here because, out there, the earth was trying to kill us. And I didn't know what to do. And they came along. The Greens, the

Evergreens. I hid from the world. I became a part of this. Not because I cared about the environment, not to make the perfect sacrifice." She shook her head. "Because I wanted to hide. So, I hid. I wanted to be safe. I made an easy, yet difficult choice. You remember the beginning. How I cried? How broken I was... might still be. And now... now I want to protect Gabby. I need to. And the other girls like her."

"Then why destroy everything we built?"

It was all excuses and mopey storytelling with her. She really was a unicorn.

"I'm not," she said. "Give them a choice." She gestured to the walls. "I wanted to give the people out there what we know. And give them a choice. He promised, you know. He said he agreed. That he wouldn't stop anyone from leaving if they found out the truth."

She was insane.

"We can't tell people that terrorists killed Shalina," Leonardo said. "They'll panic. There will be riots in the street. Shouldn't you know this?"

She shook her head. "Like right now?"

He scoffed. "You started this war. One last chance. Back down now, and I won't have to stop you."

"Last chance?" she asked.

"I didn't stutter."

"Help me, Leonardo," she said. "We don't have to break up."

Wait a second.

"You spoke to him?" Leonardo said.

"Who?"

"The Shepherd."

She breathed out. "Yes. Just hours ago. We spoke before the attacks started."

"How?"

"He asked me for my time."

"What did he want?"

"He made me an offer."

———

MR. WORTHINGTON HAD FROWNED. "Solanis Tailor will most likely try to break open BlackBox. It's uncrackable. But the act of trying makes her a risk. She's going to tell everyone that Shalina died because we were negligent. But it's not true. Everyone knows it's not true." He nodded to himself. "I am going to make her an offer. She can come to you and tell you that she wants to go outside. She can tell you that you will take her outside. She and Gabby and her boyfriend can go free."

"Sir…"

"I'm not done." He held up a finger. "That's what I will tell her. But your assignment is different. And you need to promise me that you're willing to make the perfect sacrifice to save my beauty."

Leonardo nodded. "I promise."

———

SOLANIS CONTINUED. "He said that if I wanted to, I could find you and tell you I want to leave and that you'd get me out of the Dome, and I'd be free to live my life."

Leonardo narrowed his eyes. "The coward's way out." He glanced at Walter. "Did you really think you were the only one who spoke to the Shepherd?" He felt the fire in his chest turn to iron. "Mr. Worthington gave me a mission too." He moved his finger to the trigger of the gun. "He said that when I found you and determined that you were going to destroy everything we built, I would make the perfect sacrifice. He said I should kill you."

37

BLACKBOX

Solanis

Katia emerged from the darkness of the elevator shaft and fired her gun three times, the bullets knocking Leonardo backward.

He didn't fall, but as he tried to regain his bearings, she plowed into him, the rage from her chest crackling through the room.

He fired back. Solanis flinched at the tiny piercing sound of the ricochet, as Katia dragged him to the floor. The gun clattered to the ground as Katia shoved her ruined, scarred face into his. She head-butted him. He yelled in pain. He pushed back, tossing her to the side, and scrambled to stand.

He fumbled for his tablet, his fingers grasping at the display. But Walter was faster. Walter pulled him at the waist and down. He didn't fall. He wiggled out of Walter's grasp. He groped for the tablet, but Walter lunged forward, driving his shoulder into the back of his knees and causing him to buckle. The Voice skittered to the floor. He rolled over, lifted a foot, and caught Walter square in the jaw. He kicked forward toward the dropped tablet, but Walter was once again too quick. Walter heaved himself forward, grabbed a leg, and pulled him backward. He clawed at the ground, trying to get enough friction to pull himself.

Katia ran toward the gun.

Solanis ran for the broken remnants of the cube.

Right before Katia reached the gun, she gasped and fell backward, screaming and clutching her face.

Solanis stuttered, starting toward her. "What—"

But Katia held one hand out with her palm toward her, demanding Solanis stay away. Solanis looked at the gun, still lying in front of her, and then back at Leonardo and Walter.

Leonardo had his tablet in his hand, a sneer plastered on his face as he glared at Katia. Her screams tore through the room. She had fallen to the ground, writhing in agony. For a second, she flailed for the gun, only to reveal her face melting from the left side, the skin becoming holey and torn. Small flecks of blood raced toward her chin. How were the nanobots eating her again?

Solanis couldn't get near the gun while the robots were active, so she spun back to Leonardo, who gasped as Walter landed a kick to his chest. He dropped the tablet. Walter closed the gap between them and delivered punch after punch. Leonardo put his arms up to protect his face. But Walter lunged forward, tackling him and pushing him to the ground. He struggled to get Walter off him, one hand pushing his chest back and the other grasping behind him toward his belt.

Walter refused to move.

Katia crawled toward Leonardo and Walter, dots of blood falling from her face. Her grunts straining through her teeth. Now that she was away from the gun, Solanis ran over, picked it up, and checked the weapon. It looked fine. It was loaded. Solanis aimed her weapon at the mass that was Leonardo and Walter. But it was impossible to get a good shot.

"Walter!" she yelled.

But Walter didn't hear her as he continued grappling with her colleague.

Katia continued pulling herself toward the tablet, snarling through her teeth at each movement. A trail of blood was behind her, soaking her uniform and streaking the floor.

Leonardo shoved Walter, flipping him onto his back. He was then on top of Walter, throwing punches while straddling him. He punched

Walter over and over in the face, his knuckles making a thudding noise as they smashed into his zygomatics and jaw. Walter tried to block him from his high mount and bucked to get the man off. The first buck was failure. The second, he fell backward.

Solanis aimed and fired. She missed Leonardo. She'd closed her eyes. She should know better.

Ears ringing, she tried to steady her aim again, but the blood was pulsing through her ears, and her heart was thudding.

Katia reached the tablet, stumbling to her feet. "Take it!" she yelled, tossing it toward Solanis.

And then, gasping and wheezing, Katia looked down at Leonardo and fell on top of him. She shoved her bloody face into his.

Solanis had never heard him scream before.

Solanis looked down at the tablet, the controls to the bots that were now rushing onto Leonardo's face blinked at her.

Walter scooted backward, colliding into her legs.

As they watched the little robots in Katia's face begin to eat away at Leonardo's jaw, Leonardo yelled and punched at Katia, but she clung to him.

"The tablet, Solanis!" Walter yelled. "They'll kill her."

Solanis's hand lingered over the tablet. Neither of them deserved relief. Neither of them—

Walter grabbed the Voice and tapped it a few times.

Katia fell silent.

Leonardo mewled and moaned from the floor.

The skin around the right side of his jaw was gone, the bone and ligaments lay bare to the florescent light of the room.

Leonardo went to stand, one hand still clutching his jaw, but Walter was too fast. Walter kicked him, causing him to fall backward. Walter dove to the ground after him, wrestled the gun from Leonardo's back holster, and then used the butt of the gun to deliver a hit to the side of Leonardo's face.

Again, he hit him with the gun.

And again.

Leonardo groaned.

And again.

Leonardo whimpered.

And again.

Walter was going to kill Leonardo.

An uneasiness boiled deep within Solanis, a bitter, sour sensation. Like spoiled dairy or the moment before a breakup. She couldn't let Walter kill Leonardo. He'd blame her for this death too.

She steadied the gun and pointed it at Leonardo. "Walter," she said. "Stop!"

Leonardo sputtered from his position on the floor, the skin on his face split and broken. "You're going to kill us." He spat blood to the side as he forced out the words. One hand was still pressed against his ruined jaw, blood spilling from the wound.

Katia stood.

"They'll kill you out there. *It'll* kill you out there." He gagged and rolled his head to the side. He looked past Solanis and at Katia. "You cunt."

"Shut up." Katia promptly kicked him in the head. She tossed her hair back and said, "I always come back."

He fell silent.

She collapsed, clutching her side.

But Solanis didn't care. She approached the broken key again, trying desperately to see if there was some way to put it back together. But the wires, the decorative plastic, and the circuits were hopelessly mangled.

"Walter!" Solanis yelled. "The key is broken."

Katia, breathing heavy, dragged herself over to the wall and reached up toward the panel. She slipped a bit, her weight pushing against the wall. Cursing, she said in a terrifyingly calm voice, "You'll need a way down. After the box."

Walter fired toward the elevator as the lift came back. Three SPINE agents fell dead. "Doesn't matter. We'll try something when we get up there. We have to go forward."

The doors tried to close, but a body was in the way. The elevator kept dinging and smashing into the dead man's torso.

"Walter." Katia motioned for him to join her on the side of the room as Solanis continued pawing through what was left of the key.

The fireflies danced around her discarded necklace. She grabbed it and retied it around her neck.

Walter joined Katia at the wall and propped her up as she tapped the panel. Katia gasped in pain.

"There's a way…" she said.

The elevator continued dinging, assaulting the legs of the dead man.

"They're going to climb up the shaft of the other elevator," she murmured.

Walter nodded. "Get us out of here."

"There's a way." Katia continued tapping the panel, fireflies pirouetting around her fingers. "There's always a way." She tapped the good side of her head. "I need to think. I need a second to think. Why doesn't time ever cooperate?"

Voices came from the elevator shaft.

"They're coming up." Solanis pointed her gun toward the elevator bay.

The fireflies aggressively multiplied, spreading to the darkest corners of the room. They gathered around Walter's eyes, poured from the elevator, and danced near the keypad. They excitedly crowded her vision, demanding her attention.

"Here it is," Katia said brightly, pointing to the panel. "Once the box drops, follow it down."

"You can't be serious—" Walter started.

"The floors trigger a lockdown." She tapped the display again. It went dark, and the fireflies wandered away. She slipped down the wall.

He propped her back up.

"The fifth floor will close. You just need to drop five stories. Well, two and a half, three really. These stories are narrow." She nodded. "The tunnel has pressure. Air resistance. Box can't break on the way down."

He eased her to the floor. "That's assuming we can drop the box."

"No," Solanis said. "That's not happening. We'll die. Five stories will kill you."

Katia coughed from her place on the ground. "I designed this place. My designs reach out to me."

She is losing her mind, isn't she?

"About twenty seconds after the drop. It's automatic, so you can't get down there and retrieve the box. Count to ten." She shuddered, grabbing her side. "Look at the map, Walter. I sent it to you."

Walter looked down at his tablet, the fireflies excitedly swirling around his fingers.

"Katia..." Solanis stared at the monitor. "Turn it back on."

"I don't need it," Katia said.

"Hold on." She raised her hand. She tapped the display. The embers and the fireflies came back. They rippled from the screen and bloomed to the corners and edges.

Solanis turned the display off.

The embers dissipated.

"We need to move," Walter said. His gun pointed toward the elevator shaft. "They're almost up."

She frowned. What was it about the light spectrum? Why did this feel so important?

She turned the display back on. The fire was back, dancing and blossoming.

You can see a bit more of the light spectrum than most people.

BlackBox is built off a frequency of patterns that are constantly rotating.

"Turn off the lights," she said.

Katia pulled out her tablet and tapped a few times. The lights in the room went out.

Katia's tablet clattered to the floor.

Walter kneeled next to her and shook her.

The fireflies lit up the entire room. They filled wall panels, glowed up the elevator shaft where SPINE climbed, and hovered around every electronic piece of equipment—dancing.

"I don't think I'm coming upstairs." Katia's voice was weak.

"Come on. I got you." Walter reached for her.

"No," she said. She raised her hand and made a rude gesture easy to see with the fire in the room. "No." She chuckled.

Solanis stared at the two of them, trying to connect the pieces. Would the box light up too? Was it possible?

BlackBox, it is built on a frequency of patterns. Solve the pattern, and you can turn off the box.

"Move," Katia demanded to Walter.

He didn't move.

"I'm not sorry, you know," she told Solanis. "It's why we're here. Because I wasn't wrong."

Walter looked at Solanis. "Solar," he said quickly. "Come, Solar. Come."

"I knew you'd be here. You'd do anything to save Gabby." Katia gagged, spat blood, and managed to take a shuddering breath. "You just needed to see it."

Solanis glared at her. How could she play games right now?

"Predictable," Katia's voice was steel.

Solanis gasped.

She hadn't given up.

That bitch.

"Solanis!" Walter urged.

But Solanis couldn't.

"Solar." He tried again. "She's going to die."

"I don't think I can."

Katia's laugh turned into a cough.

He knitted his brows. "Solanis, you used to be friends."

Solanis's face suddenly felt wet.

"Solanis," he pleaded.

Katia nodded in the glow of the fireflies, one shaky finger raised in her direction. "And that's the monster, the one we made." She pulled a gun from her waist. "Move."

She gripped the gun with both hands, balancing the butt on her knee.

"Go," she quietly demanded as the fireflies buzzed around her. "I'll hold them." She looked up at Solanis. "Besides"—she coughed—"I always come back. I will reach for you. For her."

There was no time for a response.

SPINE was here.

Walter fired toward the elevator shaft, pulling Solanis toward the spiral staircase.

"Move." He pulled her hard, firing again toward the glass around the spiral staircase and shattering the casing around it.

She spun and took one last look at Katia, who winked and began firing toward the elevator.

Something tightened inside of Solanis. A painful, twisted gnarled knot manifested a massive cramp that crawled up her leg.

Solanis yelled and fell in step behind Walter. She limped through the glass and chased Walter up the curved steps and through the red embers that fluttered down like phoenix feathers. She squinted and flinched as she tried to dodge the brilliance of her mind's recreation of marigold luminescence.

Could the key to her freedom be above? Could she drop the box without a key? Maybe she could knock it down. There was bound to be a broom somewhere.

She stumbled, wobbling sideways. Walter grabbed her.

"Not yet," he said, nudging her forward, past him. He turned, facing down the steps, and fired into the room below, where SPINE swarmed.

Katia was down there.

Solanis tripped forward, embers radiating from her chest, as Greg's disk cut into her. She ripped off the necklace, her other hand checking for blood.

In her hand, her brother's disk glowed as she and Walter reached the door that led into the server room.

The wall panel was still intact, demanding her handprint. Solanis complied and the door sprung open.

The techs inside panicked, trying to push their way to the door. But Walter kicked the door closed behind him, his gun corralling the workers into a group behind a massive server rack.

The server room was bright, the fireflies dancing and pulsing all around the servers, wires, and racks from RealityLife. Red fire brewed above her as she climbed the ladder to the platform above.

BlackBox was a sun in the center of the sky, thick ropes of fire protruding from its mass. It seemed to be made of two different spinning cores. A lighter exterior and a deep angry one. Flares shot out from the box as ropes of light from around the room fed into the device. It greedily swallowed everything.

Only her necklace rivaled the light in front of her.

Wait.

You'd need a key and a way to see those patterns.

Without thinking, Solanis held the disk up to BlackBox. A small black circle the size of the disk materialized on the side of the massive sun.

A dead spot that perfectly matched her brother's disk.

The disk she'd been wearing for the last decade since he was zipped into that black bag.

If butterflies still existed, real ones anyway, they might be able to see the patterns in the sun.

Solanis placed the disk on the dead spot. It vibrated and attached itself to the sun like a magnet. The disk, as if it had a mind of its own, followed the spot around the box.

Everything the disk touched turned out the lights. The black grew as the light inside the box died. It was like watching fire collide with water and fade into solitude. The dark spots wrapped themselves around the outer and inner cores until the box went completely dark.

With a slight shudder, BlackBox stopped moving.

For the first time in a decade, the Dome fell silent.

———

THE ROOM CAME RUSHING BACK.

The shadows around Solanis yelled and swirled.

The techs in the room stared up at her and Walter.

The entire server room was silent, the pulse gone.

What had she expected to happen when she shut down the box that kept all their thoughts, dreams, and ideas inside the Dome?

Maybe she expected to feel lighter, free even.

But she didn't expect to feel this crippling sensation right in the pit of the black hole that had been swirling inside of her. Now that the world's silence rushed through her, the void inside quickly became a lake, an ocean.

The whooshing of BlackBox plummeting ten stories into the vault below caused Solanis Tailor to tilt forward, but Walter pulled her back from the edge.

"Not yet," he said. "Twenty seconds."

There was a loud banging as BlackBox locked itself into the vault below.

They'd done their job.

But Walter didn't return her gaze. The crashing noise down below to her left caused her to jump and swivel around while swinging her gun toward the side door. More SPINE agents pushed into the room through the red haze, doing their best to break through the door Walter had jammed shut.

"Eleven," Walter said.

Solanis shook her head. The world was darker than it should have been now that the box was gone. Red, green, and blue waves had joined the fireflies as she struggled to get her bearings. Her legs didn't want to move. There was no way she'd be able to jump into the darkness of the pit.

"We have to risk it!" Walter yelled. "Or we'll die."

"I don't know..." she said.

He had turned again, firing more bullets toward the door. The door was slightly pried open. SPINE threatened to swarm the room.

And for the first time in a long time, he gave his half smile. Directly at her. To her. For her. True nuclear pasta.

God, how she'd missed it.

"You remember the book?" he asked her. "The real one I was reading?"

She nodded—the worn leather a distant memory.

"Remember how at the end, she jumps off Wudang Mountain because there's an old story that says the gods will grant her one wish if she does?" He fired more shots toward SPINE who were trying to enter from below. He grabbed Solanis around her waist. "We'll be fine, Solar. Make a wish. We'll be fine."

He nodded and fell sideways, still clutching her, and they tumbled into the massive hole in the center of the room. Solanis screamed as they fell, the world rushing up around them, the wind resistance pushing back at them. The fireflies fell with her.

They didn't fall for long,

They crashed into the ground, her on Walter's chest. He took the brunt of the impact.

He wasted no time and pulled her up. "Come on," he demanded, roughly limping to the next corridor. "Come on."

She clutched her shoulder in pain and fell in line behind him into the hallway, to the side door, down the concrete steps, and into the damaged lobby. He fired upward toward the balcony as he pushed her ahead of him and urged her forward.

The world was still on fire.

They reached the building's lobby with the ruins of Worthington's statue. The Shepherd's marble head faced the corner, severed.

"Did it work?" Solanis gasped as they ran. "Did it work?" The stitch in her side ached. The world was a quickly dimming fire. The shapes around her were becoming ambiguous.

Walter released a few bursts of his gun as they crossed through the atrium. LTE, SPINE, and others without allegiance were in the lobby. He let off a few more gunshots. The targets were too far away for her to know if they hit their mark. She had to squint to see his movements, even in the daylight. The fire was intensifying.

Outside, it was pure panic.

An emergency alarm sounded. Then a sequence of Klaxons. Solanis pulled out the tablet, still trying to wave away the fireflies. The screen showed her the video of Shalina imploding. Data flooded her display. On the massive screens outside, she watched over and over as Shalina fell, the bodies of the deceased on repeat.

People screamed.

But they didn't start running until the sky began to show the faces of those they'd left outside.

The sky broke into a million massive videos. Videos from family members pleading with the Evergreens to come back outside. To rejoin the world. To reject the Shepherd before it was too late.

It had worked.

Outside was in here.

The panic swelled.

Her tablet vibrated again. Directions to an exit. The tunnels.

Now that she was being jostled and pushed by the crowd, Solanis could see LTE up close. Their red, burgundy, and black outfits weren't identical, but they suggested a haphazard conformity. They carried guns as they rushed through Shamut, herding people toward the tunnels. Down the avenue, she watched as Montoya was shot in the head. The executioner was immediately gunned down by SPINE— some of their bullets striking innocent civilians. The gunfire, bodies and pleas from the outside fueled the panic. Solanis ducked her head, Walter yanked her forward.

She couldn't die now. Not when she was so close to getting Gabby out.

More gunshots.

The sky flickered off and then back on. New videos replacing the old.

Walter shoved her into a cart, sealing them from the outside noise. In the front was Heidi, who urged the cart forward through the panicked crowds. Gabby and Tatiana were in the back seat. Solanis scooped Gabby into her chest when she saw her. The tears came fast.

As they plowed forward, people dove out of the way to avoid being crushed. Her tablet wouldn't stop buzzing as messages flooded in. Videos from the population's loved ones took over the screens. Children begging their family members to come home. Friends cried, promising forgiveness. Notes of people who had died, waiting for their loved ones to see the light. Bullets pounded the exterior door. Solanis demanded Gabby and Tatiana stay low.

Walter shoved Solanis's face down into the seat. There was a loud crack as he crawled past her, kicked out the back window and leaned out, returning fire. Embers hovered around the grip of the gun when he fired.

The cart jolted to the side as the vehicle wobbled. The side door next to Solanis exploded as a man in red lunged for the open hole in the cart. Heidi screamed. The first man missed, rolling into the street. But the second clung to the seat belt. Solanis kicked him. Hard. She fired toward the cart that had aligned itself next to them. The third time she fired, the gun clicked, indicating it was empty.

"Walter!" She yelled, tapping him twice on the shoulder and flipped the gun upside down. He placed a new magazine in and tapped her back, all while the LTE mercenary clawed at her legs. Gabby and Tatiana screamed from underneath Walter, who was still firing behind them.

Solanis fired, and the bullet found its mark. The LTE mercenary was dead and rolled into the street.

Soon, their cart stopped.

Walter pulled her out. "Let's go."

The world was dimming, and her eyes were alive with the sparks of fire. In the right light, she could see Walter's scowl, his skin, and the way he was developing wrinkles near his eyes. But all of it was fading. Red embers pulsed and flickered around her, dancing as she moved through her personalized temperate furnace. Around them, people panicked, tripping over each other as they tried to figure out if they were on LTE's kill list.

And throughout the mass of people, she could hear Leonardo. "SOLANIS!" He yelled. "STOP!"

He had pushed his way through the thinning crowd. She could make out the outline of a burning cart behind him. He stood there, his uniform torn and tattered. His breathing was ragged. His gun pointed directly at her, his hair wild around his face. He was missing teeth. His essence was collapsing.

The red waves danced around him.

"You can't," he said through gritted teeth. "You can't leave me here." His hand covered his ruined jaw.

She took a step toward him. "Come with us."

"I have nothing," he cried. "This was everything. This was everything."

Walter turned back around and pulled on her arm. "We need to go."

"What about the perfect sacrifice?" Leonardo shook his head, limped forward and tapped his temple with the gun. "We were supposed to make the perfect sacrifice. This isn't it. They will all die. It's not just us."

Solanis squinted into the crowd as Shamut continued to panic, the pulse deadly high. Leonardo looked around, and his gun fell to his side. Members of LTE cut through the crowd, their guns leveled on him.

Leonardo locked eyes with Solanis and then looked down at his gun. Wide-eyed, he looked back at her and then at the oncoming LTE mercenaries, now too close to miss.

Leonardo pointed the gun at his head.

38

ALL OF THEM

Solanis

The tunnel was crowded, filled with running jostling people who were desperate to get outside. There was an irony somewhere in this mess. These people had built the Domes because the planet had tried to kill them but were now running back to the outside because the Domes were trying to do the same.

Solanis stumbled forward, one hand attached to Walter and the other dragging Gabby. Tatiana wasn't far behind.

Tatiana hadn't stopped begging for Katia.

How could you tell a little girl her mother was dead?

Was this what it felt like to kill a god? Or at least steal a god's prized possession? Surely there'd be consequences, even out here. If she was a god killer or a thief, shouldn't she feel invincible, more accomplished? Why did she feel so weak? So small.

Was she a monster? No, she couldn't be. But she didn't feel like a phoenix either.

"Solar." Walter clutched her. "We're almost there. Hang on."

She squinted at Walter, who was a little more than an outline. The light from the outdoors hardly registered to her ailing eyes. The world pulsed, light flickering in and out of her vision. But she kept moving, ignoring how the tunnel walls danced and flickered with each heartbeat. Her body fought against Haze, her eyes screaming as they had done before. The wind whipped past her ears in the tunnel. His hand was a warm granite on hers.

And then, after what had to have been hours, they were outside. The smell of the grass, sand, and ocean. A flurry of bodies, emotional noises. Some lay on the ground, dazed and confused. Others shook and cried. Some tried to run back toward the tunnels. To get inside.

Tatiana begged for her mother.

Solanis gripped Tatiana's and Gabby's hands, pulling them away from the crowds. Walter cut a line through the scuffle. Medical staff, pilgrims, and swarms of red, green, and civilians scrambled, yelling as people made their way into the light.

The stars should have been poking through the great vast curtain that was the sky. But her vision was just about gone.

She looked toward both girls, Gabby and Tatiana, determined to remember their faces.

But Tatiana squirmed away, her gaze past Solanis and back toward the tunnels. She ran into the crowd, begging for her mother. Solanis squinted, and for a second, thought she caught a glimpse of Katia stumbling through the masses, her face blank and vacant.

Figures in the dark.

Solanis's vision shuddered as the fireflies and darkness throbbed around her. She squeezed the bridge of her nose. For a second, the sinking daylight turned off, and it was just her and the fireflies.

"Gabby! Walter!" she said urgently, scared, fumbling for them. She was running out of time.

She willed the day to come back.

Gabby grabbed her hand.

The world was collapsing.

"I need to look at you," Solanis said as the two moved toward her.

Gabby stood close to her mother. "Are you okay?"

She shook her head. "I will be."

"We're safe, Mom," Gabby said quietly, stroking her hand. "You know. You say it all the time. We're together. We're safe because we're together."

Solanis nodded as the shadows grew and then shrank, morphing her daughter into a little more than an outline. "You don't need me to be safe. You're strong. Real nuclear pasta." She gripped the side of Gabby's cheek, wiping a tear that had dropped. "Can you see them? The stars?"

Gabby looked up at the sky.

Solanis willed herself to pull in as much light as she could. She needed to see Gabby one last time. She needed to remember. Every detail. Every bit of her.

"Solar." Walter's voice found her. "I'm here. I'm here."

The darkness was rolling in.

"I'm not leaving, okay?"

Of course he wouldn't.

She was broken again.

The world was just shadows and outlines. Her pulse was too fast.

But then she felt him. Walter's finger tapped her chest. Three deliberate times.

The fireflies danced in her mind.

They then settled—small little dots in the distance of the dark.

They reminded her of the stars.

All of them.

ACKNOWLEDGEMENTS

This book would not have been possible without the incredible support, insight, and encouragement of a few extraordinary people. My deepest thanks to Kate B., Joanna H., Natasha C., Dan M., Alicia O., Tirzah R., Bibi N., and Raquel F., who patiently endured my endless ideas, plot holes, and grand plans for this novel... and the ones to come. Your feedback, ideas, and belief in this project pushed me to make it better at every stage. You are the stars that light the real night sky. Your brilliance sustains me.

The world is undergoing dramatic changes, and it's not always clear how to pursue justice, equality, and fairness while protecting the people you love. How do you know when it's time to protect yourself and when it's time to stand up for your community? The impact of today will take years to understand, even after moments of shock and awe.

But here's what we do know: we cannot trade basic freedoms for the illusion of safety. Don't surrender freedom just because fear arrives. No, you don't need to become reckless, but action is a requirement. Because once they turn off the stars, it's hard to bring back the light.

This journey has been remarkable because you, the reader, chose to come along. If you loved the story, I hope you'll consider leaving a review. I read every one—and I'd love to keep exploring the world of tomorrow with you.

Thank you. Thank you. Thank you.

J.S. Thompson is a political storyteller who spends way too much time plotting how we might all survive our upcoming dystopian future. Drawing from his career in politics and advocacy, Thompson explores themes of political power, sacrifice, and survival in his work. Thompson lives right outside Washington, D.C. (where the politicians roam the Earth), has way too many plants, but is not an Evergreen. *There Are No Stars Here* is his debut novel.

Reach out to him at info@jsthompsonauthor.com. He reaches back.

Join the mailing list at www.jsthompsonauthor.com and if you loved the book, reviews are always appreciated.

instagram.com/jeremysthompson
tiktok.com/@jsthompsonauthor

—L.S. Thompson is a political story teller whose grandson A... ... (?)
joined her. Within all tat...

www.ingramcontent.com/pod-product-compliance
Lightning Source LLC
Chambersburg PA
CBHW010519100726
47903CB00011B/2808